THE

WEIGHT

OF

HEAVEN

THE
WEIGHT
OF
HEAVEN

A NOVEL

Thrity Umrigar

HARPER

An Imprint of HarperCollins*Publishers*

ISBN-13: 978-1-61523-689-3

for Anne Reid
and
Cyndi Howard,
peace and love

Shall our blood fail? Or shall it come to be
The blood of paradise? And shall the earth
Seem all of paradise that we shall know?
—"SUNDAY MORNING," WALLACE STEVENS

Sleep child, for your parents' sake.
Soon you must wake.
—"A LULLABYE," JAMES AGEE

THE

WEIGHT

OF

HEAVEN

PROLOGUE

A few days after Benny's death, Ellie and Frank Benton broke into separate people. Although they didn't know it then. At that time, all they could do was concentrate on getting through each bewildering day, fighting to suppress the ugly memories that burst to the surface like fish above water. On the day of the funeral, Frank urged himself to go up to Ellie and say something brave and consoling to her, something that would reassure her that he understood, that he did not blame her for what had happened. But he was felled by a clear, sharp thought: He didn't know how. Without Benny, he had forgotten how to make his way home, how to make his marriage whole again. Benny had been dead for less than a week, and already his marriage felt like a book he had read in high school and Ellie a character in it whose name he had forgotten. Something inexplicable happened in the days following Benny's death—it was as if a beautiful blue bowl, no, it was as if the world itself had fallen and broken into two halves. Try as he might, Frank couldn't help but feel toward Ellie how he imagined Adam had felt toward Eve after the Fall—hostile and compassionate. Sad and doomed and resentful. Above all, lonely. Above all, unable to regain that lost, broken thing.

It was not as though Benny had always been part of their marriage. He and Ellie had been married for eleven years, and Ben had been seven when he died. And that was not counting the year of courtship, when he and Ellie were inseparable. A lot of history there, as Ellie might have said to one of her clients. A lot of great times even before they had conceived *of* Benny, let alone conceived him. But a strange thing happened once Benny was born. It was as if they all ceased to be individual people. Three people merged into one and became a unit, a family. The unit traveled together or stayed home together and breathed the same domestic air. Even when they were apart—when Frank was flying to Thailand, say, to supervise a new project, or Ellie was counseling her clients, or Benny was at school, they were linked to each other, their awake thoughts full of each other. Hope Ellie remembered to fax Benny's math homework to the hotel, Frank would think while sitting in a meeting in Bangkok. Fuck. Did I remember to buy peanut butter yesterday? Ellie would wonder while listening to a client tell her about how her sister had embarrassed her in front of the whole family at Thanksgiving dinner. Little Benny would memorize a joke someone had told at school and repeat it as soon as he got home, giggling so hard that he often messed up the punch line.

And now, they were two. Benny was gone. What was left behind was mockery—objects and memories that mocked their earlier, smug happiness. Benny was gone, an airplane lost behind the clouds, but he left behind a trail of smoke a mile long: the tiny baseball glove, the Harry Potter books, the Mr. Bean videos, the Bart Simpson T-shirt, the fishing rod, the last Halloween costume. A tiny rosewood box with a few strands of his hair. A mug that read, #1 MOM. His school photo. Photographs of the three of them at Disney World. The Arts and Crafts bungalow in Ann Arbor was positively shimmering with mockery.

Even so, Frank didn't leap at the chance when his boss, Pete

Timberlake, asked if he was interested in heading the new factory that the company had bought two years ago in Girbaug, India. Four months after Benny's death he was still concentrating on the Herculean business of putting one foot in front of the other. Of making up reasons to get out of bed in the morning. He mumbled something to Pete about how much he appreciated the vote of confidence, but that it wasn't the right time in his life to relocate. But Ellie heard about the offer from the wife of another executive. And saw in it what Frank couldn't—a chance to save her marriage. To start clean in a new place. To put the baseball glove and the size-four Nike sneakers in storage, to not be slapped daily by the patter of feet not heard, by the sound of a high-pitched voice not squealing its exuberance over breakfast. And so Ellie broke the cardinal rule that she had always preached to her own clients: the one about not making any major decisions for a year after a life-altering event. Accept Pete's offer, she urged her husband. And Frank, too tired to argue, to think, let himself be guided by the faint light of hope he saw in his wife's eyes. India, he thought. He knew about the new, deregulated, globalized India that everyone was raving about, of course. The booming stock market. The billion-dollar acquisitions. The call centers, the manicured IT campuses. But he let himself dream of the old India, which he believed was the real country. India, he thought. Elephants. Cows on the streets. Snake charmers.

Above all, he comforted himself with the thought of being in a country with a new moon, a new coastline, a new sky. Of living in a house whose walls did not carry the telltale pencil marks of measuring a child's height. Whose rooms did not echo with the sounds of a boy's whoops of laughter. A country where there was no possibility of running into one of his son's teachers. Whose parks, rivers, lakes, stadiums, video parlors, movie theaters did not constantly taunt him, remind him to look at his own broken, empty hands. He went into Pete Timberlake's office on Monday morning and accepted his offer.

And so, banished from their once Edenic life in Ann Arbor, Michigan, Frank and Ellie Benton traveled east until they arrived at the Shivaji International Airport in Bombay on a cool January morning in 2006.

BOOK ONE

Spring 2007
Girbaug, India

CHAPTER 1

They had finished dinner a half hour ago, and now they sat on the porch waiting for the rains to come. The nighttime air was heavy with moisture, but it held its burden in check, like a widow blinking back her tears. While they waited, the storm entertained them with its flash and dazzle—the drumbeat of the thunder, the silver slashes of lightning against the black skin of the sky. With each explosion of lightning they saw the scene before them—the tall shadows on their front lawn cast by the coconut trees, the still sand beyond the lawn, and even beyond that, the restless, furious sea, straining against the shore.

He had always loved thunderstorms, even as a young boy in Grand Rapids. While his older brother, Scott, cowered and flinched and pulled the bedcovers over his ears, Frank would stand before the window of their shared bedroom, feeling brave and powerful. Talking back to the storm. He would deliberately turn his back on Scott, embarrassed and bewildered to see his older brother, usually as placid as the waters of Lake Michigan in the summer, turn into this fearful, unrecognizable creature. If they were lucky, their mother would come into their room to rock and calm her oldest boy down, and then Frank was free to escape to the second-floor porch that was adjacent to the guest bedroom. Being on this porch was the next best thing to being outdoors. From here, he felt closer to the tumultuous Michigan sky and violently, perilously free. Thunderstorms made him feel lonely, but it was a powerful lonely, something that connected him to the solitude of the world around him. If he stood on his toes and leaned his upper body out on the porch railing just so, the rain would hit his upturned face, the tiny pinpricks painful but exhilarating. The wind roared and Frank roared back; his hands tingled with each burst of lightning, as if it was nothing but a projection of the jagged, electric energy that coursed through his pale, thin body.

Years later, it would become one of Frank's greatest disappointments that his son had not inherited his love of thunderstorms. When little Benny would crawl into bed with them, when he would whimper and bottle up his ears with his index fingers, Frank fought conflicting urges—the protective, fatherly part of him would pray for the thunderstorm to pass, would want to cradle his son's trembling body in the nest of his own, even as a small disappointment gathered like a lump in the back of his throat.

Unlike in Michigan, thunderstorms in western India did not pass quickly. They had been in Girbaug for seventeen months now and knew how it could rain nonstop for days during the monsoon season. Now, although it was only May, the forecast called for rain tonight. Frank felt grateful to be home to watch it. He sat impatiently, waiting for the heavy, laden sky to deliver its promise. The wind whipped around them, high enough that they didn't have to rock the swing they were sitting on. Behind them, the house was dark—Ellie had turned off the lights after they'd picked up their after-dinner coffees and padded out to the porch. Every few minutes the lightning lit up the whole panoramic scene before them, like a camera flash. Frank knew that when the rains came crashing down they would come swiftly, brutally, and his body ached with anticipation. So far it had all been foreplay—the whispers of the tall coconut trees as they leaned into each other; the cloying sweetness of the jasmine bushes; the painful groaning of the thunder. Now, he longed for the satisfying release that the rains would deliver.

He turned toward Ellie and waited for the next flash of lightning to illuminate her face. They had exchanged a few aimless words since moving to the porch, but for the most part they had sat in an easy silence for which Frank was grateful. It was a contrast to most of their interactions these days, which were laced with bitterness and unspoken accusations. He knew he was losing Ellie, that she was slipping out of his hands like the sand that lay just beyond the front yard, but he seemed unable to prevent the slow erosion. What she wanted from him—forgiveness—he could not grant her. What he wanted from her—his son back—she couldn't give.

The lightning flashed, and he saw her white, slender body for an instant before the darkness carried her away again. She was sitting erect and still, her back pressed against the wooden boards of the swing. But what made Frank's heart lurch was the look on her face. She sat with her eyes closed, a beatific expression on her face, looking for all the world like one of the Buddha statues they had seen on a recent trip to the Ajanta caves. She seemed to feel none of the agitation, the exciting turmoil, that was coursing through his body. Ellie seemed far away, as distant as the moon he could not see. Slipping away from his hands. Completely unaware of the memories tumbling through his mind—Ellie and he running through the streets of Ann Arbor at night during a thunderstorm, laughing wildly and singing at the top of their lungs before arriving at the house she was renting, stripping off their wet clothes at the door and falling naked onto the couch she had inherited from the previous grad student who lived there; him coming home from work one evening and finding Ellie lying on her stomach on the floor, trying to pull their four-year-old son from under their bed where he was hiding during a rainstorm.

A savage malice gripped Frank. As was common these days,

something about Ellie's calm irritated him. Deliberately, he said, "Do you remember how he used to—"

"Yes. Of course I remember." She was wide awake now, having heard something in his voice that perhaps even he was not aware of. The satisfaction that Frank felt from having destroyed Ellie's calm was tempered by something approaching regret. Her serenity, which he used to value so much, was now a scab he had to pick away at.

"I think a year more, and he would have been fine," he continued, unable to help himself. "I'd been thinking about taking him on a couple of camping trips, y'know, just the two of us, thinking that would help with—"

"He was already getting over it," she interrupted, and his stomach dropped. Was he imagining the triumph in her voice, the knowledge that she had scored the knockout blow and that he now had no choice but to bite the bait she had set up?

Hating himself, he asked, "Getting over his fear of thunderstorms? Why didn't you tell me?"

"It was going to be a surprise. I—I trained him. Behavior modification—same thing I do with my clients."

He felt a hot surge of jealousy at the thought of Ellie and Benny alone at home, while he was flying off to Thailand, the other place where HerbalSolutions had a factory. How many meetings had he sat through, how many treks to villages in the hinterlands, how many miles logged on planes, nights spent in strange hotel rooms, all the time thinking he was doing this for them? He remembered his desperation when the cell phone signals were weak and he couldn't call in time to wish Benny good night; how he had tried to send Ellie an e-mail as soon as he got into a hotel room in whatever city he was in. How he had fought to stay connected with them even when he was across oceans and time zones. Only to learn that the two of them had their own secrets, their own rituals from which he was excluded. He tried to remember if he had always known this and if it had ever bothered him before. But he couldn't remember. Whole chunks of his memory of life when Benny was alive were gone. Or rather, the memories were there but the feeling was gone. So that he knew that he had been happy with Ellie, that they had had a good marriage, and he remembered a million acts of love and sacrifice on her part. But how it had made him feel—the sweetness, the delicacy, the intricacy—he could no longer conjure up.

"How long had he not been afraid? And how many more years were you planning to wait before telling me?"

There was a slight pause, but when she spoke, Ellie's voice was flat. "It had just happened, Frank. It stormed a few times when you were away—the, the last time. I talked him through it."

Despite the dark, Frank closed his eyes. It should've been me, he thought. I should've been the one to have calmed my son's fears. Resentment filled his mouth. "Maybe that's why he got sick," he said, spitting the words like pits from a bitter fruit. "You know, maybe the stress of suppressing his fear in front of you was what—"

"That's the dumbest thing I've ever heard you say. Even for you, that's a new low." Ellie shifted away from him so that their shoulders were no longer touching. There was a loud roar of thunder, as if the heavens themselves were emphasizing her words and she waited for it to subside. "You know, I'd like to have just one fucking evening of peace. But if you can't just sit with me and be decent, Frank, I'll go indoors, okay? Because I'm not going to sit here and wait for you to come up with one more theory of how I killed our son. If you think I don't hurt as—"

"Ellie—" His hand shot out and covered hers. "I'm sorry. Sometimes I . . . I'm sorry. It's just that watching thunderstorms is really hard, you know? It's like everything is wrapped up—" He cut himself off, wanting to say more, to reveal to his wife the altered shape of his heart, but being unable to.

In the dark, he sensed rather than saw Ellie blinking back her tears. "It's okay," she said. "Just forget it." But her voice wobbled, and his throat tightened with remorse. You're a fucking bastard, he chided himself. You think she hasn't suffered enough that you're doing this to her? Not for the first time, he wondered if he should talk to someone, to Scott maybe, to confess his miserable treatment of Ellie. He wouldn't seek understanding or sympathy—what he wanted was someone to give him a much-needed kick in the pants, to knock sense into his head, to ask him whether he wanted to lose his wife also, because he couldn't accept the loss of his son. Scott adored Ellie, Frank knew, and would defend her against his own brother. Maybe he would call Scott in New York from the office tomorrow, maybe Scott could say something profound, the one true thing, that would help him make his way back to Ellie.

He put his arm around her shoulder and pulled her back into the cradle of his arm. For a few seconds she rested stiffly against him, but then her body relaxed and she rested her head on his shoulder. They stayed that way for a few moments, and then it began to rain.

"Remember how we used to run all the way back from campus in the rain?" Frank said.

"Yup." She pulled away from him a bit, and he felt her eyes on his face. "Wanna go for a walk along the beach?"

"You mean right now?"

"No time like the present."

"I can't. We'll get soaked."

"Well, that is the point of walking in the rain—getting soaked."

"Funny. No, that is, normally I would, you know? But Ramesh is going to come over in a bit. He has a math test tomorrow, and I want to go over some problems with him."

He felt Ellie shift ever so slightly. "I see. Okay."

"What?"

"Nothing."

"Oh, say it. You're obviously unhappy about something."

She turned to face him. "You know exactly what I'm unhappy

about, Frank. I'm unhappy that we can't go for a walk because there's a little boy who's forever coming over needing something or the other from my husband. And I'm—"

He half rose from the swing. "Jesus Christ. I don't believe this. You're jealous of a nine-year-old kid. Just because I don't jump when you—"

"It has nothing to do with jealousy, Frank. It's just that you don't know what's appropriate and what's—"

"Appropriate? What the hell are you talking about? I see tremendous potential in Ramesh and so I tutor him a few evenings a week. You're the one who acts like some goddamn saint, talking about our responsibility to those less fortunate, but when I try to help the son of our housekeepers, you—"

"That's the question, Frank. Who are you trying to help? Who are you helping here?"

The phone rang inside the house, but they both ignored it. Frank sat on his right hand so that it wouldn't involuntarily curl its way around Ellie's long, graceful neck and choke it. "What the hell does that mean?"

"You know exactly what I mean. Do you know what it's doing to Edna and Prakash to have you take over their son's life?"

"Edna and Prakash? I don't believe this. You think either one of them has a clue about anything? Hell, if I could work with that boy for two years, he'd be MIT-bound, someday. Why doesn't Prakash drink less if he cares so much for his son? And why doesn't Edna stand up to him? All I'm trying to do is improve the kid's life."

"That's not all you're trying to do." The phone was ringing again, but this time they scarcely heard it. They were staring at each other, breathing heavily like boxers in a ring.

"What—?"

"Frank, Ramesh is not Ben—"

"Shut up," Frank interrupted. "Don't say it. If you know what's good for you, don't say it."

Ellie stared at him for a long second. Then, as if she'd lost some battle, her shoulders sagged. "Okay." She shrugged.

But it was too late. She had stripped him naked, Frank thought. With four indiscreet words she had torn off his clothes, removed the layers of resisting muscle and skin, and gotten to his heart. His heart that had been so dead until a dark-haired, sharp-eyed Indian boy had restored a few of its beats. A boy he had grown close to precisely because he was the opposite of his dead son—dark-skinned in contrast to the light-skinned Benny, noisy and shiny where Ben had been serene and thoughtful. Ramesh was sunshine to Benny's moonlight. Benny had been good at art and history and English and lousy at math and science; Ramesh declared that history was boring, that most books were too long to read, but was a natural at science and math. The first time Frank had helped Ramesh with his math homework, he was blown away by the boy's smarts. Within months he had insisted that the boy be transferred to the missionary school and that he would pay the monthly fees. Edna had been grateful at the time.

"Frank, I'm sorry." Ellie's voice was soft, muffled by the harsh patter of the rain. "I don't want to hurt you. Dear God, we have to stop hurting each other like this. Please, hon. I don't know how to do this alone."

He fought the urge to respond to the pleading in her voice. This time, Ellie had gotten too close, had left too deep a gash with her words. There was a time when he had thought of Ellie as his second self, someone who knew his deepest yearnings and thoughts. But everything that Ellie had given him—love, companionship, a home, and above all, Benny, holy God, above everything she had given him Benny—she had also taken away. Taken away by her carelessness, her thoughtlessness. He couldn't forget that. And now she was doing it again, with Ramesh. With the only thing in his life that gave him any solace, any sense of normalcy in this chaotic country that Ellie had come to love and that he was constantly confused and repelled by.

Well, he knew how to turn his heart into a rock. For most of his years with Ellie he had not needed to use that trick. She had softened him, made him believe that it was okay to lean on another person, to trust, to not carry himself in a constant state of war and wariness. In the years that they were a family all the old, ancient feelings— of being on guard, of believing that everything valuable had to be earned, that nothing was freely given, nothing was grace—all those feelings had vanished. But now he knew they had just gone below the surface. That he could access them, as easily as a file on an old computer.

His father had walked out on them when he was twelve. But Gerald had lived with them long enough to teach his younger son some invaluable lessons. Of how to turn his eyes blank so that no hurt would show in them. Of how to swim deep within himself, and not bob to the surface until the storm of Gerald's violence had ebbed. Of how to turn his heart into a rock so that Gerald's flinty, ugly words would bounce lightly off its surface.

Frank called on that knowledge now. Ignored his wife's upturned hand, not-seeing the sadness in her eyes or the heartbreaking curve of her mouth, not-hearing her plea for reconciliation, for going back to the way they used to be. Deliberately, he got up from the swing. "I'm going in," he said.

"You don't have to."

"Ramesh will be here soon, anyway." He collected their coffee mugs, aware of Ellie's eyes on him, knowing without looking the sadness and hurt and confusion that they held. It tore at him, this knowledge that he was responsible for the light going out of his wife's eyes, but his grief was paradoxical—it seemed to abate only if he duplicated it in Ellie, only if he caused more of it. Any moment that he spent berating himself for what he was doing to Ellie was a moment he didn't remember that he had to face the rest of his life without Benny.

The phone rang again the instant he walked into the living room, and he glanced at the clock. Eight o'clock. Could be Ellie's friend Nandita. Or Scott, for that matter. He remembered his earlier resolve to phone Scott tomorrow. Let it be Scott, he thought. He could take the call in the guest bedroom. Maybe Scott would say something that would allow him to approach Ellie again tonight, to salvage the evening.

"Hello?" he said, and knew immediately from the texture of the connection that it wasn't an overseas call.

"Sir?" the voice at the other end said. "This is Gulab Singh. Sorry to disturb at home, sir, but there's trouble at the factory."

Frank's stomach muscles clenched involuntarily. "What kind of trouble?" He hoped it was nothing serious enough to require him to go in tonight even as he knew that Gulab, who was the head of security at the factory, would not have called him at home over a trivial matter.

There was a pause, long enough for Frank to wonder if he'd lost the connection. Then Gulab said, "It's about that union chap—Anand. You remember him, sir? Anyway, sir. Problem is—Anand is dead. Unfortunately."

CHAPTER 2

Trouble's coming.

Frank had been gone for at least ten minutes, but still Ellie sat cross-legged on the swing. A dull fear was creeping up her limbs, but she was doing her best not to fan its flames, willing her mind to ignore what her body was trying to tell her. That trouble was on its way.

A particularly rude clap of thunder shattered the cocoon of mindlessness that she had built for herself and jolted her back into the world. The road leading to the factory will be dark and muddy at this time, she thought. Even though Satish was an expert driver, she was worried. She thought of calling Frank to ask him to let her know when he arrived at the factory, but the memory of the ugliness of their fight stopped her. Also, something terribly serious must have happened for them to have disturbed Frank at this hour. He did not need an anxious wife to add to his troubles.

She had had no time to ask him what was making him rush back to work so late in the evening. After he'd gone in to answer the phone, she'd heard him dial a second number—calling Satish to come pick him up, Ellie now surmised—and then she'd heard him fumble around in the bedroom before coming back to poke his head in the door and announce that he'd be gone for a few hours. She had merely nodded dully. A few minutes later, she heard the kitchen door slam and later, the sound of a car pulling out of the driveway at the side of the house.

Now, she cocked her head to hear better her body's fearful mutterings. What kind of trouble? she wondered. And was this a premonition or simply the sour aftertaste of the argument she'd had with Frank? What was frightening her so? Fear that Satish would make a wrong turn in the dark and that the car would spiral out of control? Fear that she and Frank were treading on dangerous ground, drifting apart, so that this grand experiment, this hope that India would heal them, would all be for naught? Ellie listened deeply to her body, the way she'd always advised her patients to. The body is wise, she'd often said to them. It often knows more—and sooner—than our brains do. But you have to learn how to listen to it, learn its language, the way you learn to understand an infant's gobbledygook.

But the rain and thunder were distracting her, throwing her off. The scent of the earth, the coolness of the rain-soaked air, the flashes of the lightning, were too overpowering, pulling her in too many different directions, like Benny used to when they went to the Michigan State Fair.

Still, those two words, steady as a knock in the dark. *Trouble's coming.*

I wish Frank would settle the labor dispute already, she thought, and then she was backing into the source of her fear. Almost immediately, her body relaxed as if, having relayed its message to her brain, it could now take the evening off. But what the fuck could be so wrong that they had to call him at home tonight? She realized she'd said the words out loud, but the rain coming down so hard erased the distinction between thoughts and words. Besides, she was annoyed now at how abruptly Frank had left, withholding information from her, leaving her to rock restlessly on the swing, her earlier serenity replaced by agitation and fear. "Screw you, Frank," she said loudly, making sure that the rain could not drown out her words.

Fear had made her sit still; now, a simmering anger at Frank replaced it and it made her restless. She pushed the button on the large, cheap Timex men's watch she had bought at Agni Bazaar last month, and its dial lit up in green. Eight twenty, it read. She thought quickly. If there was something going on at the factory, surely Shashi would've heard about it. As the owner of a large four-star hotel in the next town of Kanbar, Shashi employed the relatives of many of the men who worked for HerbalSolutions. And his wife, Nandita, Ellie's best friend, also kept a close watch on the situation at HerbalSolutions. Shashi went to bed early, but Nandita would definitely be up. For the first time, Ellie was grateful that all the relaxation techniques she had taught Nandita to help with her insomnia had not taken.

She had just gotten her feet into her slippers and was heading for the phone in the living room when she heard the timid knock on the door. She stopped. What the hell? And then she remembered. Of course. It was Ramesh, coming over to do his homework with Frank. In the unusual excitement of the phone call and Frank's abrupt leaving, she had forgotten all about Ramesh.

Before she could reach the kitchen, the door opened and Ramesh walked in. Ellie felt a mixture of bemusement and irritation. A few months ago, she had taught the boy that it was bad manners to walk into someone's home without knocking. So now he knocked in a perfunctory manner and then let himself in. She was debating whether it was time for Lesson 2, but Ramesh had spotted her in the living room and, dropping his books on the blue-painted kitchen table, he skipped toward her. "Hi, Ellie." He grinned. And before she could reply, "Where's Frank? I'm having *two* tests tomorrow and so much homework."

No self-respecting American boy would look so gleeful at the thought of homework, Ellie thought. But then, she knew that the enthusiasm was not so much for the homework as for the bliss of spending another evening with his beloved Frank. She smiled ruefully to herself at the realization. Watching Frank and Ramesh together made her feel like the odd man out, like the third wheel, like—what was that Hindi expression Nandita used?—something to the effect of the bone in the meat kebab. So different from the close, joint-circuit feeling she used to have when she watched Frank and Benny indulge in their usual horseplay or when all three of them walked around their neighborhood together and Benny had eyes only for his father, playing tag with him, racing up Fair Hill with him, or playing that silly game where they counted the numbers on the license plates of passing cars to see if they added up to 21. They would cajole Ellie to join in, and she, wanting only to take a relaxed, leisurely evening walk, would refuse. And father and son would mock her for not being into competitive walking and climbing and counting. But somehow even their teasing, their mocking, included her, made her feel part of a triangle, valued, a straight man to their clowning around.

"Where's Frank?" Ramesh said again, and she forced herself to pay attention to the boy.

"He's out, sweetie. I'm afraid he won't be home until late tonight."

Ramesh looked outraged. "Where he go?"

So direct, so blunt. It was a trait she had noticed in many of the Indians she'd come in contact with. Was there an Indian Miss Manners, she wondered, someone who could teach them the virtues of evasion, of subtlety, of telling the truth slant? But most of the time Ellie felt happy to be among people who did not play games, to whom the very expression "playing games" meant a vigorous game of hockey or cricket. A practical, literal people. Frank, she knew, was appalled by how bluntly his employees spoke, saw it as rudeness, crassness. And in the beginning she, too, was unnerved by it, by the lack of artifice, by the absence of the sheen of politeness that covered all interactions in America like Saran Wrap. Except for the clerks working in the fancy shops of Bombay, no one in India said inane things like "Have a nice day." Once, soon after they'd moved to Girbaug, Ellie had told Edna to have a nice day and Edna had replied, "Only if God's willing, madam, if God's willing." And Ellie had heard what Edna had not said—that having a nice day was not up to the will of mere mortals but depended upon the benevolence of a kind God. She had never used the expression again. And volunteering at NIRAL, the clinic that Nandita had started for the villagers, counseling the women about mental health and domestic violence issues, Ellie had grown to appreciate the direct, guileless way in which they spoke. Husbands were roaches and rats and *kuttas*, dogs. The women used words like *Satan* and *evil* casually and without irony. The ease with which they spoke about the devil and of evil reminded Ellie of the Christian fundamentalists in America, their vocabulary so different from that of Ellie and Frank's liberal, secular friends in Ann Arbor. When the women in the village found out that a husband had gambled away his family's life savings, they tracked down the man and removing their rubber slippers beat him with them. Last year, when a corrupt politician who had broken every promise had the audacity to visit their village before the next election, they had made a garland of their dirty, filthy slippers and placed it around his neck. The man tried to beat a hasty retreat to his air-conditioned car, but the mob of women chased him, hooting and hollering and jeering and hissing.

"Ellie," Ramesh was saying. "I'm asking and asking. Where's Frank?"

"I'm sorry, baby. He's gone back to work. I don't think he'll be home in time to help you tonight." Even as she said those words, Ellie was amazed that Frank hadn't taken the time to cross the courtyard and knock on Edna's door to tell the boy not to come over tonight. Something really serious must have called him away.

"Can you help me?" And intercepting the look of refusal on

Ellie's face, Ramesh added, "Please, Ellie. I have two big-big tests tomorrow. And in geography I'm a duffer."

She smiled at his choice of words. This boy was charming. She could see why he'd stolen Frank's heart. Still, Frank needed to be careful—and so did she. She didn't want to fall victim to Ramesh's undeniable charms. On the other hand, she couldn't refuse the boy a shot at doing well on his tests. "Well, lucky for you, I'm very good at geography. So let's do a quick revision session, okay? Where do you need to start?"

Ramesh sat at his usual spot at the kitchen table and flung open an ominously thick book. He turned the yellowing pages fast and carelessly as Ellie murmured, "Careful, careful. You must treat books with respect." But even as she spoke she noticed how used the book was, saw the passages underlined by the scores of students who had used the textbook before Ramesh had purchased it. She remembered how clean and crisp the pages of Benny's books used to look. From the time he was little, Benny had always taken good care of his books, turning the pages carefully and tenderly, as she had taught him. But God, how much easier it was to do when the books were worthy of that care.

Ramesh had opened to the section about different mountain ranges. Ellie looked at the chapter uncertainly. "So what do you want me to do?"

He looked at her impatiently for not knowing the routine, as if she were the student, and a rather slow one, at that. "I'll review the chapter quickly. And then you ask me test questions."

"Sure." She read over his shoulder and, despite herself, marveled at how fast the boy read. Frank was right. Ramesh was as bright as the Indian sunshine.

"You ready?" she said after they'd both finished. "Shall I grill you on some questions?"

"Grill me? Like a fish?"

"Very funny, Ramesh. Now listen, time to hit the books, okay?"

She caught the gleam in his eye. "And no more puns. No, I'm not explaining what a pun is. You're taking a test tomorrow in geography and math, not in joke-making." She scanned the pages of the chapter again, formulating her first question. "Outside of Asia, what is the world's tallest mountain range?"

"The Andes," he said promptly.

"Right. And what is the height of Mount Everest?" she asked, even as she wondered, Who cares? Why do they make schoolchildren in India memorize all this?

"Eight thousand eight hundred and fifty meters," he said. "Correct, Ellie?"

"Correct." She had to smile at the triumphant enthusiasm she heard in his voice. "You lied to me. You're not a duffer in geography, at all."

He made a face. "I am. There is one boy in the class who is getting the higher marks in geography than me. Always hundred out of hundred, he's getting."

"But that doesn't make you a duffer. You just have to—"

"My dada say I'm a duffer," Ramesh said. There was something in his voice Ellie couldn't quite pick up on, as if he was defying her to contradict his father, even while hoping that she would.

But before she could react, Ramesh was talking again. "Ellie," he said. "I had a card for you. But Ma said not to give it."

Ellie cocked her head. "What card?"

The boy suddenly looked bashful. Ellie noticed that he was avoiding her eye, staring at the blue table. "A Mother's Day card. We made them in school. I made one for you."

Something crept up the base of Ellie's neck. Yesterday had been Mother's Day. She had made herself forget the fact. All day long she had glanced at Frank, willing him not to acknowledge it either. To her immense relief, he hadn't. "I—" She struggled to find the right tone, unwilling to let Ramesh know how rattled she was. "Thanks," she said. "But speaking of school, let's get back to—"

"How did your boy dead?" It took her a second to realize that Ramesh was asking about Benny, and she was shocked. He had never asked her such a personal question before. But then again, she had never really spent time alone with the boy. "Die," she corrected absentmindedly. "How did your boy die?"

Too late, she realized that Ramesh was waiting for her to answer her own question. At this moment, Ellie hated this peculiarly Indian inquisitiveness. And if this had been an adult being so nosy, so brutal in his directness, she would have bristled, wouldn't have tried to cover up her outrage. But the fierce, intent expression on Ramesh's face was throwing her off stride. "He was sick," she said.

A look of such adult understanding crossed the boy's face that Ellie felt naked beneath it. "Typhoid," he said. It wasn't a question.

"No, not typhoid. A, a, rash. Do you know what a rash is?"

Ramesh glanced at his welted, mosquito-bitten hands. "Like this?"

Was it like that? Ellie tried to remember. She had been half asleep when she had first seen the horrifying purple that had covered Benny's face within a matter of hours. At midnight, when she had finally put her agitated, restless son to bed, his face had been as lovely and smooth as the moon. At four in the morning, woken out of an inexplicably deep sleep by a single cry, she had hurried to Benny's room, turned on the night lamp near his bed, and seen an unrecognizable boy sleeping in her son's bed. Even now, Ellie could remember how her stomach had dropped, the fear that gripped her, an instantaneous, icy-cold fear that she had to consciously battle with, beat down, so that Benny would not see in her scared face what she didn't want him to see. She had run her fingers over his body, one hand unbuttoning his pajama top even as the other inspected the skin on his chest, his neck, his arms. And everywhere she touched there were bumps and welts. "Are you okay, sweetie?" she had asked. "Does it hurt?" And he had nodded no, but with a rising panic she took in the heavy-lidded eyes, the hot, flushed cheeks, the hair sticking to his sweaty forehead. And when he formed his lips to say, "My throat feels funny," she saw the effort it took him to speak, heard the hoarseness in his voice. Still, she managed to keep her voice steady, as if she were walking a plank on a particularly turbulent sea. "I'm going to call Dr. Roberts again, okay, sweetie?" she said. "I'll be right back."

"Is this a rash?" Ramesh was holding his hand up for her to inspect.

Ellie glanced toward the door, willing Frank to walk through it and distract Ramesh from this line of questioning. "No, not really," she said. "*Achcha*, let's get back to the books, shall we?"

"*Achcha*," Ramesh said but the boy was in a strange mood tonight, because the next minute he stuck out his index finger and touched Ellie's wrist. Just that—the light touch of a single finger that nevertheless felt to Ellie like a lit match against her flesh. Idly she noticed the black crescent under his fingernails. They both stared at the spot where Ramesh's finger rested on Ellie's wrist. Then Ramesh said, "I am feeling so sad for your son."

And Ellie thought back to the funeral—to Father O'Donnell's rageful, heartfelt eulogy, to the whispering women clad in black, the silent, solid presence of the men, the brave, lip-trembling steadiness of her mother, the fierce, protective support of her sister, Anne, the terror on the faces of the mothers of Benny's friends, the pity on the faces of their husbands. She thought of the weeks and months that followed—the lasagnas and pot roasts dropped off by neighbors; the spontaneous hugs in grocery stores from people whose names she couldn't recall; the condolence cards from well-meaning friends who felt compelled to include pictures of Benny from their own photo albums; the cautious, careful looks she got from her own clients when she finally returned to the practice, as if they wanted to measure the temperature of her grief before they shared any of their own; the treasured, handwritten note from Robert, Benny's best friend, that read, "I will always love him." And then she looked at the dark-skinned boy with the dirty fingernails who sat touching her with one finger, and she knew that nothing that had happened in the weeks after Benny's death—not the notes or the cards or the whispered messages of courage and hope or the prayers or the homilies or the platitudes—had penetrated her as deeply as this boy's awkward, ungrammatical words. Everyone else had said they were sorry, everyone else had said it was a tragedy, a shame, a pity, a travesty, some had shaken their fists at God, others had advised her to bow to His will. But no one had told her that they felt sad for Ben. No one had understood that sentiment—that much of her anger, her rage, her grief at what had happened, was not for herself or for Frank, though, of course, their grief was monumental, almost inhuman in its size and dimensions, so that she felt as if mere humans could not understand it, only the ocean and the mountains and the wind could. No, what she felt most of all was a screaming anger for what Benny had been cheated out of, at the destiny that had been wrestled out of his tiny, unformed fist. She and Frank had lost Benny, but Ben, Ben had lost not just his parents but his unborn children; not just his best friend from elementary school but the unknown friend from college and the women he would have dated and loved, the woman he would have married. Sometimes, when Ellie thought about the enormity of Benny's loss, she was dumbfounded by its magnitude—the books he'd never read, the movies he'd never see, the symphonies he'd never hear (or compose), the geometric theorems he'd never solve, the all-night college rap sessions he'd never bullshit his way through, the junior year abroad that he'd never take, the debates about Nietzsche and Kierkegaard he would never participate in, the first kiss he would never have, the continent of difference between having sex and making love that he'd never discover, the thrilling knowledge that he'd outgrown his parents that he'd never possess, the first job, the first promotion, the first trip abroad, the first love letter, the first heartbreak, the first child—and God, so much more—the pimply awkwardness of being fifteen, the reckless giddiness of being twenty, the contentment of being forty, the achievement of being sixty, the acceptance of being eighty—none of this would be Benny's fate. Ellie understood now why people mourned the death of children. The reason to mourn the death of a child of seven (or eight, or nine) was simple—at seven (or eight, or nine) children are stupid, so unformed, so inexperienced, that they may as well belong to a different species. The true reason to mourn the young dead was not because of what they were but of what they would never be.

Now Ramesh was drawing tiny circles on Ellie's wrist with his fingernails, a shy, self-conscious gesture that she immediately recognized. Without thinking about it, she lifted his thin hand to her lips and kissed it. An American boy may have been embarrassed by this. Ramesh beamed. "I like you, Ellie," he said, but his voice was thin and uncertain with shyness, as if he was asking her permission, as if the statement had a question mark at the end of it.

"I like you, too," she said. Then, to mask her own embarrassment she added gruffly, "Now come on, enough dillydallying. You want to do well on the test tomorrow, don't you?"

"Dillydallying." Ramesh giggled. "Is that like *khaata-mitha?*"

She frowned. "*Kaataa-meeta?*"

"It's meaning sour and sweet. Like eating a green, unripe mango"—Ramesh screwed up his face—"and then eating an ice cream."

"Well, dillydally is nothing like that. It means to waste time on purpose. Which is what, you, dear boy, are doing."

Ramesh's grin was disarming. "Caught me," he said. He stretched his hands in a leisurely yawn above his head so that Ellie could see the flat, hollow stomach under his shirt. "I'm feeling lazy just now, Ellie."

"But ten minutes ago you were all frantic"—she saw he didn't

know that word—"worried about your test. Now come on, a few
more questions and then we can stop."

Outside, the music of the storm continued unabated and the
house creaked and groaned in accompaniment. When she was satisfied that Ramesh knew the answers to her questions, she got up.
"I'm going to make a cup of tea. You read another chapter, okay?"

He nodded, but each time she turned away from the kettle to look
at him, she caught Ramesh staring at the front door. He's keeping
a vigil for Frank, the same as I am, she thought, but was not offended by the thought. In fact, it touched her, reminded her of how
Benny used to wait for his father to return home at the end of each
workday. Except for Thursdays, when Ellie worked late, she always
came home by three o'clock so that for a few uninterrupted hours,
it was just her and Benny in the house. But by six the boy would be
agitated, his voice just a little louder, his playing a little more aggressive, looking out the living room window for his dad.

Ellie felt her throat swelling at the memory of those long afternoons with her son. The dappled sun climbing into the kitchen as
she cooked their supper. The stereo playing Benny's favorite song,
"Yellow Submarine." Benny climbing the tree house that Frank had
built for him, his light hair looking like spun gold in the sun. The
smell of the earth as Ellie dug a garden, Benny beside her with his
red shovel, trying to help. The two of them lying on a blanket in
the backyard, the grass green and sparkling in the afternoon light.
Golden. The memory of those years felt golden, draped in yellow
light. Although she knew that she had been as rushed and harried
as any working mom, now when she revisited that time, it felt lazy,
stretched out, like a movie reel that someone was winding very
slowly. How blithely, how casually, she had treated those years, Ellie
now thought. She had had the cavalier attitude of a woman who
expected her good fortune to last and last, who never realized that
every Eden came with its own handy-dandy snake, one who would

strike without warning and at the moment she would least expect it to.

"Frank may be late coming home tonight, Ramesh," she said over the whistle of the kettle. "I'm the best you have for now, I'm afraid."

The boy threw her a perceptive, needle-sharp look. "That's okay," he said hastily. "I like studying with you."

Ellie smiled to herself at the obvious untruth.

They studied for another two hours. When Ramesh finally left after ten thirty, Frank had still not returned home.

CHAPTER 3

Through the curtain of fog and rain, the distant lights looked like a swarm of fireflies. But as the Jeep drew closer to the factory, Frank saw that the light came from the kerosene lamps carried by the twenty or so men milling around the gate. A few of them had black umbrellas, but the majority of them were soaking wet. Their long white tunics clung to their bodies, and despite being warm and dry in the car, Frank shivered in sympathy. Or perhaps it was the ugliness that he saw on their faces as they peered into the Jeep—their eyes wide open, their mouths twisted in anger as they shouted slogans, the sound of which barely reached Frank, given the rain and the fact that his windows were rolled up—that accounted for the shiver. Or the fact that several of them beat on the Jeep with their fists or with open palms as Satish slowly drove by them, waiting for the night watchman to open the large iron gate. Without intending to, Frank found himself turning in his seat and looking back, and he saw that the crowd had surged toward the open gate but was held at bay by the armed *chowkidar*. Shit, he thought. This is not good.

The first time he had ever laid eyes on the factory, he had been embarrassed by the long, tree-lined driveway, by the green, manicured lawns, the flowering bushes, by the sheer wastefulness and display of wealth in a village marked by so much poverty. Tonight, he was grateful for the distance it put between him and the workers outside the gates. The driveway wound behind the factory to a separate building that housed HerbalSolution's corporate offices and where Satish was now headed. By the time Satish pulled up to the front entrance, the Jeep was almost out of sight from the angry gazes of the mob outside the gate. As he jumped out of the vehicle under the protection of the umbrella Satish was holding out for him, Frank felt unreal, had the feeling of being trapped in one of those movies based on a Graham Greene novel. He had needed the twenty-minute car trip here to gather his thoughts. A worker dead. What was their liability? Their responsibility? He felt totally out of his element, more of a stranger to India than on the day he had landed in the country last year. When he had gone into Pete's office to accept the assignment, labor troubles had been the last thing he'd thought of. How to deal with the aftermath of a dead worker was something they had not taught him in business school. A feeling of dread came over him, a deep resistance at having to deal with this situation. The men who were gathered at the gate during a thunderstorm were not going to forget about their fallen comrade any time soon. He knew that. This is fucked up, he thought. I come to this country just trying to do my fucking job, and next thing I know, I'm dealing with a mob that has some serious hatred on their faces.

By the time he walked through the long hallway that led to his office, anger had replaced fear. He noticed that every light in the one-floor corporate building had been turned on, and for some reason, this irritated him. Did these people think this was a picnic or something? Who the hell did they think was paying their electric bills?

He was further annoyed to find Gulab Singh sitting on his chair at his desk and using his phone. At least the man had the decency to rise from Frank's chair when he entered the room. "*Achcha,*" Gulab was saying. "Okay, no problem. First thing tomorrow morning I will be there. But the big boss just walked in. We will talk again tomorrow, *achcha?*" He disconnected the phone.

"What the hell is going on, Gulab?" Frank said before the other man could greet him. "What happened to Anand?"

Gulab took out a white handkerchief from his jeans pocket and deliberately wiped off the phone's mouthpiece before setting it down. Stupid Indian habit, Frank thought. All he's doing is moving the germs around. He forced himself to take his mind off the phone and focus on Gulab.

Frank's head of security was a big, burly man with a clean-shaven, strong jaw, a boxer's nose, and large, meaty hands. He was by far the largest Indian that Frank had ever met. Everything about him exuded power and raw, brute strength. He alternated in dress between the traditional Sikh long tunic and pajamas to occasionally showing up at the factory in a shirt and blue jeans. It was as if he changed his dressing habits often enough to remain something of a mystery. Something about Gulab had always made Frank uneasy, but he had never been able to put a finger on it. Unlike the other workers, Gulab always kept his word, was hard-working, reliable, and could think for himself. Nor was he obsequious or ingratiating like the others, traits that Frank despised. Most of the Indians he knew were either as blunt as a fist to the mouth or ingratiating as hell. But their fawning just made him feel aloof and distant. The more distant he got, the greater the intensity of the vigorous head-nodding and the smiles and the yessirs. Though, in fairness, he didn't quite like the opposite either, this new sternness and seriousness that had overcome them since the labor situation arose two months ago. Men who had seemed infantile to him just a few months ago now seemed hardened and mature, and looked at him as if they saw something in him that he himself couldn't see, as if he was something more than just Frank Benton from Ann Arbor, who had accepted a posting in a distant land and was trying to make a go of it, a working stiff (when you got right down to it) the same as any of them.

"So what's going on?" Frank said again, taking his position behind his desk so that Gulab had no choice other than to sit on the visitor's chairs facing him.

Gulab shook his head. "It's not a good situation, sir. As you know, Anand was taken in police custody two days ago. And—"

"Wait. Did I know this?"

Gulab shot him a curious look. "I informed you myself, boss." There was something in his voice Frank could not pick up on. "I think you were on your way to the weekly meeting when I told you. And your answer was—you asked me to take care of it."

Frank felt something form in the pit of his stomach. "So what did you do, Gulab?"

Gulab spoke slowly. "I thought your instructions were clear, sir. So I told the police chief to, you know, put some *dum*—apply some pressure—on the boy. He was the ringleader, see? And I thought if we could break his back, we'd break the rest of the union before things got out of hand."

"You asked them to kill him?" Frank's voice was a whisper.

Gulab looked startled and sat even more erect in his chair. "Sir. Of course not, sir. The death was a terrible accident. They were just—roughing him up—to make sure he came to his senses. God knows what went wrong. Police here know how to beat so that marks don't show, so that nothing too serious happens. This boy must've been weak for starters." Gulab's eyes darted about as he thought. "In fact, it probably was a heart condition he was having. Yes, probably had a weak heart."

That feeling of unreality, of being caught in a bad movie, swept over Frank again. I'm sitting in an office in India in the middle of the night discussing how to cover up the death of a young man, he thought, and despite the horror, the shame, the revulsion he felt, there was no escaping it—there was also a kind of excitement, a sense of being tested, of being adult and worldly in a way he never would've been if he'd remained in Ann Arbor. "So is that our defense?" he heard himself ask. "That Anand had a bad heart?"

"Defense?" This time there was no mistaking the fact that Gulab was mocking him, that he knew that Frank was out of his element, out of his depth, an innocent American boy trying to swim in murky, adult waters. Dimly, Frank remembered an earlier conversation with Gulab where the man had told him about his stint with the Indian Army in Kashmir. "I have killed men with my bare hands, sir," Gulab had said. "It was that or be killed by the Muslim swine myself." Now, he forced himself to focus on what Gulab was saying. "No need for a defense, sir. Our company is not responsible for his death. If Anand had a bad heart, he should've thought twice before becoming a union leader. Conditions in jail are such they resulted in his untimely death."

"You think they'll buy it?" And then he caught himself, heard himself becoming an accomplice in the death of a youth he barely knew, a man who had come into his office a few weeks ago with a petition demanding better pay for the workers and longer breaks. There had been nothing exceptional about Anand, no trait that had snagged itself onto Frank's memory, and it was that everydayness, that ordinariness, that filled Frank with a deep sorrow and revulsion at the conversation he was now having. "Listen," he said, faking a resoluteness he wasn't feeling, "there's got to be a better way to handle this. We can simply come clean. Say that the police tortured Anand, and that we had nothing to do with that."

"Frank, sahib. Just think. If we do this, our involvement with the police becomes clear, no? Why did they arrest him at all, sir? It's because we—I—asked them to. He had done nothing criminal. Still, they went into his house in the evening and pulled him out for questioning. And secondly, if we finger the police this time, what do you think happens when we need their help next time? For the last

year the villagers have been disputing our rights to the trees that are
HerbalSolutions's lifeblood, sir. You know that. Who do you think
helps us keep those ignorant villagers from claiming the trees for
themselves?"

Frank was aware of the simmering discontent among the villagers
about the fact that HerbalSolutions had signed a fifty-year lease to
thousands of acres of forest land from the Indian state government.
The villagers had traditionally brewed, chewed, and even smoked
the leaves of the girbal tree—the same leaves that HerbalSolutions
was now harvesting and processing to use in its SugarGo line as
an alternative treatment to control diabetes. The villagers were also
used to chopping what they thought of as their trees for firewood.
After signing the lease, HerbalSolutions had posted guards to protect the trees against poachers. But there were constant disputes and
run-ins between the hired guards and the people who believed that
despite what the government said, the trees belonged to their forefathers and were to be passed on to their children. Several times, the
police had been called to quell the unrest.

"So what do we propose we do?" Frank said, hating this feeling
of being boxed in.

"Just leave things to me, sir. I'll take care of everything."

"No, thanks. I won't make that mistake again. The last time I
asked you to take care of things, I end up with a dead man on my
hands." The words shot out of Frank, fired by the anger and resentment he felt.

Gulab stiffened imperceptibly, and his eyes went flat and hollow.
Frank could tell that he had drawn blood. He felt a small satisfaction
followed by a twinge of regret. Gulab was not someone he wanted
to turn against himself. "I'm sorry," he began. "That was—"

"No harm done, sahib." Gulab's smile was stiff, perfunctory.
"And sir. I honestly thought I was following your instruction. When
you told me to take care of the situation with Anand, I thought—"

Was the fellow trying to implicate him? Trying to ensure that

his hands were dirty—hell, bloody—too? And what *had* he meant
when he'd told Gulab to handle the situation? Just the reflexive mutterings of a harried executive? Or had there been something more
sinister—a desire for the problem to go away, to be solved by any
means necessary—in that command? He could barely remember
saying those words to Gulab. But even if he had, dear God, surely
he had not meant *murder*, had not even meant torture. Frank remembered when he had first read about the Abu Ghraib scandal. He had
felt physically sick. This is so not us. This is not what Americans
do, he'd thought. Ellie, of course, had been characteristically more
cynical. C'mon, Frank, she had said, what do you think happened
in Vietnam? Hell, what do you think happens in U.S. prisons every
day? But he had been genuinely shocked, repulsed by the pictures
on television. He looked at Gulab now, trying to think of a way to
explain all this to him, to make him see that his was not a world
of police torture and beatings and prison deaths. For a moment
he thought with longing of the house in Ann Arbor, the animated
dinner parties with friends who shared their political views, the easy
conversations where they all vowed to move to Canada if Bush won
a second term and never mentioned it again after he did. But it was
like looking into that world from a thick sheet of ice, as if his former
life was encapsulated inside one of those snow globes, delicate, frag-
ile, lovely, and he was holding it in the palm of his hand, looking at
it from the outside. After living in India for the past year and a half,
he felt closer to the American soldiers who were up to their ears in
shit and muck in Iraq, felt that he could comprehend their lost innocence and their confusion and irritation, even their contempt and
hatred for a culture they had come to save but that was destroying
them. All his liberal beliefs—that people were the same all over the
world, that cultural differences could be bridged by goodwill and
tolerance—seemed dangerous and naïve to him at this moment.
The man who sat before him right now was as unknowable as a
mountain, as impenetrable as a dense forest. The distance between

them was greater than the geographical distance between their two countries.

"Listen, Gulab," he said. "You know damn well that whatever I said, I didn't intend any violence. That's not how we do business." He looked at Gulab and thought again of how he didn't want this man as an enemy. Forcing himself to lighten his tone, he said, "Anyway. It's a shitty situation, but we'll have to face up to it. I'll back you in this. And you'll just owe me big, won't you?"

Gulab looked puzzled at this last, unfamiliar Americanism. Then, he nodded. "I'm in your debt, sir." He opened his mouth to say more, but just then there was a knock on the door.

"Come in," Frank called, and Deepak Mehta, Frank's second-in-command, walked in. "Hi, Frank," he said, ignoring Gulab. "What a tragedy, hah? I just now only got the news. Roads were bad, but I came as quickly as I could."

"You shouldn't have come in at all, Deepak. I could've handled it." Frank realized that he had not even thought of calling Deepak. You're not thinking clearly, he chastised himself. You've got to do better than this.

"Nonsense. Wouldn't think of letting you deal with this alone. Have you seen the crowd at the gate? There's about fifty people there. Including the mother."

"What mother?"

Deepak blinked. "Why, the man's—that is, Anand's mother."

"She's outside the factory?"

"Yah. I got out and talked to her. But she's not satisfied. She wants to talk to you, only."

Frank blanched, and from the slightest movement of Gulab's head, he knew that the man had seen his fear. But he was beyond caring. The thought of meeting Anand's mother, of answering her accusations, of looking her in the eye, was beyond what he could physically do. He knew his limits. Less than two years ago, he had attended his own son's funeral, had avoided eye contact with another bereaved mother, who happened to be his own wife. He couldn't do it. He couldn't.

"Frank," Deepak was saying. "It will probably help a lot if you could, y'know, go out and address the crowd. Say a few sorrys to the mother."

"I can't." Instinctively, Frank turned to Gulab for support. The man was staring at Frank in fascination, as if he was solving a puzzle. Slowly, a look of understanding spread across his face. But Frank was too anguished to register much of this. He felt like a cornered animal, actually rubbing his hand over his neck, where he felt the unmistakable bite of a noose being tightened.

"It's customary here." Deepak seemed oblivious to Frank's discomfort. "Mark of respect. You have to pay condolence to—"

"Deepak babu," Gulab said, jutting out his right arm as if to stop the flow of words. "Not a good idea for Frank sahib to face the crowd tonight. Maybe we can give the mother a few hundred rupees and send her home tonight. Later on, we shall see."

Deepak's mouth tightened. "A twenty-two-year-old boy has died here," he said. "I don't think a few hundred rupees will appease the mother."

Gulab laughed. There was something dismissive and frightening about his laugh, and it had the desired effect. Deepak looked uncertainly from one man to the other. "I'll deal with those *junglee* villagers outside, sahib," Gulab said. "Once they see that both of you have left, they will leave, also. And I'm going to make arrangements for both of you to leave from the back road, okay? No need to face that crowd again." Although he was addressing both of them, his eyes bore into Frank's, who sensed that a subtle, imperceptible shift had occurred between him and Gulab, that Gulab had spotted some essential weakness in him and was protecting him.

"Okay," Frank said. His mouth was dry, his voice weak.

Gulab shot him another look. "I'll go find your driver," he said and left the room.

"What the hell is going on, Frank?" Deepak turned to him as soon as Gulab was out of the door. "What are we going to do?"

"It turns out the boy had some kind of heart condition. Being in jail probably stressed him out. It's very unfortunate." Even to Frank, his voice sounded wobbly and untrue. But he already had the premonition of saying those words over and over again, until they would finally set, harden, become true.

Deepak gave him a long, thoughtful look. "I see. Is that what we're saying?"

Frank's tone was wooden. "That's what's true."

"I see," Deepak said again. He too sounded flat, his natural exuberance leveled into a kind of bleariness. And then, in a sudden, savage burst, "These greedy bastards. Everything was going so well. And then they had to start wanting more money and this and that."

Frank appreciated what Deepak was trying to do, incite himself, convince himself that the crowd waiting for them to appear outside the gate was to blame for the tragedy that had occurred. Out of the blue, he remembered an interview with a young soldier in Iraq whose buddies had been accused of slaughtering innocent civilians. "These mofuckin' rag-heads are treacherous, man," he had told the reporter. "One moment they're smiling at you and shit and the next they're pelting you with stones. So they bring a lot of this shit on themselves, man." Watching the interview, Frank had been ashamed and repulsed. But now, he was grateful for what Deepak was doing, understood that he would have to start thinking the same way himself.

"Deepak," he said urgently, taking advantage of Gulab's absence. "Whatever happens, I don't want to face the mother, okay?" He tried to find a lighter tone. "That wasn't part of the job description," he added, but it came out wrong, thin and whiny instead of casual and jocular.

"I already met with the mother," Deepak mumbled, shifting in his chair, averting his gaze. "Also, there will be a funeral. Someone from the factory will have to attend." His expression made it clear that he wasn't volunteering for the job.

Frank sighed. "It's late. Let's get home for a few hours and meet again in the morning, okay?" He got up from his chair to indicate the meeting was over and opened the door. Together, they walked down the hallway, only to run into Satish, who was hurrying toward them.

"You need a ride, Deepak?" Frank asked.

"No, thanks. I drove myself."

"Okay. Be careful going home."

"You, too."

In the Jeep, Frank climbed into the back seat, ignoring Satish's quizzical look. The driver expertly steered the vehicle down the side road behind the office, until they were off the HerbalSolutions grounds and could loop around again on the main road, thereby bypassing the crowd.

The rain had slowed down and the air-conditioning was on, but the vehicle still felt stuffy and hot. Frank tapped on the driver's seat. "Satish," he called. "Pull over."

He had jumped out of the Jeep before Satish could even come around to open the door for him. Running to the side of the road, he bent over and threw up. It was too dark to see the contents of tonight's dinner, but Frank had the inescapable feeling that he was throwing up more than food—that he was bringing up bruised and beaten flesh, gallons of spilled blood, the unbearable, inexpressible anguish of a bereaved mother and the lost promise of a life that he may have unwittingly taken with his careless words.

CHAPTER 4

Prakash felt as if even the sea was receding away from him. In all the years he had lived in the one-room shack behind the big house where the Americans now lived, he had always felt that the sea belonged to him. During the Olaf years, Prakash could escape to the beach to smoke a bidi or to get away from Ramesh's wailing whenever he felt like it. Olaf, the German bachelor who had built this house, had been the perfect employer—*bas*, as long as you gave him his morning coffee and poured him his evening Scotch and cooked and cleaned in between, he left you alone to come and go as you pleased. Olaf never once sat on the porch and waved to you as you crossed the lawn to take the stone steps down to the beach. As Ellie was doing right now. "Hello, miss," he muttered as he hurried past the flowering bushes and toward the steps.

The Americans seemed to spend all their time on the porch. God knows why. A perfectly nice, big house with air-conditioning in every room, and instead they preferred to bake in the afternoon sun. Unlike him, who had no choice but to be out in the sun if he wanted to avoid Edna's nagging. Some days, he wanted to burn down their one-room shack, just to get away from the shrillness of her voice.

And the disappointment that seemed to permanently reside in her eyes, like fish in a pond.

He lit a *bidi* as soon as he reached the beach. Ellie had forbidden him from smoking in his own house, lecturing him on how bad the smoke was for Ramesh. So many times he'd wanted to remind them that Ramesh was his flesh, not theirs. So many times he'd had to look away so that they would not see the anger that rumbled inside him. What was it that Rakesh had said at Anand's funeral? That the *gora*s poked their noses into other people's business so much, it was a miracle they were still attached to their faces. Prakash laughed out loud, imagining Frank without a nose. He walked along the water, moved fast, wishing to get away from Ellie's line of vision.

Ellie was nice. Polite to him and Edna. Best of all, she never mistook Ramesh for her son. And when she looked at them, she *saw* them. Unlike Frank, who looked through him and Edna as if they were air. Always searching, searching for Ramesh, like they were water he had to look through to get to the bottom of the glass where Ramesh was.

At least the *tamasha* about Anand's death had kept Frank away from Prakash's family for a few days. He was spending all his time at the factory now. For that Prakash was grateful. For several days now, there had been no *thump, thump* of the basketball in the driveway as the American and his son played game after game, jabbering away in English. Ramesh's squeals of delight felt like pinches on Prakash's body, then. And Frank was coming home too late to help the boy with his homework. Just last night Prakash had ordered Edna to help Ramesh, but after struggling for an hour, Edna had given up. He had looked away then, not wanting to see the shame and helplessness in his wife's eyes. Already, their son knew more about the world than both of them. Of this fact, they were proud— and ashamed.

Edna had not wanted to go to the funeral with him. Out of loyalty to them. The Americans. "How it look if we go?" she'd asked. "Like we supporting the union?"

"I knew Anand from the day he was born. His mother is a good woman." He didn't say the rest—that Shanti, who was several years older than Prakash, had always been nice to him. That was how Prakash judged all the villagers—who had been nice to him and who had scorned him when he was a little orphan boy, wandering from home to home.

"You go, then. I don't even know these people."

"You living in Girbaug all these years and still putting on Goa airs. You must come. A wife must follow the husband. It says in the Bible."

Edna let out a snort. "What you know about the Bible, you heathen? Illiterate as a mouse, you are."

He looked outraged. "I know Bible say the husband have right to beat his wife if she is not listening. You must go."

The truth was, he wouldn't have gone to the funeral without Edna. He had not lived in the village for years now, not since they had moved into the servant's quarters of the house by the sea. Finding it hard to feed his new bride on his auto mechanic's salary, Prakash had years ago approached the scary-looking German who had come to him with a car repair question and tried to convince him that he needed someone to clean and cook for him. "My wife very good," he had said. "All Goanese dishes she making." To his great surprise, Olaf had agreed—but on the condition that the two of them move into the shack behind his new home. It turned out that his current servant was not terribly reliable—and reliability was the great German virtue that Olaf prized above all.

For Edna and Prakash, the arrangement was perfect. Olaf doubled Prakash's salary, and they had a free place to live. In the beginning, Prakash did the cleaning and Edna the cooking, but as time went by and Prakash discovered his culinary talents, they reversed the arrangement. Olaf didn't seem to notice.

But living away from the village also meant forgoing the easy familiarity that Prakash had developed as a young orphan, the access that had allowed him to enter people's homes without knocking. He had always held a peculiar position in the village, had been an object of affection but also of pity. The villagers saw him more as a talisman or a mascot than a human being. He himself never got rid of the feeling of being the eternal outsider. If he had married a girl from the village, perhaps things would've been different. But taking the first vacation of his life, he had gone to Goa and fallen in love with Edna. They had eloped to Girbaug two weeks later, knowing that her Catholic father would never consent to her marrying a Hindu. The villagers were as shocked by their marriage as Edna's family had been.

Prakash threw the stub of the bidi into the sea and immediately lit another one. Soon he'd have to get his bicycle and go pick up Ramesh at school. He decided to linger by the water a little longer. Edna had been in a bad mood since the funeral. He himself had been unprepared for the emotionalism at the scene. He tried now to blink away the memory of Shanti beating her breasts and trying to fling herself onto the burning pyre that was devouring her son. Of Anand's sobbing sister holding her mother back. Of Mukesh, Anand's best friend, saying bitterly, "You see how 'Merica is slaughtering those Iraqis? *Arre, bhai*, they won't rest until they do the same to us."

The funeral had made him hate Frank. On the way home he told Edna, "I don't want our Ramu going over their house for studying-fudying anymore. You see now who these people are."

But Edna had turned on him like a snake. "Okay, stupid. Then you teach him. Talk to your son in your broken English. And you pay his school fees. And buy his shoes and uniform. All on your salary—which Frank sir pays, anyway."

Prakash stared at the gray waters of the sea. These days, Edna felt as far away from him as that place where the sky touched the lip of the sea. And Ramesh was always sullen around him, as if he'd picked up on Edna's constant criticism of him. If only he had the means to make the boy smile the way the *gora* seemed to be able to do without trying. A few weeks ago, Frank had knocked on their door late in the evening and presented Ramesh with a brand-new basketball. This, after Prakash had spent an hour putting a rubber patch on the old one, made it as good as new. Show off. Always buying off his Ramu with presents.

Prakash felt his nose twitch as he fought back his tears. He rubbed his nose on his shirtsleeve, then looked up at the sky. Two more hours and he could have a drink. He thought with longing of the full bottle of *daru* that awaited him at home. As if the brown alcohol had already entered his body, he felt it uncoil and relax.

CHAPTER 5

Ellie had not left the house in over a week, and now she paced the living room, anxiously awaiting Nandita's arrival. Ever since Anand's death, Frank had begged her not to leave the house, told her it was unsafe for her to be out on her own on the streets of Girbaug. And Ellie had swallowed her normal resistance and stayed at home even as she resented how little Frank was telling her about what had transpired at the police station the day that poor boy had died or about the aftermath of his death. For that, she had to rely on Edna, who, despite her cautious and diffident manner, managed to convey the mood on the street to her employer. It was Edna who had told her about the rumors being circulated by the police about Anand having terrorist sympathies, a rumor that first made the men who knew him laugh and then infuriated them and finally, after it had been repeated over and over again, muted them into a kind of baffled silence.

But what had really unnerved Ellie was the scarlet streak of betel juice on Frank's blue shirt when he returned home the day after Anand's funeral. One of the pan-chewing men at the factory had walked up to Frank, looked him dead in the eye, and spat on him. It turned out that the worker was Anand's uncle, and of course he had immediately been fired, but something of the stunned surprise that Frank felt at that moment stayed with him that evening, so that he blurted out what had happened before Ellie could even question him.

"Deepak told me to have the fellow arrested," he said. "I refused. Would just inflame an already volatile situation, y'know?" There was none of the usual belligerence that crept into Frank's voice when he talked about the factory situation. In its place was a kind of puzzled weariness.

Frank's uncertainty tugged at Ellie's heartstrings, made her decide to put all her doubts aside, the nagging voice that said, But a man is dead and all because he dared to ask for a lousy wage hike. Frank would never do anything to deliberately hurt another person, she told herself. He would never do anything that would cause a mother to lose her son, because he knows what that kind of grief does to someone. And in order to take her mind away from the path it was taking, she reminded herself of the sweet, fun-loving young man she'd fallen in love with in grad school, remembered marching alongside him in Washington to protest the first Gulf War, recalled the genuine anguish he had felt when the Abu Ghraib story first broke. Only an innocent could've been that appalled and shocked, she now reminded herself, even as she remembered that her own reaction had been more worldly, more knowing, more pessimistic. So she silenced her doubts and held her husband at night and whispered words of comfort to him. And sometimes Frank responded by clinging to her in a way that reminded her of Benny during a rainstorm. And at other times, he gazed at her with the cloudy, distant eyes of a man who had traveled in space for so long he had forgotten what life on earth was like.

It was that latter look that made it hard to sustain the unconditional support, because it reminded her of how Frank had moved away from her immediately after Benny's funeral, how he had turned into an immobile object, someone who could not bear to be touched or to touch. How it had taken her months to realize that what she thought was numbness was not; that the blankness in his eyes was pure anger, a white rock of searing rage. That all the while she was raging against the heavens, against a pitiless, merciless God, he had been raging against—her. That he blamed her for the death of their son. Not that he would ever say that aloud. Only once, six months after Benny's death, had there been a fissure in the blank deadness that he normally presented to her, and then his very voice had sizzled with rage as he said, "What kind of mother falls asleep when her son is sick?"

How to answer a question like that? Where to begin? With the fact that she had already been awake for sixteen hours when sleep overtook her? With the defense that Benny had been stable, that she had checked him just as Dr. Roberts had asked her to, before she decided to get a few hours' sleep? With the plea that he understand that she was a mother, yes, but also a human being caught in the normal, mortal needs of sleep, hunger, fatigue? With the accusation that if he'd not been on a business trip to Thailand, there would've been two of them to watch over their sleeping son? With the simple truth that when she'd retired to her room, the aspirin seemed to have worked—Benny's fever was under control, and there was not a trace of the rash that would spread like an evil lace over his body a few hours later?

There was no answer to a question like that. And the mortification she saw on Frank's face made clear that there was no need for her to answer, that even if she'd tried, her reply would've been covered up by his stricken, "I'm sorry, sweetheart. I didn't mean that. I don't know where that came from."

She thought she'd buried that memory, but when in the days following Anand's death Frank gave her that same blank look, Ellie found it hard to play the role of the loving, supportive wife. Also, India had changed Frank. Ever since the labor unrest began, he came home day after day railing about how slow the workers were, complaining about their lousy work ethic and their lack of initiative, his voice brittle with contempt. The final straw came when Frank had missed a day of work because of the stomach flu and found out the next day that they had all taken the afternoon off because nobody could figure out how to fix one of the machines that broke down and disrupted the production line. "Can you friggin' believe it, Ellie?" Frank had cried. "Even the foreman acted all helpless, like he'd never heard the word *repair* in his life. These people have no concept of deadlines or meeting orders. God, what a country."

It was that last comment, that generalization that indicted a billion people, that had made the words shoot out of Ellie's mouth, "Well, if you paid them a little better, maybe they'd care more."

Frank had turned on her, his eyes wide with hurt. "You can't help yourself, can you? It's a bad habit, right, always siding with others against me?"

The memory of that hurt made Ellie watch what she said to Frank this time. We're all alone in this country, she said to herself a hundred times a day. I'm all he has here. She had been lucky to have formed a friendship with Nandita that had in short order become as strong as any friendship she had in Michigan. Nandita had talked her into volunteering at the NIRAL health clinic and school, which she did several days a week. From the moment they had landed in Girbaug, Ellie had felt at home here, seen something on the faces of the local women that felt timeless and universal to her, seen in those brown, sunbaked faces the faces of her own sister, mother, and aunts, although she knew that her ruddy-faced Irish-American family would be shocked if she ever told them this. The fact was, India fit Ellie like a garment cut to size. Frank, she knew, found the garment too tight and oppressive, and she was sorry for him.

In the beginning, she had hoped that Frank and Nandita's husband Shashi would form a close friendship, and indeed the men spent some time bicycling together and playing table tennis at Shashi's bungalow. But somehow the friendship didn't take. Frank found Shashi too mild, not competitive enough, and Shashi—well, it was hard to know what Shashi really thought of Frank. He always seemed happy enough to see him, but there was a faint air of superiority in the way Shashi carried himself that made Frank grouse. Once, when the labor trouble at HerbalSolutions was first heating up, Frank had tried talking to Shashi about it.

"So how does one handle the labor situation in India, Shash?" he'd asked. "Any special tips?"

Shashi had turned toward him, the usual smile on his lips. "What do you mean, special tips?"

"Well, you know. You've run a successful hotel around here for many years. You must have some insight into the minds of the workers. What makes them tick, that kind of thing."

"What makes them tick is—good pay and good working conditions. Same as workers all over the world." Shashi laughed. It was impossible to know if he had just mocked Frank or mocked the entire labor class.

Frank's jaw tightened. "I'll keep that in mind," he said, and then the women had taken over, filling the strained silence with their patter until the mood at the table lightened again.

The doorbell rang, and Ellie skipped toward the kitchen door. "Oh, God, how I've missed you," she cried when she saw Nandita, flinging her arms around her.

"Wow." Nandita grinned as she stepped in. "That's a nice welcome."

Ellie had already put the kettle on, and now she poured them each a cup of tea as the two women sat at the kitchen table. "Hmm," Nandita sighed. "You've certainly learned how to make a great cup of *chai*, El."

Ellie made a face. "Well, we've only been in the country, what, sixteen months. At least I have something to show for it."

Nandita tilted her head. "What's wrong?"

"Nothing." She took a sip of tea. "Edna says they're now saying that Anand was a terrorist," she blurted out.

Nandita gave a short laugh. "Yah, this is the new India. Every two-bit criminal is now accused of being a terrorist—not that that poor kid was even a criminal," she added.

"This is not the India I'd imagined when I urged Frank to take this job, I'll tell you that," Ellie said. She could hear the bitterness in her own voice.

Nandita's tone was bemused. "What did you imagine? Cows on the streets and a guru and a snake charmer at every corner?"

"Yeah, I guess so," Ellie said. But the fact was, she had not thought much about it at all. What she had pictured was simply a country that would be the backdrop, the wallpaper before which she and Frank would enact their family drama of estrangement, healing, and reconciliation. She had certainly not imagined a teeming, heaving country that would become a player in their domestic drama. India, she now knew, would not be content staying in the background, was nobody's wallpaper, insisted on interjecting itself into everyone's life, meddling with it, twisting it, molding it beyond recognition. India, she had found out, was a place of political intrigue and economic corruption, a place occupied by real people with their incessantly human needs, desires, ambitions, and aspirations, and not the exotic, spiritual, mysterious entity that was a creation of the Western imagination.

"How was work at the clinic today?" Ellie asked, but before Nandita could reply, "I'm so tired of being stuck at home. I want to start work at NIRAL again."

"You should," Nandita said. "I mean, I don't think the situation is dangerous or anything. You may get a few dirty looks, but that's about it. I tell you, El, that's what impresses me the most about the poor—the amazing restraint that they show. Others call it fatalism, but I've worked among them for years now and I tell you, it's nothing as weak as fatalism. In fact, it's—it's fortitude. A kind of dignity. How much shit these people take from"—Nandita waved her hands to include the opulent surroundings they sat in—"from people like us. And still they don't fight back." She shook her head and managed a wan smile. "All right. Enough of my lecture*giri*, as Shashi would say."

Nandita is the only person in my life who says what I think, Ellie thought. The old Frank, the man she had fallen in love with, would've understood and felt the same way. But she knew that if Frank were here right now, he would raise his eyebrows, ask both of them if they weren't sentimentalizing the poor, and wasn't it possible that the poor were adaptive, that they had learned the art of smiling and bowing even while plotting murder against the likes of them? What happened? she asked herself. India was supposed to humanize us. Instead, it has made Frank cynical and bitter.

"Okay," Nandita said. "Enough of this depressing talk." She got up and headed for the fridge. "What has that Prakash cooked? I'm starving."

Ellie leapt to her feet. "Would you like a chicken roll? Prakash just made some more of his mayonnaise."

They assembled the sandwich together. Nandita reached on top of the fridge for a bag of potato chips. She took a big bite of the roll and spoke with her mouth full. "Why the long face, darling? Are you feeling down?"

Ellie nodded. "I think I am."

"Well, the best antidote to depression is activity," Nandita said. "You need to be engaged in the world again."

Ellie smiled ruefully. "That's exactly what I would've said to a client." She cocked her head as she looked at the woman sitting across from her. "Are you sure you're not really a therapist?"

"Oh, God, I don't have the temperament to sit still and listen to the miseries of the bourgeoisie. I'd be bored out of my mind." Nandita laughed. "No, you know what I am—a muck-raking, no-good

journalist before I became a"—here Nandita made a doleful face—
"a hausfrau."

Despite her light tone, Ellie could hear the regret in Nandita's
voice. Armed with a master's in journalism from Columbia University, Nandita had returned to Bombay and taken the world of journalism by storm, with numerous exposés of political corruption and
police brutality and bribery scandals. Although she was fêted by
human rights groups and some Bollywood movie stars, she began
to acquire a list of powerful enemies. Drummed-up charges by her
opponents had landed her in jail for three months before all accusations were dropped. She had walked out of jail triumphant, but the
damage was done—she suffered a breakdown a few months later.
She had known Shashi, the only son of a man who had made his
fortune making ball bearings, for many years but had never taken
seriously his occasional marriage proposals. For many years she
teased him for being the Son of Mr. Ball Bearings, conferred upon
him the mocking nickname Balls. She teased him for being wealthy,
for being a businessman, for having no social conscience. But while
she was recovering from the breakdown, it was Shashi more than
any of her other, progressive friends who stood by her. The next
time he proposed, she said yes. And seven years ago, when he and
his partners decided to build the Hotel Shalimar on the shores of
the Arabian Sea, she did not hesitate when he asked whether she
would consider relocating from Bombay to the small, sleepy village of Kanbar. Now she divided her time between working at the
clinic and school she had built in Girbaug and helping her husband
manage the forty-five-room resort.

Ellie leaned forward. "Can I ask you something, Nan? Are you
happy with Shashi? Are you still in love with him?"

Nandita clicked her tongue dismissively. "Shashi? Who knows?
Who cares? You Americans expect so much more from your romantic relationships, Ellie. All this talk of soul mates and all that
bullshit." Seeing the look on Ellie's face, she laughed. "Oh, God.

Forgive the blasphemy. You look, like, totally scandalized. No, but seriously? I'm happy with Shashi. He's an honorable man. I respect him, and I guess, in my own fashion, I love him. But am I head-over-heels with him? I'm not sure."

"Were you ever madly in love with him? Or with anyone?"

For a second, something flickered in Nandita's eyes. Then she looked away. "I'm not sure. It wasn't the way one was raised, with these fairy-tale notions of Prince Charmings and knights in shining armor. Anyway, one marries for companionship and, in the case of most people, for children, right? And if one decides not to have any children, then—"

Ellie had noticed this verbal tic before, how Nandita switched to the third person anytime she talked about something personal or emotionally difficult. If Nandita had been one of her clients, she would've called her on it. But some instinct told her not to push that hard, told her that Nandita was like one of those puffed, deep-fried *baturas* that deflated the instant you pierced the oily wheat exterior with your thumb.

"What about you? Are you still in love with Frank?"

"Yes." Her answer was so instantaneous it surprised even her. "I mean, we've been together since our twenties. And the relationship has certainly—sustained some blows. But even today, he's the only man who can make my stomach flip just by walking into the room."

"Wow," Nandita said. There was no envy in her voice, just interest. "Maybe it has something to do with meeting the other person when you're so young. Like what you hear about those birds—cranes, maybe?—who consider the first person they see to be their mothers. Imprinting, it's called, I believe."

"Well, we were both grad students. So we weren't quite that young," Ellie laughed. "But God, Nan. You should've seen us then. We were inseparable. Our first year together, it snowed like crazy on Thanksgiving. Frank was visiting some friends in Grand Rapids.

I had planned to cook us dinner, but one look out the window that morning and I knew there was no way he'd make it back to Ann Arbor. But at seven that evening, the doorbell rings, and there's Frank. He said he couldn't bear the thought of us being apart for our first Thanksgiving. It took him ten hours to make a trip that would've normally taken less than three."

"Yah, there's something wonderful about that kind of young love—" Nandita said.

"But here's the thing," Ellie interrupted. "Even today I know he's the one person in the world I can count on to stand at my front door during a snowstorm. Isn't that something?"

"It is."

They smiled at each other shyly and then looked away. "Nan," Ellie said. "I don't know if I ever told you this but I'm so grateful for your friendship. You're the best thing that's happened to me since—"

Nandita waved her hand to cover up her embarrassment. "Yah, and you think living for seven years in this godforsaken place without a single intelligent person to talk to was a picnic for me? Shashi always says that I would've divorced him if you hadn't showed up in the nick of time."

Ellie laughed. "Speaking of Shashi, how's he doing?"

"Find out for yourself," Nandita said promptly. "Why don't you and Frank come over for dinner tonight? I'll throw something together."

Ellie considered. "Frank'll probably be too tired to want to go out again tonight. Maybe another night would be better."

Nandita gestured toward the phone. "Why don't you call him? That way, if someone is refusing my kind invitation, it's Frank. And not his know-it-all wife."

"You're a bully, you know that?" Ellie grumbled as she got up. "God, you remind me so much of my older sister, Anne, I can't tell you." She dialed Frank's number.

Frank answered on the third ring. And to Ellie's surprise, said yes immediately. "It will be nice to get out of Girbaug for a few hours," he said, and Ellie could hear the fatigue in his voice. He's under more pressure than I know, she thought. "Did something happen at work today, hon?" she asked cautiously.

"Just more of the same labor shit. How anybody does business in this country, I don't know. Now the rumor is, they're planning a go-slow. I'll explain what that is when I get home," he added.

Nandita was gesturing toward her, asking for the phone. When Ellie handed it to her, she spoke briskly, without preamble. "Frank? Nandita. I have an idea. How about if I take Ellie home with me? And you have your driver bring you to our house directly from work? That way, we can eat as soon as you get there. I'm sure you're not getting much time for lunch these days." Her voice was even, without a trace of sympathy or judgment.

They spoke for a few more minutes and then Nandita hung up without giving the phone back to Ellie. "That's settled, then," she said. "You're coming home with me."

"Hello?" Ellie said. "Am I not to be consulted at all? Who's the know-it-all now? And what if I had some other plans?"

"You have no other plans," Nandita said flatly. "Anyway, Frank thought it was a good idea."

"Oh, I see. Frank thought it was a good idea. And what am I? Chopped liver?"

"Ellie." Nandita fixed her a baleful look. "I must say, that is the most disgusting of all American expressions. Now, do you want to get changed or are you ready to go?"

"I swear, you are such a control freak," Ellie laughed. "Man, if you were one of my clients I'd—"

"Which, thankfully, I'm not," Nandita said, as she linked her arm into Ellie's. "Another disgusting American habit—therapy."

* * *

Nandita was true to her word. Dinner was a simple meal—daal with mustard seeds and an eggplant cooked in a spicy tomato sauce. Plain yogurt and white basmati rice topped off the meal. Frank wanted to learn how to eat with his fingers, and Shashi tried to teach him, but he gave up soon after the other three picked up their forks. "This is harder than chopsticks," he declared.

Discussing Frank earlier in the day had cleansed Ellie's sour view of him, like an afternoon shower washing the grime off a window. Her heart had leapt as soon as he'd walked in the door, his six-foot frame slightly stooped, his white shirt hanging out at the sides. She noticed that the blond hair was a little overgrown and reminded herself to cut it this weekend, noticed the creases of fatigue near his gray eyes, the light shadow around his chin. Her heart softened with tenderness. So that it took no effort to push herself out of the comfortable couch and fling her arms around him as she kissed his lips. She ignored his look of surprise, ignored Nandita's bemused, raised eyebrow. She suddenly felt light, deliriously happy, as if Frank's presence was the perfect way to cap a pleasurable afternoon. In Nandita's house, away from the claustrophobic insularity of Girbaug, she felt free and safe for the first time in a week. It took her back to her grad student days, to being in someone's house, with the Rolling Stones or R.E.M. playing on the stereo and the smell of Chinese takeout food, and the sensual anticipation of an evening of booze and food and conversation.

She kissed Frank again, and he returned her kiss, deeply, sincerely. It had been a long time since he had kissed her like this, looked at her with warm eyes, without a trace of the guarded expression he usually wore. It wasn't a performance for Nandita's benefit either, Ellie knew. Nanditsa had in fact slipped out of the room after muttering a "Hi, Frank," and still Frank was looking at her intently, smiling his pleasure, as if he was memorizing her, as if he had forgotten how happy it made him to look at her.

They heard the tinkle of ice in Shashi's glass before he walked in. "Oh, hello, Frank," he said, and in her happiness, Ellie imagined that Shashi seemed genuinely pleased to see her husband. "Welcome. What can I get you? I'm having some whisky myself. And the ladies are drinking gin and tonics, I think."

"Actually, a beer sounds better than anything. It's damn hot today." Frank kept his arm around Ellie.

"A Heineken it is," Shashi said, and Ellie grinned to herself. It was one of Nandita's pet peeves, how Shashi refused to drink or serve Indian beer at home.

"Dinner will be ready in a half hour, yes?" Nandita said. "Let's sit and relax until then." She turned to Frank. "How have you been, stranger?"

He sighed. "Okay, I think. I'm sure you've heard about—the situation." He paused, took a long gulp of his beer. "It's hard. Everybody's nerves are shot." He hesitated and glanced at his hosts, as if he was unsure whether to go on. "I—I'm not really good at reading the labor situation. I don't think I've ever felt more like a clumsy Ugly American than I do these days. The way you—they—do business here is so different than—" He turned to Shashi, making a visible effort to lighten his tone. "So, any words of advice, Shash?"

Ellie felt the muscles in her stomach tighten. Please don't let Shashi be flippant, or worse, enigmatic, she prayed. Please don't let him rebuff Frank.

But Shashi's tone was sympathetic, sincere. "Hard to know what to do, Frank. It's a bad situation. My best advice would be—settle. Give them a little of what they're asking for. Make them feel like they won something. A few rupees here and there won't matter so much to your company. You can recover it somewhere else. But to these people, it will mean a lot."

Ellie had raised the same point over dinner yesterday, and Frank had bristled, told her she didn't understand the mindset of the Indian worker. So she was surprised to hear him say, "Not so easy, Shashi.

I'd like nothing more than to give in. But there's so much pressure from headquarters, you have no idea."

"Bollocks." It was Nandita. "These people live in wretched conditions—ask your wife, she has seen where and how they live. Tell her to speak to your boss in Ann Arbor about what she sees in the villages. Two less expense-account lunches a month for him will pay for their raises." Shashi tried to lay a warning hand on her, but she shook it off and turned to face Frank again. "Listen. You're my friend. So I tell you, settle this. I'm an atheist, you know that. But one thing I believe: one should only pick fights with those who can fight back. And these people can't, Frank. They're poor, hungry, weak. But don't they have the right to eat just like we do? Or any American does? HerbalSolutions makes enough profit here. Shit, you could double their salaries and still make a profit. You know that. It's obscene to—"

"Nandita," Shashi said, and they all heard the iron in his voice. She suddenly looked chastised. "I'm sorry," she said. "I'm sorry, Frank. Sorry, El. You know how I get carried away."

For a second, it was awkward in the room, with all four of them looking at the floor, but then Frank said, "That's what we love about you, Nan. You're a true friend."

It sounded so much like the old Frank, sincere and guileless, that Ellie felt teary. Despite the few bumps and moments of awkwardness, there was something restorative about this evening, she thought. "This reminds me of grad school," she heard herself say. "You know, we'd sit up nights arguing and almost coming to blows over all kinds of issues. But we were all as close as this." She crossed her fingers.

Nandita smiled slyly. "And to complete the grad school fantasy camp, we have some aids," she said. She disappeared from the room and returned a few minutes later with a carved wooden box and rolling paper. "I just got some real good weed from one of my contacts," she said proudly. "I thought, maybe after dinner?"

Shashi smiled noncommittally. But both Frank and Ellie said, "Count me in."

It was dark by the time they were done with dinner. "Just leave the dishes in the sink," Nandita told Ellie, who was helping her clear the table.

Shashi refreshed their drinks before they moved into the small sitting area off the living room. Unlike the other rooms in the house, it had no furniture, just handwoven rugs and large, cylindrical pillows on the floor, against which one rested one's back. It was Ellie's favorite room in the house. She sat crossed-legged against one of the white pillows and pulled Frank down next to her. When he sat down, she heard his left knee crack, the way it did whenever he made a sudden movement. She watched as, with great solemnity, Nandita rolled the joint, inhaled deeply, and then passed it on to her. "Wow, you weren't kidding. That's some good stuff," Ellie said, but Nandita had left the room to go plug in her iPod. Ellie smiled as Simon and Garfunkel's "Feelin' Groovy" wafted over to her from the next room. The perfect song for the evening, she thought, and from the way the others were looking at her, realized she'd spoken out loud.

"She's high already," Frank laughed. "I can tell."

"Am not," she said, grabbing for the joint as it made its way around, afraid that they would cut her off.

"You're a lightweight, babe," Frank teased. "Admit it."

"Well, *I* wasn't the one who got drunk the first time we went to a party together," she said loftily.

"Hey, no fair. There's got to be a statute of limitations on the dredging up of old stuff."

"All's fair in love, sweetheart," Nandita said. Her dark eyes were bright, sparkling. "Spill the beans, El."

Ellie opened her mouth to speak, but her tongue suddenly felt like it was made of cotton wool. It took too much energy to tell a story, she realized. "You tell it," she told Frank. "Tell on yourself." The last phrase struck her as hilarious. She giggled and pretty soon, she heard a fellow giggle and, turning her head, realized it was coming from Shashi. That only made her laugh more.

Frank groaned. "Oh, no. There she goes. Once the giggling starts . . ."

"Tell on yourself, Frank."

He turned to Nandita. "It's nothing, really. The first party we went to together—and she'd put me through hell before she even agreed to go out with me, let me tell you—was at the apartment of an ex-boyfriend of hers. Or so I believed, at the time. Turns out he wasn't her ex, after all. But I didn't learn that till later." He shook his head, looked at the lit joint that Ellie had passed him, and then took a deep drag.

"Frank," Nandita said. "What the fuck are you talking about?"

"Damned if I know." He stared at Nandita hard, as if trying to solve a puzzle. "Yeah. Jealousy. That's what we're talking about here. Anyway. So naturally, I did what any red-blooded male would do. I got roaring drunk. Every time I caught her talking to old dickhead, I took another swig of my beer. Somehow Ellie managed to get me to her apartment that night. And I passed out on her couch. Imagine. I'd lusted after this woman for weeks, and I'm finally in her apartment and I'm snoring soundly on her couch, like a good altar boy."

"So now we don't drink to excess," Ellie said happily. "Now we just get high to excess. Moral of the story."

"So," Frank said. "How did you and Shashi meet?"

Shashi spoke before Nandita could. "I saw her picture in the newspaper once. And fell in love with her. Small black-and-white picture it was." He turned to Nandita, who was looking at him openmouthed. "I never told you this. Anyway, I made some inquiries. Found out who her friend circle was, wormed my way into it."

"And I thought I was the only investigative reporter in the family," Nandita muttered.

"Shashi, you're a sly one," Ellie said. "And romantic. Such a romantic."

"Withstood years of her ignoring me," Shashi continued, as if speaking to himself. "When she did notice me, it was only to ask me for money for some cause or the other. I had almost given up." He suddenly looked up at them. "But then, one day, she said yes." He sounded delighted, as if Nandita had said yes to him yesterday.

Ellie had the strangest feeling that as Shashi spoke, the physical space that separated him from her disappeared. She felt that she was entering the body of this man who had always felt a little aloof to her, so that she could relive his long-ago anticipation at having finally met a woman whose picture he'd fallen in love with, his crushing disappointment at her rejection of him, his steady doggedness at hovering at the periphery of her life, his triumph at having won her over at last. She suddenly knew what it felt like to be Shashi from the inside—his sadness at the knowledge that he would always love Nandita a little more than she loved him, his delight at having a brilliant, beautiful woman as his wife, his ambivalence, that mixture of pride and bashfulness at the way she barged ahead in life, shaming and chastising his rich relatives and business associates into donating money to whatever cause she was championing. Ellie felt she had a glimpse of what it meant to be a man who was married to a cloud—ever-shifting, hard to pin down, filtering light but also holding rain.

Something was shifting, the mellow happiness of earlier making way for a sweet sadness. But before the melancholy could descend on her any further, she felt Frank's arm around her. "Hey, baby," he said softly. "You okay?"

Ellie wished suddenly that someone would invent an album for filing moments, just as you could photographs. If so, she would file the imprint of Frank's warm hand against her sleeveless arm, the quizzical smile that played on his lips, the breath-stopping expression of curiosity and love that she saw on his face.

"Beyond okay," she said, snuggling closer to him.

It was almost one o'clock when they got up to leave. At the front door, Nandita gave each of them a hug. "You come and see us soon, okay?" she said to Frank. And then, with her voice lowered, "And you know you can always ask Shashi for advice, right? He'll help you in any way he can."

"Thanks, Nan," Frank said lightly. Ellie noticed that even the reference to work didn't yank Frank out of the languid, mellow mood he was in. Weed therapy, she said to herself. I'm going to ask Nandita for some.

"And you should start coming to the clinic," Nandita said to Ellie, loud enough that Frank could hear. "You'll be absolutely safe, I promise." Both women waited for Frank to react. He didn't. "I'll come pick you up at eleven tomorrow," Nandita said.

Satish had brought the Camry to pick them up, and they rode in the back seat together with Ellie cradled in Frank's arms. They rode quietly in the dark, and after a few moments, Ellie heard the sound. At first she thought it was Frank humming, but then she realized what it was. Frank was snoring lightly, rhythmically, even while he kept his arms wrapped around his wife.

CHAPTER 6

Prakash glanced at the big clock in the kitchen again. It was only ten thirty in the morning, too early to sneak into his shack and have a drink. Edna was in a foul mood this morning, and it was making him jittery. He could tell by the way she was sweeping the floor around where he was standing in front of the stove. Usually, she would wait respectfully for him to lower the flame and move away from the stove before sweeping near him. But today she sat on her haunches and hit his bare feet with the thick end of the *jaaro*, grunted an abrupt, "Move." He resisted the urge to strike her on the head, aware of the fact that Ellie memsahib was still in the house, rushing from the living room to the bedroom as she got dressed. But he stood his ground, even though his hands shook. "No eyes to see I'm cooking?" he muttered to her. "So-so much in a hurry you are. Late to meet a boyfriend or something?"

She looked up at him, her eyes barely hiding her disdain. "After you, I swear off men. Even a rat would be better than you."

As usual, he looked away first. It hurt when she talked to him like this, brought back memories of his childhood when he used to wander from house to house, exposing himself to whatever mood a particular resident was in. Never knowing whether the women would chase him away with a curse or welcome him in with a sweet. And the worst part was, the children themselves picked up on the moods of the adults, so that one day they would invite him to play kabaddi or hopscotch with them and the next day they would chase him around the village calling him names—Orphan Boy, Long Face, Cursed One.

"Move, men," Edna said. "You deaf or what?"

"You deaf or what?" he imitated but heard the feebleness of his counterattack and got no satisfaction from it. He went and stood in the doorway.

There was a time when Edna would've killed herself before talking so rudely to him. She had been only twenty-three when they'd met; he, almost ten years older. Enthralled by a Bollywood movie shot in Goa, he had impulsively asked his boss at the auto shop for two weeks' leave, borrowed a motorcycle from one of his clients, and taken off for Goa.

He met Edna on his second day there. She was working as a maid at the run-down, ten-room motel where he was staying. He was immediately smitten, although in those days he spoke little English, and he thought her Goanese Hindi was hilarious. She told him of cheap places to eat and what beaches to visit. On the third day of his visit, she had the day off and airily proposed that she show him around. By the fourth day, he was sure that she was the woman he had to marry. They eloped two weeks later, after Edna had convinced him that her Catholic father would never give his blessings to her marrying a Hindu. She was right—neither her parents nor her older sister ever saw her again.

"Are you wanting me to convert?" she had asked him after they'd been married for about six months. "Will that make you happy?"

"Why for?" he'd replied, in the broken English he'd started learning soon after meeting her. "I marry knowing you are Christian."

She flung her arms around him. "Thank you," she whispered. "You Hindu fellows have so-so many gods, it would make me giddy, trying to decide which one to worship."

In the early days, he would come home from the auto shop, go for a swim in the sea, and then help Edna with the evening meal. He discovered an aptitude for cooking, and Edna delighted in teaching him the Goanese and continental dishes that her mother had spent a lifetime making for the British babu who had visited Goa forty years ago and never left. Sometimes they would go for a night show at the village's only cinema and ride home on Prakash's bicycle, him pedaling standing up and Edna perched on the seat. If they overheard the tsk-tsking of the neighbors, saw someone looking at them askance, they ignored it, accepting the villagers' judgment at their intermarriage as the price of their happiness.

The first time he had made her *bebinca*, the Goanese pancake made from coconut milk, she had wept with gratitude, told him it tasted better than her mother's even. He had last made the dessert for her two months ago. This time, Edna had chastised him for trying to add fat to her hips, ignored him when he protested that she was as beautiful as ever, accused him of stealing her family recipe, and told him it didn't taste as good as her mother's, anyway.

Standing in the doorway, eyeing his wife, Prakash thought he knew exactly when things had begun to sour between them—it was after Ramesh's birth. Edna had not informed her parents of her pregnancy, as she had wanted to surprise them after the birth of their first grandchild. For nine months she had pictured the reconciliation—her teary parents cradling the infant in their arms, welcoming Prakash into their family, her mother covering Edna's face in kisses, telling her how much she'd missed her. But the telegram she had sent them announcing Ramesh's birth was answered by one that said, "We have no grandson. Stop. Because we have no daughter."

Prakash had held her in his arms for hours that day, a wailing infant on one side and a sobbing wife on the other. "They will change, *na*, Edna," he said. "We have one miracle, our Ramu. Second miracle take time."

She had shaken her head. "You not knowing how stubborn my papa is." She picked up Ramesh and held him to her breast. "It is decided—my son will pay for my sins."

Something had turned cold inside him then. Sins? Edna thought of her marriage to him as a sin? The old childhood names—Cursed One, Bad Luck—came back into his mind. He saw himself clearly at that moment—a skinny, ungainly man with a third-grade education, who had few prospects and little to offer his son and young wife.

"Sorry," he said, rising to his feet. "Your father right. You marry trouble."

"Prakash," she cried. "I'm not meaning anything bad." She set the baby down and cradled his face with her hands. "You—you never my trouble. You are my joy. You make me so happy."

He shook his head. "I have nothing to give this boy. Nothing more than my hands."

"Is enough, Prakash," she said fiercely. "We will love our son enough for everybody."

But it hadn't been. It was the great source of sorrow in Edna's life, that Ramesh was growing up without knowing his elders. Maybe that was why she had seemed so pleased when Frank had first taken an interest in Ramesh. And Prakash had not minded either, when, a few months after the Americans had moved into the beautiful bungalow with the pink stucco walls and the bougainvillea growing up those walls, Frank had offered to pay Ramesh's tuition so that he could attend the missionary school in Kanbar. But now Ramesh was spending more time at the main house than with his own parents. When he'd mentioned this to Edna last month, she had turned on him. "Stupid idiot," she'd said. "Jealous of your own son. Should be glad someone so powerful paying him attention but no, jealous instead."

"Let him mind his own business. His son dead, so he's trying to buy my son."

"Shameless, shameless man," Edna had replied. "The devil is talking from your lips."

Some days Prakash found himself missing his old boss, Olaf. He was the first pink man that Prakash had ever seen, much less spoken to. Olaf spoke little English and no Hindi and took absolutely no interest in Ramesh. Every few days the German would go to the market to shop for fresh fish and vegetables—a task that he refused to hand over to Edna after he'd hired her—and that was the extent of his communication with the local people. The village children followed him at arm's length, giggling and nudging each other, as he bought his okra and eggplant and pomfrets. The vendors quoted him absurd prices that would've drawn a sharp rebuke from Edna if she'd been allowed to accompany him, but he didn't seem to notice. He just drove back to the house, set the bags on the kitchen counter without a word, and then withdrew to his typewriter and resumed his *click-click-click*. Over time, Edna had figured out that Olaf wrote books, but that was about all they knew about him. Once, Prakash had tried questioning him, but Olaf had spoken such gibberish, half in English and half in German, that he'd given up. Still, Olaf was kind—he left one peg for Prakash in the bottle of Scotch he downed every two or three days, winking as he handed the bottle over.

Prakash still remembered the day Olaf had come into the kitchen and announced he was leaving. Going back to Germany. He had been stunned. But being from Goa, Edna wasn't too surprised. It was a common enough occurrence—Europeans coming to Goa for a visit and falling in love with the beauty of the place and the warm friendliness of the people, which they mistook for a childlike innocence. Next thing you knew, they were buying up beachfront property on their accountants' and nurses' and plumbers' salaries. They lived in Goa for years until one day, a sudden urge to eat fish and chips at the Blackheath pub or to see the Seine at dawn or to revisit the Cologne cathedral came over them, and they heard themselves tell a nephew or a niece they had last seen thirty-five years ago that they were coming home.

"Why you looking like someone dead, men?" Edna had said to Prakash. "The old man has to go home, no?"

Prakash shook his head. "I thought his home here."

Edna laughed. "He live here twenty-five years and never speak the language. And you think this his home? At least Olaf is a decent fellow—told me today he giving us ten thousand rupees. The British gent my mama cook for for years, you know what he leave her? A picture of himself. Say he not want to insult their friendship by giving money. Can you imagine?"

Before leaving, Olaf also told them in his broken English that he'd sold the house to an American company called HerbalSolutions and that someone from the company would soon be living there. He had highly recommended Prakash and Edna to the new owners. The ten thousand rupees was to tide them over in the eventuality that there would be a delay in the arrival of the new occupants.

Now, thinking of Olaf as Edna finished sweeping the kitchen, Prakash said to her, "Do you remember—"

"Do you remember, do you remember?" she mimicked him. She got up from the floor and straightened herself. "All I remember is you come home at eleven last night, like an ordinary ruffian. Drunker than the devil himself."

He had to look away from the fury he saw in her eyes. How to explain to her what had made him stagger out of the house and head to the bootlegger's joint, last night? He had been in the courtyard pruning the bushes when Ramesh had returned to their shack after knocking and knocking on the door of the main house. "*Arre, bewakoof,* I told you they not home," he'd called out to his son.

Ramesh's forehead was creased with worry. "But I am needing help on a maths problem, dada," he said. And then, "How come you cannot help me?"

The shame had risen in him, like acid from the stomach. Unable to speak, he had instead smacked his son on the head. "Go inside and study," he said. He lingered in the courtyard for a few minutes, knowing that he was not going into their one-room shack, that he was too embarrassed to face his son. He gave the bush one savage clip, put away the shears, and walked to the village instead.

Edna was still staring at him. "In Goa they at least have AA meetings," she said. "In this godforsaken place, nothing."

"Goa, Goa," he said, forgetting to keep his voice down. "If your Goa so good, pack your bags and go. See who will marry an old *boodhi* like you."

"And who made me an old *boodhi*, you rascal? So young and plump I was when I met you . . ." And Edna was down the road that she walked at least once a week, a path full of recriminations and accusations and blame and nostalgia for the Goa of her youth. Usually, he simply ignored her, made his mind fly like a kite to some other place, but today he felt pity for his wife, heard in her lament for her lost youth something that he himself was feeling. Stopping her mid-sentence, he put his arms around her. "*Chup, chup*, Edna," he said softly. "I understand the reason for all this *gussa*. You is just missing your mummy and papa."

Her eyes filled immediately with tears, and he knew he had diagnosed the problem accurately. But how to solve it, he didn't know. Not for the first time, he cursed the pigheaded father-in-law he had never met.

Feeling her relax and soften, glad that he had been able to interrupt her tirade, he continued. "Listen, my bride," he said to her in Hindi. "Our son doesn't lack for anything, does he? Together, we provide him with all the love in the world."

She pulled away from him. "Yah, and what are you knowing about family love, you stupid orphan?"

He flinched and moved away from her, the same expression on his face that the stray dogs wore after they had been kicked in the ribs by one of the village children. "Prakash," Edna began, but he shook his head fiercely.

"Go," he hissed. "Get out of the kitchen. Take your sad face out of my sight."

"I didn't mean—"

"You go, I say. Before I lift my hand to you."

She picked up the broom and left the room. He stood in the kitchen for a few moments, forcing the sting of her words to lessen. He noticed that the rice was done and turned off the burner. He heard Edna and Ellie in the living room. It sounded like Ellie was giving Edna some instructions. He eyed the door.

It would take only a minute to cross the courtyard to their shack and take a long swig of the *daru* bottle that he had hidden in the kitchen. He could come back and finish cooking the rest of the food before Edna was done talking to the memsahib. He moved stealthily across the floor and shut the door quietly behind him.

CHAPTER 7

Ellie crossed the courtyard behind the house and opened the wooden gate that led to the driveway where Nandita was waiting in her car. Edna followed behind her. "What time will you be home, madam?" she called.

Ellie felt a wave of irritation. She hated how Edna kept track of her all the time. "I don't know," she said.

Nandita leaned over to give her a peck on the cheek after she climbed into the car. "You know, I think you're wise to not have live-in help," Ellie grumbled as Nandita backed out of the driveway.

"Why? What happened?"

"Oh, Edna's so fucking controlling at times. And witnessing this hostility between her and Prakash gives me a headache. It's like— shit, it's hard enough to run my own marriage, without having to watch those two every morning."

"Uh-oh. What has happened to my kind-hearted, high-minded friend this morning? How come she's sounding like the rest of us mortals?"

"Oh, shut up."

"Wow. You *are* a grouch today. But speaking of marriages . . . you and Frank seemed pretty lovey-dovey last night."

"It was the weed."

"Bullshit. You two were making eyes at each other from the moment he walked in." She looked away from the road to glance at Ellie. "So. Did you get some action last night?"

Ellie laughed. "You're baaaaad."

"Avoidance of a question is not the same as answering it."

"And what is that? Something you read in a Chinese fortune cookie?"

"Yup. Confucius say: Avoidance of a question is not the same as answering it."

Ellie laughed again. "You must've been one heck of an investigative reporter."

"That I was. Guilty as charged." Nandita paused for a moment. "Speaking of which. I got a call from a journalist in Mumbai this morning. He works for a small political weekly. I'm sorry to tell you this, El, but he was asking me what I'd heard about the death of a young political worker in police custody. And what the mood in the village was and all that."

Ellie suddenly had a sour feeling in her stomach. "What did you say?"

"I didn't know what to say. So I told him I was a friend of yours and that it would be a conflict for me to talk about the situation. He wasn't too happy."

Ellie knew what it must've cost Nandita not to help a fellow journalist, not to weigh in on an incident that ordinarily she would have done her best to publicize. She felt a lump form in her throat and waited for it to clear before she spoke. "Thank you, Nandita," she said. "I know that must have been really hard for you. And I'm sorry you're getting dragged into this mess."

Nandita shrugged. "I've been dragged into worse messes, believe me," she said lightly. "And anyway, I never took a pledge to help every journalist who comes looking for me. So to hell with it. I'm sitting this one out." She patted Ellie's thigh. "Now, cheer up, won't you? Otherwise I'll regret having said anything to you."

"Don't. You know me. I don't care how painful the truth is—I'd rather know something than be in the dark."

"I'm the same way." Nandita smiled, swerving to avoid an on-coming car. "I think that's why I became a reporter."

As always, a crowd of children gathered around the car as they pulled into the dirt road that led to the NIRAL clinic. "Hello, Binu, hi Raja," Ellie called as she recognized some of the children who had come to greet them. "How are all of you?"

In reply, she heard a chorus of voices say, in that singsong manner of theirs, "Fine." The way they stretched the word out into two syl-lables made Ellie laugh. She was happy to be here, had missed this place and these children more than she'd known, she realized.

Several of the kids grabbed her forearm so that they looked like a round cloud of dust as they made their way into the classroom at one end of the building. Ellie looked over to where Nandita was standing with her own young charges. "Shall I run the class with the children first?" she called. "Meet with the women later?"

"Sure. I have to do some paperwork, anyway. Ordered the vac-cines this week, and I want to make sure they're here. I'll send Rakesh out to let the women know you're in today."

"Make sure he informs Radha," she called as she opened the blue wooden door that led to the small classroom. "She was really having a hard time the last time I saw her. I want to follow up with her today."

It was hot inside the room. Ellie opened the single window and turned on a table fan. "Haven't you been meeting in here last week?" she asked and was greeted by a chorus of, "No, miss."

"So Asha didn't run the class?" Asha was a shy nineteen-year-old villager who had finished high school and was now employed by NIRAL to tutor the younger kids.

"No, miss."

"Well, then we have a lot of work to do." She looked over the class, which had students ranging from four to twelve. She sorted the children according to their reading proficiencies and began with the first group. Some of the kids were learning the alphabet; others were reading on their own; a few of the really bright ones were able to comprehend the science and history textbooks she had purchased for them. Anu, one of the older girls, raised her hand and asked for permission to work on a jigsaw puzzle while Ellie was tending to the younger kids. Ellie hesitated, loath to give up any more valuable reading time, but the pleading look on Anu's face made her say yes. "Ten minutes on the puzzle," she instructed them, ignoring their groans of protest. "Then, start reading."

An hour and a half later, Asha entered the classroom and stood in the back, Ellie's cue to wrap up the class. "Okay," she said. "See you all on Wednesday."

She and Asha walked out of the stuffy classroom into the bright light of the day. "How come there was no class last week?" Ellie asked.

Asha looked at her dust-covered feet. "We were too busy with the AIDS prevention class, miss," she mumbled.

Shit. She had forgotten. Last week had been AIDS education week. And Nandita had been too decent to mention it to her.

"Shall we start our rounds, miss?" Asha asked. "Many-many women waiting to see you today."

"Sure," Ellie replied. "But listen, did you find Radha? She was here two weeks ago. I need to spend some extra time with her." Radha had come to the clinic bearing black marks on her chocolate brown skin, signatures of her husband's violence. Those big, dark eyes, glistening with unshed tears, had haunted Ellie, had made her want to confront Radha's husband, even while she knew that doing so would only make life harder for the girl.

"She afraid to come to the clinic, miss. Says we should come to her house."

Ellie glanced at her watch. "Okay. Let's attend to the women at the clinic first. I'll make sure to keep some time to go see Radha after that."

It was almost three thirty by the time they got done at the clinic. As always, Ellie left the building drained in a way she never had been even after spending a full day at her practice in Ann Arbor. The problems of the women of Girbaug seemed so intractable to her—impoverished mothers-in-law demanding more dowries from the penniless girls who married into their families; drunken husbands who routinely beat their wives and children to relieve their frustration at being squeezed by ruthless landlords and moneylenders; women who had given birth to three consecutive daughters being shunned by the community; middle-aged women who cried for no apparent reason and carried themselves in that listless way that Ellie recognized as depression.

Most of the time, Ellie was at a loss as to what advice to give them. All the things that she had suggested to her mostly white, middle-class clientele in Michigan seemed laughable here. What could she ask these women to do? Go to the gym to combat depression? Take Prozac when they could barely afford wheat for their bread? Join Al Anon to learn to accept the things and behaviors they couldn't change? These women were masters of acceptance—already they accepted droughts and floods and infections and disease and hunger. As for asking them to change their own behaviors, what would that do? There were no shelters for battered women that they could go to, no twelve-step programs that their husbands could enter, no social institutions to support women who deviated from the norm. So Ellie mostly listened while they spoke their woes, nodding sympathetically, sometimes cradling them as they sobbed and cursed their bad luck. She told herself that simply giving these women, who nobody saw as anything beyond mother-sister-wife, a chance to vent was worth something. Once in a while she suggested some small behavior modification, and mostly they told her why that wouldn't work, but sometimes a woman returned the following week with a story of minor success, thanking Ellie for the suggestion. Those small victories Ellie carried around with her the rest of the week.

Now, she staggered out of the clinic with Asha, who acted as her translator, by her side. She squinted at the sun and at the dry, dusty road that stretched before them. Despite the recent rains, the land looked as parched and thirsty as ever. "Where does Radha live?" she asked.

"Very close by, only," Asha said.

As always, Ellie was impressed by the simplicity and cleanliness of the mud huts that stood near each other as they entered the main area of the village. A few dogs were lying on their sides under the shade of a large tree near the cluster of houses, but they merely raised their heads and yawned luxuriously as the two women walked past. Ellie recalled what Nandita said—how rural poverty looked much cleaner than urban poverty—and, remembering the slums that she'd seen during her visits to Bombay, she agreed. Radha's house had a traditional grass roof, one of the few of its kind. Most of the houses around hers had metal sheeting, which raised the indoor temperature much more than the cooling grass. But Asha had explained to Ellie that the grass roof had to be replaced each year, and in the last few years, the grass was not growing as abundantly as it always had. A few chickens pecked near their feet as Asha knocked on the door. A weak voice answered in Hindi, asking them to enter. They opened the bamboo door and walked in.

It was dark inside the house—like many in the village, Radha's house had no electricity. A kerosene lamp blazed in front of the girl, who sat on her haunches on the floor, which Ellie knew the villagers made out of a plaster of mud and cow dung. Despite the darkness in the room, Ellie sensed that the girl appeared even more dejected than a few weeks ago. *"Namaste*, Radha," Asha said, and the girl replied, *"Namaste,"* as she rose off the floor. Her voice was dull, her movements slow.

Ellie grabbed the girl's hand and squeezed it in greeting, noticing the marks on her forearm as she did so. "Please to sit," Radha said, her glance including both Asha and Ellie, and all three women sat on the floor, Radha and Asha on their haunches and Ellie cross-legged. "How are you, Radha?" Ellie asked, Asha translating for her.

In reply, Radha lowered the *pallov* of her sari and opened a button on her blouse so that the other two could see the marks on her chest. Ellie swallowed the gasp of horror that sprang to her lips. Instead, she asked, "Has he always beaten you, Radha? And how long have you two been married?" She looked around the hut. "Who else lives here?"

"We married when I was sixteen, *didi*," the girl replied in Hindi. "And first few years my husband was very nice. After the birth of my son, we were very happy." Her face fell. "But what to do, *didi*? He lost his job six months ago, and now we have no income. All day he goes out looking for the leaves, but the guards chase him away."

"What guards? What did he do for a living?" Ellie asked, marveling at the sudden torrent of words that spilled from Radha's mouth. She looked expectantly at Asha, waiting for her to interpret Radha's words. But Asha looked uncharacteristically embarrassed. "All rubbish she's saying, miss," she mumbled.

"Hey," Ellie said. "I need to know what Radha said. Otherwise, we can't help her, can we?"

Radha continued to speak and Asha gazed quickly from one woman to the next before translating. "She says her husband used to cut leaves from the *girbal* tree, make a bundle, and sell to other villages nearby, miss," she said. "Villagers use the paste of those leaves for medicine. But then the company say that the trees now belong to them, not to the villagers. Put up big signs saying, 'Private Property. No trespassing.' So he is trying to steal some leaves when the guards are not looking, but they find him and give him a beating. Now he is afraid to go back, miss. So no moneys in the family plus peoples getting sick without the leaf paste."

Ellie felt her heart pounding. "What's the name of the company?" But before Asha could reply, "It's HerbalSolutions, isn't it?"

Asha bowed her head. "Yes, miss," she said simply.

Despite herself, she heard herself asking, "Does—does she know my husband is—that he works for the company?"

Asha was twisting the *pallov* of her sari in embarrassment. "That I don't know, miss."

Ellie stared into the flame of the kerosene lamp, aware that Radha was looking at her, waiting for her to speak. There was a sour taste in her mouth. Who are you kidding? she said to herself. Pretending to help these people when your very presence, perhaps even your very existence, causes them grief and misery?

The door opened, and a tall, gaunt-looking man with a drooping mustache walked in. Ellie saw that it took a second for his eyes to adjust to the dark room, but as his eyes fell upon them, his slack face grew suddenly animated. He turned to Radha and spoke to her in rapid-fire Hindi, all the while locking eyes with Ellie. Radha answered him in a dull, heavy voice, staring at the floor the whole time. Ellie took advantage of this exchange to whisper to Asha, "Is this her husband?" to which Asha nodded yes.

But the man must have heard her because now he loomed over her, his breathing heavy and jagged. Wagging his index finger, he spoke to Asha, a deluge of angry words, hard and biting, that brought a scowl to Asha's usually calm face. She tried to interrupt him several times, but he cut her off, gesticulating wildly, and finally Asha gave up and grew silent. The man went on and on, occasionally slipping in a word that Ellie understood. She thought she heard him say "company" and "police." After what seemed like an interminable length of time, he finally fell silent, although his eyes were still wild-looking. Nobody spoke for a second, and then he said, "*Bolo*," to Asha, pointing to Ellie with his chin. Ellie knew that *bolo* meant to speak, so she understood that he wanted her to translate for him.

But she would not give him that satisfaction. Leaping to her feet, she grabbed Asha's hand. "Come on, Asha," she said. "Let's go."

"Go, go," the man said, having understood what she'd said in English. And then, deliberately, looking her straight in the eye, "America, go home."

A small crowd had gathered outside Radha's hut, but nobody said a word as Asha and Ellie emerged. Even the children and chickens seemed subdued. The two women walked rapidly and silently away from the cluster of houses. Behind them, they could still hear the man shouting from the doorway. Ellie felt a twinge of fear at having left Radha alone with her angry husband but comforted herself by believing that the crowd would intervene. It struck her that that could be a strategy that she could teach the village's many victims of domestic abuse—they come to each other's help. Could they? Would they? she wondered.

They were at a safe distance from the houses, now. She turned to the young woman walking next to her. "Asha, I need you to tell me everything the husband said. Please, don't be embarrassed. You won't hurt my feelings, honest."

Asha didn't seem too convinced. "He's mad man, miss," she started, but seeing the look on Ellie's face, she stopped. And started again. "He says the company ruin him twice—first it take away his leaf business and also, it kill his best friend. He says that Anand, the boy who was killed by police, was his best friend since day he was born. So he hate the company." Asha looked shocked and afraid, as if she was the one who had expressed these sentiments.

"Go on," Ellie said. "Tell me everything."

"Nothing more to tell, miss. He says he doesn't want us entering his home again. Says English peoples brings bad luck wherever they go—in Iraq and in Girbaug."

"Oh, please," Ellie said. "That's a bit of a stretch."

Asha was not familiar with the expression. "Excuse, miss?"

Ellie shook her head. "It doesn't matter. Tell me, do—do the others in the village feel the same way about me?" She was surprised to hear the tremor in her voice.

"All the women like you, miss," Asha said eagerly. "They say you help them. But ever since Anand die, there is much anger. Peoples say, our life do not matter to the big sahibs. And we all use the *girbal* tree our whole lives, miss. We boil it in our tea, make paste out of it. Some of the older peoples chew it. They our trees, miss. How can a company come and buy our trees?"

Ellie was quiet, unsure of how to answer that question, unable to tell Asha that she had asked the same question of Frank.

Asha touched Ellie's shoulder. "That man is total stupid," she said. "You stay with us, miss."

Ellie heard in the young woman's voice the desire to appease, the natural hospitality and generosity that seemed to come so naturally to the Indians she'd met. She smiled. "I'm not going anywhere," she said lightly. "Don't you worry."

Nandita was walking rapidly toward them as they approached the clinic's compound. "What happened?" she said. "Why didn't you tell me you were going to Radha's house?" She looked angry.

"Wow, news certainly travels fast in these parts," Ellie said. Turning to Asha, she said, "Thanks for all your help today, sweetie. You worked so hard. I'll see you Wednesday?"

"Okay, miss," Asha said. "Good evening." The woman glanced at Nandita, nodded, and walked briskly away.

"What happened?" Nandita said again, as soon as Asha was out of hearing range.

"I'll tell you in a minute. But can I have a cup of tea first?"

Nandita must have heard something in her voice because she was immediately solicitous. "Of course. Come on."

In Nandita's small office, Ellie blew on the hot glass of tea she had been handed on their way in. She took a few sips, trying to get her emotions under control before she told Nandita about her encounter with Radha's husband. When she finished, Nandita looked at her for a full minute and then exhaled loudly. "I'm so sorry, Ellie. I don't know what we could've done to prevent this."

"Don't be ridiculous," Ellie protested. "You had nothing to do with this, Nan." She closed her eyes for a second, trying to gather her thoughts. "I don't even know who to blame for this mess. I know Pete Timberlake, the guy who started HerbalSolutions. I've known him for years. He and Frank went to college together. Pete's a great guy. He'd be shocked if he knew how much grief he's brought into the lives of people like Radha and her husband. If I know Pete, all he knew was that he'd bought a bunch of trees that nobody wanted and that seemed to have magical properties that helped Americans with diabetes. And yet, having met Radha and the others, I'm mad that people like them always seem to pay the price for someone else's ignorance."

"But it isn't an isolated instance, El," Nandita said gently. Her voice was strained, as if she was torn between trying not to injure her friend's feelings while also speaking the truth. "The West has such a terrible history of—"

"I know. God, Nandita, you think I don't know that? Even this poor, ignorant man, her husband, even he made some reference to our involvement in Iraq. And there's nothing I could say to him. Except that I don't think I'm a dirty imperialist pig. And I don't think my husband is, either. And that I'm every bit as appalled at what my country is doing in Iraq as, as, any of you."

She was close to tears now, her body shaking as she recalled the contempt on the man's face as he'd entered his home and found her sitting on the floor next to his wife, his angry, accusatory words, the embarrassed, conflicted look on Asha's face as Ellie had forced her to translate sentiments that, it now occurred to Ellie, Asha probably agreed with.

"Hey, hey," Nandita said, coming around her desk and crouching low so that she could hug Ellie. "Come on now. You can't work at NIRAL if you have a thin skin. Nobody's blaming you for this situation, El. This—this stuff is bigger than any one person."

But the complicated combination of guilt and defensiveness followed Ellie home that evening. In the car, the two women rode in almost total silence, each one lost in her thoughts. Ellie had a terrible headache by the time she got out of Nandita's car and went into the house to wait for Frank to get home.

CHAPTER 8

At exactly six a.m. the following morning, there was a tentative knock on the door. Frank leapt to his feet and threw the door open before Ramesh could knock a second time. "Shhh," he whispered, holding his index finger to his lips. "Ellie is sleeping. We have to be quiet." He led the boy through the living room and toward the porch. Flinging open the wooden porch door, they stepped down onto the lawn. It was a pleasant morning, with a weak sun and a cool breeze blowing off the sea. The tall, stately coconut trees were rustling in that breeze, but Frank and Ramesh didn't hear them. The dew on the grass tickled their ankles as they moved quickly to the left of the front yard and then climbed the seven stone steps that led to the beach. Ramesh bent and picked up a pebble to fling at a crow who was pecking at something inside a brown paper bag on the sand. "Hey," Frank said putting out a restraining arm. "Throw that stone away."

"I hate crows," Ramesh replied. That was a big difference between Ramesh and Benny—Benny was forever wanting to nurse sick squirrels and birds and wanted to bring home every puppy or kitten he saw. Ramesh's attitude toward the natural world was more—well, more utilitarian.

"Anyway," Frank continued. "You're here to train so that you can be on the school soccer team, right? Or do you want to be a champion crow-killer, instead?"

It worked. Ramesh tossed the pebble away. Frank permitted himself an imaginary pat on the back. He had come to know this boy's psychology really well, knew how competitive and vain Ramesh was about doing well in school as well as in athletics.

"What do we do?" Ramesh asked.

"First you do some push-ups," Frank said. "Move to the flat part of the sand—it'll be easier. Okay. Like so."

He watched the little bulge in Ramesh's triceps as he lifted and lowered himself. This kid is strong, he thought and felt a kind of parental pride, as if the boy had inherited *his* muscular structure, *his* genes.

"Good," he said. "Okay, ready to jog? Let's go."

He had first grown aware of Ramesh over a year ago, after they'd been in Girbaug for about four months. It was a Sunday, and Ellie was out with Nandita. Frank was in his bedroom taking an afternoon nap when he was disturbed by the steady thud of a ball in the driveway outside his window. Occasionally, a thin voice cried out, "Score!" He tossed and turned for a few minutes, gnashing his teeth in frustration, and finally threw back his covers and leapt out of bed. Moving swiftly across the living room and kitchen, he threw open the door that led to the courtyard that divided the main house from the housekeepers' shack. Pushing the small wooden gate, he went out into the driveway, barefoot and dressed only in a white T-shirt and shorts. Ramesh was racing the length of the driveway, dribbling a basketball, occasionally reaching high and jumping to throw the ball into an imaginary net. "Hey," Frank yelled. And when the boy didn't hear him, "HEY, you." Remembering the boy's name, "Ramesh. Stop."

Hearing his name, the boy froze in place, cradling the ball in his open palm, his eyes wide and startled. Frank saw that he had scared him, and the realization drove away his anger. Walking up to the boy he said in a softer voice, "I was trying to sleep. You woke me up." He imitated the dribbling of the ball. The boy stayed motionless. "Oh, forget it," Frank said almost to himself. "You don't speak any English, do you? The few times he'd seen Ramesh he had been with Prakash, speaking to him in Hindi as he helped his father around the yard.

He was about to turn away when the boy said, "I speak good-good English, teacher say. Best in class."

Frank smiled. "You do, huh? So you go to school?"

The boy looked offended. "Yes, of course."

Something about his affronted expression made Frank laugh. It reminded him of the look Benny used to get when Ellie or he teased him. "Well, are you a good student?" he said.

"The bestest in my class."

"That's the best in my class. Not bestest."

The boy threw his basketball down and flexed his muscles, looking like a scrawny body builder. "But I am better than best," he cried. "Bestest."

This kid was a hoot. Frank was laughing out loud now. "Oh, yeah? What are your favorite subjects?"

The boy didn't have to think. "Maths," he declared.

"That was my favorite subject in school, too," Frank said. "What else? What about reading and writing?"

Ramesh screwed up his face. "I hate geography. And reading-writing is boring." His face brightened. "I love history. And sports."

"What sports? Cricket?"

"Cricket, yes. But also basketball. You know Michael Jordan?"

"Sure I know Michael Jordan." Frank crouched low so that he was almost at eye level with the boy. "But can I tell you a secret? I'm better than Michael Jordan."

Ramesh's eyes grew wide. "Better than Michael Jordan?" he

breathed, his voice hoarse with wonder. He stared at Frank, his eyes searching his face. "No," he said finally. "Impossible."

Frank pretended to be outraged. "Impossible?" He straightened to his full height. "Them's fighting words, my man."

"Challenge," Ramesh said.

"Challenge?" Frank walked slowly toward the ball, picked it up swiftly, and leapt up to the rim of an imaginary net. "There. Did you see that? The beauty of that dunk? And that? And that?"

Ramesh was squealing with joy as he tried to hit the ball out of Frank's hands. Frank pretended to defend the ball but yielded it to the boy after a few seconds. "Oops," he said. "You really are very good."

Ramesh looked magnanimous. "Best of ten, best of ten," he yelled. He pointed to a medium-sized tree to the side of the driveway. "Hit top of that tree. First person to hit ten, is winning."

So that's what the boy had been doing while he had been trying to take a nap. Remembering the well-lit basketball courts that he had played on as a teenager in Grand Rapids and the hoop that he'd installed on the top of their garage in Ann Arbor, Frank was touched by Ramesh's desperate ingenuity. He realized that he had no idea how much money Ramesh's parents earned—they had simply come with the company-provided house and were paid by HerbalSolutions. He resolved to supplement their income with an occasional tip here and there. And first thing tomorrow he would send Satish to buy a basketball hoop for this boy.

Ramesh was tugging at his T-shirt, trying to get his attention. "Scared?" he said.

"Scared?" Frank roared in mock indignation, knocking the ball out of Ramesh's hands. "Not me." He rose on his bare toes and threw the ball high so that it touched the top of the tree. He grabbed the ball and did it a second time. But before he could get his hands on the ball again, he felt a sharp elbow in his side. "Oww," he yelped. "Why, you dirty little cheat." He pretended to nurse his injured side while Ramesh giggled his pleasure and took four consecutive shots.

Now, knowing how competitive Ramesh was, he told himself that if they were to stop jogging, he'd have to be the one to call it quits. The boy had done well keeping up with him as they ran along the shore, but his breathing was getting more ragged and the sweat was pouring off his face. Also, Ramesh was running barefoot, having shaken off his plastic sandals at the base of the stone steps. "Where're the sneakers I bought you last month?" Frank gasped.

"Dada said too good to wear on beach."

Frank felt the familiar wave of irritation whenever he thought of Prakash. Typical stupid advice. "I want you to wear them for jogging, okay?" he said. "They will help you run faster."

Ramesh shot him a cocky look. "I running very fast, already," he said.

Frank tapped him lightly on the back. "Very clever." He stopped. "Okay. Let's head back. I have to be at work and you have to be at school. I don't want you to be late."

Ramesh shrugged. "I can run more and more."

"Yeah, I know." He glanced up to where the sun was heating up the day and wiped the sweat off his brow. "But take pity on an old man, okay?"

Ramesh got that solicitous, serious look on his face that Frank had come to love. Benny used to get that gentle, absurdly adult look also, when he thought somebody needed his care or protection.

"Okay," Ramesh said. "We stop." He took Frank's hand, as if he was helping an elderly man cross the street.

They were far away from the house, so he didn't have to care about Ellie or Prakash being jealous of the fact that he was walking on the beach holding Ramesh's hand. Ramesh's grip was tighter, different from Benny's, but it made him miss his dead son with a sharpness that took his breath away. Still, it felt good to hold a child's hand again. Something softened and relaxed within Frank, and he realized how stiffly he had been holding himself ever since Anand's death. He was thankful that upon seeing Ramesh in the courtyard last evening, he had suggested this morning's run.

As they walked back toward the house, Frank determined to get back into the routine of helping Ramesh with his schoolwork. The child should not have to suffer because of the chaos of the adults around him.

A few hours later Frank picked up the phone to call Peter Timberlake from his office. He didn't want to go through another day without getting Pete's permission to give in to some of the workers' demands. He was hoping Peter wouldn't put up much of a fight, but somehow he didn't think so. Pete had been stunned when Frank had called to report Anand's death and the ensuing furor. "Jeez," he'd breathed. "How the hell did that happen?"

He was dialing the country code for the United States when he found his fingers dialing Scott's number instead. Scott was a broker on Wall Street, and Frank trusted his business acumen even more than Pete's. Plus, he needed his big brother's help in rehearsing what exactly to say to Peter when he spoke to him.

"Hello?" Scott said.

"Hey, possum," Frank replied. "How are you?"

"Well, hi there, squid. What's new with you?"

They had called each other by these nicknames for so long that neither one of them remembered when or why they'd come up with them. Frank felt his neck muscles relax at the sound of his brother's deep baritone. "I can't talk too long," he said. "Gotta call Peter before he zonks out for the night. Whatcha doing? How's Mom?"

"She's fine. Says she tried calling you this week but there was no answer. Anyway, I took her out to dinner last night. Oh, and I finally met the mysterious Barney." After not dating anyone in all the years since their father had left, Lauretta was now dating a man who lived in her apartment building. Neither Scott nor Frank could quite get over this recent turn of events.

"How is he? Does he treat her nice?"

"He's nuts about her. And she—she seems happier than I've ever known her to be."

Frank laughed. "Goddamn. Wait till I tell Ellie."

"How is El?"

"She's fine. She's great."

A minuscule pause. "You guys doing all right?"

"Yeah. Sure." Frank exhaled heavily. "It's only that—things are tough here right now, Scott. In fact, if you have a minute, I wanted to run something by you."

"Go ahead."

"Well, we had a situation here where this young guy—he was a bit of a troublemaker, a union leader type—well, we had him arrested. I guess one of our men told the police to, y'know, rough him up a bit and they got carried away or something. And the guy died in police custody and—"

"Holy shit."

"Yeah. Exactly. And needless to say, everybody's tempers are inflamed, and I don't know, the whole situation is pretty explosive."

"I'll say." Frank could tell that Scott was thinking, could picture him with his eyes closed and forehead creased. "Have you made any overtures to the family?"

"We did. We sent the mother a check for ten thousand rupees, and she refused to accept it. Said it insulted her son's memory."

"Ten thousand . . . that's like what? Two hundred dollars or something? Well, can't say I blame her. I'd be insulted, too." Scott cleared his throat. "Fact is, kiddo, your company's profits are soaring. I follow the stock daily. I think you guys can afford to be more generous, don't you? And what exactly are their demands?"

"Oh, the usual—a pay raise, more breaks during the day. That sort of thing."

"I don't see what the problem is. So give in to some of their demands, squid. I mean, this situation sounds untenable."

Frank was surprised to find that he had tears in his eyes. He clung to the phone, not daring to speak. Scott sounded as reasonable, as calm and responsible, as ever. Frank remembered the day after Benny's funeral, when Scott asked him to go to lunch. But instead of lunch, Scott had driven to a state park and they had walked for two hours in almost complete silence. On the way back, in the car, Scott had turned to face Frank, his eyes steady on his younger brother's face. "You will survive this," he said. "I know you think you won't, but you will."

"You still there?" Scott was now saying.

"Yes," he whispered, not daring to say more.

"Listen. Call Peter and tell him—don't ask him, tell him—you're gonna give them part of what they want. You're in charge there, it's your ass on the line, not Peter's. So you make the decision, okay?"

"I miss home," Frank blurted out. "I just miss—you know, life in the States."

"So come back. How much longer are you two gonna stay there, anyway?"

"I don't know. Until things are stable, I suppose. And Ellie loves it here. She's built a life for herself here, Scotty. Whereas me"—he was teary again—"I don't know if I'll ever be at home anywhere again, Scott." Now he was sobbing, silently but hard. "Oh, God, Scott. I don't know what's happening to me. I'd really hoped that being in a new place would help me heal. Just when I think I'm getting better, getting over him, I—I miss him, Scott. I feel like they buried me alongside him. I'm trying so hard, but I don't think it's getting any easier."

"Frankie," Scott said, his own voice hoarse. "Frankie, don't."

"I just keep *remembering* things. Like what the hair on his forearms felt like when I caressed him. Or that bump on the side of his head, remember? He had that since birth. And that squeaky giggle that he had? Remember how you used to play that silly game with him when he was little, Scotty?"

"Stop. Don't do this to yourself, kiddo."

But he couldn't stop. He talked about Benny so rarely. And Scott was one of the few people whom he trusted with Benny's memory, one of the few who knew how sacred that memory was and how one wrong statement could defile that. "I can't talk to Ellie about this," he said. "I don't know why—God knows she tries. But I can't, Scott. I think I still blame her for her negligence. If only she'd—"

"Frankie, that's bullshit. She did nothing wrong. The doctor said there was no way she could've possibly known. I heard him myself. In any case, how does it help your marriage, man, to blame Ellie?"

"Well, she blames me, too. Hell, just the other day she accused me of using Ramesh—the little servant boy who lives with us, Scott—to get over Benny." He felt fresh outrage as he remembered Ellie's words.

"Frank. Ellie's your wife. She adores you. She's all you got. And vice versa."

There was a knock on his door and before he could respond, Rekha, his secretary, walked in. "Not now," he barked, embarrassed to be seen in this disheveled state. "How many times do I have to tell you people? You don't enter my office unless I ask you to."

He heard Scott gasp at the other end, even while he registered the look of startled fear on Rekha's face before she slipped out of the room. "Easy, easy," Scott was murmuring.

He fought to control his emotions. "Sorry," he said finally. "I just lost it for a second."

"Frank, listen to me. Here's what you're gonna do. First, nip this whole labor thing in the bud. Fix it—and fast. That's the first order of business. Second, get out of town for a few days. Take Ellie and go somewhere. You're gonna have a breakdown if you go on like this, kiddo."

He felt more clear and resolute after he got off the phone. He immediately dialed Pete's number, afraid of dissipating any of that resolution if he waited. To his relief Pete was amenable to a settlement; the news of Anand's death had rattled him up more than Frank had realized.

He heaved himself out of his chair after he'd hung up and opened the door to his office. Rekha was at her desk. "I'm sorry about yelling at you," he said. "I . . . It was an important business call, you know? But I shouldn't have yelled at you."

Rekha looked so relieved and eager-to-please, it made him want to cry. You're a jerk, he told himself. You really scared her. "I'm sorry," he said again before making his way out of the building.

The workers were on their half-hour lunch break when he reached the factory. He smelled the sharp, pungent smell of the crushed girbal leaves as he entered. He inhaled deeply and walked over to where Deshpande, the foreman, was sitting against a machine. The man, who was eating a simple lunch of a roti dipped in daal, jumped to his feet when he saw Frank approach. "Good afternoon, sahib," he said in his thickly accented English.

"Afternoon," he said. Out of the corner of his eye, he could see the other workers staring at him. "Listen, Desh. I have some good news. I've decided to raise everybody's salary by two rupees a day, effective next week. And we're adding an extra fifteen-minute break to each day. Okay?" He waited for an expression of delight to cross the man's face, but Desh was expressionless. Damn poker-faced bastard, Frank thought.

Desh finally spoke, lowering his voice. "We should also offer a good sum to Anand's mother, sahib. Will help tensions a lot."

To his surprise Frank realized that the foreman was talking to him as an equal, as if they were partners brainstorming a business strategy. The guy really cares about this place, he thought, and found the notion comforting and oddly touching. A feeling of good cheer spread across him. "Tell you what," he said. "You recommend what you think is a fair amount. I'll leave that to you." He was rewarded by a shy grin.

Desh waited until Frank exited the factory to break the news to the others. On his way out, Frank heard the men erupt into cheers and whistles. He smiled to himself. As he walked back to his office, he couldn't help but think that maybe he'd turned a corner.

That night, the chicken pot pie tasted delicious. "How does he do it?" Frank gasped. "I mean, the guy looks like Howdy Doody but cooks like Wolfgang Puck."

Ellie giggled. "He does look a bit like Howdy Doody, doesn't he?"

"Yup. He should teach Ramesh how to cook. Good skill to have if the kid's gonna study in the States someday."

"You really think Ramesh is that good?" Ellie asked. "That he could hold his own in the U.S.?"

He waited to see if he detected any hostility or sarcasm in her voice and decided there was none. "I think the kid's brilliant, Ellie," he said. His voice was sincere, even-keeled. "With the right kind of parents, the sky would be the limit—"

"But that's just it, babe," Ellie said. "His parents are a bright but passive mother and a father who seems more interested in booze than anything else. Those are the cards he has to play."

Not if I play a stronger role in his life, Frank wanted to say. And I would, if I didn't have to watch over my shoulder and gauge your reaction all the time. But he swallowed the words even as they formed on his lips. As he did the thought that followed: How come Ellie is so damn liberal about global issues—the rights of women, the obligation of rich countries to help poorer countries, even what should be done at HerbalSolutions—and so pinched and narrow when it came to solving the one problem they actually could—helping one poor boy live up to his full potential?

Frank felt a little pinch on his shoulder. "Hey, you," Ellie said. "I'm still here. Where did you go?"

He immediately felt guilty about his ungenerous thoughts. Ever since that lovely evening at Nandita's, things had been sweet between him and Ellie, and he didn't want to upset the cart. Just last night he had made love to her for the first time in weeks, and it had not been the cautious lovemaking that they'd slipped into since Benny's death. He had fallen asleep pleased that they had not lost that electric connection, that they were still capable of fucking like they were twenty-five.

"I'm here, babe," he smiled. "I was just thinking . . . how about if we go somewhere for the day on Sunday? Might do us good to get away for a few hours."

"That's a great idea. I've missed you this week. And you've been working such long hours that I worry about you." She squeezed his hand. "Tell you what. How about we pack a picnic and go to a nice beach somewhere along the coast? Would you like that?"

He began to grin his approval and then stopped, struck by a thought.

"What?" Ellie said.

"Nothing. Only that, I'd promised Ramesh that I'd spend a whole day at the beach with him soon. So if we go, we can't tell him where we're going, okay?"

Ellie's face was expressionless. "I see," she said and again, that awkward, infuriating silence grew between them.

"It's okay," he said hastily. "Really. I shouldn't have even brought it up. It's just that—he's so sensitive, that boy. I don't want to hurt his feelings. But as long as we don't tell him—"

"Well, we can just have him join us," Ellie said. "That would solve it, wouldn't it? Would you like that?"

Would he like that? Despite his best efforts to keep his face blank, Frank could feel it inflame with joy. From the look on Ellie's face, he knew that she'd noticed it too and felt ashamed. But the fact was inescapable. The thought of Ramesh joining them made the proposed picnic immediately more pleasurable. With just him and Ellie at the beach it would be sweet, but with the ever-present possibility of awkwardness or even hostility. But Ramesh would liven things up. There would be no room for silences, for strained conversations, for the deliberate avoidance of subjects that could trigger sad memories.

Ellie was staring at her dinner plate, getting the last of the chicken pie onto her fork. Frank sensed that she was looking away out of kindness, embarrassed for him and his naked need for this young boy. He also knew that her question was a test of sorts.

Saving his marriage was more important than an idle promise to Ramesh, he decided. He remembered Scott's reminder about Ellie being the most significant thing in his life. "Listen," he said. "Let's forget I even mentioned Ramesh. Let's just you and I go and have a good time, shall we?"

For a second, Ellie looked tempted. Then, as she got up and picked the empty plates off the table, she said, "It's okay, hon. Invite him. I know you'll feel better if he's there—that way, you don't have to break your promise to him," she added hastily. She kissed the back of his head as she carried the dishes to the sink.

He sat alone at the table, feeling that he had failed her test despite giving her the correct answer. But even while he was chastising himself, a thin, sharp feeling was piercing him. He recognized it as anticipation at the thought of spending the whole day at the beach with Ramesh.

CHAPTER 9

Edna seemed thrilled at the prospect of her son's outing with Ellie and Frank, but Prakash was a different story. The man had come over at nine to put together their picnic basket, and a little later Ramesh bounded into the kitchen. "Dada," the boy said, "Ma wants to know if—"

"*Chup re,*" Prakash hissed, slapping the back of Ramesh's head. "Stupid boy. Turning my brain to yogurt with your Dada this, Dada that."

From the living room, they saw Prakash's gesture. Ellie felt Frank tense. "If he touches that kid one more time, I swear I'm gonna deck him," he said.

"Frank, just ignore it," Ellie whispered. "He's just—who knows what his problem is? He's just acting out for our benefit. Anyway, we'll be out of here in no time." All the while thinking, that she knew exactly what Prakash's problem was—the man was jealous. Jealous and ashamed, because on his salary, he could never put together a lavish picnic, could never treat his son to a day on the beach in the style that they would. She marveled again at how obtuse her usually perceptive husband became when it came to matters involving Ramesh. The boy was truly his blind spot.

They heard Prakash raise his voice again. "You come home, *jaldi-jaldi*, understand? Lots-lots homework to do. No waste whole day on beach like a *mawali*."

"But Dada—" Ramesh's voice sounded anguished.

Before Ellie could stop him, Frank strode into the kitchen. She followed him, standing in the doorway between the living room and the kitchen. "You knew we were going to be gone the whole day," Frank was saying. "What's all this fuss now? In any case, the boy's all caught up on his homework. So what's the problem?"

Prakash kept his head bowed as he concentrated on the chicken sandwiches he was assembling. A long moment passed. "Prakash," Frank said, as Ramesh looked tearfully from one man to another. "Is there a problem?"

The cook finally looked up. His eyes glittered with—anger? Malice? "No problem, sir," he said. And then, with a sudden grin that had not a trace of joy in it, "Have a nice day."

Frank stared at Prakash for another moment—a moment too long, Ellie thought. There's no need to humiliate the man in front of his son, she thought to herself, willing Frank to walk away, ready to intervene if he didn't. Just as she was about to, Frank let out a short sigh and turned away. So that he didn't see—but Ellie did—the quick, furtive look that Prakash threw toward Frank. This time, she had no trouble reading the expression on the man's face. It was pure hatred. Her stomach dropped.

As if he knew he had been caught, Prakash expertly smoothed his expression into the mask of pleasant blankness he usually wore around them. "You wanting pickle with food, madam?" he asked. "Me pack pickle?"

"No thanks," she said. She couldn't imagine eating the tangy, spicy lime relish with the other foods they were taking.

"Put some for me, dada," Ramesh said as she walked toward her bedroom to find the sunscreen.

"Shut your mouth," she heard Prakash hiss. "Bad boy. Getting father into much trouble with the *feringas*." *Feringas*. Foreigners. So that's how they think of us. Although she knew she was being ridiculous, she couldn't help feel disappointed.

The interaction with Prakash had put a damper on their spirits as they got into the car but not for long. "Good morning, Satish," Ellie said to the driver and was gratified to receive a smile that was warm and genuine.

"How are you today, madam?" Satish asked. His eyes fell on Ramesh. "He's coming?"

"Yah," Ramesh said. He turned to Frank. "I want to sit in the back, in between you and Ellie."

"Well, good thing we're taking the Camry then." Frank laughed. He looked over Ramesh's head at Ellie. "That okay with you?" he mouthed, and she nodded.

Ramesh scampered into the back seat. "Bye Ma, bye Dada," he called to his parents, who were standing by the gate of the driveway.

"Good Lord," Frank whispered to Ellie before making his way to the other side of the car. "You'd think we were away for a week rather than a damn day."

As he backed out of the driveway, Satish got into the spirit of things. "You're sitting in the back," he said mournfully to Ramesh. "I'm all alone in front. No company for me, *yaar*."

"Want me to come to front?" the boy asked promptly. "I can climb over the seat."

Satish looked at Frank and Ellie in his rear view mirror and laughed. "No, *ustad*, it's okay. I'm just taking your *firki*."

"What's that mean? That last thing you said?" Ellie asked.

"Taking someone's *firki*? Like making fun, you know?" Satish grinned.

"*Arre*, I'll take your *firki* double," Ramesh said. His accent was

thicker and his manner less diffident in Satish's presence. She wondered if Frank had noticed, also. "My three best friends and I are
teasing each other all day at school," he announced.

"You have three best friends?" Ellie said. "How is that possible?"

Ramesh looked puzzled. "Why not possible, Ellie?"

"Well, you can have many *good* friends. But there can only be
one best friend, right?"

The boy considered for a moment. Then, "But if I have only one
best friend, then what happens to my other best friends?" He looked
so pleased with himself that the others laughed.

"Wah, wah, ustad. You are a champion arguer."

"I'm also champion at maths. And basketball. And history." He
turned toward Frank. "Tell him."

"He's right," Frank said. "Ramesh is a champion eater. And a
champion tall-tale teller. And a champion nose-picker."

"Hey," Ramesh yelled, hitting Frank on his arm with his fist.
"Stoppit."

"Such talents, Ramu," Satish said. "I'm impressed."

Ellie could tell that the boy was hovering at that point between
giggling and getting whiny. She knew if she didn't intervene, the
two men would continue teasing the boy until they'd have a full-
blown tantrum on their hands. "So which beach are we going to?"
she said, changing the subject. "Where should we go, Satish?"

"You wanting to go to Foreigner's Beach, madam?" he asked.
Foreigner's Beach was the local name given to the beach that Hotel
Shalimar and the other, newer resorts overlooked. Ellie considered.
If there was another American couple on the sand, they would feel
compelled to come up to the Bentons to chat. Frank would hate sharing his time with Ramesh with anyone else. Plus, she was hoping
that if Ramesh fell asleep in the afternoon, she and Frank could go
for a walk.

"No Foreigner's Beach," she said. "Something more—quiet, maybe? With just local people?"

"No locals on the beach in daytime, madam," Satish replied promptly. "They go during sunset."

Ellie remembered. Indians hated to sunbathe and came to the beach wearing their regular clothes, although she had seen the affluent Indian tourists who visited the resorts out on the sand in T-shirts and shorts. Even that, Nandita had told her, was a relatively recent trend.

Satish drove them to a pretty, secluded beach with a grove of coconut trees behind them and huge boulders where the water curved in to meet the sand. "This is beautiful," Ellie gasped.

"Thank you, madam," Satish replied. The young man helped them carry their beach chairs and the large rainbow-colored umbrella that would protect them from the bubbling sun. He and Frank pounded the metal pole of the umbrella into the sand. Then he straightened and looked at Frank. "What time should I pick you up, sir?" he said.

For Ellie, this was always the awkward part, after Satish had dropped them off someplace and disappeared until he was summoned again. For a moment she contemplated asking this nice young man to join them for the day, but she knew Frank would not forgive her if she invited Satish to intrude upon their day. No, better to get through the momentary embarrassment, which, for all she knew, only she felt. Satish was probably glad to get away from them and have the day to himself. Though where he went, she didn't have a clue. Despite herself, she found herself asking, "Will you have someplace to go?"

"No problem, madam," he said. "Village is close by, only. Some friends there I'll be seeing." This was Satish's stock answer. He apparently had friends every place they ever went, including Bombay. Ellie suspected he was just being polite, not wanting them to feel discomfort on his behalf, the way the have-nots always seemed to protect the sensibilities of the haves.

"I'm hungry," Ramesh announced as soon as Satish had left.

"Boy, your mother told me you'd eaten breakfast," Frank said. "You must have worms in your stomach."

"I have a nail tree growing in my belly," the boy said seriously.

"A nail tree?" Frank and Ellie asked simultaneously. "You mean, like, metal nails? Shall I hammer them out?" Frank grinned.

"No, no. Fingernails." He held out his chewed nails for them to inspect. "I biting my nails. Ma says it makes a tree grow in your stomach. Maybe that's why I'm eating all the time."

"That's just an expression," Ellie started to say and then thought better of it. For all she knew, Edna probably did think her son had a tree in his belly. This was a country where the lines between metaphors and reality, fact and fiction, were virtually nonexistent because strange, improbable things happened all the time. She remembered the first time she'd visited Bombay—she'd seen a cow, an elephant, a snake, and a monkey in the streets on the very first day. And all these animals coexisted peacefully with the mechanical animals—the Jaguars and the Dodge Rams and Ford Mustangs—parked on the street. Edna was forever telling her strange stories—of how her aunt once saw a crocodile and a cow fall out of the sky while it was raining; how, when she was a little girl and traveling with her father in a bullock cart on some rural road at night, they had seen a cobra in the middle of the road. They had stopped, and before their very eyes, the cobra had turned into a beautiful woman who disappeared into the nearby woods. If one of her patients in America had told her this, Ellie would've tested him or her for various mental conditions. But here in India, she was learning to take such things in her stride, was beginning to realize that reality was more multidimensional than she had ever suspected in Cleveland or Michigan.

She pulled out a sandwich and handed it to Ramesh. "Will this tide you over until lunch?"

He cocked his head. "Tide me?"

"It's an expression," she said again. "It just means—"

"Time and tide wait for no man," Ramesh intoned slowly. Ellie thought he looked like nothing so much as a wise owl at that moment. The boy turned toward Frank. "Have you heard that saying?"

Frank was poker-faced. "I think so," he said. "A few times." After a few minutes, he got up and lifted off his T-shirt, blocking the sun for a moment. "Speaking of tides, how about a quick swim?" He tagged Ramesh. "Last one in is an elephant's turd."

Ramesh threw the last of his sandwich into his mouth, squealing as he scrambled to his feet, tossing sand onto the blanket. "*Ae,* you cheating," he yelled after Frank, who was running toward the shoreline. Unbuttoning his blue cotton shirt, he began to follow Frank, looking back at Ellie. "He cheating, Ellie." He hit the water a few seconds after Frank did.

Ellie dusted the sand off the blanket and then sat with her hands across her knees, looking at the two of them frolicking in the water, splashing and dunking each other. Even from this distance she could hear Ramesh's yelps of delight and Frank's deep laugh. He's happy, she thought with wonder and realized she had tears in her eyes. It had been so long since she'd seen Frank like this, young, carefree, and genuinely joyous. The sullen, cautious shell of a man that he'd turned into the night that Benny had died seemed to have been cast away, as if the waters of the Arabian Sea were baptizing him in a new faith. Never mind that this faith was rocky, that it was built on a foundation as unstable as this sand that shifted below her. Never mind that this new religion that he was finding was being led by a nine-year-old boy who belonged to two other people who, despite their short, abrupt manner with him, loved him very much. That the nine-year-old belonged to a father who was already uneasy with what he saw as a usurpation of his powers and authority, who sensed in Frank a challenger to the unconditional love he expected from his son.

And suddenly Ellie felt something darken the sun, as if a shadow had leaned across it, and she became acutely aware of Benny's presence. Her stomach dropped and, unable to help herself, she looked to her right, knowing that Benny was sitting right there. But when she looked, there was nobody on the red and green blanket, just the sandals Ramesh had kicked off before heading for the water. Still, she couldn't shake off the feeling that Benny was right next to her. "Ben?" she whispered, staring straight ahead now, not knowing whether Frank could see her lips moving from this distance but not wanting to take the risk. "You here, Benny?"

There was no answer, just the low hum of the universe, which always seemed more audible on clear, cloudless days at the beach. The afternoon air shimmered like cut glass. But even as Ellie felt foolish, she couldn't let go of the feeling that, like her, Benny was watching the antics of the man and the boy in the water. Her heart ached for her dead son. Did he believe that his dad was replacing him with another boy? Did he feel forgotten, ignored, neglected? Did he feel—*dead*? Or was he aware of how sharply, excruciatingly alive he was in their minds and lives? Did he know that they thought about him a hundred times a day, that each of them had a picture of him beside the bed that they kissed first thing in the morning? That there were certain foods that they could not eat to this day because they were his favorite foods, that neither one of them had eaten a watermelon or Chinese fried rice since his death, that they turned off the radio if "Yellow Submarine" or "Octopus's Garden" came on, that they never entered a Nike store because that was his favorite brand of shoe?

Ellie felt her throat tighten as another thought struck her: Did Benny, oh, dear God, did Benny hold her responsible for his dying? Did he think—as Frank had occasionally let slip he believed—that she had been a neglectful mom? That he would still be alive if only she'd rushed him to the ER at the first sign of fever? Did he blame Frank for being away in Thailand, convinced that his pragmatic, eagle-eyed father would've spotted the danger signs faster than his more relaxed and easygoing mother? Oh, but what about the scores of times when she'd nursed her boy through fevers and sore throats and head colds while Frank was away? How could she have possibly known that this time was different? She'd followed the doctor's instructions—she'd put the wet rags on his head, given him the baby Tylenol, brought him a Popsicle for his sore throat, checked his temperature every two hours. And more: she'd put on some soothing music on the portable CD player in his room, opened the windows to let in some fresh air, sat holding his hand and telling him how much she loved him. Did he remember all this? Didn't he remember this? That she'd only left him after his fever was down to normal and he was asleep, his sweet chest rising and falling gently as he breathed? That his skin was smooth and flawless, without any of those purple blossoms that would bloom just a few hours later? That his eyes were shut and he was smiling in his sleep as he often did when he was having a funny dream? That he had his fingers locked together across his chest as he slept and she'd noticed the perfect fingernails and as always, her heart had swelled with love at the sight of those tiny, smooth hands, brown as a small loaf of bread?

She did. She remembered all of it. The single, strangled cry from Benny that had woken her out of a deep sleep so that she was in his room before she could even remember waking up. The turning on of the night lamp and the horrific first discovery of the rash. The sweaty, disoriented look on Benny's face. The terrified phone call to Dr. Roberts. The longest five minutes in the world waiting for him to call her back. She had already used those five minutes to get out of her nightdress and into clothes, knowing that Dr. Roberts would ask her to take Benny to the ER. The shakiness of her hands as she dialed 911. The cool, calm efficiency of the paramedics. Riding in the front of the ambulance—despite her pleas, they wouldn't let her ride in the back, where they'd already started Benny on an IV—and watching the Mott Children's Hospital building looming like a spaceship in the night as they approached. The resident doctor talking to her, asking her questions, barking out orders at a nurse, asking her to page Dr. Masood, the infectious disease specialist. Dr. Masood had arrived a short while later. After Ellie had answered all his questions, he had touched her shoulder lightly. "We will do our best for your son, Mrs. Benton. We are running some tests right now. But I'm ninety-nine percent sure this is meningococcus. There's nothing you could've done to prevent this. So I want you to understand, you did nothing wrong."

Ellie wished she could say those words to Benny now, plead her case while at the beach on a blindingly bright afternoon. But the strange thing was, she could only feel Ben's presence if she looked straight ahead at the water. If she glanced in the direction where she was sure he was sitting, she felt nothing, saw only the blanket and the sun shimmering on the grains of sand that Ramesh had deposited when he'd tossed his sandals off. Besides, no time now to explain anything because Frank and Ramesh were climbing out of the sea and heading toward her, shaking their heads to shake off the water, looking like two happy dogs as they did so. With every step they took, the sensation of Benny being nearby left her. Now they were almost upon her, and even though the wetness had darkened Frank's blond hair, she noticed how it glistened in the sun, took in the long, angular face, the big, wide grin, which was also her son's grin. The grin took her breath away because for the first time she saw what others had always commented upon—Benny's strong resemblance to his father.

But no time now to ponder this because Ramesh's wet, dark body was shivering uncontrollably despite the sun. She threw him a towel, but Frank grabbed it and roughly rubbed the moisture off the boy's slender body before wrapping it around him. When they sat down, Frank kept his arm around the still-shivering boy, occasionally rubbing his back to breathe more heat into him. The gesture reminded Ellie of Frank bathing Benny when he was a toddler. Ben hated baths, used to scream holy murder every night when Frank carried him into the tub. But once he was in the water, he would settle down and splutter with laughter as he splashed around. Father and son would inevitably look like they'd both had a bath, as a soaking, dripping Frank would rub his son down and then carry him in his towel into his bedroom to change into his pajamas.

Ellie marveled at how effortlessly Frank was performing the same task with Ramesh. For the past two years, she had believed that Frank was the one stuck in the muddy cesspool of grief, that she was the one who was coping with the death of their son. Now, she wasn't sure. While she sat on the beach talking to her dead son, Frank had found a new son to love.

Something of her shock at this last realization must have showed on her face, because she saw Frank stiffen as he said, "He's cold." She heard the defensiveness in his voice, as if her husband was fighting back some unspoken accusation.

"I know," she said mildly. Smiling at Ramesh, who sat beaming, oblivious to the sudden tension, she added, "And they say the perfect meal after a swim in the ocean is—potato chips."

"Yessssssssss," the boy said, and they all laughed. Frank had a habit of pumping his fist and exclaiming every time he scored a point at basketball, and Ramesh had picked up the gesture from him.

"Hey, I'm hungry, too. Can I get something to eat?" Frank said.

Ellie smiled. "Who are we kidding? May as well break into the food right now." She rummaged through the picnic basket, taking out each of the dishes Prakash had packed for them. "Wow. Prakash must've thought we were taking half of Girbaug out on the picnic with us."

Ramesh suddenly slapped his knee and squealed with laughter. "Half of Girbaug," he said. "You're funny, Ellie."

Frank and Ellie eyed each other quizzically. "It's not *that* funny, Ramesh," Frank said finally. "Now stop laughing or you're gonna choke on your sandwich. "

But that only made Ramesh laugh even more. "Ignore him," Ellie murmured to Frank. "Best thing to do when they get like that."

Ellie's hand touched something squishy at the bottom of the basket. Removing the small piece of wrapped aluminum foil, she unwrapped it. There was the lime pickle relish that Ramesh had requested from his father.

"My dada didn't forget," Ramesh yelled with delight. The boy opened up his sandwich and spread the relish on top of the chicken salad. Then he took a big bite.

"Ugh," Frank and Ellie said simultaneously.

"Hah?" Ramesh said.

"Ramesh, that's gross. How can you ruin the taste of the chicken with that?"

Ramesh smacked his lips. "The pickle makes the sandwich good. Otherwise, it's too boring."

"Guess it's no different than mustard on a hot dog," Frank said to Ellie. He let out a sudden groan. "God. What would I give for a nice, juicy hot dog right now?"

"You eat dog?" Ramesh looked so outraged that Ellie burst out laughing.

"It's not a dog. It's just called that. It's actually a—" Her mind went blank. What exactly was a hot dog? Beef or pork? "It's just meat," she added lamely.

"And boy, let me tell you. On a hot summer's day like this, nothing tastes better." Frank was still waxing nostalgic.

Ramesh chewed with his mouth open. "Let's cook it for Christmas this year," he said. "I'll tell my dada to make it."

"No, no, no. You don't have it for Christmas. It's summer food." Frank closed his eyes. "It's what you have on the Fourth of July. A nice, cold beer, a fat, juicy burger, and a hot dog."

"Stop," Ellie smiled. "You're making me homesick."

"The Fourth of July is American independence day," Ramesh declared. "I learned at school."

"Right-o," Frank said.

"When is Indian independence day?" Ramesh asked. "You know?"

Ellie and Frank looked at each other, startled. Did they know? They remembered being in Bombay last year because it was a bank holiday and the factory was closed. "I know it's in August," Ellie stammered, little embarrassed. "Is it August seventeenth?"

"August fifteenth," Ramesh yelled. He glared at them. "I know America's independence day, but you don't know India's," he said.

"Okay, buckaroo. You've made your point," Frank said. "Now let up."

Ramesh's ears perked up. "Bukaroo? Like a kangaroo?" He bent his hands at the wrist and held them toward his chest. "Want to see me hop, hop, hop?" Before they could reply, he was struck by another thought. "*Ae*. Let's cook hot dogs for your independence day. I'm sure Dada knows how to make them."

Frank shuddered visibly, and Ellie knew that the thought of Prakash making hot dogs was sacrilegious to him. But to Ramesh, he merely said, "Afraid not, bud. We're going to be in Bombay for the Fourth of July."

Ellie looked at him inquiringly and then remembered. The American consulate was throwing a bash for American expatriates in and around Bombay. Knowing of her reluctance to attend such gatherings, Frank had bribed her with a boat trip to see the Elephanta Caves if she agreed to go. She'd said yes mostly because she knew he wanted her to.

"Bombay?" Ramesh screamed. "You're going to Bombay? Can I come?"

Ellie watched as Frank's face went through several contortions at those last words. First, he looked startled, as if the thought had not occurred to him. Then, the prospect of Ramesh's company made it light up. Immediately, though, the light vanished, dulled by the reminder that Ellie would probably not look too kindly at this intrusion. This realization was followed by a sharp, stabbing resentment at having to sacrifice his pleasure out of a sense of duty toward his wife. Finally, he threw a blanket of blankness over it all and turned to face Ramesh. "I wish you could, buddy," he said. "But not this time."

But Ellie had seen the wistfulness on Frank's face. And beneath his cursory denial of Ramesh's request, she heard the anguished regret at refusing not only the boy but also his own heart's desire. She couldn't bear the thought of being the reason for that refusal. That much she loved him. That much she owed him—the right to occasional happiness that only a bright Indian boy, who belonged to other people, seemed to bring him. Also, she felt an immense sadness as she watched the suddenly downcast Ramesh, saw his bent, disappointed head. She remembered all the places Benny had seen by age seven—Disneyland, New York City, Florence, Captiva Island, Boulder, Cape Cod—and compared that to the fact that Ramesh had never left his hometown, had never seen the giant metropolis that lay less than a few hours away. And who knew what seeing Bombay might do for the boy, what lurking dreams it might arouse, what horizons it might expand? Ellie remembered how going to Barcelona when she was eleven had affected her. "You all go home," she'd said to her parents when it was time to leave. "I'm gonna stay here." They had laughed, and of course she'd gone to Shaker Heights but some part of her—the ambitious, cosmopolitan, worldly part—had been shaped forever by that trip. And she was the daughter of a history professor, had grown up in a home with maps and atlases and books, no stranger to the glories and splendor of the wider world. How now could she deprive Ramesh of his one chance to step outside the confines of his life? What she and Frank could provide for Ramesh without the slightest sacrifice, with a mere flick of their wrist, would take Prakash and Edna a lifetime of scrimping and saving and hardship. A trip to Bombay was the least they could do.

"Why can't he go with us?" she asked.

Frank's head jerked up, and there was a light in his eyes that Ellie had not seen in two years. "I . . . I just assumed . . . I guess . . . no real reason why he can't . . ."

"I mean, do you think the embassy people might object?" she said, enjoying this power to make Frank happy, prolonging it.

"Hell, no. I mean, the invitation said children were welcome. It's just a picnic, anyway, a casual affair." Frank's left eye twitched, and Ellie watched in fascination. His eye generally twitched only in times of stress. How badly he wants this! she thought in wonder. And how hard he tries to hide this need from me! For the first time, Ellie felt grateful for Ramesh's presence in their lives. Perhaps this boy could be the rope that pulled her drowning husband out of his grief. Perhaps he could be the silken thread that reconnected her to Frank.

Her thoughts were interrupted by the whoops of joy emanating from the boy sitting next to her. "Yesssssssssssssssss, Ellie," Ramesh yelled. "Thank you, thank you. Always I've wanted to see Mumbai. I am wanting to meet Shahrukh Khan."

"Who's Shahrukh Khan?" Ellie said and heard Ramesh's gasp.

"You don't know Shahrukh Khan? He's the bestest actor. My own favorite." Ramesh leapt up from the blanket, and striking his best macho pose, began to recite dialogue from Khan's latest film. They listened to the boy for a few minutes, and then Frank turned toward Ellie. "Thank you," he said simply.

She squeezed his hand. "It's no big deal. Besides, it will be fun to have him around."

"I wonder if he'll like the city? Or be afraid of it?" Frank smiled. "Do you remember when we took Ben to New York? How he wanted to go into the peep shows because he thought there would be chickens there?"

She smiled back. "Sure. Remember the visit to Saint Patrick's?"

They had wandered into the magnificent cathedral on Saturday afternoon. Despite their Catholic childhoods, neither Frank nor Ellie was particularly devout, and as they walked down the aisle and took in the stained glass windows, the high ceilings, and the ornate altar, they scarcely noticed the small clusters of people who sat in the pews with their heads bowed and eyes closed. Ellie lit a candle on behalf of her mother and then turned to her five-year-old son and asked if he was ready to leave. "But we haven't prayed yet," Benny replied. And before they could react, he raced ahead and sat in a pew next to a disheveled-looking man, who was wearing a tattered coat and staring into space. His eyes tightly closed, Benny sat beside the man, who reeked of alcohol and urine, for close to ten minutes. Occasionally, his lips moved. Finally, the boy opened his eyes, said a loud, "Bye," to his ragged companion, and joined his parents. "Okay, I'm done talking to God now," he said.

For the rest of that day, Ellie had looked at her son with something approaching awe, realizing that the whiny boy who only wanted fried rice for dinner that night and wanted his dad to carry him back to the hotel was also a mysterious, spiritual being whose individuality was already beginning to assert itself.

She had thought about that strange incident many times, especially since Benny's death. "You remember?" she now asked Frank.

He nodded. "Of course." He paused, looking out to where the sea spread before them like a large banquet table. "He was quite a little man, our Benny."

They both looked away, eyes stinging with tears, afraid to speak until the moment passed and they could control their voices again. Ellie covered Frank's hands with hers. "I bet you Ramesh will love Bombay," she said at last. "How could he not? It's fast, busy, exhilarating—just like him."

Frank sighed. "It's still almost a month away. Wish it was sooner. I could really use a long weekend off."

CHAPTER 10

Ellie gritted her teeth and swore to herself. Edna was standing before her and wailing, beating her forehead and cursing her bad luck for marrying a stupid wreck of a husband. Despite the fact that the woman's anguish seemed genuine enough, Ellie couldn't dismiss the feeling that some of the high drama was for her benefit, that Edna was trying to cover up her embarrassment at her husband's obstinacy with her wailings and mutterings.

Prakash was being an ass, no question about that. It was three days before they were to leave for Bombay, and the man had suddenly changed his mind about letting Ramesh accompany them. Edna had crept up to Ellie about a half hour ago with the news. "What to do, madam? The fool is becoming more-more stubborn in his old age. God only knows what got into his head last night, but he saying he won't let Ramesh go."

"Have you told Ramesh?"

Edna wailed even louder. "No, madam. If that mule wants to break his son's heart, let him tell him. That boy has been excited as a firecracker over this for weeks."

"I see." Ellie didn't know which would be harder, Frank's despondency or his rage when she told him the news. She suddenly felt fed up with the whole situation, this weird dance in which she was caught between the egos and insecurities of two warring men. And Edna was getting on her nerves. Such drama, so early in the morning. Now Edna was evoking the memory of her mother, wishing she had listened to her admonishments about marrying a non-Christian. "These Hindus, madam," she sniffed. "Not the same as us. Sooner or later, they show their true nature. My mama was correct. This man is a total loss."

Despite herself, Ellie laughed. "Edna, please," she said. "This is a simple case of a father not wanting his son to go with us because he's—well, who knows why? Let's not turn this into a religious war."

Edna looked injured and continued to mutter darkly about Prakash's ways. But at least the wailing had stopped. In that silence, Ellie decided to act. "Is Prakash home?" she asked Edna.

"Of course, madam."

"I want to speak to him," she said. "Can we go to your house?"

She caught Edna's startled look. She had never before crossed the courtyard and entered Edna's house. The realization that she had no idea what her servant's home looked like, despite the fact that they shared an address, made Ellie blush. "Let's go," she said gruffly.

The one-room shack had two cots on either end. A third mattress lay on the floor beside one of the cots. A half-partition made way for a little kitchen, and Ellie surmised that the bathroom was behind a yellow door at the far end of the room. Two decrepit-looking chairs were propped against a wall, and a small television set rested on one of them. Even though she knew that Edna's living quarters were much better than those of many of the villagers, Ellie was shocked at how spartan a life her housekeepers lived. No wonder poor Ramesh was always looking for an opportunity to spend time in their home. She wondered what the boy thought of their house. She also felt a twinge of apprehension at taking Ramesh to the Taj, where they would be staying during their time in Bombay. The five-star hotel would be something beyond what the boy's imagination could conjure up. She half wondered if insisting on the boy going with them was a mistake, but then she saw Prakash sitting on his haunches in the kitchen area, and her temper spiked.

Prakash stayed on his haunches, but Ellie caught the murderous look that he flung at his wife at this intrusion. She knew Edna would pay for this barging-in, but right now she couldn't think of that. She just wanted the matter resolved before Frank found out about it. "Prakash," she said sharply. "Edna told me you were against Ramesh going with us. I was so shocked, I knew there had to be a mistake. So I wanted to hear it from your own mouth."

Prakash stared at the floor. "No mistake," he mumbled. Then, looking up at her he repeated more loudly, "No mistake."

Ellie heard the defiance in his voice. "I see," she said, stalling for time. "May I ask why?"

Now, Prakash was openly sneering. "What the world come to," he said to nobody in particular. "Father must give reason for something concern his own son." Behind her, Ellie heard Edna gasp.

"Prakash," Ellie said. "You've known for weeks about this. We have made arrangements, booked hotel rooms." She did a quick calculation and decided to call his bluff. "Who will pay for the hotel rooms?" she asked with fake indignation. "Hundreds of rupees it will cost us."

Still the man did not budge. "That not my *mamala*," he muttered.

His insolent manner was getting on her nerves. "Every time we take Ramesh somewhere these days, you make a fuss. Do you want us to wash our hands of him? We'll be happy to do so." She could tell from Prakash's face that he had not understood her meaning. But Edna did, and she emitted something that sounded like a growl.

"Look at him sitting there with his dung face," Edna said. "Not caring for own son's future." She prodded him with her bare foot. "I'll go," she cried. "I take Ramesh, and in the middle of the night, we'll run away from you."

Prakash threw her a malicious smile. "Where will you go?" he said to her in Hindi.

Edna exploded. "Anywhere. To Goa. I'll beg my mother to take us back. Or I'll drown Ramesh and myself in a well. But away from you."

Prakash raised his hand and made to get up off the floor. Seeing this, Ellie's frustration developed a muscle and hardened into anger. "If we lose our hotel money, I'm going to dock you for it," she cried. "I'll take it out of your salary until you've paid the whole amount, you understand? Is that what you want?"

The cook sat down with a heavy thud, as if pushed back to the floor by the gust of rage coming from both women. "You cannot take salary," he mumbled. "That our money."

Ellie could tell that the spirit had gone out of him, and she felt a faint triumph. "But I will, Prakash," she said. "If you push us too much."

Edna came and stood between her and Prakash. "*Chalo*, don't waste more of madam's time," she said. "What's your decision, you?"

Prakash stared at the wall. "Whatever you wish," he said finally.

But Ellie was not done. "This is not a game, Prakash. Now, no more of this nonsense, *achcha*? You understand?"

"Understand."

"Okay." Ellie exited from the house with Edna walking a pace behind. The two women crossed the courtyard and entered Ellie's kitchen. "Madam," Edna said excitedly. "You showed him good-proper. What you say about cutting pay was very clever." And despite Edna's exuberance, Ellie thought she detected something, a thin thread of anxiety, as if the woman wanted assurance that Ellie had just made an idle threat.

"I was just fooling about that," she said. "Y'know, calling his bluff."

Edna nodded vigorously. "I know, I know. Good you did that, madam. That lump of dung was afraid he wouldn't have moneys for his bottle. He care more about his drink than food for his family."

Edna went on and on, expressing delight at how Ellie had knocked Prakash out, deflated him like an old tire, but Ellie felt none of the exhilaration that Edna apparently did. Reviewing her performance, the imperial manner in which she had spoken to the cook, the way she had used the whip of wealth and power to flay Prakash into submission, she felt nauseous. How easily she had slipped into the role of mistress, of the white memsahib. She remembered all the times she had chastised Frank for doing the same thing with his minions, had turned away in embarrassment when he had exercised his power over his workers. And here she had done exactly the same thing. She tried to imagine a situation where someone—a neighbor in Ann Arbor or a teacher or a relative—could've bullied Frank and her into reversing a decision they had made about Benny. She couldn't come up with one plausible scenario. Surely Prakash had the same rights to decide what was best for his family, surely fatherhood gave him at least that authority, to decide whether his son should go on an out-of-town trip with people he barely knew or liked? Why had she so easily trampled on that right? What made it so easy? But even as she asked that last question she knew the answer: it was her wealth and privilege.

But surely there was also the issue of being correct? Surely it was okay to expect Prakash to keep his word, to let the man know that he could not exploit their affection for his son, that they would not be tossed around on the winds of his whims? Surely that was what they would've said to anyone—a neighbor in Ann Arbor, say—who treated them with such little regard? Ellie tried to sink into the comfort of this line of thinking. But she was shaken by the memory of the tone of her voice, the stiffness of her manner, her threatening words. She had sounded more like Frank than herself, she realized.

Frank. He was the reason behind the whole confrontation with Prakash, anyway. It was her fear of Frank's distress at the thought of Ramesh not joining them on their holiday that had made her speak to Prakash in the first place. For a second she resented her husband for turning her into a person she didn't want to be. Then her sense of fairness corrected that impulse. He had not asked for Ramesh to accompany them to Bombay, had in fact tried hard to conceal his desire from her. And he had not urged her to barge into Prakash's house and have her little temper tantrum. No, Frank's manner of dealing with Prakash would've been much cleaner, less psychologically fraught—he would've grabbed the man's scrawny neck in his clean, white hands and choked him. Ellie grinned and then, seeing Edna's curious expression, stopped.

She shook her head. "I'm tired, Edna," she said. "Can you come to clean in maybe an hour? I just want to rest."

Edna was immediately solicitous. "Of course, madam, of course. Beg pardon." She hurried to the door and then stopped. "Madam, please to forgive my husband." She smiled softly. "He's not a villain, madam. He just—he loves his son and he's scared."

Scared of what? Ellie was about to ask, but she didn't. She knew. She had heard what Edna was too polite to say: my husband is scared that your husband is making a claim on our son that he has no business making. He's scared of his only child being seduced by your wealth, by your world of privilege that we have no defenses against. He's scared of your introducing our son to a life of such finery and luxury that he will never again be at home in our world. And what will happen to Ramesh then? He will become a ghost, an exile, at home in no place. And that is a subject that my illiterate, orphaned husband knows a lot about. He will die before subjecting his son to that fate.

A look passed between the two women. Ellie was the first to turn away. She felt as if with the gentlest of touches, Edna had chided her, accused her of stealing something. She was confused. A half hour ago, Edna had been wailing in her kitchen, cursing Prakash and his shortsighted ways. She had helped Ellie with the barrage of words that had toppled Prakash from his perch of righteousness and inflexibility. And now, without saying a word, she was making Ellie see into Prakash's tormented heart. But suddenly, Ellie got it. Edna was just like her, a conflicted woman—caught between the desires of her own heart, and an overpowering, almost maternal need to mother her husband and protect him from his own demons. She took in the woman's worried, sallow face, the creases on her forehead, the hair prematurely turning gray. She tried to picture what Edna must've looked like as a young bride and saw a jovial, warm, openhearted, headstrong young woman who believed in the redemptive power of love. And she saw Edna over the years, the soaring hope for family reconciliation after the birth of her son and the graying of that hope when it slowly became clear that Goa was a permanent paradise lost. And Prakash, too, being cast away from the bosom of the community that had raised an orphan boy together, once he came home with his new Goanese bride. Ellie felt their loneliness, their isolation, their forced turning to each other for all sustenance and support and the inevitable crumbling of a marriage from the weight of such insularity. And Ramesh becoming the vessel into which they poured all their crumbling dreams, the only reason why their union still made sense. Ellie imagined their pride and hopes when she and Frank first exhibited an interest in their shiny boy. And she imagined that pride turning into concern and then resentment and then hostility as Frank overstepped his bounds, monitoring Ramesh's homework, playing basketball with him, taking the boy to the restaurant at the Shalimar, where a meal cost more than what they earned in a month. And now, the final insult—taking their nine-year-old boy to a city that was a dream, a mythical place to them, as remote and impossible a place as Paris or England was, a city where they imagined movie stars strolled along the streets, bursting into song whenever inspiration hit them.

"Edna," she said gently. "I know Prakash loves his son very much. Of course, I—we—know that. And one thing you should know. We will never do anything to harm your son. We know what he means to you."

Edna let out a small cry and crossed the length of the kitchen. She took Ellie's hand and held it to her wet eyes and then kissed it. "God bless you, madam," Edna cried. "May God be very kind to you."

Ellie felt a faint shock at this breach of etiquette. In all these months, Edna had been very careful to maintain the distance that all Indian servants kept from their mistresses. She was also moved by the sincerity of Edna's gesture. Hesitantly, she touched Edna's shoulder and then stroked her arm. "It's okay," she murmured. "Don't worry so much. Everything will be fine."

But this was a mistake. Now Edna was sobbing almost uncontrollably. It tore Ellie's heart up, to hear such deep sorrow. "So lonely . . ." Edna was saying. "No one to talk to. Miss my family. Your kindness. So happy you're here, madam. Only person I can talk to. My husband . . . has own worries. In marketplace, everybody say how kind you are, madam. God will reward you."

Ellie sighed. She had so much to do. Counseling Edna had not been on the agenda for the day. Neither had confronting and humiliating poor Prakash. She eyed the sobbing woman in front of her. "Edna," she said firmly. "Listen to me. You go sit in the living room. I'll make us a cup of tea."

Edna stopped mid-sob, shocked at this unnatural reversal of roles. Wiping her eyes with the back of her hand, she said, "No, madam. You sit. I make the tea."

"Okay," Ellie said. She went into the living room and sat on the couch, holding her head in her hands. She stayed that way until she heard the rattle of the tray that told her that Edna was heading into the room.

CHAPTER 11

Bombay.

Such a deceptive word, so soft-sounding, like sponge cake in the mouth. Even the new name for the city, Mumbai, carries that round softness, so that a visitor is unprepared for the reality of this giant, bewildering city, which is an assault, a punch in the face. Everything about the city attacks you at once, as you leave the green tranquillity of the surrounding hills and enter it—the rows of slums that look like something built for and by giant, erratic birds rather than humans; the old, crumbling buildings that have not seen a lick of paint in decades and many of which are held up by scaffoldings; the new, tall buildings that rise from the wretched streets and point like thin fingers toward a dirty, polluted sky; the insane tango of auto rickshaws and cars and bicycles and scooters and bullock carts competing for their inch of space, creating their riotous din of blaring horns and yells and invective; the beggars—armless, legless, fingerless, eyeless, and the lepers, dear God, even noseless—darting in between the vehicles, the legless ones perched on a homemade skateboard, making it hard for the drivers to spot them; and above all, the people, the constant, ever-present mass of people, thousands of them on every street, spilling from the slum-invaded sidewalks onto the roads, zipping in and out of traffic, curving around the hood of a car to avoid being hit by it, and constantly moving, moving, a procession of humanity in motion. You enter the city from the sub-urbs, which have none of the green tranquillity of the American 'burbs, and pass street after street of small restaurants and shops selling everything from jeans to gold jewelry to the ubiquitous betel leaf concoction known as *paan*, which every Indian male of a certain class background seems to chew. Occasionally, there is a shop with a name you recognize—Sony, Wrangler, Nokia—and it is impossible not to notice the billboards that say Coke or Pepsi, part of the Cola Wars being fought across the country. But mostly, nothing registers because your attention is pulled in multiple directions—here is a taxi coming up to your right and about to hit your Camry and you try to control your reaction, bite down on your tongue, but at the last minute yell to Satish to watch out and feel the quiet press of embar-rassment when the taxi misses your car by inches—as they always seem to—and Satish flashes you a grin in the rearview mirror. And here you are stopped at a traffic light and your car is surrounded by scores of tired-looking young women with children on their hips, beating on the windows with their open hands as they beg for money, and you feel hot and flushed and don't know where to look, know it is dangerous to make eye contact but staring straight ahead feels pretty untenable, also, and on top of this Satish is admonish-ing you not to weaken, not to toss out a few coins because there are always more beggars than coins. So you sit in your air-conditioned car, ignoring the sound of hands beating on the window, feeling like a chimp in a zoo, remembering that other time a couple of months ago when other, angrier hands had beaten on your car, feeling that lethal combination of pity and aggravation that India always seems to arouse in you. And then, at the last minute, you sense that your wife can't take this anymore and she reaches into her purse for a few one-rupee coins and, watching this, the crowd outside your car gets frantic, you can feel it even though you're safely inside, and suddenly their numbers seem to double, just like that, like ants at a picnic. And Ellie lowers the window just as Satish starts moving, and now the outstretched hands are in the car, grasping at the money that Ellie is tossing out, and some of them are running after the moving car, in and out of the heavy traffic, fixated on the single coin, with no thought to the safety of life or limb. "Put the window up, madam," Satish yells, even as he handles the control of the automatic window himself. And not a moment too soon, because the lowered window has let in more than the dark, desperate faces of the women and children, it had let in the stench of the city, a peculiar eye-stinging, nose-filling, throat-gagging combination of urine and exhaust and sweat and black smoke. This burning, rubbery smell is everywhere, though it dissipates a bit as you make your way from the inner rings of hell—Parel, Lalbaug, Bhendi Bazaar—into the outer rings—Crawford Market, Flora Fountain, Colaba.

It was while the car was stopped at yet another traffic light at Parel that Ramesh burst into tears. "I want to go home," he sobbed. "I hate Bombay. Too much poor people."

Ellie put her arm around the boy. "I know, baby," she said. "But it will be okay. We'll be at our hotel soon. There's a swimming pool there. We're going to have a good time, okay?"

Ramesh looked at her tearfully, as if he couldn't imagine having a good time in this city. "But Ellie, that boy is having no hands," he said, as if that explained everything. The clamor of the beggars surrounding them grew as they witnessed the scene inside the car. Even with their windows rolled up, Frank could sense the excitement outside. They were jockeying for some advantage, looking for a loophole through which a few coins would slip out and make their way toward them. He felt a grudging admiration. The entrepreneurial spirit at work, he thought.

But the truth was, he was happy at the sight of his wife sitting with her arm around Ramesh. As far as he knew, this was the first time Ellie had done this. He found himself opening his wallet and removing a ten-rupee note. "Tell you what," he told Ramesh. "You can give this to that boy's mom. How's that?"

As the beggars saw the white man reach for his wallet, the beating on the car window grew more frenzied. Satish raised his voice. "Don't open the window, sir. Please to wait until the car is moving. Then you can throw money out. Otherwise, no peace while we're at this traffic signal." He lowered his window a fraction. *"Chalo. Jao,"* he yelled threateningly at the crowd, and the ones closest to him moved away a few inches, his voice creating a ripple in the crowd, and then, the next second, the ripple died and they closed in again.

Ramesh sat clenching the note in his hand. "How will I make sure he only gets the money?" he asked. "What if someone else take it away?"

"You want me to do it?" Frank asked, wishing the goddamn light would change already, but Ramesh shook his head vigorously. "No. I want to give him."

They lowered the window a fraction when they were finally moving again, and Frank hoisted Ramesh onto his lap so that he could hand the money to the sad-eyed woman. Scores of hands tried to push their way into the opening, but although he was scared, Ramesh held on to the note until he could shove it into the hand of the mother. And then they were gone, leaving behind a swarm of squabbling, jostling beggars to descend onto the next car.

Inside the car, with Ramesh still in his lap, Frank touched the boy's sweaty forehead and then put his right hand over the boy's heart. As he had thought, Ramesh's heart was racing, beating fast. Frank let his hand remain until he felt the boy's heart slow down its frantic jabbering. It was a trick he had discovered with Benny, how simply laying his hand on his son's small chest could calm the boy down. Out of the corner of his eye he caught Ellie staring at him and knew that she, too, had remembered the times he'd tried this with Benny, suspected that she resented this easy (in her mind) substitution of one boy for another. But at this moment, he didn't care. They hadn't even reached their hotel yet, and already he was experiencing a feeling of liberation at being in Bombay with Ramesh and Ellie. He hoped that Ramesh would come to see this also—how, despite the fact that the city felt like a trap and caught its citizens in a death-like vise, its sheer size, its mindless momentum, conferred upon you a kind of anonymity and freedom. It occurred to him that he wanted Ramesh to return to Girbaug a citified boy, realizing his hometown's limitations, chafing at its smallness, feeling its squeeze, like a pair of shoes one has outgrown. Someday, the boy would see New York, London, and lose himself in the paradoxical freedom that big cities conferred upon their residents.

But he was getting carried away. The first task was to console Ramesh, prep him for the wonders of the old colonial buildings of South Bombay, prepare him for the opulence of the hotel room that they would occupy in less than an hour. And also, to draw Ellie into the fold again, make her a part of this adventure, so that for a few precious days they could pretend to be a family. He gave Ramesh a light shove. "You're getting heavy," he grunted. "All muscle."

As he had predicted, the boy beamed. "Yes," he said. "That's why only I'm beating you at basketball." He moved off Frank's lap onto the seat. "I beat him six games in a row, Ellie," he added.

Ellie smiled. "That's good," she said, but her voice was absent-minded, distant.

"Whatcha thinking, hon?" Frank said.

"Nothing, really. Just about all this." She swept her hands to indicate the sprawl of humanity all around them and then leaned forward. "You have family in Bombay, right, Satish?"

"Correct, madam. My sister's family live in Mumbai. Close by to where we are now, actually." He lowered his voice. "She married to a Muslim man, madam."

"Muslims eat cows," Ramesh declared.

They ignored him. "Your parents okay with that?" Frank asked. He stretched his arm so that he was cradling Ramesh as well as pulling Ellie close to him. She rested her head on his arm and he smiled at the familiarity of the gesture. He remembered a winter's night in Shaker Heights, on a double date with Ellie's sister Anne and her husband, Bob. They had gone to Nighttown to listen to jazz and on the way home, he and Ellie had sat in the backseat, Ellie leaning her head on his arm.

Satish turned to give Frank a quick glance. "Better now, sir. At first, lots of fightum-fighting. My mother say she will never see Usha again. But after first baby born, my mother ask me to take her to Mumbai to see baby."

Frank sighed. While in college, he and Pete had once rented a Bollywood movie, curious to know what all the fuss was about. They had hooted with laughter at the sappy dialogue, the exaggerated gestures, the caricature of a villain, the melodramatic reconciliation between mother and son, and of course, the interminable musical numbers. But after living in India, none of this seemed as exaggerated or unrealistic as before. Every family, every home, in India seemed to have its own saga of melodrama and heartache. For the second time, he opened his wallet. This time, he took out two hundred-rupee bills. "Buy some chocolates for your sister's children from us," he said, leaning forward to hand the money to Satish.

"No need for this, sir," Satish protested, but Frank noticed that when he looked at him in the rearview mirror, the driver was smiling.

"I want some chocolates too," Ramesh said, and Frank smacked him lightly on his hand.

"How're you going to be a world-class basketball player if you get all fat?"

"I'm not fat," the boy said indignantly, and they all laughed.

"No, you're *doobla-sukla, yaar,*" Satish said.

"What does that mean?" Ellie asked.

"Like this, like this," Ramesh explained, holding up his little finger. "Thin-thin."

"I see," Frank smiled. "Tin-tin." He was always teasing Ramesh about his inability to make the *th* sound.

"No, not tin, *thin*." Ramesh caught the smile on Frank's face and punched him on his shoulder. "Stop making fun of me." He turned to Ellie. "Make him stop."

"Stop," Ellie deadpanned, and they grinned at each other over Ramesh's head.

The car pulled into the arched driveway of the Taj Hotel. Getting out of the car, Ramesh pulled his head all the way back to take in the tall tower of the Intercontinental, nestled against the original domed building. "Frank," the boy breathed. "We're living in a palace?"

Frank laughed. "Yeah, I guess we are, kiddo." He tried to pick up a suitcase from the open trunk, but Satish came racing back and looked affronted. "Leave it, sir," he said, nodding his head to where a skinny bellboy was standing dressed in a heavy red uniform. "He will take." The driver lingered long enough to make sure that the bellboy had all their belongings and to make final arrangements with Frank as to where and when to pick them up for tomorrow's picnic. Handing the keys of the Camry to the valet, Satish walked briskly away to catch the bus that would take him to his sister's home.

Striding into the Taj's opulent lobby, Frank kept a protective hand on Ramesh's shoulder. The boy was subdued, though his eyes were wide with awe as he took in the enormous chandeliers, the clusters of white-skinned businessmen and tourists, the soft-spoken, dazzlingly beautiful women receptionists, the unmistakable scent of luxury and opulence that the place exuded. He waited on one of the leather couches with Ellie while Frank got them checked in. He was quiet even as they rode the gilded elevator that led to their room. Once they were in their large room, he silently toured the carpeted bedroom with the large, comfortable bed, the red-and-gold mahagony chaise longue near the large window that overlooked the Arabian Sea, the marble-tiled bathroom with the tub and a vanity dresser in one corner. Then the boy sat down heavily on one of the antique chairs and, for the second time that day, burst into tears.

"What's wrong?" Frank asked. "Ramesh, are you sick?"

The sobbing boy shook his head. "Not sick." He tried to say more, but he couldn't. Frank made a move toward him, but Ellie stopped him. "Let him cry," she whispered. "He's just overwhelmed. He needs to get it out."

While Frank looked at her uncertainly, Ramesh dug into the pockets of his pants. He fished around and finally came up with a dirty-looking note, which he held out to Frank. They noticed that the boy was keeping his eyes on the ground.

"What's this for, Ramesh?" Frank asked, smoothing the creased twenty-rupee note.

The boy kept staring at the ground. "Ma gave it to me," he said. "As spending money." He finally looked up and around at the room and was attacked by a fresh bout of sobs. "But this room must cost so-so much money, Frank. You take this."

Ellie reached him first. "Oh, honey," she said. "It's okay. We can afford this." She kissed Ramesh on his head. "It's very sweet of you to offer. But you keep this money, okay?"

The boy shook his head vigorously. "No, I want to give it. You take it."

"Tell you what, kiddo," Frank said. "How about you save it for us? And maybe you can buy us all ice cream later today?"

Ramesh thought for a moment. "Okay," he said. The three of them sat on the bed in silence for a moment. Frank threw Ellie a look. See this boy's character? the look said. See how sensitive Ramesh is? But Ellie gazed back at him expressionless, and he was perturbed by the fact that he had no idea what she was thinking.

"Where am I sleeping?" Ramesh asked. "On the floor?"

"No, bud." Frank laughed. "We'll have a cot brought in for you. That okay?"

"Okay."

Frank rose from the bed and stretched. "Well? What do you guys want to do the rest of the afternoon?" He knew what the plan for the weekend was—attend the picnic thrown by the consulate general tomorrow afternoon and then visit the Elephanta Caves, which Ellie so badly wanted to see, on Sunday. But that still left the rest of the afternoon open today.

"I'm going to take a nap," Ellie said promptly. "I'm tired."

Frank was about to protest but then thought better of it. It would be nice to spend some time alone with the boy. "How about if I take him out for a couple of hours?" he asked. "Show him the Gateway to India, maybe take a quick swim in the pool? Will that give you enough time alone?"

Something darkened in Ellie's eyes, but when she spoke her voice was noncommittal. "It's not that I want to be alone, hon. I just need a quick nap, that's all."

"I understand," he said quickly, afraid that she would change her mind and decide to accompany them. He looked at her, wondering if she had caught the pulse of eagerness in his voice, wondering if he was imagining the fact that the air between them suddenly seemed charged and tense. There was a time when Ellie's face had been like a movie screen, so that it registered every emotion she was feeling and her thoughts. When had she learned to slam her face shut like a door? Or had he simply lost the ability to read her? He remembered what he'd whispered to her on their wedding day—You are part of me; you live on my skin. He had repeated those words to her a million times since. And yet here he was today, trying to shake her off, trying to sneak a few hours of guiltless enjoyment with Ramesh.

He turned away, afraid of letting any of this register on his face. "We'll see you later," he said and then, over his shoulder, "Come on, Ramesh. Put on the swimming trunks Ellie bought you, under your shorts."

How lovely it was to see the beautiful stone arch of the Gateway of India and share its history with Ramesh, what a pleasure it was to tell him about the similar-looking Arc de Triomphe in Paris, to describe to him the Parisian bakeries and bistros. How wonderful to stroll down the sidewalk beside the sea, dodging the beggars and the peanut vendors and the balloon sellers who were following them. Frank looked down with affection at the shiny head of the shiny boy who walked beside him. "You okay, bud?" he said. "You're not scared, are you?"

Ramesh shook his head. "No," he said. "I like this Bombay. Even the beggars here are nice. Less sick."

Frank laughed at Ramesh's perceptiveness. "You're right, sweetie. This is a wealthy area. So, I guess, even the beggars are richer."

Ramesh giggled. "You called me sweetie."

"So?"

"So . . ." The boy lowered his voice to guard from the most persistent street urchins who were still following them, "only boyfriend-girlfriends is allowed to call sweetie." He gave Frank a look that was equal parts bravado and shyness.

Frank pretended to be outraged. "Ramesh. You naughty boy. Who taught you about girlfriends and boyfriends?"

"A girl in my school," Ramesh said. "She say she will marry me."

"And do you like her?"

He shrugged. "She fine."

Frank grinned. "She's fine? Fine? That's not enough to marry someone." He suddenly grew serious. "Besides, my boy, you have to focus on your studies, right? No time for girlfriends, you hear?"

Ramesh nodded vigorously. "I know, I know." He glanced up at Frank again, as if trying to gauge something. Then, "She kiss me once. On my nose."

"She kissed you on your *nose?*"

"Don't laugh." Ramesh sounded cross. He stopped walking

and putting a hand on one hip, looked up at Frank in exasperation. "That's what mother-father do," he explained. "Before a baby is born."

Frank heard the frustration and something else—uncertainty—in Ramesh's voice. He stopped walking, too. "Come here," he said, drawing the boy toward the cement wall. "Let's sit for a moment." He kept his arm around him as he considered his choices. Was this the right time to teach this boy about the birds and the bees? Was that even his place? Did Indian parents have these conversations with their children? Prakash and Edna had obviously not, and the thought annoyed him. Surely the boy was old enough to know the workings of his body? Ramesh had always struck him as less mature than his American counterparts, but still, it was ridiculous to think that a woman got pregnant from a kiss on the nose. He suddenly wished Ellie was here. She'd know how to handle this.

"Who told you that a woman can have a baby from a kiss?" he asked cautiously.

"Parvati did," he replied. "My school friend."

Frank saw his opening. "And is Parvati going to have a baby? Because she kissed you?"

Ramesh looked at him as if he was an imbecile. "No, Frank," he said patiently. "*She* kiss *me*. To have the baby, the boyfriend has to kiss the girlfriend."

Frank gulped hard and looked out at the water. "I see," he said. It occurred to him that he would have never had to have such a difficult conversation with Benny. He and Ellie had always been candid with their son, and Ellie had on more than one occasion told their son matter-of-factly that a daddy had to stick his penis inside a mommy for a baby to be born. Ellie had been emphatic about sparing their son any confusion and puzzlement about sex. Even some of their friends had been a little shocked at their pragmatic approach. Frank remembered the time Ellie's mother, Delores, was visiting them in

Ann Arbor and had insisted on bathing her three-year-old grandson. He and Ellie had heard their son announce, "Grandma, that's not my pee-pee. That's my penis." The look on Delores's face, they agreed, was, as the commercial said, priceless.

Still, with Ramesh, he hesitated. How much easier this would be if Ramesh was his son. If he knew that this boy would grow up in the progressive, intellectual environment of Ann Arbor. But the fact was, Ramesh was someone else's boy. He belonged to a father who seemed content to let the boy raise himself. And besides, Frank knew how weird Indians were about sex, was aware of the odd combination of female prudery and male aggression that was the hallmark of Bollywood movies and, for all he knew, the culture itself. It was not his place to educate Ramesh about sex, and his heart sank at the realization.

Ramesh was wriggling beside him, eager to resume their stroll, and Frank took the hint. "Listen," he said as they walked. "No getting distracted by the girls, okay? You have to focus on your studies, remember?"

"I remember," Ramesh said.

Frank hesitated for a second and then set free the words that had formed at his lips. "Besides, if you're to study in America you have to have good grades."

"I am already first in my class, Frank." Ramesh's voice was plaintive.

"I know, kiddo. But it's very, very difficult to get into good schools." He pointed to where a group of obviously affluent, westernized college students were leaning against a Honda. "You see those people? That's who you will be competing against even to go to college in Bombay."

Ramesh stared at the group of boys in their blue jeans and thin cotton shirts. His eyes grew big and his chin trembled, and seeing this, Frank cussed himself for his stupidity. "Luckily," he continued brightly, "you don't have to worry about this today." He stopped and cocked his head as he looked at Ramesh. "Want to walk more? Or shall we go for a swim in the pool?"

Ramesh tore his eyes away from the group of laughing boys. "Let's go pool-swimming," he said, and Frank remembered what the boy had told them on the way to Bombay: that he'd never swum in a pool before.

"Okay," he said. "And then let's go wake Ellie up and go out somewhere. We have to celebrate your first trip to Bombay."

Ramesh held his hand as they crossed the street.

CHAPTER 12

The Fourth of July picnic was held on the grounds of a large stone house in Malabar Hill. Frank and Ellie exchanged looks as Satish pulled up to the wrought-iron gate. Frank whistled. "Man. I could get used to living in these digs." He turned to Ramesh. "This neighborhood is where the governor has his house. Can you imagine what *his* house must look like?"

Ramesh looked small and scared inside the car. He pulled on the collar of the light green shirt Ellie had bought him for the occasion. Like Frank, he was dressed in cream-colored chinos.

Satish stopped and lowered his window as a young American carrying a clipboard hurried up to them. He was accompanied by an intimidating-looking man in a suit and wraparound sunglasses. The young man leaned into the car. "Hi," he said. "Welcome. May I get your names?"

Frank lowered his window and handed him the invitation card. The young man checked off their names on his list. "Welcome, Mr. and Mrs. Benton," he said smiling brightly. Then the smile left his face as he peered into the car and spotted Ramesh. "And who is this?"

"He's with us," Frank said. "Hope that's not a problem."

The young man frowned. "I don't understand," he said scanning his list. "He's not on here. And your RSVP says two attendees."

Frank felt the heat rise to his face. "He's my son," he said. "He—we didn't decide to bring him until the last minute. And the invitation said kids were welcome." He felt Ellie put a warning hand on his thigh. "Would you like me to take this up with Tom Andrews?" Tom was the U.S. consul general to Bombay, and the host of this party.

"There will be no need for that, sir," the young man said smoothly. "Glad to accommodate your—son. Have a wonderful day."

Frank realized his teeth were clenched as Satish eased the Camry into the long, curved driveway. Beside him, he heard Ellie swear. "Friggin' bureaucrats. These were exactly the kind of people we spent our whole lives avoiding. And now we have to spend the whole day with them."

Ellie's words broke the tension, and he laughed out loud. Also, he was grateful for the fact that she was directing her anger at the man with the clipboard and not at him, that she wasn't hurt by the fact that he had referred to Ramesh as their son. "You better behave yourself, babe." He grinned

"Arre baap," Ramesh breathed as they pulled closer to the house and saw its opulence. He looked up at them. "Does the maharaja of Mumbai live here?"

But there was no time to answer because someone was flagging them down. They got out of the car, and Satish handed over the car keys. "I will pick you up later, sir," he said. "Enjoy."

They stood in the driveway, torn between wanting to join the crowd that had already gathered on the lawn but knowing that protocol demanded that they first seek Tom out and say their hellos. They walked up the five marble steps that led into an enormous room with a mosaic-tiled floor and a high ceiling. Tom Andrews was standing there, surrounded by a gaggle of the other guests. Frank shook hands with many of the other American businessmen as they slowly approached the consul general. He didn't expect Tom to remember his name and so was astonished when he heard him say, "Hey, Frank. Good to see you again. How the hell you been? And this must be your lovely wife. Ellie, is it?"

A politician's game, memorizing names, but Frank was impressed, nevertheless. "Ellie, this is Thomas Andrews," he said.

The consul general grinned. "Call me Tom. And happy Fourth of July." He gave Ellie a quick peck on the cheek and then looked around. "My wife is somewhere around. You'll enjoy meeting her."

Someone else jostled for his attention, and Tom began shaking another set of hands. But he turned around one more time and said over his shoulder, "Go on outside. That's where the real party is." He winked. "Real, honest-to-goodness burgers and hot dogs. Flown in especially from home."

Frank had wanted an opportunity to introduce Ramesh to Tom, knowing that they might need the latter's help if Ramesh was ever to visit the States with him. But this was not the right time. He took Ramesh's hand and said, "Come on, let's go outside. You hungry?"

The boy shook his head.

Frank bent down. "Are you scared?"

Ramesh nodded. "A little. I'm not knowing anyone here."

"You know us." Frank and Ellie spoke together. Ellie grabbed Ramesh's other hand. "Come on, honey," she said. "Nothing to be scared of."

They stood on the marble steps, scanning the scene on the front lawn. To the distant right were five barbecue grills where the chefs were grilling an array of meats, their faces hidden behind the rising clouds of smoke. Next to them was the bar, and even from this distance, they could see the sun reflecting off the bottles of hard liquor lined up in a row. Right in front of them were two white tents set up to accommodate the diners, and off to the left was the children's area, with an old-fashioned lemonade stand and a smaller tent with rows of tables and a woman who appeared to be doing face paint-ings. Frank noticed that several of the children were walking around with their faces painted red, white, and blue. He also noticed the few Indian guests, much more formally dressed than the Americans, the women in their saris looking like royalty walking among the peas-ants. Below the hill the house stood on was the breathtaking view of the Arabian Sea curving from the sandy beaches of Chowpatty to the tall office buildings of Nariman Point.

"You want to go play with the other children?" he asked Ramesh.

The grip on his hand got tighter. "No."

"What if I were to go with you?"

The grip slackened. "Okay."

The three of them walked over toward the children's tent, where a dozen blond and sandy heads were bent over coloring books. Out-side the tent, a group of kids were playing a vigorous game of water balloons, smacking each other hard and erupting in laughter each time a balloon burst. Ramesh seemed drawn to the game, but Frank tugged him toward the line where children were waiting to get their faces painted. While they waited, a waiter came around with a tray, and both Frank and Ellie picked up a glass of white wine. Ellie or-dered a Coke for Ramesh, and the boy gulped it down eagerly when it arrived.

Finally, it was Ramesh's turn. The gray-haired woman smiled at him. "Well, hello, love," she said in a strong British accent. "What would you like a picture of? I can do the flag or the American Eagle."

Ramesh looked up at Frank and smiled bashfully. Frank could read his face—the boy hadn't understood a word that the woman had said. "I think he'd like the flag," he told her.

Ramesh stood still as the woman deftly mixed her palette and began to apply blue paint. But as the brush touched his face, he let out a yelp. "*Ae*, why you painting me blue? Flag is green, *na*? Saffron, white, and green."

There was a short silence, and then there was a loud guffaw to their right. It was Tom Andrews, his arm around his wife, Elisa, a thin, good-looking woman much younger than him. "Now there's a spirited boy" He grinned. "So you want the colors of the Indian flag, huh? Well, Mabel, can we accommodate his request? No?" He made a rueful face. "Sorry about that, my man. Think you could endure the red, white, and blue? It is Fourth of July, after all."

Frank put his hand on Ramesh's shoulder. "It's fine," he said. "Just give him the usual. He'll be fine."

"But Frank—" Ramesh started, only to be silenced by the look Frank flashed him. "Okay," he mumbled.

While Ramesh was having his face painted, Frank turned toward Tom. "Needed to ask your opinion about something, Tom," he said quietly. "If you'd let me know whenever you have a moment, I'd appreciate it."

"No time like the present," Tom said graciously. "Excuse us, ladies." He put his arm around Frank and escorted him away from the line. Something about his body language, the way he leaned in to hear what Frank was saying, communicated to the other guests that they were not to be interrupted, a fact that Frank was grateful for.

"It's about the incident involving the union leader, isn't it?" Tom said, and it took Frank a second to realize that Tom had misread the situation.

"No, not really. I mean, that situation seems to have quieted down, thank goodness. No, this is more of a personal matter." He stopped and then started again. "This involves Ramesh, the boy you just met. He's . . . he's someone we know from Girbaug. A very bright kid. But his parents are very poor. But this kid is incredible, Tom. A math whiz. I think with the right education, the sky would be the limit for him." He noticed that Tom was looking at him strangely, fixing those deep blue eyes on him. Slow down, he told himself. Don't botch this up. And for God's sake, don't get emotional.

"Anyway," he continued, trying to strike the tone of a mildly interested well-wisher, "I want to take the kid with us the next time we visit the States. Just show him around, see how he fits in, that kind of thing. And I was hoping that getting a visa wouldn't be an issue."

"Is that why you brought him here?" Tom said. "To see how he'd fit in?" There was something in his voice, a tremor that Frank couldn't place. Surely it wasn't anger?

"Well, no," he stammered. "I mean, we were bringing him to Bombay anyway, and—"

"His parents know you're thinking of taking him to the States?" Now there was no mistaking the sharpness in Tom's voice.

Frank let the fact that he was offended register on his face. "Well, of course, Tom. I wouldn't be having this conversation with you if I didn't—"

Tom raised his hand in a truce. "Okay. Okay. Sorry. Just checking. You don't know how many awkward situations we've been placed in here." He lowered his voice. "Two years ago, there was this couple. Came to India to visit some guru at an ashram for like, two weeks. One of those dial-a-guru types that America seems to churn out so regularly." He rolled his eyes. "In any case, they fall in love with this beggar child who lived on the street across from the ashram. So they just make off with the child one day and come to us asking for a visa. Can you fucking imagine? This kid had parents and siblings, but they felt entitled to him." He rubbed his hands over his eyes. "It was a fucking nightmare, getting that kid back to his home."

"Well. I can assure you that Ellie and I are not going to kidnap Ramesh," Frank said dryly.

Tom patted him on the back. "Okay. We'll do everything that we can do to help. Just do me a favor. If you're thinking of going home around Christmas, give me enough lead time. It's a zoo around here, then."

Frank wanted to head back to Ellie and Ramesh, but Tom was apparently not done. "Listen. I gotta tell you. What happened with that union leader was not good. This goddamn war in Iraq is killing us around the world. I've been in this business for twenty-four years, and it's never been this bad in terms of our image. We have to tread very lightly wherever we are. So whatever concessions you gotta make—"

"We made them, Tom. We gave in to their demands. Everything is normal, now."

Still, Tom lingered. Frank noticed with a start that the blue eyes were suddenly red around the edges. He wondered if Tom had been drinking since earlier this afternoon. "I'm a Republican appointee," Tom said. "He's my president. But there's no question—this Iraqi situation is a mess. A wholesale PR disaster."

"Well, it's more than just a PR disaster. It's a moral disaster, too." It was Ellie, escorted by Tom's wife. The two women had come up behind him, penetrated the invisible circle that Tom had drawn.

Frank felt his stomach muscles clench. Did Ellie never know when to keep her friggin' mouth shut? He tried to think of something that would lighten the mood and take the sting out of his wife's words but before he could, Tom bowed. "Touché," he said.

But Ellie was not done. "Do folks like you ever get to talk to the president? Tell him what you see in the real world?"

Tom smiled but didn't answer the question. The old master diplomat at work, Frank thought. "Where's Ramesh?" Frank asked Ellie, hoping to change the subject. She nodded toward the cluster of kids engaged in the water balloon fight. "Let's go get him," he said, taking his wife firmly by the hand. He smiled at Tom and Elisa. "Thanks for taking the time, Tom," he said.

"That's what we're here for," Tom said. "Come see us next time you're in Mumbai."

They strolled away, Frank still holding onto Ellie. "You can let go of my hand now," she said dryly. "I'm not going to give poor Tom any more lectures."

"I should hope not. Putting him on the spot like that. Sometimes I really wonder about your judgment, El."

She shook her hand free. "Maybe you should worry less about my judgment and more about your president's judgment. Or your judgment for that matter, for wanting to hobnob with these pricks. And for putting me in situations where I can't speak my mind."

He was careful to keep his voice lowered. "You're being ridiculous. Tom has been very good to HerbalSolutions, helping us negotiate with the Indian government and a million other things. And he's got nothing to do with Iraq." He felt his temper spike. "You really need to stop lecturing people about their morals, Ellie. It's becoming an irritating habit."

She looked hurt for a moment and then made a wry face. "Okay. I'm sorry. I'll behave." But he wasn't appeased. "Come on, let's not fight. I—I just feel uncomfortable around so many healthy, beefy-looking white people."

"There you go again," he started, but realized that she was laughing and, against his will, found that he was laughing too. "Damn you, Ellie," he said but he took her hand again, and this time his grip was light and friendly. "I swear, you're gonna have to go through a debriefing when we get back to the States."

She turned around to look him squarely in the face. "Right now, I can't even fathom going home. I feel like this is where we belong, here in India. Don't you?"

Did he? The truth was, he belonged nowhere. If he belonged at all, it was to people, not countries. He felt the ties of family and history when he called to speak to his mom once a week. The night after the dinner at Nandita's, he had felt that old connection with

Ellie, felt with absolute conviction that his place was in her arms, that he could build a home for himself in those deep dark eyes. And last week on the beach with Ramesh, the two of them playing in the water, he had felt that he belonged under the wide open sky and in those churning waters of the Arabian sea, as long as he had this little boy by his side.

He leaned over and kissed Ellie on the cheek. "Right now, I belong in front of a hamburger stand," he said. "C'mon. Let's go collect Ramesh and then go eat."

They found Ramesh engaged in an aggressive water balloon fight. His clothes were soaked and hair was plastered on his forehead, with the paint running down his face. He had taken off his shoes and was racing around barefoot, screaming like a hellion, dancing like a demon, dodging the balloons and throwing them back with gusto. Some of the American families stood watching the skinny brown boy who was twirling around, with bemusement. "Hey," Frank called. "Ramesh. Stop for a minute."

Ramesh released the balloon he was holding at the backside of a tall, brown-haired boy. "Ow," the boy yelled as the balloon burst and Ramesh pointed to him and laughed uproariously. But he stopped in mid-laugh as a young girl rushed up to him and threw a balloon at him at close range. "Stop hitting my brother," she screamed, her face red. The poorly aimed water balloon fell off Ramesh's chest without breaking, but Ramesh froze, taken aback by the fierce expression on the girl's face. Seizing the moment, Frank stepped in, pulling Ramesh out of the circle of laughing, screaming children.

"Look at you," he mock-admonished the boy. "You're soaking wet."

Ramesh was still looking back at the girl, who had resumed her playing. "She's angry at me," he said.

"Forget about her," he said. "She's just a spoiled brat." He caught Ellie flashing a warning look at him and heeded her silent message not to aggravate the situation further. "Anyway. Are you hungry, you walking-talking puddle of water? How are we ever going to dry you off?"

"Let's throw him in the dryer," Ellie teased. "He'll be dry in no time."

"Noooooooooooo," Ramesh yelled. "If I'm in the dryer, I'll be like the clothes, I'll go like this-like this," and shaking off Frank's hand, he did a couple of somersaults on the lawn. Droplets of water fell from him onto the grass.

Frank turned to Ellie. "You started this," he said as she lunged for Ramesh and grabbed his hand. "Okay, now," she said. "Behave yourself." She turned toward the food area. "Let's go eat, *achcha*?" she said. "I'm starving."

"I want some tandoori chicken," Ramesh said. They had introduced him to the grilled chicken dish at the restaurant at the Shalimar, and now this was his favorite meal.

"You ate that at Khyber last night," Frank chided. "In any case, this is an American picnic. I want you to try some American food." He stopped, struck by a thought. Ramesh was a Hindu and didn't eat beef. What on earth would he eat here? But as they walked toward the grills, he noticed that one of the cooks was grilling chicken.

They were halfway through their meal—chicken, hamburgers, hot dogs, potato salad, baked beans, corn on the cob—when they saw a flurry of activity and sensed that the U.S. ambassador to India had arrived. Frank groaned. "Guess I'd better go stand in line to say hello."

"Just sit here and finish your meal," Ellie said. "What do you care about the stupid ambassador?"

"It's good for business, Ellie. Some face time."

She rolled her eyes. "Whatever. But the line's gonna be so long, you may as well keep eating."

He eyed the jostling that was going on around the tall, silver-headed man, and decided Ellie was right. He took a big bite of his hot dog and closed his eyes in pleasure.

"What're you thinking?" Even with his eyes closed, he could hear the smile in her voice.

"Detroit Tigers," he said promptly. "Best seats in the house, right behind home plate. Scott buying me one of those big stadium dogs with mustard, ketchup, the works. The Tigers beating the pants off the Yankees that day." He sighed. "I was fifteen years old."

"My dear Frank," Ellie said. "You sound homesick."

And suddenly he was. He wanted to feel the cool, summer breezes off Lake Michigan, wanted to walk with Ellie on their Ann Arbor street taking in the mad, riotous colors of October, wanted to celebrate, as always, Christmas in New York with Scott and his mom and New Year's Eve with Ellie's family in Cleveland. Suddenly, he wanted baseball games and movie multiplexes and spotlessly clean malls. He wanted art house movies, good theater, poetry readings at the U of M. He was dimly aware of the fact that his nostalgia was for a life he had not actually lived in a long time. But he didn't care. He was happy missing the Michigan of his youth, of his college days, of his early life with Ellie when he had graduated with an MBA and gone to work for a small company while she worked on her Ph.D. They had planned on waiting until she was done with her degree before getting pregnant, but life had a different plan for them, and Benny had been born two weeks after Ellie had earned her doctorate.

"Remember Alex?" Frank now said, and Ellie spluttered with laughter. "Oh, boy, do I ever," she replied.

"What, what?" Ramesh asked, looking from one to another. "What is LX?"

"Not LX. Alex. It's a person's name. He was a babysitter—he used to come watch our son when we were at work. He was this goofy musician guy—he could do all these tricks. He used to play music using our broom and dustpan."

Ramesh was excited. "How he do that, Frank?"

"I dunno. It's hard to explain. He could also make these noises that sounded like a whole band was playing."

Ellie grinned at him. "Remember my mom's face when we first introduced her to Alex? You know how he used to dress, in those pink and purple jeans. And that hair. Jesus, that hair. I think she was this close to reporting us to Children's Services."

"Yeah, I've always thought Delores had something to do with Alex deciding to seek his fortune in Alaska."

Ramesh pulled at Frank's sleeve. "Stop talking about old things," he said. "I'm feeling alone." His tone was peevish, but it tugged at Frank.

"Sorry, bud," he said. "We're losing our party manners."

"My dada and ma do this, also," Ramesh said. "Talking about things before I was born. It's boring."

For a moment Frank pictured Edna and Prakash discussing their youth, the early days of their romance, before life coarsened their love. He remembered Ellie telling him that Edna had eloped with Prakash and that her family had disowned her as a result. He felt a sudden flash of sympathy with the couple but fought the temptation to soften his hostility toward Prakash.

"Okay. What do you want to talk about instead?"

The boy didn't have to think. "About me," he said.

Ellie burst out laughing. "I diagnose a budding narcissist in the making," she said. And before Ramesh could react, "Now, calm down, Ramesh. Remember, we're at a party."

The boy was about to respond when a young man with a harried expression trotted up to the tent where they were eating. "Excuse me," he called. And when no one paid him any attention, he raised his voice. "Excuse me," he said again. "The Honorable Bill Richards is here. He would like to say a few words, starting in two minutes. Can you kindly follow me into the house?"

Frank looked at the food on his plate longingly. "Lousy timing," he whispered to Ellie, but he was already rising to his feet, his eyes imploring his wife to get up also.

Ellie eyed all the abandoned plates as everyone around them rose and followed the young aide. "Our tax dollars at work," she muttered but accompanied Frank and Ramesh as they crossed the front lawn and climbed the marble steps again.

The ambassador had already started speaking as they made their way into the foyer and stood against the doorway. A light breeze blew in from the open front doors and played with the corners of Ellie's cotton skirt. Thinking of the burger getting cold on his plate, Frank prayed that the speech would be short. Judging from the periodic bursts of laughter from the crowd surrounding the ambassador, the speech was funny. There was a moment of uncertainty after Richards got done speaking, a low rumble rising from the crowd as people resumed their conversations and shuffled on their feet, unsure of protocol. Frank was about to turn to Ellie and ask whether they should return to their tent when they heard it—a voice as clear as glass singing words as familiar as a loved one's name. "Oh, say can you see?" the voice sang and they all turned their heads to see a slender young boy, no older than eighteen, dressed formally in a white linen shirt and dark pants, strolling toward where the ambassador stood, parting the crowd with the clarity of his voice, with the sincerity on his face. In a moment, the crowd joined in, singing the words in a low pitch, careful not to douse the sweet flame of that single voice. Frank found his spine straightening, felt goose bumps covering his arms. His right hand automatically made its way to his heart. He felt Ramesh tug at him, but he ignored the boy, swept up in the delicacy of the moment. And at his favorite juncture—that juncture when the anthem took that delicious turn and became a poem and a prayer, that plaintive, wistful moment when it asked the question of the ages, "Oh, say does that star-spangled banner yet wave?" he turned toward Ellie, wife and fellow citizen, his heart aching with love for his country, for all the people gathered

here. And was shocked by her posture. He noticed immediately that
Ellie stood with her hands by her side. And that there was a curious, academic look on her face, as if she were studying a natural
phenomenon. Dammit, Frank thought. She looks like a goddamn
anthropologist or something. More than anything she had said earlier today, this passivity, this silent irony, offended him. He knew
she found expressions of patriotism to be simple and easy, almost
farcical. But there was nothing cheap or easy about the powerful
emotions that had coursed through him at the first recognition of
his country's national anthem. He felt defensive and hated her for
making him have to defend his pride in his country.

"Could you at least pretend?" he hissed at her.

"Pretend what? That we're not committing terrorism in the
world? That we're really the land of the free? Do you ever read the
newspapers?"

She had done it. She had succeeded in shocking him, repelling
him in a way she'd never been able to do when she'd engaged in
spirited debates with his brother, when she'd denounced the very
idea of business management while having dinner with the dean
of U of M's business school, when she had chastised him for what
HerbalSolutions was doing to Girbaug's economy. Their marriage
had been a long intellectual conversation—over the years he'd
argued with her, sometimes been scandalized by her, often been
amused by her, had called her a damn Communist when she went
too far. Mostly, he'd agreed with her, and even when he didn't, had
been proud of his independent, rebellious wife. But he'd never felt
the kind of seething anger that he felt right now. All these years,
Ellie's critiques and criticisms of America had felt tolerable because
they felt like the angst-filled laments of a mother whose brilliant
child was not living up to its promise. But this was something different, something new. He didn't recognize this cold, ironic Ellie. And
he knew that it was their location, the soil they were standing on,
that made all the difference. India had done more than radicalize his

wife. It had embittered her and positioned her differently. She now saw America the way the rest of the world did. It was no longer a critical but maternal look at a wayward child. Now, it was the accusing, harsh look of a stranger.

"What?" she said. "You have nothing to say?"

He turned away, apprehensive of the resentment that he was feeling. He had only hated her like this one other time—the day Benny had died. Now, all his old feelings from that day came rushing back. "Let's just drop it," he said brusquely. "There's no point in talking to you when you're in this mood."

They walked back to the picnic area. Frank got a fresh plate of food, but the corn now tasted insipid and the meat was charred and chewy. He was suddenly self-conscious of the conspicuous consumption—the mounds of grilled meat, the steady flow of alcohol, the piles of discarded plastic plates and glasses—all around them, and he hated Ellie for forcing this awareness upon him. He pretended to listen to Ramesh's nervous chatter, exchanged banter with Bob, the ruddy-faced businessman sitting next to him, but his heart was not in it. For an unguarded moment, his eyes lingered on Georgie, Bob's skinny, peroxide-blond wife, who had the kind of hair and figure that he had lusted after when he was fifteen. As he grew into a serious young man, he had been turned off by women like Georgie, had felt a desperate loneliness when confronted by their empty, vacuous chatter, but today he thought—Jesus Christ, at least Bob never had to worry about his wife insulting the consul general. Ellie had satisfied him in every way—sexually, intellectually, emotionally— but for a moment he wondered what being with Georgie would be like, how it would feel to be in the kind of marriage where he could turn around after a good fuck and fall asleep instead of living with a woman who spoke of terrorism and genocide at a friggin' Fourth of July picnic. He looked up and saw that Ellie was looking at him. As their eyes met, she raised one eyebrow and threw him a slow smile. He flushed, knowing she'd read his mind. He felt flustered and exposed. He wanted to wipe that smile off her face—wipe it off with the whack of his hand.

He got to his feet abruptly, cutting Bob off mid-sentence. "I'm sorry, we've got to go," he said.

Bob stared at him. "You've got to be kidding. Man, the party's just getting started."

"I know." He pulled Ramesh up. "But we've got another engagement." He looked at Ellie, imploring her to play along. She rose to her feet slowly, keeping her eyes locked onto Frank's.

"It was nice chatting with you'all," she said. "Happy Fourth."

"Hopefully, next year we'll all be celebrating in the good old U.S. of A.," Georgie said. "I can't wait to get out of this godforsaken—" she noticed Ramesh and amended, "lovely country."

Twenty minutes later, they had said all their good-byes, shaken hands with Tom and Elisa as well as the ambassador, and were in the Camry with Satish at the wheel.

"Did you eat anything, Satish?" Ellie asked as soon as they were out of the gates.

Satish looked bashful. "Actually, I did, madam. All of us drivers were out in the parking lot, but somebody came and gave us lots and lots of food. The chicken was tops."

"I'm so glad someone thought of serving you dinner," Ellie responded. Frank noticed that she had not said a word to him since they'd said good-bye to Bob and Georgie.

"Americans are good like that, madam." Satish seemed unusually talkative, and Frank wondered if dinner had come with a glass of wine. "Always thinking of us. If this party had been at the Indian consulate, food only for the guests."

Frank smiled grimly. At last someone who appreciated Americans. He told himself to slip Satish a hundred-rupee note for his unexpected help in his silent argument with his wife.

CHAPTER 13

Ellie leaned her head against the car door and stared at the rain outside. Behind the dappled glass wall of rain, the trees were a blur of green. She had already told Satish to slow down a few times, chided him for driving so fast in these weather conditions, but to no avail. So she had given up, much as she'd earlier given up on making small talk with Frank. In any case, Frank and Ramesh were both fast asleep, Frank with his mouth open, Ramesh snoring softly, a trickle of drool running down his chin.

Disappointment had a taste. She had never known that before. It tasted like ashes, feathery and dry. She had left Girbaug for Bombay three days ago with hope and was returning with regret, as if a fresh bouquet of flowers had withered in her hands. A simple gesture, a look that she was not even aware of at the picnic, followed by some intemperate comments, had unleashed a cold fury in Frank. And she couldn't help thinking that it was merely the echo of an older, more repressed fury. The weather had not helped either. The outing that she had so looked forward to, visiting the Elephanta Caves just outside Bombay, had been canceled yesterday due to the rain. No boat operator was intrepid enough to carry a boatload of tourists from the Gateway of India to the nearby island that housed the caves that held the ancient sculptures. Instead, they had spent Sunday mostly hanging out at the Taj, Ellie reading a book in the room while Frank and Ramesh visited the hotel's many boutique shops and then had lunch at the Golden Dragon. Despite Frank's unhappiness with her at the picnic on Saturday, Ellie had been surprised to find that his anger had extended into the next day. She had tried to focus on the novel she was reading, but her heart leapt each time she heard a sound in the hallway, hoping it was Frank coming to get her, anticipating that any minute he would walk into their room to tell her how much he was missing her company, ask her to shut her book and come join him and Ramesh in whatever they were doing. At about four in the afternoon she was tempted to go for another bath, but she lingered, afraid of missing him if he poked his head inside their room. Finally, at five, she called him on the cell. "Hey. It's me. What're you guys doing?"

"Nothing much," he answered. "Just sitting in the lobby talking to another guest."

"Is she beautiful?" she asked, half jokingly but the long, pained silence told her that her words had hit their mark. She took a sharp breath, the pain of being unexpectedly right stronger than she'd imagined. She heard Frank say, "Excuse me," imagined that he'd stepped away from the woman, and then, "What do you want, El?"

"Nothing. I just wanted to see what you guys were up to. And whether we had plans for dinner. Unless you—you have other plans," she stammered, suddenly unsure of herself.

She heard the exasperation in his voice. "I'm on holiday with my wife and a nine-year-old boy. What other plans could I possibly have?"

Despite his sarcasm, despite the fact that he sounded cold, she had felt a rush of joy. Obviously, Frank was not so mad at her that he was planning on staying away for the rest of the evening. She realized that this is what she had been dreading all day long.

"Good," she had said. "Well, I'd be happy to go wherever you want to go."

He must've heard the submission in her voice because his voice was gentler when he spoke. "No. Today was meant to be your day until these stupid rains ruined everything. You decide where you want to go to dinner."

"I don't care." She felt teary, wanting to end this horrible frostiness between them. "I just want to be with you."

"Let me go find Ramesh," he said promptly. "We'll be up in five minutes."

She had hung up, relieved that there was still enough of the old spark—or at least, enough goodwill—left between them that he could detect and respond to her need for him. And sure enough, the door opened a few minutes later and Ramesh came bounding in, followed by Frank. The boy was carrying three new shirts for himself and a silk scarf for his mother that Frank had let him believe he had purchased from his twenty rupees. Ellie's stomach clenched as she pictured Prakash's reaction to these extravagant gifts. She doubted that the cook had ever been able to afford to buy his son three shirts at one time. And if they'd bought a gift for Edna, why not buy a small token for Prakash? She wondered if Frank was even aware of the slight. Prakash would surely be, would read all kinds of things into it. Any other time she would've pointed this out to her husband, her voice gently chiding. But not today. Instead, she determined to slip some money into Prakash's hands, telling him they had not known what to get him. The money would evaporate like the vapors of the alcohol he'd surely purchase from it, but that couldn't be helped.

Frank was polite and attentive to her during dinner, and Ellie was miserable. His politeness stung more than his anger had—he was treating her like a stranger with whom he was compelled to break bread. She was thankful for Ramesh's lively presence and nonstop chatter throughout dinner. A few times she wanted to chide him for talking with his mouth full, but each time she stopped herself, suddenly nervous, unsure of her role in this relationship. Watching Frank interact with the boy over dinner, she sensed a shift, realized that something had happened before her very eyes. If this had been another woman competing for Frank's affections, she would've known what to do, how to compete. But as it was, it was a disarming nine-year-old who had stolen her husband's heart. And it had happened on her watch, was happening even now, and she had no way of preventing the slow erosion of her status in this strange new dynamic that had sprung up between the three of them. With Benny, the effect had been the opposite—he had completed Frank and her, bound them to each other, welded them together. Then, she had felt important, vital, aware that it was her maternal, womanly body that linked her husband to her son. But sitting through this dinner, Ellie was miserably aware of how heavy and *useless* her body felt, how she could not use it to forge a bond between herself and Ramesh because she was not his mom. In fact, she was nobody's mother and probably would never be again. Her one pregnancy after Benny's birth had resulted in a miscarriage, and although no doctor had ruled out the possibility, she had never gotten pregnant again.

After Benny's death, Frank had insisted that she get back on her birth control pills. She had not fought him on this because the truth was, she was scared. And tired. The process of taking a wailing, prune-faced infant and raising him into an intelligent, vivacious seven-year-old had been joyous but also difficult. Everything in those seven years had revolved around Benny—breast-feeding, teething problems, potty training, measles, birthday parties, sleepovers, homework, day camp. Watching *Shrek 2* instead of *Before Sunset*, *The Three Stooges* videos instead of the art movies at the Ann Arbor Film Festival. Seven years of not making a plan or a decision without putting Benny's needs first, and it turned out that none of it was enough. Being a good, diligent parent was not enough of a talisman against the cruelty of a snarling universe. She had looked away for a split second, and in that blink of time, he was gone. The earth had swallowed him up, turned him into dust, and then Ellie had laid in bed at night, wrestling with the thoughts of worms eating at Benny's fine, precious body until she felt like the worms were inside her brain, feeding on her. Months after they'd buried her son, she had struggled with this image of the worms, waking up in the middle of the night with her scalp itching, dreading the slow descent back into sleep. Every day she would wake up with dark circles under her eyes and drag herself through another day of listening to the sad stories of her clients. Once, only once, did she unburden herself to a client, a retired schoolteacher who had lost a child twenty-five years ago, and the woman had assured her she didn't mind, but Ellie was appalled. She had insisted on not charging the client for the visit, and when Lois Shaffer, the psychologist who owned the practice where Ellie worked, asked her why they were not billing for her time, she'd told her. Lois had looked at her for a long time and then said quietly, "I thought you returned to work too soon, my dear. But even now, if you want to take some time off, it'd be fine. We'll find a way to cover for you."

Remembering Lois's words, Ellie shifted in her seat. She had not taken Lois up on her offer then, but when, a few weeks later, she'd gotten wind of Pete Timberlake's proposal to Frank, she had insisted that Frank not dismiss it without thinking it through. And the more she spoke to Frank about it, the more convinced she'd become that it was the right thing to do, that starting life afresh in India, a country where they knew no one and where nobody knew them as Benny's dad and mom, was what they needed to do. And much to her surprise, everyone on both sides of the family—with the exception of her mom—had agreed with her. The resistance that she'd expected from her dad and from Frank's mother never came. Perhaps the dark circles under her eyes, the fact that she battled with images of her son's skull at night, were more obvious than she'd known. Only Delores had balked. During one of their late-night phone conversations she told Ellie, "Moving to India won't change the fact of what's happened, honey. It's like that saying—you gotta go home with them that brung you to the dance."

"I don't know what you mean, Mom," Ellie had said frostily. Her mind was made up; it was late. She didn't want to deal with her mother's enigmatic statements tonight.

"I'm just saying, darling, that whatever you and Frank need to work out, you should do it here at home. Where there's family and friends to hold you up. Who's going to take care of you in India, my darling?"

Now Ellie bit down on her lip as she remembered her dismissive answer to her mother. "I don't need anyone to take care of me, Mom," she'd answered. It had been a reflexive answer, a throwback to her years as an independent-minded, rebellious teenager chafing under the watchful eye of an overprotective mother, but riding in a car speeding through the Indian countryside, Ellie regretted her arrogant words. Today, she felt far removed from that traumatized but hopeful woman who had believed that India—*India*, land of yogis and yoga and the Ganges and the holy city of Benares—would be the answer to the spiritual and emotional crisis that Benny's death had inflicted upon Frank and her. Now, she was simply a woman in need of comfort—and she couldn't turn to her husband, who right now was sleeping in the back seat with his mouth open, his shoulder cradling the head of a boy he had recently referred to as his son. Everybody had somebody to call their own, it seemed to Ellie—somebody that they had loved or married or adopted or birthed or simply borrowed. Everybody except her. She suddenly longed to hear her mother's voice, hungered for the nuggets of hard-earned wisdom that Delores dropped without seemingly meaning to. She might no longer be a mother herself, but she would always be somebody's child, and at this moment, Ellie was profoundly grateful for that fact. She would call her mother tonight once they reached home.

Satish turned a corner, and for a second the sun peeked out from behind the heavy clouds, bathing the countryside in an artificial-looking white light. Ellie barely noticed it. Instead, she took in the shivering trees, their leaves battered by the relentless violence of the rain, and the occasional cow, emaciated and wet, seeking shelter below one of those trees. Although it was warm and safe in the car, Ellie felt one with those living things outside, beaten by the rain, unprotected and unsafe in a dangerous world.

Her heart full of misgivings, Ellie eyed the road stretched out in front of them. She imagined it looked like her future—dark and endless and lined with ominous, threatening rain clouds.

BOOK TWO

Summer and Autumn 1993

Ann Arbor, Michigan

CHAPTER 14

He wanted to buy her.

Later, ashamed of his initial reaction, he would try to remember the truth differently, tell himself that his first reaction upon seeing Ellie had not been that crass or politically incorrect. Later, he would amend that to believe that upon first setting eyes on Ellie he had felt a strong urge to possess her or even that he had known in that first instant that he wanted to marry her. But the fact was, before his mind could censor his thoughts, he had wanted to buy that beautiful woman in the sleeveless black shirt and baggy pants who was bent over her cello, her straight dark hair falling across what he thought was the most finely sculpted face he had ever beheld. Wanted to buy her, the way one would want to buy a delicate bone china vase in an antique store or a painting one fell in love with at an art gallery.

He turned away, embarrassed by his own thoughts, but the next second he turned back, mesmerized this time by the men's watch that she wore and by the improbably rich blue veins running down her thin, tanned wrists, enchanted by the way she was cradling the awkwardly large cello, those long fingers coaxing the instrument into doing her bidding. He had a sudden flash of what this woman would be like in bed, how she would hold her lover lightly but firmly, how those fingers would coax from him a different kind of melody. He imagined himself kissing the inside of her wrists, kissing the narrow strip where her watch had left a band of white against the rest of her tanned flesh. He imagined her body like a cello, a rich, golden instrument, her long, delicate neck, the smooth, polished torso, imagined plucking at her small, firm breasts with his lips, holding those narrow hips against his. He told himself to memorize this woman's face and body in case he never saw her again, so that the next time he was tempted to sleep with the pretty, inconsequential girls who seemed to be everywhere at the University of Michigan, he would remember what his ideal woman looked like.

Aware that he was staring, Frank forced himself to look away and at his surroundings. It was a beautiful afternoon in June. Ellie was playing in a string quartet hired by Wilfred Turner, whose parents were throwing him a belated graduation party on their large family estate. Wilfred was a year ahead of Frank in the MBA program at the University of Michigan.

The quartet was working through the Brandenburg Concerto No. 2, but Frank scarcely heard the music as he rummaged his way through the guests milling around the enormous backyard, looking for Wilfred. "Good party, big guy," he said. "How you doing?"

Wilfred made a face. "I'll be better after all these folks leave, and we can go down a few beers at McLarry's. Most of these are mater's friends."

Frank nodded noncommittally. He pretended to look around. "Nice music," he said, keeping his voice light. "Where'd you find them?"

Wilfred laughed. "Forget it, kiddo," he said. "You're the sixth guy who's asked. From what I hear, she has a boyfriend."

"Who are you talking about?"

"Oh, knock it off, Frank. You're not fooling me. Either you're suddenly interested in classical music or you've developed a sudden fondness for middle-aged men," Wilfred said, pointing his chin in the direction of the three other musicians.

"Fuck you, Wilfred," Frank said, walking away.

He heard Wilfred laugh behind him. "For what it's worth, they call themselves the Moonbeams."

He spent the next hour prowling around the lawn, making small talk with the other students, avoiding Wilfred and his mother, picking up an occasional hors d'oeuvre from a passing waiter's tray and sipping white wine. Finally, the musicians took a break, and Frank made a beeline for where the cellist was standing, stopping long enough to grab a fresh glass of wine.

"Hi," he said. "I'm Frank. And you must be exhausted. Care for a drink?"

She accepted the proffered glass without so much as glancing at him. "Thanks," she said and began to walk away.

"Wait," he said, and as she stopped and looked at him quizzically, he found himself saying, "A friend of mine is looking for a musician for a—a birthday bash he's having. Do you have a card or something?"

She gestured with her head. "You should talk to Ted. He does all the bookings."

Out of the corner of his eye, Frank could see the other guys milling around, waiting for a chance to talk to the girl. "Well, the thing is, my friend's place is small. He only wants to hire one musician." Even to his own ears this sounded lame. "Do you happen to know someone who can perform solo? You know, classical guitar or something?"

"Well, I play the harpsichord."

"Harpsichord? Why, that would be perfect. He—my friend— has a small place. So, let me call you. Do you have a card?"

She looked amused. "Sorry, no card. I just do this on the side, to earn some extra money. Grad school's not cheap, you know."

Frank's eyes lit up. "You go to U of M? Music school?"

"Nope. I'm starting on my Ph.D. in psychology in the fall."

"Oh, wow. That's cool." Frank saw Wilfred waving to her as he approached them. "So let me get your phone number," he said, pulling out a pen. Wilfred was almost up to them now. He scribbled it on his palm as she recited it.

Wilfred walked over and kissed the girl once on each cheek in the European way. Frank felt a surge of jealousy run through him. Goddamn pretentious prick, he thought. "How you doing, sweetheart?" Wilfred said. "Is my buddy here bothering you?"

Frank spoke before she could. "I should let you two chat," he said. He smiled at her. "Nice meeting you."

He nodded to Wilfred and held up his hand as if to scratch his ear so that he could see the phone number written on his palm. "Good party, Wilfred," he said. "I think I'll go chat with your—mater."

He had to control the lift in his step as he walked away. It was only when he had gone to the bar to get another drink that he realized that he didn't know the name of the woman he had just lost his heart to.

Which made it awkward when he called her the next day. He could've asked Wilfred for her name, of course, but he didn't want to give him the pleasure of lording it over him, teasing him, or worse, lecturing him. He didn't want to talk to Wilfred at all. In fact, he didn't want to talk to anyone except the girl, the girl, the girl who had slithered her way into his dreams the previous night, the one who was responsible for the thudding of his heart and for the dampness of his pajamas when he woke up. The girl who had reduced him to being a callow teenager again, who had no control over his own body. Like a love-struck teenager he had copied her number down on a piece of paper when he got home from the party and then traced its outline again on his palm, not wanting it to fade away.

He tumbled out of bed at nine the next day, brushed his teeth to get rid of the morning hoarseness, and dialed her number. She answered on the fourth ring. "Hello?" she said, and the single word made Frank's body ache with longing.

"Hi," he said. "This is Frank. We met at Wilfred's yesterday? I talked to you about playing at my friend's party?"

There was a slight pause and then she said, "Yup, I remember."

Couldn't she sound a little *glad* or something? Frank thought. But hey, at least she remembers. "Great," he said. "Well, I was calling to follow up on it. He definitely wants to hire you."

"What date is the gig?"

Date? Shit. "He doesn't know yet. That is, it's sometime in July, but he's not sure when."

"Well, he should let me know as soon as he knows. July's a busy month. Everybody wants to get married then."

Had he detected something in her voice? Some edge, some sarcasm? Was she against marriage? Against love, romance, men in general?

"Hello?" the voice at the other end said. "You still there?"

"I'm here," Frank said. He thought fast. "You know, before I introduce you to my friend, you and I should come up with a list of dates when you're available and go over the musical arrangements. Are you free to meet for coffee or something this week?"

"You want to go over what music I'll play?" This time there was no mistaking the bemusement in her voice. But before he could respond, she said, "Okay. I'll bring my calendar with me, and we can pin down some dates. I can also show you a list of selections. But shouldn't your friend meet with us?"

Damn. This lying business was treacherous. He was already beginning to feel like a dirty old man. "Don't worry about that. I— we're sort of cohosting this party together."

"But I thought—" she started before changing her mind. "Whatever."

"Listen," he said. "I have an idea. I was gonna grab a quick lunch at Ali Baba's at one o'clock today. You know where that is, on State Street? Would you like to discuss this over lunch?"

The slightest of hesitations and then, "Sure."

Sure? It was that easy? Frank exhaled and realized that he had been holding his breath the whole time they'd been on the phone. "Great," he said hoping she hadn't heard the slight tremor in his voice. "See you at one."

The instant he hung up, he realized he still hadn't asked her her name.

At noon, he caught himself changing his shirt a second time and stopped himself. Enough preening, already, he told his reflection in the mirror. Either she'll like you or she won't. You're not auditioning for a part. The way he was behaving brought back memories of lingering on the front porch of the house in Grand Rapids, dressed in the suit he wore to church every Sunday, looking for his father to return. For five months after his father left, he kept a vigil after church every Sunday, wanting to be dressed in his finest when his dad came back. And then one day he *saw* himself, a twelve-year-old boy dressed in his brother's hand-me-down suit, rocking himself on the big white rocker, his heart jumping every time a car came down the quiet street. Saw the futility of the hope that burned in that boy's chest. And he went inside and got out of that suit as quickly as he could.

He had grabbed an outdoor table at Ali Baba's and was paging through a library book when he looked up and saw her standing in front of his table. And he knew that she had seen the look of stunned pleasure that crossed his face when he spotted her. She wore a simple white dress with wide lapels and big black buttons in the front, her sunglasses resting on her head. Surrounded by men and women in T-shirts and shorts, she stood out like a flower in the desert. Frank's mouth went dry as he stood up to greet her.

"Hi," she said.

"Hey." He smiled, knowing that his smile was too deep for the occasion but not really caring. He was happy to be sitting across from this lovely woman and he didn't care who knew it.

"I grabbed an outdoor table. Hope that's okay."

"It's perfect." She looked around and flung one arm out. "It's a gorgeous day."

"It is," he said. "A perfect day." And she must've heard something in his voice because she looked at him before lowering her eyes.

She ordered an iced tea and a felafel sandwich. Frank ordered a chicken pita and hummus for them to share.

"Okay, I have a confession to make," he said when the waiter left. "I don't even know your name."

"Oh, I'm sorry. It's Ellie."

Ellie. He tried it out in his head and decided it was like swirling a rich, red wine in his mouth. "Nice to meet you, Ellie," he said.

"You, too. So. Shall we look at our calendars?"

He tore a piece of pita and dipped it in the hummus. "Let's wait until after lunch," he said. "Small table."

"Sorry. That makes sense."

"Though if you're in a hurry?"

"No, I'm fine. I've nothing planned for today, thank God."

"So why psychology?" he asked, while thinking, If you don't sleep with me I'm going to spontaneously combust.

"It's what I've always wanted to do. Help people heal their lives. I think it's one of the reasons I've always been drawn to music, too."

"Yeah. Hearing you yesterday, I'm surprised you're not studying music. You were fantastic."

"Thanks. When I was younger I used to think I'd be a professional musician. I was a music major as an undergrad."

"Where'd you go to school?"

"Oberlin."

"That's where you're from?"

"No, I grew up in Shaker Heights, near Cleveland. But my dad taught at Oberlin, so . . ."

"I've heard of Shaker Heights. Do your parents still live there?" Frank was aware that he was being rude by asking so many questions, but he couldn't stop himself. He was charmed at how easily Ellie spoke. She had none of the guarded self-consciousness that often afflicted beautiful women.

"Your childhood sounds happy," he said, and hated the trace of wonder and envy he heard in his voice.

She looked embarrassed. "It's that obvious, huh? Guess I'm going to have to keep this a closely guarded secret from my clients. But it's true—I had a happy childhood. Go figure."

She smiled, and he felt himself getting flustered. Everything about this woman was throwing him off stride. He didn't know what to focus on—her flawless, tanned skin, the radiance of her face, the careless way she pushed her shiny hair out of her eyes, the way she moved her hands as she spoke, the rich, silver words that tumbled out of her like a waterfall. Frank knew that he was good-looking. While growing up, he had strangers at the mall telling his mother how cute her little boy was; had Jenny Waight, the girl next door, give him his first kiss when he was twelve; had his male roommate profess his love for him while in college. But he suddenly felt as nervous and uncertain of himself as he had been the night Jenny Waight had kissed him behind the garage.

"Did you hear a word of what I said?" Ellie was saying.

"Oops. Sorry. Guess I wandered off for a minute."

She pulled a face. "Is the company that boring?"

He realized she was flirting with him, and the realization made him laugh. "Not at all."

"I was asking about where you grew up."

"Grand Rapids. A little over a hundred miles from here. That and a universe away."

"How do you mean?"

He looked at her, unsure of how to explain. "I was born in Grand Rapids," he said. "But I never felt like I belonged there. It was—there was something defeated about the place. But my first day here in Ann Arbor, I felt like I was home."

She nodded. "How about your parents?"

"My mom wasn't too crazy about the town either. But she still lives there. My dad—" He stopped for a slight second, wanting to ensure that his voice would be smooth and matter-of-fact when he spoke. "My dad—he left when I was twelve. So I have no idea what he thought."

The dark eyes held something in them now, a sharp, probing intelligence. "I'm sorry," she said simply.

He looked away, afraid of seeing pity in her eyes. He thought back to the day he'd come home from school and found his mother weeping in her bedroom. He had immediately blamed himself, thought back to how defiantly he had spoken to his dad when he'd been ordered to clear the table the previous week, was convinced that he had inadvertently conveyed to his father the growing contempt and animosity that he was beginning to feel. For weeks he had sat on the front porch bargaining with God. In school, he gave Tommy Hefner a bloody nose for asking if he was okay, now that his father had left.

"It was a long time ago," he now said. His tone was measured, pleasant, as if he was telling her about a recent picnic.

"I see," she said. She opened her mouth as if to say more, and he stiffened imperceptibly. "Well?" she continued. "Should we go back to discussing the matter at hand?"

He stared at her blankly. "What's that?" he blurted.

She laughed. "The party? At your friend's house? I thought I was auditioning for the part? Don't you want to come up with some dates and look at the music selection?"

Did she know that he had made the whole thing up? He couldn't tell. At this moment, he hated himself for having made up this cock-and-bull story. Maybe he would've been better off if he'd told her the truth—that he would *die* if she didn't sleep with him. But just as he was trying to decide whether this was the moment to sit back in his chair and say that he had a confession to make, she pulled out her calendar and something about the gesture told him that she had no idea that there was no friend and no birthday party.

Something stirred in him, a deep tenderness at this trusting, gullible girl with her head bent over her large appointment book. Now she was leaning into her bag and pulling out a notebook and he realized that she had written down possible musical selections. He pulled his chair closer to hers, saying, "Let's take a look," and his voice was so husky with sexual desire that he was surprised that she didn't notice. He felt like a pervert, getting his jollies merely from inching closer to a pretty girl.

She told him a little bit about each musical piece and he half listened in a semi-delirious state, happy to be smelling her shampoo, inhaling the subtle sweetness of her perfume, glancing at her face every chance he got. "You know what?" he said finally, knowing that she was waiting for him to respond to her many suggestions. "You decide the music. I have implicit faith in your—good taste." And this time he let his eyes linger lightly on her face, her neck, the sweet place where the white of her dress met her chest. She blushed and looked away, but when she spoke her voice was light and jaunty. "Not a problem. Let's come up with a date, though."

"Tell you what. Why don't you give me three dates and I'll—run them by my friend?"

"Great."

He felt a sudden panic at the thought of saying good-bye now that lunch was over. Leaving Ellie would feel like coming down from a drug-induced high. "Hey," he heard himself saying. "I was thinking of walking down to the art museum. Do you know about the new Chagall exhibit? Any interest in joining me?"

"I've already seen it," she said, and the sun disappeared as if someone had plucked it out of the sky. "But I adore Chagall. If you're going, I wouldn't mind seeing it again," and the sun assumed again its rightful place in the sky.

"Cool. Let's go," he said, setting down a twenty-dollar bill, and when she reached for her handbag, he touched her hand lightly and said, "No way. I asked you. This is my treat." And all the while his mind was saying, Remember this moment. It's the first time you touched her.

They spent three happy hours at the museum. When they left, Ellie wanted a Coke, so they went to a nearby café and soon Frank was talking about this wonderful Chinese restaurant that had recently opened up on Main. Ellie said she loved Chinese food and he invited her to join him for dinner. It was nine o'clock when they finally parted, after Ellie refused Frank's repeated offers to drop her off at her home. He walked down the streets to his apartment whistling to himself. A first date that had lasted for eight hours, as long as a workday. While the other schmucks in the city were punching clocks, appeasing bosses, putting in a full day at work, he had just spent eight hours in the company of a woman who seemed to get lovelier with each passing moment. Eight hours. Not bad for a first date, Frankie boy, he told himself, not bad at all.

He phoned her the next day, but Ellie was going out the door and couldn't talk. But she phoned him back that evening and they talked for three hours. Just before hanging up, he asked her casually if she was free for lunch on Saturday. She wasn't, she was playing in a wedding, but she had to go to Borders on Sunday to pick up a book she'd special ordered, and did he want to go with her? He did indeed, but what about grabbing a quick lunch before that? Maybe do Ali Baba's again, if it wasn't too soon.

He showed up at the restaurant intending to confess his deception to her. He had practiced keeping his tone light, making a rueful face, admitting to being a little starstruck. She was already at the restaurant when he got there. "Hi," he said brightly, and she turned to face him, but her eyes were cold. He sat across from her, a sudden feeling of dread enveloping him.

"What's up?" he said uncertainly, but she interrupted him. "I want to ask you something. And I want you to tell the truth. There's no friend, is there? No birthday party that I'm to play at?"

He shook his head, trying to find that rueful, puppy-dog expression that he had practiced. But suddenly he saw it as she did—not as a playful ruse by a love-struck man but a ploy by a man ruthless enough to lie in order to get what he wanted. "I'm sorry," he said. "I was going to tell you today."

She shook her head angrily, and he saw that what he'd earlier seen as coldness was actually rage. "One thing about me, Frank. I hate being lied to. Even so-called white lies." She shook her head again. "God. I feel like such a loser. Can't believe I fell for such an obvious move. I figured it out this morning. Anyway. Guess the joke's on me." She pushed her chair back and got up.

"Where—where are you going?"

Her voice was low but deliberate. "Away. From. You." She moved away and then looked back. "Please don't call me ever again."

He sat at the table transfixed, watching her stride away until he could not see her anymore. He did not feel sad. He felt angry. Angry at himself for having blown this, for having told a lie in order to get something that he thought he had no realistic chance of getting any other way. Only to lose her, anyway. And he was angry at her for not understanding this, for treating him as if he was a goddamn stalker or something, instead of just a twenty-three-year-old guy with a serious crush on a woman. Screw her, he told himself. She's not worth it. Probably snores in her sleep. He hardened his heart, became again the twelve-year-old boy who, after he'd stopped keeping his vigil for his father, didn't allow himself to miss him again. His anger protected him, allowed him to leave the restaurant without dissolving into tears.

The tears came as soon as he turned the key and entered his apartment, which suddenly felt as empty and desolate as a grave. He collapsed on his futon, his mind leafing through the many snapshots he'd clicked in the past few days—Ellie with her head bowed over her notebook, Ellie bent over the cello like a lover, Ellie searching his face with her all-knowing, probing eyes—and then he was a boy again, sobbing his losses, his pain at the loss of his father coming at him fast and evil, like a madman with a knife, and merging with the pain of this most recent loss. His rational mind tried to tell him that this was insane behavior, that he barely knew this woman, that he was crying over a phantom, but it did him no good. He turned on the stereo so that the neighbors couldn't hear him, and then he sobbed, dimly aware that the sounds he was making were not so much the sounds of a grown man but of someone much younger. He thought of phoning Scott, but that would have required words, and he felt beyond words at the moment.

He didn't eat for a full day after the talk with Ellie. Didn't shave for four days. Barely left the apartment. Ignored the two messages that his mother left on his answering machine. Played Jim Morrison on the stereo each night and drank two beers before collapsing in bed.

On the fifth day, he woke up early, shaved, and got dressed. He resolved to stop acting like a goddamn imbecile. He decided to go for a bike ride down to the river. After the ride, he ran into some friends and hung out with them. He was pleased with himself when he finally wound his way home at about four in the evening, proud to have under his belt a day without lamenting the loss of Ellie. He took a shower, and when he came back into the living room, he noticed the flashing light on his answering machine.

"Listen," Ellie's voice said. "Just because I asked you to never call me again doesn't mean that you should—you know, *never* call me again."

He was dialing her number before he'd heard the rest of her message.

CHAPTER 15

All that fall, it smelled of watermelons. And burning firewood. The air was glassy and transparent. Ellie and Frank walked in a daze that autumn, under skies that floated like a blue, fast-moving river above them. Some days it seemed as if they were standing at the edge of the earth, barely keeping their balance, about to fall off. The streets, littered with drying, dying leaves, added to the askew feeling. The promiscuous trees bled yellow and red and gold with such an obscene lavishness, it made them blush. Michigan had never seemed this beautiful or this lonely. They spent hours that fall walking through the littered Ann Arbor streets, hiking on the banks of the Huron River, following the walking trails at the Arboretum. On weekends they shunned their friends and took Ellie's yellow Ford to nearby campgrounds and slept under the stars, staring at moons that went from being plump and round, to a silver scratch in the sky. And inevitably, they made love, made love with such ferocity and passion that it seemed as if they were engaged in some silent, never-ending argument. Their lovemaking left them exhausted, hollow-eyed, spent. They tried to take a break away from each other and found that they couldn't. Found that they couldn't keep their eyes, their mouths, their hands, away from each other's bodies, found themselves acting in ways that shocked and embarrassed them.

Ellie blamed it on the weather. She waited for the weather to turn, for the chill in the air to harden into ice and release them from this tableau of ridiculous passion that they were stuck in. Autumn was not a sensible season—it made everybody act a little intoxicated and loopy. She ignored the fact that her loopiness had started in June, after she'd met Frank for the second time at Ali Baba's and told him she never wanted to see him again. She had marched off that afternoon full of righteous anger and indignation, but by that night she had felt an ache in her body so acute, she'd thought she had the flu. And four months later, that ache had not dissipated. No matter how many hours she spent with Frank, no matter how many nights they stayed up talking, no matter how many times they made love, roughly or gently, urgently or languidly, it didn't seem enough. She still felt thirsty for this man, ached for his presence in her life.

She had been in love before, and that was why she was so unprepared for this. Blamed it on the weather. Waited for the spell to break, like a dreamer awakening from a dream. She thought it was only a matter of time before she'd tire of this man, waited for the morning he would get out of bed and she would not raise her head from the pillow to drink in his beauty. Prayed for the day his beautiful, chiseled body—the long, muscular legs with the thin scar on the left knee, the tight, dimpled buttocks, the heartbreaking curve of his lower back, the shoulder blades that flared like angel's wings, the coiled, animal strength of his long neck, the face that was rescued from an almost feminine loveliness by the saving grace of a broken nose—would leave her indifferent. But that day was not yet. Sometimes, when she looked at his naked body she felt a kind of brusqueness, a violence, an arousal that she'd always imagined was male. It terrified her, this degree of carnality, this nakedness of feeling, this lust, because it defied every notion of what she thought of as femininity.

Being with Frank made her feel powerful, and it increased all her appetites. She played Scrabble with more of a killer's instinct, laughed and talked louder, even ate larger meals in his presence. She sat in his living room with her legs uncrossed, letting her lust register in her eyes until she saw it flare in his. Yet there was nothing coy, nothing about the femme fatale about her behavior. Rather, there was something egalitarian, clean, about their sexual intimacies. She often left his apartment in the morning wearing one of his shirts, smelling him on her body as she drove home, savoring the soreness of her breasts and vagina, reveling in each scratch or mark that he'd left on her body. Once in a while, her reaction and thoughts embarrassed her. But for the most part, they didn't, because nothing she ever did with Frank cost her her self-respect. If he'd ever suggested she dress up in a certain way or entertain some stupid boyish fantasy of his, she would've lost interest in him. But he never did. He was just there, ready to meet her, standing on equal ground, the simple intensity of his gaze the only sexual aid she needed.

Although she had never been this loopily in love with anyone before, she convinced herself she had, sifted through the past and came up with names of boys barely remembered and conferred upon them an intensity of feeling that she'd never had at the time she was dating them. David. Sean. Richard. Jose. She told herself she'd been crazy about each one of them and reminded herself of how abruptly she'd fallen out of love: David because he'd told her he didn't see any need for the Equal Rights Amendment. Sean because he had farted during the most important scene when they'd rented Bergman's *Persona*. Jose because he confided that he'd seen *Love Story* twelve times and had the movie memorized. Richard because the sex had become predictable, boring. She waited for something like that to happen with Frank, counted the days for autumn to turn into winter and for the delirium to end, for the fever to break.

Instead, he asked her to go to New York to meet his brother Scott in early November. His mother was still living in Grand Rapids at the time, but he didn't seem anxious to make that introduction. She sensed that her meeting Scott was important to Frank and therefore was about to refuse. But what came out of her mouth instead was a proposal—that if she agreed to drive to New York to meet his brother, they would stop on the way back to see her family in Shaker Heights. That way, I won't feel too guilty not going home for Thanksgiving, she told him, but the reality was she wanted to introduce this bewitching man to her older sister, Anne, knowing that with a few well-chosen, sarcastic words, Anne would help the scales fall off her eyes.

What she hadn't counted on was loving Scott. Nothing that she knew about him—Republican, fan of Reagan, pro-life conservative, Wall Street banker—could've prepared her for that. What she'd also been unprepared for was the physical resemblance to Frank—despite Scott's being a few years older, a little heavier, with darker hair and a more stolid manner compared to Frank's catlike sexiness, there was no question about them being brothers. But what bowled her over was the protective, almost fatherly manner that Scott had around Frank. Until she saw how protective Scott was toward Frank, she had had no idea that Frank had needed protection. It made Ellie realize that the offhand, bare-bones way Frank had told her about his family life—dad had left when he was twelve, mom had raised him and his older brother while running an antique-furniture store in Grand Rapids—had been a deflection, a way of smoothing over pain that he was still vulnerable to. For the first time, Ellie asked herself a dangerous question: could her wild lust for this man ever be tamed into something as steady and consistent as love?

The trees in Central Park were bare by then, and Ellie felt their trajectory echoed the path of her relationship with this enigmatic man. They had met in the full lushness of high summer when the air was warm and rich, continued their passionate romance through the mad drunkenness of fall, when the trees themselves were a distraction. But now it was almost winter, and the bare bones of the universe were already exposed. It was put up or shut up time. She decided to shut up.

"Why is my favorite Commie so quiet today?" Scott teased as the three of them walked around the lagoon. "Has she lost her talking points from Chairman Mao's Red Book? Why the sudden silence?"

She hit him on the shoulder. Hard. Three days with Scott, and already he felt like family. "Who can get a word in edgewise when the Benton brothers are together?" she said. "And when it's so damn cold that you can see the words freeze as they come out of your mouth?"

And then it happened. As soon as Ellie admitted to being cold, both men, one on either side of her, instinctively moved closer, and each put his arm around her. They all laughed, Frank and Scott in embarrassment, Ellie in delight. She suddenly felt like she was a little girl again, crawling into bed on cold Cleveland nights, snuggling under a comforter with Anne. To make sure they did not pull away from her, she threw one hand around each man's waist, keeping them close to her. Frank turned and kissed her on the top of her head. "Thanks." She smiled and he smiled back, and the scene froze, became one of those perfect, cherished moments where the brain takes a snapshot and files it for later use.

It was a new feeling, tenderness. It scared her, made her doubly glad that they were leaving for Cleveland, where her big sister would turn her skeptical eye on her newest boyfriend and bring her to her senses. This relationship with Frank had already gone on too long, she decided. She had just started her doctoral degree, which was going to need all her attention. It was never advisable to start a new relationship while working on a Ph.D, everyone knew that. The future that she had envisioned held no room for a man whose real shape, the depth of his childhood hurt, was only now beginning to emerge. The day after the walk in Central Park she had woken early and decided to fix herself a bowl of cereal. But Scott was already in the kitchen, making them all French toast, and there was nothing to do but pull up a bar stool and offer to beat the eggs for him. And before she knew it, he was talking to her in that soft, deep voice of his, thanking her for making his brother so happy, telling her about Tina, Frank's last girlfriend, and how unsuitable he'd thought she was for his baby brother. Tinsel Tina, he'd called her. And then he'd turned those blue eyes on her and said, "But you're the real deal, Ellie. You're the first person Frank has dated that I think is deserving of him." She had tried to tease him, make light of his stout love for his brother, but Scott was having none of it. He remained serious. "I'm not kidding," he said. "I know this boy can come across as if he's all light and play, but he's not." And then he told her about the months that followed their dad's leaving, the porchside vigil his brother kept, the promises and bargains with God that he'd overhear as he walked by Frank's bedroom. Ellie shook her head, wanting and not wanting to know. But Scott's words had their effect. The image of the twelve-year-old boy sitting on the front porch day after day weaved its way into her head.

Which may be why as soon as they pulled out of the city, she picked a fight with Frank. He looked stunned at first, tried to ask her what was upsetting her so, but she wouldn't—couldn't—tell him. Soon, his temper flared to meet hers, and they drove all the way to Pennsylvania in almost total silence. Once, he turned on the radio and struggled to find a station with good reception. As soon as he found it, she reached out and turned the radio off. He looked exasperated but didn't say a word.

They sort of made up after lunch—Frank even made a half-hearted attempt to put his hand up her skirt—but the damage was done. By the time they pulled into Cleveland at five in the evening, their only thought was to get away from each other. Ellie decided she no longer needed Anne's help in breaking it off with Frank. She jumped out of the car and raced up to the red brick house as soon as they pulled up into Anne's driveway.

"He's gorgeous," Anne whispered to her as the sisters escaped to the kitchen to fix Frank a gin and tonic.

"Yeah, and he's vain and self-absorbed."

"Really?" Anne's eyes were curious. "I thought he was really nice."

Ellie pulled a face. "He is. Most of the time. We just had a bad fight on the way here."

Anne reached up and pulled out a bottle of gin. She splashed a generous serving in each of their glasses. "What did you two fight about?"

"Honestly, I don't even know. Just one of those silly—" Her face suddenly crumpled. "I think I'm trying not to fall for him, Anne. I just can't afford to be involved with someone right now. I have so much on my plate."

Anne added the ice to their glasses. "Good luck trying to resist him," she said drolly.

When they reentered the living room, Frank was standing at the window. "It looks like a pretty street," he said politely. "A lot of kids, I see."

"It's a very kid-friendly neighborhood," Anne agreed, handing him his glass. "Do you like children, Frank?"

Ellie gasped, shocked by her sister's obviousness. But Frank didn't seem particularly offended. "I adore them," he said. He looked out of the window again. "Your street reminds me of the neighborhood I grew up in. We played outdoors day and night." He turned to face Anne. "Do you and your husband want children?"

What were they doing, engaged in a contest to see who could ask the more personal question? Ellie wondered. She looked from one to the other and realized that they were smiling at each other, oblivious to her presence. She didn't even try to hide the sarcasm in her voice. "Speaking of your *husband*," she said, "what time is he getting home? And what time are Dad and Mom coming over?"

Anne looked at her as if she were a particularly irritating fly disturbing a successful picnic. "What?" she said vacantly. "Oh, didn't I tell you? Bob's out of town. Last-minute business trip." Ellie noticed darkly that she didn't seem too perturbed. "And the folks will be here around seven." She turned back to face Frank. "Which leaves us plenty of time for another drink."

"Sure." Frank smiled at Anne. Ellie thought he looked devastatingly handsome, more beautiful than she'd ever seen him. Frank reached out and touched Anne's hand lightly. "But let me help you fix the next round." And with that her boyfriend and her sister left the room and walked toward the kitchen. It didn't escape her notice that neither one had offered her a second drink.

The evening only got worse. By the time her parents arrived, Anne was saying, "Jeez, Frank, you've almost convinced me about the virtues of a business management degree." Ellie shook her head in disbelief. Anne was practically a Marxist, for crying out loud.

Her mother immediately fell for Frank's charm. And even Ellie had to admit that his manners were impeccable. He insisted on helping Anne in the kitchen. He spoke knowledgeably about the last presidential campaign with her father. And even though he was still flirting shamelessly with Anne, he did it in a manner that was not apparent to anyone but her. The conversation during dinner flowed surprisingly easily, unlike some of the stilted dinners when she'd brought previous boyfriends home. Halfway through the meal, Ellie had a sudden realization. He's playing us all, she thought with awe. It's like he's conducting an orchestra— an attentive nod here, a smile there, a joke somewhere else. No wonder she'd spent the summer and autumn wild about this man.

But this was ridiculous—Frank was absolutely promiscuous in how he flirted with her entire clan.

Her parents, who always went to bed by ten o'clock, finally left to go home at eleven that night. She noticed how vigorously her dad shook hands with Frank on their way out.

Anne made them a big breakfast the next morning and then packed them sandwiches for lunch. As they stood around in her driveway, Anne reached up and kissed Frank on the cheek. "You come see us again, you hear?" she said. Frank beamed.

They made desultory conversation the rest of the way home. When they got to Ellie's street, she emitted a few long yawns. "Well, that was fun," she lied. "But man, am I tired."

"You don't want me to come up?" he said immediately.

She turned to face him as he eased the car into a tight spot. "If you don't mind, hon, I'll have so much work to do. I'll see you around?"

"See you around?" he mimicked. But he didn't argue with her decision.

She felt a sense of letdown almost immediately after she let herself into her apartment and shut the door behind her. Also, now that Frank was gone, she couldn't quite understand what he had done to justify her coldness toward him. She walked around the apartment puzzled by her behavior, not quite sure what had happened to sour her mood ever since they'd left New York for Ohio. She turned on the television and, after a few minutes, turned it off. She ate a cup of yogurt. She changed out of her clothes into a pair of sweats. She told herself the least she could do was keep her word and get some schoolwork done.

At seven that evening, she called the Amazing Wok and ordered some Chinese food to be delivered. When the doorbell rang a half hour later, she went to the door, her credit card in hand. But instead of Lee, the seventeen-year-old delivery boy, it was Frank. Her heart lurched when she saw him, and it was all she could do to not fall into his arms. But his stern expression stopped her. Her heart lurched again, this time in fear. "What's wrong?" she said, wondering if he'd come to break up with her.

"Nothing," he said, stepping into her living room without asking for permission. He turned to face her. "Everything."

"What do you mean?"

"I mean that ever since we've met, you've been looking for a reason to leave me. I thought meeting my brother would convince you that I'm not—you know, a werewolf or something. But instead, it's done just the opposite. I don't know what Scotty said to you, but it's scared you something fierce. And the least you can do is tell me why exactly you're dumping me."

She stared at him, unable to speak. She had posed the same question to herself a few hours ago. "I'm scared," she heard herself say. And then, to cover that up, "and you were flirting shamelessly with my sister. My married sister."

"Don't be ridiculous. You know I can't so much as look at another woman these days. And I was only being nice to your sister to impress you."

They were on safer ground now. "That's bullshit," she said. "You were just being a jerk, and what's more—"

"Ellie," he said as he took a step toward her and grabbed her by the shoulders. "Stop. Just stop. This is a diversion and you know it. Just tell me the truth—what have I done to deserve this?"

"I don't know," she cried. She tried to move out of his hands, but he simply tightened his grip on her. "I don't know," she repeated.

"Listen," he said, shaking her slightly. "I wasn't looking for this either, you know? I didn't plan to fall in love with you. But I did. And Ellie, all I can think of is, any day that I'm not with you is a day I don't want to face."

"What are you saying?"

"That I want to marry you. That I want to spend the rest of my life with you."

"How can you be so sure? I mean, we're young, Frank. What if—what if we meet someone else six months from now?"

He eyed her sadly. "If you have to ask that question, then I guess that tells me something."

She looked away from the sadness she saw on his face. I never want to cause this man a day's sorrow, she thought. She leaned forward and rested her head on his chest. "I'm sorry," she said. "I don't even know what I'm saying. I don't know why I'm so scared. I've just never felt this close to anyone before, and it's freaking me out. I guess I'm afraid of trusting it because I feel it will be snatched away. You know what I mean?"

He stroked her hair. "El, listen to me. I know I'm not much of a bargain, right now. Heck, I don't even know how long it will take me to get a job after I graduate. But I promise you this—I will always try to make you happy. And you will always be able to depend on me. I will never abandon you."

And he had been true to his word. They were married a year later, and Ellie could always rely on him. Always, until that fateful night of Benny's death, when she needed him more than ever before, and he abandoned her to tend to his own ruined heart.

BOOK THREE

Summer 2005

Ann Arbor, Michigan

CHAPTER 16

The world had never seemed crueler in its bounty and largesse than it did the day Frank sat fidgeting in his plane seat. Come on, move it, he thought, his hands gripping the seat rest as he leaned forward, as if the sheer momentum of his impatience could force the jet to fly faster. He remembered how, when Benny was little and rode in the back of a car, he used to dig his feet into the front passenger's seat and push, believing that the action made the vehicle go faster. Benny. Just the sound of his son's name on his lips made Frank's heart tremble with love and fear. Nothing could possibly go wrong with Benny. Nothing. He'd never be able to survive it. Hell, he had almost passed out when Ben had broken his wrist at the playground a few years ago. Just the thought of his lovely boy being in any kind of pain brought out something in Frank that he had no name for. And also, a feeling that he did recognize—a sense of failure. After all, the boy was his to defend and protect. His job, his responsibility, his precious cargo. He was more than a father—any asshole could be a father, and didn't he know all about that? He was a dad. And dads did anything to protect their families, paid any price. Which he was willing to do. Pay any price, with his life if need be. But please, dear God, Benny had to be okay. Had to be sitting up in bed and laughing, eating a quart of ice cream by the time he got home.

Not home, he corrected himself. To the hospital. That's where Benny was. They're talking of moving him to the ICU as soon as he's stable, Ellie had whispered during her first phone call from the emergency room. And Frank, they have a breathing tube up his nose. He had hated her then, for saying those words. Felt an anger that was new and old. New because he'd never felt anger toward Ellie before. Old because it was how he'd felt toward his mother in the months after his father had left. If you'd loved him more, he wouldn't have left, he'd once spat at her, and was mortified and pleased to see his mother go pale in the face. Now he felt that kind of anger toward Ellie. For giving him this news on the phone at six o'clock on a quiet Bangkok evening. He'd been sitting in the hotel bar having a drink with Mr. Shipla, who was HerbalSolution's man in Thailand. "Hi, hon," he had answered brightly, pleasantly surprised that Ellie was calling him this early in the evening, forgetting for a second that it was not even dawn in Michigan. And then, listening to her quiet, worried voice, the gin that he'd been sipping suddenly burned in his stomach. And he felt that sharp, helpless anger toward Ellie, as if he wanted to cup her mouth with his open hand and shove the words back into her throat—The doctors say he's very sick, Frank. They're pretty sure its meningococcus. You better come home.

Shipla had been wonderful. Worked the phones like a madman, trying to get him a flight out of Bangkok that same evening. I need to get out of here, he'd said as he paced the hotel room frantically, throwing whatever clothes he found into his large duffel bag. They'd finally put him on a flight to Paris, with Shipla promising to get him a connection to Detroit before Frank landed at Charles de Gaulle. "Call Pete," he'd said to his Thai colleague as he got out of the car at Don Muang International Airport. "He'll know what to do." He had a seven-hour layover at de Gaulle, and Frank had never hated the airport as much as he did that day. He was offended by the martini bars, the bright, glitzy stores selling duty-free perfumes and chocolates, all these people rushing around, looking bright and cheerful and active, while his son lay in a hospital bed chained by plastic tubes. He glanced at the digital clock on the wall every few minutes and caught himself swearing out loud. Get a grip, Frank, he chided himself, but there was nothing to get a grip on. His very core seemed to have collapsed, and in its place he felt a fear that was vaporous, a gas filling the cavity of his body. His hold on the world itself seemed to have loosened. He couldn't believe it. While he sat at the airport in Paris, surrounded by all the riches and material things the world had to offer, his son was in an existential fight with— He shook his head. He wouldn't let his brain conjure up the dreadful word.

He fished for his cell phone, to call Ellie again. He'd already tried her six times since landing in Paris, but she wasn't picking up, and after leaving her an irritable message the first time, he'd realized that she probably couldn't use the phone in the hospital. He'd left her a second message, gentler this time, repeating his flight arrival information, telling her to hang in there, that he'd be home soon and they'd all be together again. This time, he dialed her number with no hope of her answering and felt a dip in his stomach when she said, "Hello?"

"Babe? It's me. How are you? How is he?"

"I just stepped out to call you back," Ellie said, and even at this distance he could hear how raw and weary she sounded.

"So . . . how's it looking?"

"Not good." He heard the sob in her voice. "Not good. I'm scared, Frank. I think he's not—he may not—make it."

His jaw locked, but his voice was gentle as he spoke. "Hush, baby," he said. "Don't say that. This is not the time to give up. It's up to us to save him. Those doctors don't know everything."

"He asked for you just before they moved him to the ICU," she said, and he felt the world collapse around him. He looked up with bloodshot eyes, and everything seemed transformed—the spotless, shiny stores melted into rivulets of gold and molten glass; the busy, rosy-cheeked people rushing around seemed absurd and foolish. His son had asked for him, and he was not there. His son was sick— even dying—and he wasn't at his side, holding his hand, talking to him, pulling him back to the land of the living.

"Frank?" Ellie asked. "You there?"

He blinked a few times before he trusted himself to speak again. "Tell him I'm coming," he whispered. "Tell him to—hold on until I get there."

There was some background noise at Ellie's end, and then he heard her say, "They're paging me. I gotta go."

"Call me," he yelled. "If anything . . . happens, leave a message on my phone."

When they finally took off, Paris looked green and tranquil from his plane window. He didn't trust it. The world suddenly felt sinister, evil, a place where a young boy with the sweetest smile in the world could be fighting for his life. He felt as if he was staring into the bleached bones of the universe, into the ugly pit at the center of all existence. A pit that was usually covered up by grass and trees and butterflies and sunflowers. He felt foolish to have ever believed that the world was a benign place, ruled by a kind, benevolent God. He saw it clearly now—the beauty of the world was a distraction, a sleight of hand, meant to make bearable the irrefutability of death.

I need a drink, he thought. Until now he had refused the free alcohol that the smiling stewardesses had tried to ply him with. But now, he pushed the call button and ordered a Bloody Mary, to still the tremors that kept attacking his body in icy waves and to dull the jagged edges of his thoughts.

After his second drink, something loosened in him. He picked up the phone on the back of the seat in front of him and dialed Scott's cell number. "Scotty?" he said as soon as he heard his brother's voice. "It's me."

"Hey." Scott sounded breathless, as if he'd just run a mile. "We're walking into the hospital right this minute."

"You're in Ann Arbor?"

"Yup. Just got in. Didn't Ellie tell you?"

"No. I've barely managed to reach her. Keep missing each other. How'd you—is Mom with you?"

"Yup, sure is. Wanna say hi to her?" And before he could react, Frank heard his mother's voice say, "Sweetheart? How are you?"

He was trying not to choke up, uncomfortably aware of the fact that the Italian man across the aisle was listening to every word he said. "I'm fine, Mom," he said. "Trying my damnedest to get home quickly." He gulped hard. "Kiss him for me, will you, Mom?"

His mother's tone was calm. "I sure will, honey. And I want you to stop worrying. Benny's gonna be just fine, now that his grandma is here. You just wait and see."

His heart sank as he realized that he didn't believe his mother's words. Still, he smiled faintly into the phone. "Thanks, Mom. Can I, can I talk to Scott for a second?"

There was a rustle, and then he heard Scott's deep tone again. "Does Ellie have your flight schedule, Frank?"

"Believe so. I left it on her cell phone." He hesitated. "Scotty, I want you to do me a favor. You go see Benny, and you tell him that his daddy is on his way and that he should—he should hold on."

He heard the crack in his brother's voice. "You just get here, kid," Scott said gruffly.

"I'm trying. If I thought hijacking a plane would make it go faster, I would." Too late, he realized that he'd chosen an inopportune place to say those inflammatory words. But when he glanced at the woman sitting to his left, he noticed the ear buds sticking into her ears. She hadn't heard. Nor had anyone else, thank God.

"Be safe, Frankie," Scott said. And then, "He's in God's hands, Frank. Pray."

And Frank did. Prayed to God, fought with God, argued with

God, on the long flight from Paris to Detroit. He reclined in his seat with his eyes wide open, staring into the dark cabin. Listen, he said, I haven't asked you for anything in a long, long time. Not since Dad left, to be precise. So I have a few chits coming due, don't you think? Though to be fair, you haven't given me much reason to ask for things over the years. All in all, you've been pretty generous. I have everything that I want, really—a great wife, a good job, a gorgeous son. And that's all I'm asking for, to keep what I have. I don't want anything extra. Because if you take away what you've granted us, well, that's a dirty, cheap trick, don't you think? You're better than that, right, God?

He heard the anger, the defiance in his voice and checked himself. Scott had asked him to pray, to beg, and what he was doing was snarling at God. And so he tried. Sweet Jesus, he started again. Don't take my son from me. I won't be able to survive that, please God. You punish me in any way you want to, dear God, and I'll take it. But not this. Not Benny. He made a few more attempts to continue in this vein, to promise things to God, to strike bargains, but soon gave up. Because it reminded him too much of those awful months after his dad had left. He thought back to that young boy pacing the front porch or lying in bed at night listening for the slamming of car doors, and his stomach turned at the indifference of a God who had stood by and watched silently. What kind of a father treated his children so shabbily? How could someone all-powerful, someone with the ability to perform miracles with the flick of his wrist, perform so few of them? How could an omnipresent being not know the whimpering frailties of the human heart, and if he did, how could he not be moved with pity? How could he bear to witness all this suffering if he had the power to end it? In a human being, these qualities would be contemptible, would be seen as the epitome of evil, the stuff tyrants and war criminals and psychopaths were made up of.

Well, if he could not plead with God or bargain with him, he would fight him for Benny's life, would wrestle with him for the right to keep what was his. Because Benny belonged here, on mortal earth, with him and Ellie. He would walk into that hospital in a few more hours and keep vigil by his son, not leave his bedside for as long as it took. He and Benny would leave that hospital together.

He called Scott again as soon as the plane landed in Detroit, willing his brother to answer the phone. "How is he?" he asked as soon as he heard Scott's hello.

"He's alive," Scott replied, and Frank's body went slack with relief. Benny was alive. And now he was in the same city as his son, instead of hovering in the heavens, keeping company with a deity he didn't like very much at the moment. "Where are you?" he asked.

"At the airport, outside of baggage claims. I'll see you in a few minutes."

Pete Timberlake had accompanied Scott to the airport. Frank saw the two men startle as they took in his appearance—the crumpled clothes, the unshaven jaw, the bloodshot eyes—and felt a moment's embarrassment. "Hey," he said to his brother, who took his bag from him and popped open the trunk. "Thanks for coming, Pete," he added.

Pete grabbed him in a bear hug. "Are you kidding me?" he said. He took a step back. "You holdin' up, bud?"

He shrugged and got in the car just as Scott came around and slipped his bulk into the driver's seat. He was off before Frank could even buckle his seat belt. Frank glanced at his older brother. "How's Ellie?" he said quietly.

Scott threw him a quick look. "She's hanging in," he said. "Anxious for you to get there."

He nodded. "Did you . . . did you give Ben my message?"

"I did." Scott chewed on his lower lip. "But Frankie, I gotta tell you. He's pretty out of it. The doctors say he's not technically in a coma. But I can't tell if he can hear anything we're saying. And I just want to prepare you for this—he's . . . they've put him on a ventilator."

Frank looked out of the window, afraid that he was going to lose control of his body. He willed his brain to forget what his brother had just said, cleared his mind to get rid of the horrifying images that were rooting themselves in there. He felt Scott's hand on his thigh but ignored it. His task was to sweep out of his mind the debris of Scott's words. He was so involved in this benign task that he heard the awful sounds coming from his mouth at the same time the other two did and was therefore as startled as they were. He sounded like an animal with a bullet in its leg, which is how he felt, wounded, crippled, helpless.

The car swerved. Scott was half turning in his seat, one hand on the steering, the other on his brother. "Frankie," he said. "It's okay, boy. It's okay. He'll be all right. He has a lot of people praying for him."

But the animal noise didn't stop. Frank bent from his waist and leaned forward, his hands clenching his stomach. The sounds that came out of him were as old as the world itself. He had never known that the human voice was capable of this range. He knew he was worrying Scott, felt he should reassure him, but human speech seemed beyond his ability at the moment. He was gripped by a fear so large, it was swallowing him alive. It felt almost prehistoric, existential. It no longer seemed as if Benny had only been in his life for seven years. He felt as if Benny had lived within him forever, had been part of his flesh, carved his initials on every cell of Frank's body for all of eternity. It was as though Benny had begun to exist from the moment of Frank's own birth, that they had grown up together, irreducible, and the prospect of losing his son was the prospect of losing his own skin. There was no human language large enough to hold such a loss. There was only sound. Like the howling of a demented dog, the neighing of a horse with a broken leg, the squealing of a pig with a slit throat. But older, less specific than even that. It was the sound of an orphaned universe. A wail, a rant, a moan, a keening, that seemed to come from the very bowels of the earth.

"Frank," Scott said finally. "You want me to pull over?"

"No," he managed to gasp. "Go as fast as you can. I want to be with my son."

Scott ran three consecutive red lights as they approached the hospital. He pulled up at the front door, and Pete jumped out of the car with Frank. "This way," Pete said and they walked the long hallway that led to the children's ICU.

The waiting room outside the unit was packed. His mother was there, of course, and Bob and Anne and Ellie's parents. Half of their friends and neighbors were also there, and it seemed to Frank that none of them dared to make eye contact with him as he went in briefly to hug his mother. He felt his throat tighten with a resentment he knew he had no business feeling. Why were they all here? He only wanted them to/gather this way to celebrate happy occasions—Benny's birthdays, his high school graduation, his college graduation, his wedding day. He had not invited them to this event. "Where's Ellie?" he asked his mother, but Pete was already ushering him out of the room and through a set of enormous metal doors. As soon as they entered, Frank noticed how low the lights were in here and how quiet the unit was. A cold fear gripped him as they walked down a short hallway toward Benny's room.

He almost cried out when he saw Ellie, who was talking to a nurse in the hallway. He had only left for Thailand five days ago, and he was coming home to a different woman. She had shrunk. Gotten older. There were lines on her face that had never been there before. Her shoulders were bent at an angle of defeat. Her mouth curved downward. But what killed him were her eyes. Magpie eyes, he'd always called them, full of mischief and fun. The eyes that looked at him now were friendly but dead. She looked at him with recognition, with gratitude, love even, but behind that look was another.

And it was that second look that scared him. That told him how desperately sick his son really was.

He went up to her and kissed her cheek. "I'm here," he said. He wanted to say more but his voice broke. "I'm here, babe," he finally said. "We're going to pull him out of this."

She rested her cheek against his shoulder for a quick second. Then she looked at him, her eyes searching his face. "I don't want you to freak out when you see him, okay? You promise?"

"I promise," he said, and it was a good thing he did, because it took every ounce of self-control not to cry out loud when he saw Benny in the hospital bed, when he found his son's tiny body under the city of tubes and drains that ran across him. He heard the steady whoosh of the ventilator and thought he'd never heard a more ominous sound. But what really undid him was the rash on Benny's hands, neck, and face. When Ellie had told him about the rash over the phone, he had pictured something delicate and subtle, like a purple lace handkerchief placed on Ben's face. Nothing had prepared him for the brutality of what he saw. This rash, these purple blotches, looked like an assault, like an invasion by a genocidal army. He bit down on his lower lip as he looked at Benny's hands and saw the blackened fingers. How he had loved those hands. It was the first part of his son's body he had ever kissed, minutes after Benny had been placed in his arms for the first time. He had loved the puffy rise of puppy fat on those hands when Ben was a toddler and later, the smooth stretch of skin. He had kissed those fingers individually and bunched up together. Now, he picked up Benny's limp hand and held it to his lips. And before he could complete the gesture, he knew that this was one of the last times he would ever touch his son's alive, breathing body.

Beside him, Ellie made a sound, like the cry of a small animal. He turned his stricken eyes to her, unable to prevent his last treacherous thought from registering on his face. All his earlier resolutions of striding into the hospital and bringing comfort to Ellie, of bending down and whispering in Benny's ears and asking him to fight, *fight,* left him now that he'd seen the terrible face of reality. He felt paralyzed, thankful that his legs were still holding him up. He looked at Ellie, who obviously needed him, with something approaching resentment. He was spent, hollowed out, in shock. The burden of her expectations weighed heavily on him, as did the dismaying realization that he was not up to the challenge of comforting her, that he would fail her on this count. He stood silently at the side of his son's bed, his eyes darting between the monitor and Benny's bruised, marked face. "Ben," he whispered. "Benny. I'm here. I'm home, Ben. And I won't leave you now, not even for a minute." Gingerly, careful not to tug at one of the tubes, he stroked his son's hair.

"Until a few hours ago, I couldn't even touch him," Ellie said in a dead monotone. "He was still contagious, they said, so we had to wear a mask. And they started all of us on antibiotics, too. Like I care. Like I want to live if something happens to Ben."

"Don't say that," he hissed furiously. "Nothing's gonna happen to him." Out of the corner of his eye he saw that Scott had entered the room. He watched as his brother put his arm around Ellie's shoulder. The simplicity of the gesture filled Frank with shame and longing. Ellie's been up for almost thirty-six hours, he reminded himself. Eyeing the couch at the far end of the room, he said, "Ellie. Why don't you take a nap for a few minutes? I can take over now."

She ignored him. "I didn't know how much to tell you over the phone," she said. "Didn't want to scare you. In any case, the rash didn't look this bad when I brought him in. It's grown a lot mo—"

He knew what he had to do. "When was the doctor last in? I want to talk to him. Maybe we can transfer him to a bigger hospital. The fact that they can't even get the fever under control is ridiculous."

Scott turned to face Frank. "We've already been through all that, Frankie," he said quietly. "Ben's actually getting top-notch care here. And two, I don't think it's a good idea to transfer him anywhere in this condition. This is a pretty great hospital. You know that."

He opened his mouth to protest, but Scott held his gaze, and Frank was the first to look away. "So what do we do?" he mumbled, unable to look at Ellie.

"We wait," Scott said. His eyes were bright as he looked at Frank, and when he spoke again his voice was gentle but firm. "And we do whatever is right for Benny."

At five that evening, Ellie suddenly fell asleep halfway through a sentence. "She's exhausted," Scott mouthed to his brother. "Let's let her nap for a few hours. We can wait outside."

He rose reluctantly, knowing that Ellie needed the sleep but reluctant to forfeit his place in Benny's room for even a few minutes. When they reached the door, he turned to Scott and whispered, "You go ahead into the waiting room. I'm gonna just sit quietly by Ben's bed. I won't wake Ellie up, I promise."

He silently pulled up a stool and sat with his hand on his son's wrist. He stared at Ben's ghastly face, looking for a sign, for the tiniest gesture, the slightest movement that would give him a reason to keep hoping. But Benny's eyes remained closed, his mouth forced open by the clear plastic ventilator tube that was keeping him alive. He kept staring at the beloved face behind the purple mask smothering it. Except for the gurgling of the ventilator, the room was silent. Frank had been up for over thirty hours himself, and the undertow of sleep tugged at him. He fought it off, forcing his eyes wide open, moving his eyeballs from side to side. He felt himself drifting and, for the first time since he'd received the terrible news, felt a strange peace. He was home. He was in a darkened, quiet room with his son and wife. And Benny was alive. They were in a bubble together, adrift on a strange, dark island, surrounded by strange plastic sea monsters. But they were together. And Benny was alive. That was the main thing. They were all alive, even if a cold mechanical being was drawing his son's breaths for him. I could get used to this, he thought, spending my days here keeping a bedside vigil. Dear God, even this, these days of talking to and touching a son who could not talk or touch back, would be better than not having Benny in the world. I would settle for this if this were the best you have to offer.

You selfish bastard, he chided himself. Is this a life you would wish for your son, this misery of being chained to a machine? He remembered what Scott had said—that they had to do whatever was best for Benny. Please God, he prayed. Do not put me in that position. Don't let that time come, ever. Do not ask of me what should be asked of no man. Just let me walk out of this hospital with my boy, and I'll never ask you for another thing again.

Benny died a little after six in the morning the next day. They were all gathered around his bed. Ellie and Frank sat on either side of his bed, each of them holding his hand. In a low, quivering voice Ellie sang, "Kisses Sweeter than Wine," one of Benny's favorite songs. Next, she kissed his damp, fevered forehead and said, "It's okay, baby. You've been a real brave boy, but you don't need to fight anymore, okay? You can let go."

Frank had wanted to stop her then, because even after the night doctor had told them at two o'clock that morning that it was time to bring the family in to say their good-byes, even after Dr. Brentwood had come in and told them that the latest lab test had shown overwhelming sepsis, even after he, Frank, had left the room to go call Scott to tell him to drive everybody back to the hospital, he had clung to some strand of crazy hope, had held out for a miracle. He wanted to tell Benny exactly the opposite of what Ellie was telling him: instead of asking that he let go, he wanted to urge his boy to fight, to wrestle with that dark demon, to rise from his deathbed and assume his rightful place. You don't belong in this stinking hospital room, Ben, he had wanted to say. You belong in the Little League baseball park and swimming at Seaflower Lake and going to school at London Elementary. You belong in bed between your mom and me on Sunday mornings and next to me in the car on Saturday afternoons when I take you to baseball practice. You belong on the beach at Hilton Head during the summers and on your little sled on the hill behind our house in the winter.

He closed his eyes, almost smiling to himself at the thought of an exuberant Benny flying down the hill on his blue sled last winter, his blond hair glistening in the light of a wintry sun the color of weak tea. While his eyes were still closed, he heard Ellie cry, "Oh, God, Ben, no." By the time he opened his eyes, his son was gone.

The room tilted, then straightened, then tilted again. Through the tilt, he saw Ellie fling herself on Benny. Careful, he wanted to say, but there were spiderwebs across his mouth and he couldn't speak. And now the webs were being spun across his eyes because his eyes had become slits and he could only see half of the world. Scott was saying something, but he could only hear every fifth word, like a bad cell phone connection. He blinked, tried to focus on what Ellie was saying to him, tried to see her full face, but it looked like a Cubist painting—he could see her pained, open mouth, took in the terror in her right eye, followed the path of a single tear. But he couldn't put it all together.

What finally broke the spell was Ellie's hand. She reached across Benny's reclining body and took his hand in hers. "Frank," she moaned. "Frank, talk to me."

He saw a funnel cloud of words leave his mouth. He noticed Ellie's expressive face react and knew that he was saying all the right things. And he was glad. Proud of himself and the comforting funnel cloud that he was producing. Because inside, *inside*, he was gone. Wandering through the punishing straits of his dry, acrid heart.

CHAPTER 17

The disappointment was a new feeling. From the first day he had met Ellie, he had always been proud of her. Ellie was one of those people who excelled at whatever she did—she was an accomplished cello player, had graduated summa cum laude from her Ph.D. program, had been a well-respected therapist. Not to mention a loving, wonderful partner to him and a devoted, vigilant mom. Which is why he couldn't understand what had made her doze off after knowing that Benny had a fever. He believed her when she'd said that the fever had come down by the time she'd fallen asleep, but surely she could've slept in Benny's room for one lousy night? The worst part was, he couldn't mention this resentment to anyone. He had tried voicing his thoughts to Scott the day before the funeral, but his older brother had stared at him before saying, "It's not Ellie's fault, Frankie. It's nobody's fault. You heard what the doctor said. A few hours wouldn't have made any difference." But he couldn't accept that. A few hours might have made all the difference in the world. A few more hours of antibiotics, fluids, blood pressure medicine—who knows how much that would've helped? If nothing else, he would've received Ellie's phone call sooner, and that would've perhaps meant an earlier flight home and more precious time at his son's bedside.

He turned in bed, knowing he should go downstairs to be with Ellie, who had gotten up hours ago. But he didn't, pinned onto the bed by another memory, one that he had previously swept away into an unlit corner of his mind. But now it fueled his simmering resentment against Ellie. The night before the miscarriage, he remembered, she had gone out with some friends from grad school. They had gone to a dance club where a salsa band was playing. Ellie had come home at two that morning, happy and tired and bragging about how she had danced for three hours straight. Six hours later, the spotting had begun. She had miscarried the baby a few days later, and although no doctor had ever made a connection, he had dimly wondered if the dancing had contributed to the miscarriage. Now, he felt a fresh wave of anger at the memory. Careless, she's so careless, he muttered to himself, even while the rational part of his brain told him that he was being unfair. But he also felt anew the freshness of the loss of the baby. At the time, they had been devastated but not inconsolable—Benny was the bright star in their lives, and they told each other that they would try again and even if it didn't take, they were already blessed with a beautiful boy. But now, Frank felt the absence of the baby. How much more bearable this Sunday would be if there was a reason to get out of bed—a little blond-haired girl, maybe, who would've come in and kissed her daddy and urged him not to sleep away the morning.

He opened his eyes and peered at his watch. Eleven o'clock. He groaned and closed his eyes again. He couldn't remember a day when he'd slept in this late—it would've violated every doctrine in the Church of Benny to have let either of his parents laze around in bed until eleven. But this was the first Sunday in seven years that he was home without Benny in the house—Ben jumping up and down on his parents' bed until they realized that asking him to quiet down was like asking a gushing fire hydrant to suck back its water, and grumpily submitted to his demands; Benny racing through the house until the walls shook with the sound of his excitement; Benny pestering Ellie to make waffles and pancakes for breakfast until she gave in; Benny making a list of all the things he wanted them to do with him that day before they'd even had a chance to say good morning to each other. And best of all, best of all, Benny climbing into bed with them at six o'clock on Sunday mornings and snuggling between both of them. If it were winter he would burrow his tiny body into Frank's, looking for all the world like a little kitten seeking shelter in a warm kitchen. And then Frank would feel something soft and liquid in his chest, something almost feminine, what he imagined was what a woman felt like when she was breast-feeding. Cuddling with Benny made him reappraise everything, re-shaped his body, made him realize that everything that he thought had belonged to him—his muscles, his heart, his strong hands, his broad chest—actually belonged to his son. It gave his body a different purpose, as if his hands were designed for the sole purpose of cradling Benny; his stomach a burrow where Ben could wiggle in for warmth; his chest a pillow for Ben's sweet head. He would lie awake, stroking his son's hair, smiling at Ellie on the other side of the bed, knowing that she was feeling the same intensity of emotions that he was. It bound him to her, this knowledge, in a way that he had never felt connected to another human being. Their love-making had always been a language, expressive, full of words and pauses and the resuming of an ongoing conversation. But even that communion paled before what he felt toward Ellie when they shared their bed with their son. Benny completed the conversation he had started with Ellie years ago.

He heard a loud crash downstairs and was on his feet before he had even opened his eyes. Damn, he thought as he raced down the wooden stairs. Ellie's hurt herself. His stomach muscles clenched at the thought of finding Ellie injured or in pain. "El?" he called. "Where are you?"

There was no answer. But instead, he heard another crashing sound and raced toward the kitchen. At the doorway, he froze. Ellie was standing in front of the sink, surrounded by shards of broken glass. Every few seconds, she was systematically picking up a dinner plate or a glass and dropping it into the stainless steel sink, barely flinching as the object shattered and glass flew toward her face. By the look of it, she had already destroyed a considerable number of plates. Her face was red and streaked with tears, her hair wild. Frank took one step toward her and then stopped as his wife brought another plate crashing into the sink. "El," he yelled, and seeing that she had not heard him, "Ellie. Stop. Stop." He covered the distance between them and grabbed her wrist, making her loosen her grip on a wineglass. "Babe. Stop. What're you doing?" He tugged at her wrist, turning her toward him and making her step away from the sink.

The sound of the splintering glass was replaced by the sound of Ellie's broken, anguished sobbing. "I miss him," she said. "I can't stand the silence in this house."

He pulled her toward him, and she buried her face in his chest, crying loudly. He flinched, each sob landing on him like a blow, reminding him of his own impotence and powerlessness. His wife was in anguish, and he had no way of helping her. He, who from his meager grad student stipend had bought Ellie a new car when her yellow Ford finally bit the dust. He, who had bought this gorgeous Arts and Crafts bungalow simply because Ellie had fallen in love with it while they had walked past it one evening. He had approached the owners the next day, and as luck would have it, they were an elderly couple who had been thinking of moving into a retirement home. By then, he knew Ellie's tastes well enough to know that she would love the dark wooden floors, the crown molding, the cherry cabinets. And so, even though he knew the money would be tight, he went ahead and purchased it. Surprised her with the deed to the house on their first wedding anniversary. Early in their marriage he had made a promise to himself—that he would do everything in his power to make sure that Ellie never regretted her decision to marry him.

But now she was asking him to resurrect their dead son, and he had to look into those dark eyes, eyes that were mad with pain and anguish, and admit failure. His own grief, his own sense of loss, was already unbearable. He felt his body sagging under its weight and had no idea how he could hold up under the weight of Ellie's torment. He looked away. He felt burdened by the desperation that he saw in his wife's eyes. Not this time, he wanted to say. He had been there for Ellie when Anne had had a breast cancer scare. When her father had needed a bypass. When one of her patients had attempted suicide. Each of those times he had been able to prop her up, to rise to the occasion, to ask the right questions of the doctors, or say the right words to his wife. But now she was asking him to fill the silence of a long Sunday afternoon that uncoiled before them like barbed wire, and he didn't have a clue how. Now she was asking him to make up for the absence of Benny, and his toolbox was empty, his hands broken.

"Babe," he groaned. "Oh, my God, Ellie."

They stood in the middle of the kitchen, holding each other. Sunlight poured in, danced on the shards of broken glass, and mocked their misery. Moments passed. Frank felt a shudder start at the base of his spine and travel up the length of his body. He held himself rigid, but it was too late. His body spasmed and then he was sobbing in loud, open bubbles of grief. He shook in Ellie's arms, arms that felt like a boat built out of twigs, unable to carry the oceanic power of his sorrow. "I'm sorry, El," he blubbered. "I don't know what to do or say to help you. I can barely manage to . . ."

She covered his face in kisses. "I know," she said. "It's okay. You don't have to be strong for me."

But he did. And failing to be strong made him feel ineffectual, less manly. He ran his palm over her face, wiping away her tears, and realized the futility of his gesture even while he did so. There will always be more tears, he thought. This is merely the first Sunday in a lifetime of Sundays to come—open, unplanned days that would have no purpose or shape or meaning. Days stretched before them like a banquet they had no appetite for. "I'm going to call Jerry and Susan," he mumbled. "Maybe we can go over there for a few hours."

She turned to him with the expression of a stray, wounded puppy. "Bertie's home," she said simply, and he knew immediately what she meant. Bertie was twelve, but his loud, shouting presence would inevitably remind them of Benny. He cast his mind around, searching for a harmless Sunday afternoon activity that would divert their attention, that would make them forget for ten minutes what had happened. He came up with absolutely nothing. He resented having to be the one to come up with a plan.

"Frank," she said suddenly, an expression on her face he'd never seen before. "I had a weird dream last night. I dreamed that—this will sound weird, I know, but I dreamed that we both drink this pink liquid—it looked like Pepto-Bismol or something—and we're able to see Benny again."

He knew immediately what she was saying, what she was asking, what she was proposing, and his heart raced. Ellie was too proud to actually say the word *suicide* but he knew her well enough to know that she was testing the waters, feeling him out, measuring the depth of his desperation. He knew what it had cost her to share this with him, saw from the sly, crazed expression on her face how little she was in control of her own emotions, how fervently she was hoping he would agree even while praying that he would not. Ellie was a therapist—by profession and by personality she believed in the endless, bountiful possibilities of life, in redemption, in affirmation, in hope as a moral obligation. For her to even think about suicide, let alone mention it, meant that she had stared into the heart of the universe and seen only black. That, like him, she could only imagine the stupefying blankness of an endless row of aimless Sundays. Followed by six more days each week. That, like him, waking up without Benny was like waking up knowing that the sun would not be in the sky that morning. Pointless.

He reached out and raised her chin so that she was looking deep into his eyes. "No Pepto-Bismol for us," he said. "We're not those kind of people." Something flickered in her eyes, but he couldn't read it. "Are we?" he added and when she didn't answer, "El. Are we?"

"No, I guess not."

He stared at her for another moment. "You're all I got in this wide world," he said quietly. "If you have any feelings for me, you gotta make me a promise right now."

She said nothing.

"Ellie."

She shook her head. "Forget I ever said anything. Like I told you, it was a weird dream." And then, "I promise."

He realized he'd been holding his breath. "Okay."

"Can I ask you something?"

"Sure."

"Can we go for a long drive somewhere?"

He let out a sigh of relief, glad to be asked for something he could deliver. "Sure, baby. Anything you want. Tell you what. You go shower, okay? And I'll—I'll just sweep up this mess in the sink."

Ellie made a rueful face. "I'm so sorry."

"Don't be."

They left the house an hour later to go for a drive. That became their new weekend ritual—driving long distances to go to places where nobody knew their name, where expressions of pity and sympathy didn't greet them on the streets and in the grocery stores.

In this way, they got through the first four months of their new life.

CHAPTER 18

She wanted him to laugh. But that seemed impossible. So she wanted him to cry. Crying would be healthy, she thought. Crying would be a prelude to talking, the first step toward getting Frank back.

Benny had been dead for four months. And Frank had glided away from her as silently as a cloud in the sky. Ellie felt acutely the loss of both men in her life. The last time Frank had broken down in her presence, had let her see the depth of his anguish, was the afternoon she had shattered the dishes. Since then he had built a shell around his body, a shell so hard and brittle that if she so much as touched it with her finger, it gave off a white dust. It made her feel lonely, more lonely than she'd felt the morning in the hospital before the first of family members had arrived, more lonely than she'd felt at the funeral where she'd heard the kind words of the mourners as if they were speaking to her from the other side of a glass door. And because she knew something about that deadness of the spirit, that numbness that could spread like a drop of iodine on the tongue, she was worried about Frank. The new Frank, she'd taken to calling him. The new Frank was guarded, secretive, almost shy around her. She had hoped for a comrade, a fellow traveler who could help her navigate this new continent of grief. Instead, she was dealing with a stranger, or worse, an adversary, who planted his harvest of pain on his own plot of land, and seemed resentful when the borders of her sorrow brushed up against his. And because of this, Ellie felt that permission for her to cry and break down in his presence had also been withdrawn.

Last night they had made love for the first time in four months. And it had been terrible. There was a tentativeness, a formality, to their lovemaking that was alien and new. She had tried to tell herself that Frank was being tender, solicitous, but she knew what he really was—watchful.

She had initiated the lovemaking. Turned to him in the middle of the night and pressed herself upon him. Taken his hand and placed it on her breasts and later, between her thighs. Kissed him on his lips with a mounting desperation that she pretended was lust. And he had responded. Had kissed her back passionately. Their bodies worked their way toward each other as effortlessly as they always did. But Ellie sensed some reserve on Frank's part, a hesitation, a missed beat. She had intended their lovemaking to be a cleansing, an act of oblivion. She had wanted to cry, to break down, to claw at the veil of an uncaring universe. To dissolve in a mess of sweat and tears. Had wanted to seek and deliver forgiveness, to replace this hard, cold silence between them with something alive and affirmative. Had wanted the friction of skin to warm their frozen blood. Instead, Frank rolled away after she climaxed, back to his corner of the bed. Instead, she lay there for the longest time, feeling more alone than she had ever felt before. Instead, she stared into the darkness, feeling more distant from her husband than she had the last four months.

She woke up the next morning with a new kind of resolution. Instead of worrying about Frank, she was now worried about herself. She recognized how close to the edge she had walked these past few months and knew herself well enough to know that she could not sustain that degree of misery. That she wanted to belong again to the world and wanted to be made large by her grief, not shrunk by it. That she didn't want to use the tragedy that had befallen her as a crutch, or worse, as a stick to beat up others with. Rather, she wanted to be softened by her grief, made more human. Even if it meant opening herself up to new wounds, new vulnerabilities. She felt capable of this now, felt a new willingness to give up the soft gauze of numbness from which she had peered at the world for the last several months. She would not shrivel, would not become a snail living in her shell, like Frank. And most important, she would not let herself believe that grief was a tribute to her dead son, that she was honoring his memory by not living a full life. How often she had seen her clients fall to the lure of this sweet myth—women who did not date for decades after a divorce, adult children who would never touch ice cream again because their elderly mothers had craved it on their deathbeds, women who had been left by their husbands making a virtue out of celibacy. As if misery was ever the antidote to misery. No, the best way to honor the dead was by living. They had failed Benny these past few months. If their sunny, joyous son was indeed in heaven looking down at them, he would not recognize the people they had become.

She was determined to change that. She didn't see her first client until one o'clock today, and so there was time to drive to the florist and come home armed with a large bouquet of flowers. She arranged them in a large red vase that she placed on the kitchen table.

On the drive to work, she allowed herself to roll down the window and let in the beauty of the world. For the first time in months, she noticed how delicious the sun felt against the skin of her forearm, how delicate the afternoon breeze felt as it slipped into her car, observed the tinkling loveliness of the tiny yellow and blue wildflowers along the side of the freeway. By the time she got into work, her face was flushed with heat and life.

As luck would have it, her first client was Amy Florentine. Amy was a retired schoolteacher, a tall, gruff woman in her late sixties.

She and her longtime husband, Fred, had first come to Ellie four years ago to work through some marital problems. Long after they'd quit couples counseling, Amy had taken to stopping in three or four times a year, for what she referred to as her tune-up sessions.

But this was the first time that Amy had been back since Benny's death, and Ellie wondered if her client had heard the news. She didn't have to wonder for long, though, because as soon as Amy walked into Ellie's office, she extended her hand and said how sorry she was.

"Thank you," Ellie said. They sat facing each other, and Ellie fought the urge to pull the blinds so that Amy couldn't see the motorcade of emotions that crossed her face at the mere mention of her son.

"Well, how have you been?" she started but Amy cut her off. "You remember I lost my son Jim almost twenty-five years ago," she said. "And I tell you honey, there's days when it's still real hard. So be real gentle with yourself."

Ellie did remember. A diving accident where Jim jumped into a lagoon and hit his head on a rock. Fred and Amy had mentioned it to her during their very first session, and Fred had reached over and held his wife's hand all the while they were talking about it. She had liked them immediately, but had been amazed that a couple who had gone through so much together could still have marital problems in their late sixties. Now she knew better.

She also knew better than to lay her burden at a client's feet. But Amy's face was luminous with sympathy and understanding, so different from the faces of those whose lives had been untouched by tragedy, who made all the right sounds and murmured their condolences and then hurried back into the bright lights of their good fortune. And so she found herself asking, "Does it ever get any easier?"

Amy Florentine looked at her for the longest time. Then she shook her head. "You're asking the wrong question. What you're trying to do, Ellie—what we all do—is you're trying to salvage something of your past life. But it doesn't work that way. What the death of a child does is that it wipes everything out. Clears the decks. The plain truth is, honey, what you once had is gone. So what you have to do is build a new life. From scratch. And the bitch of it is, you're not left with much. So you gather in every miserable twig and leaf that you can find and you build with that."

"I still get tricked all the time," Ellie said. "Every morning I wake up, and my first thought is, Benny's gonna be late for school, or Damn, I forgot to pack Ben his lunch. And then I remember, and it's like dying a little bit all over again."

"That part will go away," Amy said. "But I'll tell you something right now, Ellie, that nobody else is gonna tell you—the pain will never go away. It's always there, even years and years later. And there's so much pressure to bury it. It's just the way our culture is— even grief comes with an expiration date, you know? You're supposed to nod and smile because raw emotion embarrasses other people."

"I sense it already," Ellie whispered. "I ran into Benny's old teacher at the store the other night, and when she asked how I was doing, I told her the truth. Not good, I said. And she immediately changed the subject."

"I know. My Jim was twenty when he died. All his friends who were with him that night at the lagoon, boys who practically grew up in my house—nothing. They all turn their heads away when I approach." She fixed her gaze on Ellie. "I'm telling you all this so that you won't take it personally when it happens to you. It's just human nature, honey. They don't mean anything by it."

Ellie smiled. "I feel like I should be paying you for this session."

"Nonsense," Amy said immediately. "Fred and I came to you in the first place because we'd heard you were a real person. Not one of those know-it-all, theory-sprouting robots who call themselves thera-pists." She rolled her eyes. "Oh, honey, don't make me name names."

"I know what you mean," Ellie said. "I went to school with some of them."

She didn't get done until six that evening, but she walked into the house charged with a new feeling of resolution. Frank was already home and was sitting on the couch sipping a glass of wine. She went and sat beside him. "That looks nice." She sighed, eyeing his wineglass. The old Frank would've immediately offered her a sip from his glass. The new Frank jumped off the couch and got up to pour her her own glass. She made herself not notice the difference. "Thanks, hon." She smiled. "How was your day?"

He shrugged. "Nothing special. Same old, same old." He didn't ask her how her day had been. She made herself not notice.

She finished her wine and then got off the couch. "Cyndi Sheehan is speaking on campus tonight. I was thinking of going after supper. I don't suppose you would want to go?"

He stared at her. "What're you talking about?"

"You know who she is, right? She's the peace activist who lost her son in Iraq?"

"I know who she is, Ellie. Obviously. What I don't understand is why you would want to subject yourself to more sad stories when we are barely—" He cut himself off. "Forget it."

"No, finish what you were saying."

He turned to face her, his eyes shiny with anger. "I'm finished."

"What are you so mad about? Why are you treating me like this?"

"Don't start on me, Ellie. You've been itching for a fight since the moment you walked in. From before that, even."

He was giving her a headache. "Frank, what the hell are you talking about? I was actually in a good mood when I came in today."

"I see that," he yelled. "I noticed. As if anyone could miss the red vase in the kitchen. And the goddamn flowers."

Ellie looked at Frank, fearful for his sanity. "That's what's set you off? The fact that I bought flowers? I was just trying to cheer myself up."

"Cheer yourself up by making the house look like a goddamn

funeral home? It's been four months since we buried our boy, and I still see him in his coffin every night. And you, you . . ."

She flew back to the couch and threw her arms around him. "Oh, honey. That was the last thing on my mind. Oh, God, Frank. I can't live like this. I can't live in a home where flowers remind us of death instead of life. Please, babe."

He leaned into her for a moment, and then he stiffened. "Just leave me alone," he mumbled. "I—I just have to deal with this in my own way." He reached for his wineglass, using the movement to get out of her arms.

"Can't we just talk?" she tried, but his aloof expression when he turned to face her was the answer she needed.

They sat on the couch in silence for a minute, and then Ellie pushed herself off. "Listen," she said. "I don't feel like cooking supper tonight. How about if we both manage on our own? There's leftovers in the fridge."

"So you're going to go to this peace rally thing?" he asked.

She wavered for a moment, wondering if this was his way of reaching out to her, asking her to spend the evening with him. But then she remembered the conversation she'd had with herself earlier today, about wanting to be enlarged by tragedy rather than shrunken, about using her loss to connect her to the lives of others. Besides, if Frank needed her to stay, he had to learn to ask.

"Yes," she said, and turned away first.

BOOK FOUR

Autumn and Winter 2007

Girbaug, India

CHAPTER 19

The drumming was thrilling—loose and wild and yet totally controlled. It brought out something in Ellie that she hadn't felt in a long time—a nervous excitement as well as a deep happiness, the kind she normally felt only when faced with the vastness of the ocean or in Big Sky country. This is India, she kept saying to herself, I'm in India. As if she had just arrived.

Before her, Asha, carrying a short red stick in her hand, danced with a man from the village. All traces of the demure, shy girl who acted as Ellie's translator were gone. In her place was a whirling, twirling, gyrating seductress who rhythmically struck her baton or *dandiya* against the one her dance partner was holding, who moved and swayed to the incessant pounding of the *dhols*. Along with maybe two dozen other villagers, the couple was dancing in the clearing in front of Nandita's school and clinic.

All of Girbaug's residents seemed to have turned out in their finest clothing for the Diwali celebration this November. Ellie snuck a sidelong glance at Frank. He had been reluctant to come, afraid of the reception he would get from the villagers. But Nandita had marched into their home a few nights ago and told him sternly that he had to attend, that the villagers would take his absence from their most important holiday celebration as a slight. "Besides, Frank, you might actually have a good time," she'd added sarcastically. And Frank had grinned and told Nandita that she sounded exactly like Ellie and that he could fight one of them at a time but once they ganged up against him, he had no goddamn choice but to acquiesce.

Ellie was glad he was here. And, judging from the way his fingers were involuntarily tapping against his thigh as he kept time to the music, so was he. In his open white shirt and dark green pants Frank looked gorgeous, she thought. The sun was setting behind them, and it lit up Frank's golden hair like a streetlamp.

She wasn't the only one who had noticed, apparently. A cry went up from the crowd as Mausi, the village's oldest resident at ninety-two, got to her feet and hobbled her way to the clearing where the dancers were gathered. She was supported on either arm by two boys who were Ellie's students and whom she assumed were Mausi's grandsons. But as the three-person procession moved up to the front row, where Frank and Ellie were sitting with Ramesh, Nandita, Shashi, and a few other westerners who were visiting Shashi's resort, Mausi stopped. Shaking off the boy who was holding her right arm, she reached out one bony hand and ran her gnarled fingers through Frank's hair. Frank froze, his eyes darting toward Ellie for help. But then Mausi removed her hand, gathered her fingers together, put them to her lips, and flung a kiss at Frank, who had turned three shades of red. All around them, the crowd roared with laughter. Hoots and whoops rose in the air.

But Mausi was not done. Still standing beside Frank, she pantomimed that she wanted him to escort her to the dance floor. Frank looked as if he'd been drilled into his chair. It didn't help matters that Ramesh, sitting between Frank and Ellie, was bouncing up and down yelling, "She is wanting you to do *dandiya* with her, Frank."

"I can't," Frank said finally. "Tell her, I can't—I don't dance."

But just then two of the drummers strayed from the clearing and made their way to where they were sitting. *"Chalo ji, chalo,"* one of them chanted, and the pounding got even more fervent and loud.

Nandita leaned over. "Guess you have no choice, Frank," she grinned over the noise of the drums. "Mausi always gets to choose her first partner."

Mouthing a silent *fuck* that only Ellie could hear, Frank let one of the drummers pull him to his feet. The crowd roared. Mausi grinned, showing all of her three teeth. The dancers opened up a space for the newcomers. One of the men handed Frank a baton and showed him a few steps.

He looks like a clumsy-footed white man, Ellie thought with bemusement as she watched her husband struggle to clink the baton in time with Mausi's. It didn't help that Mausi, bent with osteoporosis, came up to his waist. What Ellie had always loved about Frank was his lithe, catlike surefootedness, which made him a wonderful dance partner. But here, dancing in the open air under a darkening sky, surrounded by brown-skinned men and women dressed in a dazzling array of reds and greens and yellows, he reminded her of an elderly man in those checked green pants at a golf outing.

Nandita must have read her mind. "You have to go help him," she said. "He looks miserable out there." And before Ellie could answer, Nandita was pulling up both Shashi and Ellie. "Come on. I'm dying to dance."

Ellie didn't need to be asked a second time. From the time they'd arrived here for the feast and celebration, from the second she had heard first the Bollywood music over the loudspeakers and later the beating of the *dhols*, from the instant she had taken in the dazzling beauty of the village women and seen the laughing excitement of the children as they set off their fireworks—the rockets that raced in a zigzag line toward the sky, the fountains that erupted in a shower of red and blue sparks, the spirals that spun in an orbit of light and color before dying out—she had felt something relax within her, felt an expansive, giddy joy. Also, a sense of belonging that she didn't quite understand. Yesterday, while visiting the homes of some of the village women who couldn't come to the clinic, she had noticed that each mud-baked hut had a clay *diva* at its entrance. The simplicity of the tiny earthenware oil lamp had brought a lump to her throat. She thought of them as emblematic of the quiet, simple dignity of the people who lived in those homes.

She had tried describing Diwali, or the Festival of Lights, to her parents last year. Imagine July Fourth lasting for a week, she'd said, but she knew that didn't quite capture the sheer lavishness, beauty, and generosity of the festivities. Just the universality of the offering of food—there was no way to explain that to her middle-class parents. Every home in Girbaug bought or made sweetmeats for Diwali and distributed them among neighbors, friends, and visitors. All the women who had come to see her at the clinic yesterday brought her a few pieces of sweets. All of them, no matter how poor. The mothers of the children who came to school also sent an offering of some kind. In one case, a child had simply given her a single piece of rock sugar. It was like Christmas, except you exchanged gifts with the whole town.

Now she was trying to control the sway of her hips, trying hard to resist the tug of the pounding drums that were making her lose her inhibitions, making her want to dance manically, the way she used to in nightclubs when she was in her teens. But that was the beauty of the *dandiya* dance—it celebrated the paradoxical joy of movement and restraint, of delirium within a structure. This was not about individual expression but about community.

Frank turned to her with something akin to relief. She saw the beads of sweat on his face. "Hey," she yelled, above the music, tapping his baton lightly with hers. "Having fun?"

"I've had better dance partners before," he said wryly, but then he grinned, as if he was having a good time despite himself.

Nandita and Shashi made their way up to them, Shashi shaking his hips in such an uncharacteristically uninhibited way, it made

Ellie giggle. There was something nerdy and a little absurd about Shashi, and she loved that about him.

Nandita, on the other hand, was all business. "Come on, Frank, move," she said, striking her stick smartly against his. "You're dancing like a fucking mortician."

They danced in a small circle for a few minutes and then were joined by the other westerners. They expanded the circle to let them in, but Ellie almost immediately lost interest, felt a kind of deflation. She also became aware that they had unwittingly formed a cocoon, their own private circle that excluded the villagers. As soon as she could, she stepped away and began to dance with some of her younger students. Frank followed her in a few minutes. She saw that he had abandoned his stiff posture and was genuinely enjoying himself now, sweating freely, loosening the buttons of his shirt. "Boy, do they ever let up and take a break in between numbers?" he grinned. "This is like dancing at one of those techno clubs."

"Close your eyes," she yelled back. "Just dance with your eyes closed. It's a wonderful feeling."

"And risk clobbering that old lady on the head with my stick? No thanks."

"No," she said, looking closely at him. "Just dance with me. You'll be able to do it, you'll see."

So they did. For a full five minutes they danced with each other with their eyes shut. To their astonishment, they were completely in sync, never rapping each other on the knuckles with their sticks, never missing a beat. Ellie opened her eyes first. She took a step closer to him, and as if sensing that movement, his eyes flew open. "You see?" she said, as if she'd scored an important victory, transmitted some essential information to him.

"I see," he replied. "And I love you. Very much."

"You're my guy." She felt she was being maudlin, sentimental, about to cross that thin line between happiness and melancholy. But she didn't care. It suddenly seemed like the most important thing on earth that Frank knew what he meant to her.

"I know," he said quietly. And then, "Thanks for bringing me here. This is quite wonderful."

She flung her arms wide open, smacking the man dancing next to her. "This is my India," she said dramatically. "Now you see why I love it here."

Even above the music she heard the envy in his voice. "You're lucky. The India I deal with every day is nerve-wracking."

"Don't think about that tonight. Just . . . enjoy."

A rocket whizzed over their heads and landed on the ground just past the dancers. Frank looked nervously over to where a group of teenaged boys were setting off the firecrackers. "I hope these kids know what they're doing," he said. "That was a little too close for comfort."

Just then, one of the boys lit a cone-shaped firecracker. A shower of blue and red erupted from its mouth and came cascading down in colorful streams. "God," Ellie shouted. "I love these fireworks so much more than the ones back home. These are so much closer to the ground and—I don't know—this feels more democratic, some- how."

Frank smiled. "Methinks you're in love with India."

She smiled. "I am." She waved her arms again. "Look around. How could you not be in love with a country with so much color and vigor?"

Ramesh came dancing up to them. The boy was wearing a white cotton kurta and pajamas with a maroon vest. Ellie thought he looked more beautiful than she'd ever seen him. The boy was car- rying himself with a self-consciousness that she knew came from wearing new clothes, and she was glad Edna had bought him this outfit for Diwali. She resolved to use Christmas as a pretext to buy Ramesh a bunch of new outfits. Now she turned her head and looked around for Edna and Prakash, but they were lost in the crowd that sat behind them. She had offered to have the housekeepers ride with them earlier this evening, but Edna had whispered in a conspiratorial tone, "No, thank you, miss. Prakash is in a foul-foul mood today. Better you go alone, only. Just take Ramesh."

"I love this jacket," she now said to the boy over the music, and was gratified to see Ramesh beam.

"It's velvet," he replied seriously, fingering the soft material.

"Yeah, you look like a young prince," Frank said. His tone was light, teasing even, but Ellie could detect the pleasure in his voice as he inspected the boy dancing next to him.

"When I grow up, I want to be a prince," Ramesh said. He cast Frank a mischievious look. "I know, I know. In order to be anything I wanting to be, I need to study today."

Frank threw back his head and laughed. Behind him, a rocket soared into the inky black sky and then showered back to earth in splinters of color and light. Ellie caught her breath. Her mind photographed the moment—Frank with his head tilted back, his hair damp with sweat against his forehead, framed by a cascade of tiny lights, held in time and space by the loud, incessant pounding of the thunderous drums.

"Made you laugh," Ramesh said. It was a new game between the two of them, their own version of tag. Somewhere, Ellie supposed, one of them was keeping score on who made the other laugh more.

Like someone breaking off a conversation in mid-sentence, the drumming stopped. Momentum kept Ellie's body moving for a full second after the music ceased. She looked around and saw that some of the other dancers looked as dazed as she felt. *Danceus interruptus*, she thought to herself, and then giggled at her own silliness.

A thin, tall man whom Ellie recognized as the *doodhwalla*, the milkman who came to their door every morning, strode into the middle of the clearing. "Brothers and sisters," he said in Hindi. "It is time to share a meal together." The crowd stirred, but he silenced them. "But first, we must honor the guests in our midst." Turning to where Ellie and Frank stood panting, he glanced at them and then sought out Nandita and Shashi. "Please," he said. "You will lead us to the food."

Ellie looked around for Nandita, who immediately came up to her side. *"Shukriya,"* she called out. "We are honored to be here." She turned to Ellie and Frank. "They want us to be the first at the table. Come, let's go." Ellie smiled at the milkman, to ensure that he knew they understood.

The staff at the clinic had cleared the desks from the classrooms and set up a long dining table for the westerners in their midst. The villagers squatted on their haunches on the floor and were served on the traditional banyan leaves. Ellie watched in amazement as Mausi bent her ninety-two-year-old knees and squatted on the ground. She thought of Josetta, another therapist in her practice, who had had two knee replacements at the age of fifty-two. For a second she thought of suggesting that the rest of them join the villagers on the ground, but Frank and the couple from Germany were already seating themselves, and she thought better of it. Ever since the fight she and Frank had had at the July Fourth picnic, she was trying very hard to tone it down, not to put Frank on the defensive for being what he was—a middle-class white American. Besides, she was not sure that her untested knees could survive a long dinner spent squatting on the floor.

However, despite the best of intentions, she could not abide the thought of sitting next to the German couple for dinner. They were headed to Dharamsala in a few days to spend a couple of weeks at an ashram and talked incessantly about finding spirituality and enlightenment as if these were items they could buy from a catalog. When she'd first met them earlier this evening, she'd thought they were kidding, playing at being caricatures of the clueless Western tourist. But watching the carefully constructed blankness on Nandita's face, it had dawned on her that they were serious about believing that they would leave India after two weeks having found what they were looking for. She much rather preferred the wry humor of Richard Thomas, the gay British journalist who was traveling through India. Now she looked around for Richard and, upon spotting him, lunged toward him. "Shall we sit together?" she asked, ignoring the frantic looks Frank was throwing her way, as he silently pointed to the empty chair beside him.

Richard arched an eyebrow. "Ingrid and Franz getting to you?"

She grinned. "Naaaawww," she drawled. Next, she turned toward Nandita. "Get Shashi to go sit next to Frank," she implored. "I'll owe you, forever."

She dared not meet Frank's eye as she sat down next to Richard. But a few moments later, her guilt at abandoning Frank to Ingrid's earnest spirituality evaporated, carried away in the aromas of the steaming food she was being served. She bit into an onion pakora; tore a piece from a light, flaky roti; dipped the bread into a thick, spicy curry; cooled her tongue on some cucumber yogurt; picked up a tender piece of fish with her fork. She felt a little spiritual herself, swept up in a kind of rapture at the intensity of flavors. "How on earth can one country have so many wonderful foods?" she gasped.

"You asking *me* about good food?" Richard said. "I'm British, remember?"

She laughed. "London has some great restaurants."

"Yeah, and they're all Indian."

One of Ellie's older male students came to their table, carrying a large stainless steel tray full of glasses. "You will have a lassi, miss?" he asked.

She took a long gulp of the cool yogurt drink. "I think I'm having an out-of-body experience," she said.

"Easy there," Richard said. "Your husband's boring holes into my back, anyway. I wouldn't want him to think I'm the reason for this look of ecstasy on your face."

"I like you, Richard. You remind me of my brother-in-law."

"Your brother-in-law is gay?" Richard deadpanned.

Ellie spluttered, blowing lassi out of her nose. "Oh, stop. Look what you've made me do." She turned to him, a pleading look on her face. "Can't you stay with us here in Girbaug? I can talk Shashi into giving you a really good rate at the hotel."

Nandita, who was sitting at Richard's left and had been talking to Franz, turned toward them. "What on earth are you two *guss-puss*ing about?" She leaned over to face Ellie. "Frank's going to kill you on the way home, darling. You pulled a really dirty trick on him."

Ellie looked rueful. "I know. But I can't deal anymore with stupid foreigners." She glanced at Richard. "Present company excepted."

"Who're you calling a foreigner, you Yank? My people were here in India while yours were—"

"I know. Swinging from trees."

"Something like that."

"Nice to hear you two imperialists arguing about your claims to India," Nandita said. Her tone was bemused, her eyebrows raised, and they all chuckled.

Frank came up to her as soon as dinner was over. "I'll pay you back for this," he said, but his tone was light, his eyes friendly.

"I'm sorry. I'm a rotten wife." She shot him a look of sympathy. "Was it absolutely excruciating?"

"Well, it's all a matter of perspective. I'm sure a brain tumor or hemorrhoids would be worse."

She was still laughing when Nandita came up to them. "Don't hate me for inviting them," she said to Frank. "They insisted on getting the 'full cultural experience.' Poor Shashi had no choice."

"I'll forgive you for the price of a few invitations to dinner," Frank said promptly. He stopped, a frown on his face. "Speaking of dinner, this was quite a lavish affair. How can these folks afford this, Nan?"

Nandita looked embarrassed. "Well, actually we, Shashi and I, we sponsor this celebration. I mean, it's always been traditional for the villagers to have a communal feast. But in the last few years, well, the hotel is doing so well, that we offered to—chip in."

Frank nodded. "That's good," he said vaguely. Then, "I tell you what. If I'm still here next year, I'll make sure HerbalSolutions becomes a cosponsor of this feast. That is, if you will have us."

Both women spoke simultaneously. "What do you mean, if you're here next year? Why won't you be?"

"Whoa, whoa." Frank laughed, stepping back from them. He turned to face Ellie. "In case you've forgotten, babe, I've only signed a two-year contract. Everything has to be negotiated again soon."

"Oh, bullshit," Ellie said. "Pete's not gonna refuse you if you tell him that's what you want to do."

Frank grinned and placed one arm around his wife. "I'm gonna have to pry this one loose when it's time to leave India—and I'm hoping that won't be for a few more years," he added.

Nandita stepped closer to Frank and rubbed his back. "Glad to hear it," she said. "I can't imagine Girbaug without the two of you."

"Likewise." Ellie heard the sincerity in Frank's voice and was glad for it.

But her mood had soured slightly. They lingered at the feast for another half hour, watching another fireworks display, watching the young people dance as Hindi film music blared from the loudspeakers. Nothing has changed, Ellie kept telling herself, you are here, be present, live in the moment. But just the talk of returning to America had cast a pall on the evening, made her realize the impermanence, the precariousness, of their life here. The thought of returning home produced nothing but a dull sadness in her. Just a few days ago, her mother had asked on the phone whether they had bought their tickets for coming home for Christmas, and she had heard the joy and anticipation in her mom's voice and felt compelled to fake an enthusiastic response. The fact was, she was dreading the ten-day trip. She had already made it clear to Frank that she would not visit Ann

Arbor. The plan was to fly into Cleveland and stay with Anne and Bob. Unlike past years, Scott and his mother were coming to Cleveland for Christmas. Frank would drive to Ann Arbor for a couple of days to check on the tenants they were renting their house to and to meet with the folks at HerbalSolutions. He would take Ramesh with him.

Yes, Ramesh. It had been Frank's idea, of course, to take Ramesh home with them. When he had first suggested it to Ellie in early October, she had demurred but not put up much of a fight. She was counting on several things—the fact that it would be difficult to get a visa for the boy, the fact that Prakash would throw a fit at the thought of being away from his son for ten days, the fact that Edna, being a Christian, would want to have her son with her over the holidays, even the fact that Frank would realize the awkwardness of returning to his family in America with Ramesh.

What she had not counted upon was desperation. First, there was Edna's desperation to provide her son with every opportunity that she knew that she and her alcoholic husband could not, her pent-up desire to give her son what she saw as his birthright—the love that his grandparents should've showered upon him and that he had been deprived of. Now, she saw Frank and Ellie as an unexpected answer to her prayers, de facto guardians of her son, with the means to offer Ramesh opportunities even her parents could've only dreamed of. Edna became a tigress, clawing at her husband's resistance, chomping up his protests. "He's going," she declared. "My son will be first in Girbaug to go to America. No one will stop him."

Then there was Frank's desperation. Unable to face the long flight to America, with its echoes of that terrible flight from Thailand; unable to imagine sitting down for Christmas dinner without seeing the boy who was missing; paralyzed at the thought of going to the Ann Arbor house to check on the renters, knowing that the house would echo with the voice and laughter of his dead son; terrified at being under the same American sky, breathing the same chilly air, walking on the same hard ground, that his son had. So he had first gotten Ramesh a passport and then called Tom Andrews to request the embassy folks to issue the boy his tourist visa.

Finally, there was Prakash's desperation. Unable to think straight, not knowing what this strange new force was that had entered his life in the guise of a tall white man who was obsessed with his son, he vowed every morning to stop drinking so that he could be sober long enough to solve this puzzle. But he reached for the bottle almost absentmindedly as the day, with its countless humiliations and chores and demands, ground him down. Stung and hurt by the venom with which his wife spoke to him, believing her threats to leave him if he didn't give in to her demands, Prakash hovered between bravado and capitulation. The prospect of losing Edna terrified him. So he reluctantly agreed to offer up his son to the Americans for ten days, in exchange for keeping his wife forever.

"What's wrong?" Frank said to Ellie on the way home. "Your whole mood has changed."

"Sorry." She thought for a moment and then decided to come clean. "I'm nervous about the upcoming trip to the States."

Frank sighed. "I thought so. I thought you got quiet after the conversation about leaving India." He shifted in the car seat so that he could face her. "You really love this place so much?"

"I do. Though right now, it's all mixed up with the dread of going home. Of facing everybody. I don't know what to expect— on one hand, I'm dreading any reference to Benny, any expressions of sympathy. On the other hand, if my parents try to sweep it under the carpet, if they don't speak his name, that will infuriate me even more. It's like I'm not being fair to them, you know?"

"It will be almost two years since we were home, Ellie," he said quietly. "We have to face up to what has happened to—to the fact that America is home."

Easy for you to say, she wanted to say. I see how well you're doing facing up to reality, losing yourself in the company of a nine-year-old boy we are practically stealing from his parents, unable to bear the thought of going home without having him by your side. But she could not, would not, say this out loud. She wanted Frank to retain whatever delusions brought him comfort, wanted to allow him to decorate his life with whatever streamers of hope he could.

"You're right," she said. She felt tired, unable to capture the thrilling excitement she had felt earlier this evening.

Frank put his arm around her and pulled her close to him. "Don't worry, Ellie," he murmured. "It's only a short visit. And it will be good to be with family again."

She rested her head on his shoulders, allowing herself to be lulled by the promise of his sweet lie.

CHAPTER 20

Ellie heard it first. A chattering, a sound that appeared to be organic, part of the natural world, like crickets in the dark or birds at dusk. Only, it was now dawn. She and Frank were still in bed, but she awoke sensing something outside their bedroom window, a disturbance, an unrest, an uneasy shift of the wind. She sat up in bed, rubbed the sleep out of her eyes, and looked out the open window. And saw nothing except for the green expanse of the front lawn and, beyond it, the sea.

But then came a different noise, and as if in response, the hair on Ellie's arm stood up. It was an unearthly sound, loud and continuous, a keening that hung in the air. And under the high-pitched wail was accompaniment—a deep rumble that provided the percussion to the wailing. Ellie's feet hit the ground. Grabbing her robe around her, she walked through the living room to the front porch. Her stomach dropped, and she gasped. For a split second, she thought that perhaps she was still asleep and the scene before her belonged in a nightmare. Then she smelled the salty sea air, felt the sweat forming on her forehead, looked at the woman who was keening, and knew it was the worst kind of nightmare—one that was real.

A crowd of about thirty had gathered on the front lawn of her bungalow. She recognized many of the men from the Diwali celebration just a few days ago. On that day, their faces had been slack with pleasure and warmth. Today, they were looking at the house as if debating whether to burn it down, their faces pinched and tight with anger and resentment. All except for the woman who had collapsed on the grass, slithering on the ground like a snake, occasionally raising her head toward the heavens to let out another cry. Despite her shocked reaction, some part of Ellie took in the painterly quality of the scene in front of her—the pale gray morning light and the trembling sea in the far distance, a still life of tight-jawed, frozen men and in the close-up, a writhing, wailing woman half singing her grief to the disinterested heavens.

One of the men spotted her on the porch, and the painting splintered and then rearranged itself. The man let out a cry and pointed toward her, and within a second, at least a third of the men had struck the same pose, pointing at her. Despite being inside her house, being separated from them by a good twenty feet, Ellie suddenly felt exposed, naked, as if the house was built of paper and rags and one angry breath by the mob could bring it crashing down. She watched in horror as one of the villagers bent down and picked up a small rock and then hurled it toward the house. Toward her. She ducked, although the stone missed its mark by several feet. But the attack brought her to her senses, and she fled indoors, screaming for Frank to wake up. The mob jeered her as she retreated into the house and then the chanting began.

"HerbalSolutions *murdabad*," they shouted.

"Shame, shame, 'Merica go home."

"Down, down with HerbalSolutions."

"Long live Mukesh bhai."

And soaring above their political slogans, as if giving the truest expression to their anger and sorrow, the keening.

"Frank," Ellie yelled as she raced through the house. She reached the bedroom and saw that he was still asleep. "Frank," she said shaking him roughly. "Wake up. Wake up. We have a riot outside our house."

His eyes flew open and he sat upright in bed. "Huh? What? What's going on?"

"I don't know, but you better come see." Ellie could hear the hysteria in her voice and struggled to control it. "Come see," she repeated.

Frank stumbled into the coffee table on the way to the porch, gnashed his teeth, and followed his wife. He gasped at what he saw. The crowd had swelled by another ten men. But what arrested their attention was the body laid out on their lawn, to the right of the wailing woman, who had crawled over to the dead body and was sobbing over it, beating her breast with her open hand. As the crowd spotted Frank, a shout went up. "Frank sahib *murdabad*," a few of them shouted.

"Frank," a stunned Ellie stammered. "What's happening? I think that man is—dead."

Frank's face was white. He looked more scared than Ellie had ever seen him. "I don't have a fucking clue," he replied hoarsely.

A youth broke out of the crowd, his face twisted with rage. He stepped around the prone body and approached the porch. Instinctively, Ellie took a step backward. But even in her terror, she noticed that Frank was standing his ground. As the young man came closer, Ellie recognized him as one of her students. But her brain wouldn't unfreeze long enough to remember his name.

The student was pointing to the body of the man. "Look," he spat. "Mukesh dead. Kill himself by hanging. From *girbal* tree belong to us. But your guard not allowing him to pick leaves. He and his family starving. He kill himself."

And suddenly, in an awful moment, it all fell into place for Ellie as she recognized the keening woman. It was Radha, her client, the domestic abuse victim whose house she had visited. She remembered the encounter with the woman's husband a few months ago. What had Asha told her about what he'd said? That he had earned his livelihood plucking and selling the leaves of the *girbal* tree, which was now off limits to the local people.

But no time now to think because amazingly, incredulously, Frank was moving away from her and toward the mob. "Frank," she screamed. "What the hell are you doing?"

"Phone Deepak," he hissed at her. "Go in now and call him. Tell him to send the police over *now*." But Ellie couldn't move. She stood transfixed as she saw Frank move closer to the edge of the porch and looked down at the crowd. "Listen," he yelled. "I'm sorry for the— for what has happened. But HerbalSolutions had nothing to do with this. You need to go home now. We don't want any trouble."

Ellie moved indoors and toward the phone. "Come in, Frank," she called. "Get out of there."

Her hands shook like birds in a rainstorm as she dialed Deepak's number. She hung up as soon as she'd asked him to send the police over. Frank had followed her into the house, and they stood in the living room, staring at each other, not pretending to hide the fear on their faces. "What'll we do if they come in?" she began to ask, and then stopped as she heard Radha's voice call her name. "Ellie bai," the voice said, followed by a long tirade in Hindi. Other, male voices took up the chant. "Ellie bai, Ellie bai." Then, a loud, "Miss Ellie. Radha wanting to talk you."

Frank read her mind. "Don't you even think about it," he said. "You're not stepping out there."

The chanting started again. "HerbalSolutions, shame, shame."

"Frank sahib *murdabad*."

"Long live Mukesh bhai."

"I know her," Ellie gasped. "The woman who is . . . the widow. Maybe I should go talk with her."

"Don't you dare," Frank began. "You hear those stones pelting the porch? There's no telling—"

They huddled together on the couch, looking at each other in incomprehension. Just when the cacophony got unbearable, their ears took in a new sound. For a moment, it sounded like whips striking the air, and then there was screaming and someone yelled, "Po-lice. *Bhago, bhago*, run."

Ellie felt her whole body shake. "Do something," she cried. "Make them stop."

But Frank sat down heavily on the couch and held his head in his hands. He looked small, diminished, as if something had collapsed within him. "I can't believe this," he muttered. "We have a fucking riot in our front yard."

The screams got louder and more agonized. They heard a series of piercing whistles and orders being barked. And then suddenly, abruptly, it was silent. For a second Ellie was thankful, but as the silence sustained itself, it began to sound creepy, ominous. "What's going on?" she said. She forced her legs to stop shaking and inched closer to the porch again. She was in time to see a swarm of khaki-colored policemen roughly herding the villagers down the stone steps. She looked for Radha but couldn't see her. They must've arrested her first. She flinched as she saw the indifferent, brutal way in which two of the policemen wrapped the corpse in a white sheet and carried it away. Her eyes fell on a tall, burly man in civilian clothes who seemed to be orchestrating the whole scene. She watched as he curtly spoke to the men removing the body, noticed the crook of his index finger as he pointed toward the house. As if he had felt her staring at him, the plainclothesman looked up and smiled. Ellie shuddered. She felt voyeuristic, corrupt, implicated. Still, she stood her ground, fighting the urge to scuttle into the house and get back into bed and pull the covers over her head, pretending that the last half hour had not happened. The India of the Diwali celebration— the gentle, generous India, the country of red flared skirts and twirling dancers, of clay lamps and firecrackers that emitted light and beauty—that India seemed as dead as the corpse in her front yard.

She suddenly saw India as Frank had grown to see it—corrupt, unpredictable, volatile, and even sinister. Like the man who was walking toward the porch, with lips that smiled and eyes that were as cold as a January morning in Ann Arbor.

"Memsahib," he said, nodding at her as he came up the stairs.

"Stop," she said. She had no intention of letting this man into her house. "Who are you?"

The lizard eyes grew colder even as the smile grew. "No need to be afraid, Ellie memsahib," he said. "I'm Gulab Singh. Head of security at HerbalSolutions."

Gulab Singh. Ellie racked her brain to remember why the name sounded familiar. And then she remembered Nandita telling her about Gulab's reputation among the villagers. "I wish Frank hadn't hired this fellow to head security, Ellie," she had once said. "He's a disgusting man. Grew up in the village and then went away for a few years—I don't know, says he was a big shot in the army or something. In any case, all the village folks are terrified of him."

Now, eyeing Gulab, Ellie felt her mouth twisting with dislike. "What's going to happen to those people?" she said, wondering where Frank had disappeared. "Where have they been taken?"

Gulab made a dismissive cluck. "Don't worry about them, memsahib," he said. "They'll be dealt with properly." Something about his manner, his refusal to make eye contact with her, told Ellie that he had sensed her dislike of him. But before she could respond to his contemptuous dismissal of the fate of the villagers, she saw him straighten and smile broadly. "Good morning, Frank sahib," he said, and Ellie felt Frank behind her.

"Not a good morning, Gulab," Frank said curtly. "Not a good morning, at all. What is going on here?"

Gulab was on the porch now, and Ellie smelled a faint but cloying scent. Women's perfume, she thought with wonder. This jerk has women's perfume on. "A thousand apologies, sir," Gulab was saying, his manner as cloying as his scent. "I was at the factory when I heard the news. I had no idea these scoundrels were planning this. Would've bashed their heads, if I'd known. But it seems they found him—the body—early this morning. What I am now needing to find out is which mischief maker decided to come to your good home and disturb your sleep."

"Listen," Frank said. "I don't want any more violence, you hear? The last thing we need is more trouble." He paused for a moment and ran his hand over his tired face. "Who is this guy, anyway? What did he kill himself for? And why the fuck are they angry at me? What did I have to do with this?"

"Frank sahib," Gulab said. "You go get some rest. And please, not to come into the factory today. I will take care of everything."

"That's bullshit." Ellie's voice was louder and sharper than she'd intended. "My husband is not a child. He needs to understand what is going on." She looked at Frank, silently urging him to side with her, to demand an explanation from this man whom she disliked and distrusted more with each passing moment.

Frank looked from Ellie to Gulab, as if just picking up on the hostility that ran like a black wire from one to the other. "What's going on?" he said. "Who was that man?"

"A known Communist, sir," Gulab replied. "Hating Americans. Best of friends with Anand. Hung himself because he knew we were watching him."

Ellie was incredulous. Who the hell was this man who was treating Frank like a puppet? Did he himself believe a word of what he was saying? Did Frank realize that he was being fed fiction? Would he acquiese or protest?

"This is such crap," she said. "I know this guy." She turned to Frank. "I didn't tell you. I met this man who . . . who has died . . . when I was at the clinic a few months ago. His wife is one of my clients. He went into a tirade when he saw me in his home." She saw Frank's eyes widen but forced herself to continue. "I didn't want to worry you at the time, sweetie," she said. "Anyway, he went on and on about how he used to earn his living selling the leaves from the *girbal* tree. And something about the guards not allowing him access to the trees. He was very frustrated."

Frank exhaled. "I see." He looked at Gulab, not bothering to hide his distaste. "Well, you better come in. We have to come up with a strategy to deal with this mess." He turned to face Ellie. "Thanks for letting me know. Just wish you'd mentioned this at the time."

Ellie saw something gleam in Gulab's eye and knew that he had picked up on Frank's mild rebuke. She felt her jaw muscles clench. This man was a snake. She could only pray that her husband saw this. "Well, I guess I should leave you two alone," she said at last.

She walked toward the kitchen, and the two men followed her into the living room. "Sit down," she heard Frank say, and then she could only hear a low murmur of voices. "Ellie," Frank yelled after a few minutes. "Any chance I could ask you to make us a cup of tea?"

Her stomach muscles clenched at the thought of serving tea to Gulab. But she said, "Sure."

Frank was scribbling something on a notepad when she entered the living room with the tray. "Can you tell me what will happen to those people they arrested?" she asked Gulab.

Instead of answering, Gulab turned toward Frank, who stared at the floor. "Frank," she said sharply. "There's a woman in jail who has just lost her husband. What do you intend to do about it?"

He looked up at her with a sigh. "What do you suggest I do?" he said. Despite her mounting anger, she heard the fatigue—and something more than that, a trace of confusion—in his voice.

"I suggest you get this guy here," she pointed her chin at Gulab, "to get them out of jail. Immediately. This morning. Before"—and here she thrust in the knife, deliberately, calculatingly—"someone else gets hurt in police custody, like earlier this year."

Frank fixed her a baleful look. "That wasn't necessary."

But it was. It was necessary to wake Frank up from the comatose state that he was in, to snap her fingers and break the diabolical
spell this horrible man was casting on her husband. She saw that
Gulab was looking back and forth between them, knew that he was
picking up on the tension between husband and wife, knew he was
exactly the kind of man who would file this knowledge away to use
at some later time. But she couldn't be concerned with that right
now. The task of the moment was to make Frank say the words that
would spring Radha and the others out of jail. She was stunned that
Frank himself couldn't see that, beyond the simple morality of the
issue, it was also the absolute best thing for HerbalSolutions, the
only prudent, political thing to do. A man is dead, she wanted to
scream at Frank to get him out of his catatonic state. A man has died,
hung himself from a tree that was part of his childhood inheritance
and that is now owned by a company headquartered eight thousand
miles away. A man has hung himself to prove the irrefutability of his
belonging to a piece of the natural world that we have taken away
from him.

"You know I'm right," she now said, her voice cracking with
urgency. "I—I know the villagers better than you do. The arrests
will pour gasoline on the fire, Frank."

Something in her words, her tone of voice, clicked. He turned
his head toward Gulab and said, "Call the police chief. Have them
release all of them."

"But Frank *seth*—" Gulab began.

"Don't waste any more time," Frank cut him off. "Just make the
call. Ellie is right. It will save us grief in the end."

Gulab rose to his feet and bowed slightly. "As you wish, sir."
His manner was calm, imperturbable. "But best if I go down to the
police *chowki* myself." He nodded toward Ellie. "Good making your
acquaintance, madam."

She forced herself to nod back.

At the door, Gulab turned around. "Better if you don't come in today, sir," he said. "There may be some—trouble—at the factory."

Frank closed his eyes for a moment. "Okay," he said. "But call me if anything is wrong. I want you to stay in touch with me during the day, understand? And tell Deepak to call me as soon as he can."

"Yes, sir. Get some rest, sir."

They sat on opposite couches, staring at each other, after Gulab had left. Neither one of them spoke for a few moments. Then Frank said, "Still think coming to India was a good idea?"

She looked at him, unsure of how to answer. "I certainly didn't expect any of—this," she said at last.

He shook his head. "I'd better call Pete and let him know," he said. "Seems like I'm giving him more bad news each time I call." He suddenly punched the palm of his left hand with his right fist. "Goddamn it. So we settle with the workers in May in order to buy ourselves some friggin' peace. I give in to most of their demands. But how the fuck can I anticipate that some yokel from the village is going to kill himself and then blame us?"

Frank's look of outrage reminded her of the expression on Benny's face if he felt somebody had been unfair to him. Despite her anger, her heart went out to her husband. "How did they know his reason for committing suicide?" she asked. "Did Gulab say?"

"Yeah, apparently he told some of the village youth that his wife had had to beg her parents for money for cooking fuel. The guy had not worked in months." His face crumbled. "Jesus, Ellie. What the fuck am I supposed to do? How can they possibly hold Herbal-Solutions responsible for something like this? I know these folks are dirt-poor. But we didn't create their poverty. And we're a business, goddamn it, not some social service agency."

She looked away, knowing that what Frank needed from her right now was unconditional support and not a self-righteous lecture. Beside, some part of her agreed with him. She knew Frank and Pete well enough to know that destroying the local economy or ruining a man's life was the last thing they'd have anticipated when they were negotiating for the grove of *girbal* trees. She remembered how Pete had rushed to the hospital when Ben was dying, how he'd looked as bleary-eyed and ruined as the rest of them at the end of their vigil. Pete was a loving dad, a generous friend, a good citizen. And so was Frank, a good man, despite his growing disenchantment and callousness. You shouldn't judge him, she chastised herself. She didn't have to deal with the stupefying Indian bureaucracy, with the sullen, erratic demands of the workers, the casual disregard for deadlines by the suppliers. For all practical purposes, Frank lived in a different India than she did.

She pushed herself off the couch and went and sat next to him. They sat leaning into each other. "I'm sorry, baby," she murmured. "But it will be okay. Don't worry. Everything will be all right."

She didn't know if either one of them believed her comforting words.

CHAPTER 21

The young woman sitting across from him reminded Frank of Ellie. That is, Ellie from twelve years ago, the fiery, impulsive woman who had been willing to right every wrong in the world. There was some of that in Sunita Bhasin, the journalist who had come into his office a half hour ago. Frank couldn't help but like her, even though he was painfully aware of the fact that she saw him as one of the wrongs she was trying to right.

He had blown her off the first time she'd called seeking an interview. He had been stunned to find out that Mukesh's death—and the ensuing strike by HerbalSolutions' workers—had made news in the Bombay newspapers. They were also dredging up the incident involving Anand's death in May. He had been shocked at how one-sided and unfair most of the coverage had been—hell, I'll never bitch about Fox News again, he'd groused to Ellie. So when Sunita, who worked for an English daily in Bombay, had first called him, he'd hung up on her. Days of negative coverage followed, and the stories never failed to include the line, "Officials at HerbalSolutions refused to comment." It was maddening. And thanks to the glories of the Internet, Pete was following every blasted story. To top things off, the alternative paper in Ann Arbor had gotten wind of the news, also. Every day now there were phone calls from Pete or one of the other executives in Ann Arbor, demanding that he stop the beating they were taking in the press. Demanding that he do something to end the strike.

"What the fuck would you like me to do, Peter?" he'd finally asked. "You wanna return the bastard trees back to them? That's what it will take."

There was a short silence. Then Pete said, "Can't do that. The antidiabetes pill is our number-one seller these days. But you have to do something, Frank. I was at Joe's baseball practice last night, and another parent stopped and asked me about the situation in India. That's bad."

"So what would you like me to do?" he asked again.

"I don't know, Frank." Pete didn't bother to hide the irritation in his voice. "You figure it out. That's what I pay you to do."

He was shaking when he hung up from that phone call. Pete was his friend. In all their years together, Pete had never thrown his weight around, had never reminded Frank of the fact that he was the head of the company. Also, the casual reference to Joe's baseball game, with Pete's indifference to the memories of Benny that it would inevitably arouse in Frank, stung. He thought for a few minutes and then dialed Sunita Bhasin's number. "If you still want to interview me, I'm willing," he said.

He had expected a middle-aged professional journalist and so was pleasantly surprised when a young, attractive woman of about twenty-five walked into his office two days later. She was dressed in the way many of the educated, college-age women in Bombay did—a white kurta over blue jeans and carrying a long cotton bag. Straight black hair framed an intelligent-looking face. His heart lightened. She looked like someone he could talk to, someone who clearly came from an educated, westernized background.

But half an hour later, he was conscious of the faint trickle of sweat running down his face. He fought the urge to wipe it off, not wanting her to see the effect her tough, matter-of-fact questioning was having on him. They had already engaged in a spirited but general debate about the pros and cons of globalization, and as long as the conversation stayed at an abstract, theoretical level, he felt sure of himself, felt that he was on safe ground. But now she was asking him about the circumstances of Mukesh's death.

"Do you think it is ethical for a foreign company to own natural resources in another country?" Sunita asked.

Frank made an exasperated sound. "Oh, for God's sake. The land was leased to us by your own government fair and square. If we'd have known there would be all these problems, why, we wouldn't have even bid on it."

"The government is corrupt," Sunita said matter-of-factly. "Everybody knows. In fact, we are reviewing all the contracts." She looked away for a moment and then stared at Frank dead in the eye. "How much in bribes did you have to pay to the officials?"

Frank half rose from his chair. "I'm not going to sit here and be insulted, Miss Bhasin," he said. "I gave you the interview in good faith—"

"Okay," she said hastily. "I withdraw the question. I'm sorry."

"Besides, the deal was made long before my involvement with the Indian plant," Frank continued. "I was not part of it."

"Okay," she said again, looking down at her notebook. "One other question. Are you planning on offering Mukesh's widow any compensation for her loss?"

There was something so smug and self-congratulatory about her expression, he wanted to slap her face. "Let me remind you of the fact that Mukesh was not our employee. In fact, until he made this—unfortunate and tangential connection between him and us, we had never heard of the man."

"I didn't ask about your legal responsibility," Sunita said softly. "I asked about your moral responsibility."

"Touché," Frank replied. "In fact, I don't believe we have a moral responsibility toward this man's family. Now, this is not to say that we won't—"

A flame of color shot into the woman's face. "It is exactly this kind of callousness that these villagers are fighting," she said. She swallowed hard and asked, "Mr. Benton, do you have a family?"

"I have a wife," he replied cautiously. He had no idea where she was going with this line of questioning.

"But no children?"

He thought for a moment. "No."

"I thought so," Sunita said. "See, if you had children you would feel differently about all of this, about your responsibility to the natural world, to those trees that you are stripping bare, to this poor woman who will now have to raise her child as a widow. I think that's what children do, no? They sensitize us to the miseries of the world."

He fought the urge to physically lift this smug, pious, ignorant woman off her chair and throw her out of his office. It was a typical Indian trait—this unforgiving inquisitiveness and then this unbearable, smug superiority. As if they fucking knew your life better than you did.

"Listen," he said, his eyes blazing. "Don't you dare sit in judgment of me. You don't know shit about me. I lost my only child a little over two years ago. My wife and I are still recovering from that loss, you hear? So don't you dare lecture me about suffering and misery. If you think I'm not torn up about that poor son of a bitch who hung himself, then, well, you don't know anything about me. But I have other responsibilities. I have a company to run. Which is a heck of a lot more difficult than cowering behind the protection of a notebook and making up shit to put in the next day's newspaper."

To his horror, Sunita's eyes filled with tears. "Oh, my God," she gasped. "I am so sorry."

He shook his head brusquely. "Forget it."

"No, I'm really sorry. My mummy always criticizes me for this—for how easily I pass judgment on others."

He listened in amazement as Sunita indulged in a feast of self-recrimination. This whole interview was surreal. He thought with nostalgia of Dave Kruger, the business reporter at the *Detroit Free Press*, who had interviewed him on numerous occasions and always maintained his brisk, professional manner. For all of his and Ellie's skepticism about objectivity in journalism, he was suddenly thankful to those journalists who at least tried. He had no idea if Sunita was typical of her profession or not. But one thing he knew—even after a two-martini lunch, Dave Kruger would not be indulging in the kind of self-chastisement that Sunita currently was.

The other thing he knew: he had lost control, had allowed this woman to rile him to the point where he had lost control of his emotions. He had exposed to a perfect stranger the raw nerve that rested just under a thin layer of skin. It scared him, the realization of how close to the edge he lived, of how it had taken the slightest of pushes to topple him. For the first time, he admitted to himself how unsettling Mukesh's suicide had been, how it had jarred his memory of those awful days following Anand's beating at the hands of the police. And how each such incident reopened the trauma of Benny's death.

"Miss Bhasin," he said finally. "No offense taken. Really. But I have another appointment scheduled for now. So if you have no more questions. . . ."

To his relief she jumped to her feet. "Of course, of course. I'm so insensitive. Sorry. Thank you for your time. And once again, please accept my apologies."

They shook hands, and he escorted her to the door. But just before leaving, she turned to face him again. "How—how old was your son?"

His eyes filled with tears before he could control them. "He was seven. His name was Benny."

She nodded. "It's a good name," she said. There was something old and mature in her face, a new understanding.

"Thanks for asking."

The strike lasted another two weeks. Pete called daily during that time, micromanaging in a way he had never done before. Frank forbade Ellie from volunteering at the village clinic during this time, knowing that it wasn't safe. She complied without much protest, and he suspected Nandita had given her the same advice. However, Ellie attended Mukesh's funeral without telling him. She only informed him after the fact, and before he could protest, added, "It's good that I went. Radha was very grateful to see me. I earned you some goodwill, Frank. And they all treated me with great respect."

Nandita and Shashi came to dinner during those two weeks. "So what do you hear about the situation in the village, Nan?" Frank asked. "Are things quieting down?"

Nandita looked down at her plate where the chicken tikka masala lay untouched. "It's pretty bad," she said. "These people have no safety net, no savings. So the strike is killing them."

"Then they should come back to work."

She smiled sadly. "I'm sure they will. Eventually."

"They'd rather starve than come back to work?"

"They want access to their trees, Frank."

"You mean, *our* trees."

Nandita looked him in the eye. "No. I mean *their* trees."

The room was silent, except for the roaring Frank heard in his ears. He felt angry, embarrassed, humiliated.

Shashi cleared his throat. "This is silly," he began.

"*Chup re,*" Nandita hushed him. She looked across the table at Frank. "You know I care about you," she said quietly. "I know how smart you are, and I know you have a good heart. So I will never disrespect you by feeding you lies. I'll tell you the truth, even when it's painful."

He forced himself to look at her, hoping she couldn't see the color infusing his cheeks. "So what's the truth?"

"The truth is, they should have access to trees their forefathers planted. The truth is, this is a community that has never seen a case of diabetes, thanks to the leaves. The truth is, it's downright immoral to treat diabetes in the West at the expense of the people who gave you the treatment."

"But your truths are all subjective," Frank said. "The fact is, these people had not undertaken any reforestation programs. They would've stripped the trees bare in a couple of generations. We will actually protect them by planting new trees."

"And what good will that do them if they can't benefit from it?" Ellie asked.

It hurt, the fact that Ellie, too, was siding with them. Although Shashi had not said anything, Frank suspected that he agreed with his wife. He thought he'd never felt more alone in all the time he'd been in India. "Well, we can't just hand the grove back to the villagers," he said.

"Nobody's asking you to. Just share some of the harvest with the local people. Believe me, you won't even notice."

"Let me think about it," he muttered.

He went into work the next day, armed with a proposal for Pete. It didn't take much to convince his boss to agree with his recommendations. Working through the village *panchayat*, or council of elders, Frank announced that henceforth the villagers would get a fraction of the harvest from the *girbal* tree. A small group of workers trickled back to work the same day. With Pete Timberlake's blessings, HerbalSolutions also gave a check of fifteen thousand rupees to Mukesh's widow. Finally, a fund was set up to help build a new wing for Nandita's clinic. It was to be called the Mukesh Bhatra

Clinic. The last of the workers returned to work, and the strike was officially declared over.

Sunita Bhasin wrote a laudatory story about how HerbalSolutions was at the forefront of a new consciousness on the part of foreign companies operating in India. Frank read the story on the plane to Chennai, where he was to negotiate buying a machine that would replace about a third of his workforce.

CHAPTER 22

Frank looked at his watch again. It was ten o'clock. Gulab was already fifteen minutes late. It was Sunday morning, and he was waiting for Gulab to drop off a stack of letters for him to sign. He had returned from Chennai on Saturday, and Deepak urgently needed him to get a head start on the pile of papers awaiting his signature. Ellie had left an hour back to meet Nandita for breakfast, which was the only reason it was possible to have Gulab deliver the papers. Since the day of the riot, Ellie had made it quite clear she didn't want Gulab in her house.

Prakash was in the kitchen making lunch when the doorbell finally rang. The cook looked up inquiringly. "I'll get it," Frank said curtly. "I'm expecting a visitor."

What he didn't expect was the look that came over Prakash's face when Gulab Singh walked into the kitchen. The man blanched. Gulab, however, didn't seem to notice as he looked at the cook imperviously. "*Kaise ho*, Prakash?" he said.

"*Theek hu,*" the man mumbled, keeping his eyes on the counter.

"Good," Gulab replied in English. Turning to Frank, he smiled. "Good to see you, sir." He glanced at the briefcase he was carrying. "Deepak sahib has sent many-many papers for you to sign."

"That's all right," Frank said. He led the way to the living room and was about to sit down on the couch when Gulab said, "Shall we sit on the porch, sir?"

"If you like."

"I used to come to this house a lot, sir," Gulab said conversationally as Frank led the way. "I knew the previous owner well. Did some . . . jobs . . . for him."

"What sort of jobs?" Frank asked, even though he didn't really want to know.

"He was German, sir. Unmarried. I used to procure women for him."

Frank felt his stomach turn. A typical Indian habit, he thought. Always giving you more information than you need. When they're not being inscrutable, that is. "I see," he said primly. "Huh. Well. Let's begin—"

Gulab eased his bulk into a wicker chair near the porch swing. "That fellow in there," he continued, "his wife used to get real angry. Blamed me for corrupting her little Olaf uncle. So I told Prakash to take her to a movie or something when the women came over."

"That how you know him? Prakash, I mean?"

Gulab snorted. "Prakash? I've known him since he was running around in his bare bottoms. Little chit of a fellow he was, always coming around our house for scraps of food my mother used to throw at him." He straightened in the chair and looked at Frank. "He was an orphan, you know. Mother died in childbirth, and father a few years later. So he ran around from one house in the village to another. My mother had a soft spot for him for some reason. Always giving him our old shirt-pants and feeding him. Such a pasting I used to give him, trying to chase him away. But always, like a stray dog, he'd show up at dinnertime." Gulab threw back his head and laughed.

Frank felt an intense revulsion for the man sitting next to him. If this were anybody else Gulab was talking about in this manner, he would've thrown him out of his house. But his own dislike for Prakash found a home in Gulab's casual cruelty. "Well, I guess him being an orphan explains why he's such a lousy father," he said. Despite himself, his voice softened at the thought of Ramesh. "Pity is, he has a wonderful son. Bright as anything. Could run a company such as ours some day, if he had the proper guidance, instead of this—this—jealous, petty fool for a dad."

Gulab's eyes narrowed, and Frank knew the man had heard the bitterness in his voice. Careful, he said to himself. This man is your employee. No point in telling him too much.

"Yah, I know the boy. Seen him around the marketplace with his mother. A sunny nature he is having." Gulab paused. "What is making that old fool jealous, sir?" he asked. His voice was casual, almost disinterested.

But the simple question unleashed Frank's pent-up frustration. "I am. Can you imagine? The idiot is jealous of my friendship with his son. Thinks I'm going to steal him or something."

"You should." Gulab's voice was smooth, almost seductive.

"Excuse me?"

"You *should* steal him. Take him with you to America. Give him a good life. Over here, sir, he will just rot." Gulab lowered his voice. "Plus, sir, parents are mixed marriage. And for many years now, they are living in this house, away from the village people. The boy will face much difficulties as he gets of marriageable age. No one will want his daughter to marry a mongrel."

Frank flinched and felt his temper rise. As if he'd read Frank's mind, the older man held out his hand in front of him to deflect the blame. "That's not my opinion, sir. I'm just knowing the mentality of these villagers."

He nodded, to let Gulab know that he understood. But his mind was elsewhere. With a start, he realized that for the last few months whenever he'd imagined Ramesh five or ten years from now, he'd imagined him in America. Seen him as an American boy. He had told Ellie so often about how this boy could be MIT-bound with just the right support that he had begun to believe it. The thought of Ramesh remaining in this tiny hellhole of a village, dropping out of school to work some miserable job, remaining a bachelor because no illiterate, ignorant villager thought he was worthy of marrying his vacuous, illiterate daughter and taking care of his worn-out mother and ingrate father as they aged, filled Frank with despair. For months now, he had believed the story he had spun for himself, a story that had him rescuing the boy from his fate, plucking him like a flower and transplanting him into fertile soil, where he could bloom. But Gulab's succinct words had robbed him of that illusion, and he now had to imagine Ramesh as the villagers saw him—as a boy of dubious pedigree, the product of a transgression most of them frowned upon. If there was anything special about the boy that caught their attention, it was not the fact that he was sharp and warmhearted and gifted. It was the fact that his Hindu father—an orphan boy who they had raised on the crumbs of their charity—had married a nonlocal Christian girl whose own family had disowned her over this dishonor.

"These people are idiots," Frank said, the venom in his voice surprising even him. "I thought Ramesh only had that fool in the kitchen to contend with. I didn't know there was a village full of them."

"You should take him, sir. To America, I mean. Give him a good life there."

Frank made a face. "And what do I do about his parents? They give me shit if I ask to take him to the beach for a day. He's supposed to go to the States with us for ten days over Christmas. From what my wife tells me, getting Prakash to agree to even that was like pulling teeth. I can imagine what his reaction would be if—"

He stopped, halted by the dismissive sound Gulab made, a cross between a hawk and a hiss. "Forget them, sir." In a distinctively Indian gesture, Gulab brought all five fingers together and then made them fly apart, as if he was discarding something. "They are nothing. I can make them disappear."

"Huh? What do you mean, disappear?"

Gulab's dark eyes fixed themselves on Frank for a full moment. In that moment, Frank remembered what Gulab had once told him—I have killed men with my bare hands. He shivered. But before he could say anything, Gulab smiled, a slow, secretive smile. "When you are ready to take the boy with you, sir, then ask me. I will tell you what I mean." His voice was low, mesmerizing, and Frank felt suddenly sleepy and dull, as if he was being drugged by Gulab's seductive voice. A vein throbbed in his forehead as Gulab held his gaze. He shuddered and looked away, disturbed by what he saw in Gulab's eyes.

He yawned and shook his head, feeling the spell cast by Gulab break as he did so. "Okay. Enough of this crazy talk," he said, forcing his voice into a lightness he didn't feel. "We'd better get down to work."

Gulab was immediately formal. "Of course, sir. Lots of papers for you to sign."

They worked for about twenty minutes, and then Frank heard Prakash's nasal voice in the doorway. "Soup is ready. Shall I bring out?" Looking up, Frank saw that although Prakash was addressing him, he was looking at Gulab as if transfixed, his eyes wary and fearful. He's petrified of Gulab, Frank thought. This bastard must've terrorized him when they were boys. And despite himself, his heart filled with pity.

"Just leave it in the pot," he said. "I'll warm it up when we're done." He was about to ask Gulab whether he wanted something cold to drink when he stopped himself. Somehow, he knew that asking Prakash to serve a Coke or a Limca to his old nemesis would be more than what the cook could bear. Beside, some instinct told him to keep his head of security at arm's length, not to let the man forget his place too much. Even as small a gesture as offering him a drink would signal a familiarity, a collegiality, that he was not willing to confer on Gulab.

"You can go home," he told Prakash, his voice less harsh than it usually was. "Go get some rest." Out of the corner of his eye, he saw Gulab's head shoot up, but when he looked over, the man was looking at the papers in front of him, again.

"As you wish," Prakash said and turned away.

"He's a good cook," Frank said after Prakash had left. Even to his own ears, the words sounded defensive, as if he was trying to justify his earlier kindness to Prakash.

Gulab's eyes were flat. "There's a saying in Hindi. It means, the shit of even a chicken feeds flies. Even *bevakoofs* have their virtues, sir."

Frank laughed. "Never heard that one before." He turned back to the stack of papers. "Okay. Let me go through these to see what else needs my signature."

He had barely read two letters when he looked up and saw Ramesh walking on the stone wall between the front lawn and the beach. Gulab spotted the boy at the same time and made to get up from the chair. "Some ruffian on your property, sir," he said. "I'll go chase him away."

"Leave him be," Frank said. "That's Ramesh. He lives here."

"Yes, of course, my mistake," Gulab began, but Frank wasn't paying him any attention because Ramesh had spotted the two men and was now running barefoot across the lawn toward them. "Hi, Frank," he panted as he came up to them. "Can you play basketball today?"

It felt wrong to have Gulab witness his interactions with the boy. He wanted to cover Ramesh's innocent, open face from the other man's probing, all-seeing eyes. "Not today," he said curtly. "I have to work right now, Ramesh. We can talk later, okay?"

"Okay," Ramesh said, but Frank could tell he was hurt. It didn't matter. More important to get this boy away from Gulab Singh and his watchful gaze. "Bye," he added. "Go on, now."

Ramesh ran away, looking back once but never breaking his stride. The two men watched as he hopped back on the wall and then jumped onto the sand on the other side. "Sweet boy," Gulab said. His tone was neutral. "He calls you Frank? Not sahib or sir?"

"My wife doesn't like formality." He had almost said servitude, but knew that Gulab would think of that as a weakness on Ellie's part.

The man smiled. "Americans. Informal people. When I was in Virginia, same thing. Very informal in dress and speech."

"You were in America? When?"

"When I was in the service, sir. Special training mission, with the American government."

Frank thought for a moment. "You were in Virginia? Working with the CIA?"

Gulab turned his head so that he was gazing at the sea. "Secret work, sir. Even my mother-father didn't know where I was for three months." He proceeded to tell Frank what had taken him to Virginia, but the tale was so convoluted and Gulab used so many acronyms that Frank was unfamiliar with that he soon grew tired of trying to keep up. He had no idea if the man was telling the truth. Everything that he was saying sounded incredible, but Frank knew enough about politics to know that governments got away with what they did because they counted on ordinary citizens dismissing events as being too incredible and implausible. He looked pointedly at the papers in front of him, and Gulab, attuned to his every nuance, stopped abruptly. "Anyway, sir. This is all past. Old history."

Picking up his pen, Frank started going through the papers. Gulab handed him more to read and sign. At one point, he went into the kitchen and returned with a glass of water. "Drink, sir," he said.

"Water important in this heat." While Frank worked, the other man leaned on the railing of the porch and stared at the sea.

The stack had gotten considerably shorter by the time Ellie came home. They both heard the doorknob turn and Ellie say, "Hon?"

Shit, he thought, she's home a lot sooner than I'd imagined. "Over here," he yelled. "On the porch."

Ellie walked in, her face flushed from the heat. She was removing her straw hat as she walked in. The smile on her lips froze as she spotted Gulab, who had risen from his perch on the railing. "Oh," she said stiffly. "I wasn't expecting—"

"Hello, memsahib," Gulab said.

She did not acknowledge Gulab's greeting. Frank felt his face flush, embarrassed by his wife's rudeness. Ellie turned to face Frank. "Why are you working on a Sunday?"

"I was only signing some papers," he said, willing her not to create a scene, not to come across as a hen-pecking wife in front of Gulab. To his relief, she turned around to leave.

"Nice to see you again, memsahib," Gulab said, but she didn't respond.

"She's annoyed that I'm working," he said, trying to gloss over Ellie's inexplicable rudeness.

Gulab's face was impassive. "Of course, sir."

The man left a half hour later. Frank escorted Gulab to the door and then walked into the bedroom where Ellie was lying in bed, reading. "Hi," he said. "How did breakfast go?"

"Fine," she said, looking up from the book she was reading. "Why'd you let that awful man back into our house?"

"I told you. I wanted to get a jump start on things."

She rolled on her side and sat cross-legged behind where Frank was perched on the bed. Reaching over, she began to rub his shoulders. "We stopped at the market, and I purchased a few things for Ramesh to distribute as Christmas gifts to folks in Ohio."

"You did?"

"Yeah, I figured it would be awkward for him to not participate in the gift exchange."

He turned around and kissed her. "You're wonderful." He rose from the bed. "I think Prakash has made us some chicken corn soup. Want some?"

"Sure. I'll be there in five minutes. I just want to finish this chapter. Oh, by the way. Nandita wants us to go to the Shalimar for tea this afternoon. Wanna go?"

"Sure."

He went to the kitchen to heat the soup, his heart lighter than it had been in days. He knew Ellie was not thrilled about going home for the holidays, but he now dared to hope that perhaps having Ramesh with them would be good for her, also. He caught himself whistling as he placed the pot on the stove.

Some part of his brain kept wanting to stray to the strange exchange he'd had with Gulab, wanted to try and decode the man's evasive but vaguely sinister words. But he forced himself to focus on the steady, quiet flame of happiness that Ellie's gift-buying spree had lit in his heart, much like the blue flame of the gas stove that he had just turned on.

Chapter 23

Prakash tried lifting the pot from the stove but couldn't. His hands were shaking too much. Even though the *badmaash* Gulab had been gone for several hours and Frank and Ellie were out for the afternoon, he still felt the man's vile presence hanging like black smoke over the house.

Too much. He was being asked to put up with too much. First there was the American trying to take over the life of his son. And now he was letting into the house the man who had darkened his childhood, a bully whose hands had never failed to curl into a fist when Prakash was around. Every child in the village had feared Gulab, who was a few years older than most of them. But most children had a father or a mother to protect them, to grab Gulab by his ears and drag him to his mother's house to protest. The old woman would slap her son's head, and for a day or two, he would stop his terror. Prakash alone had no one to defend him, and Gulab made the most of this. Punches. Pinches. Kicks. Slaps. Head butts. And worst of all, the cruel jokes and the laughter.

"*Ae*, Sad Face," the teenage Gulab would call out. "What's wrong, *yaar*? You look like your mother-father have died."

Prakash would try and slink away, would pray for invisibility, but silence only infuriated Gulab. "Come here, you motherfucker," he'd continue. "Tell me, who died today?"

There was no correct response. Answering back invited violence. So did silence. And besides, the physical pain was tolerable. What was intolerable was the humiliation. The way the other boys looked away while he was being tortured, the contempt and pity he saw on their faces. Without witnesses, the abuse would not have mattered. But Gulab always made certain that there were spectators to his torment. And no one ever spoke up for Prakash, no woman, man, or child. There was not even a family pet, a dog who would bare his teeth at Gulab.

He had been so relieved when Gulab had disappeared from the village for several years. Rumor was that he had joined the army and was fighting in Kashmir. "I hope the Muslim scum kill him and eat his bones," he'd said to his friend Amir when he'd first heard the news. Amir had looked shocked for a second but then grinned, showing red, paan-stained teeth. "May they choke on his bones," he'd agreed.

But demons were hard to kill, Prakash thought, as he washed a frying pan in scalding hot water. Gulab had come back to the village a few years after he and Edna had moved in with Olaf. During those years Gulab stopped by at least once a week, to bring Olaf a new woman each time. And now he was back, let into the house by the American. Still tormenting Prakash by his very existence.

The door creaked, and Edna came in. "*Baap re baap*," she said. "Such-such noises you're making. Are you washing the pot or killing it?"

He shot her an ugly look. "Don't talk," he said. "Just sit *chup-chap*, if you must be here."

"What *bhoot* got into you tonight?"

Prakash set the pan down with a bang. "Gulab was here today," he said. He knew Edna disliked the man, also. "See who your 'Merican lets into his home? Such low-class people."

For a happy moment he thought Edna was going to agree with him. Then her eyes narrowed and she said, "Gulab does security for the company. Of course Frank sir have him come here on business. Why that sticks in your gullet?"

"Why for he give him the job? People in village say Gulab ordered that poor Anand to be beaten in the police *chowki*."

"People in village say moon come out in the afternoon. You believe them?"

He hated this about her, how she blindly sided with the Americans over her own family. "You shameless. Not siding with your own countrymen."

"Countrymen? Those fools ignore me from the day I come to this godforsaken village. Now they become my fellow men?"

He stared at her in frustration. For years he had let her believe that his aversion to Gulab stemmed from the fact that the man pimped women for Olaf, unable to let his wife see the smothering shame and terror that he felt each time he was in Gulab's orbit. "You the fool," he said lamely. "Blind by your loyalty to these foreigners."

"Ellie miss treat me better than anyone in Girbaug ever did. Frank sir teaches my son. Only you ungrateful to those who feed you."

He picked up the pot of curry from the stove and set it on the kitchen counter with such force that a little of the liquid sloshed over. "I feed *them*," he yelled. "They not feeding me." And before he could think, he swirled a nugget of saliva in his mouth and spit into the curry.

Edna looked at Prakash in shocked silence. "What—what did you do?" she said finally. "Have you gone total mad? Spitting in their food? *Arre baap.* God save you, man."

He suddenly felt teary, unclean. He had never done such a dirty thing before. She had pushed him to this point of fury. "I . . . See what you make me do, woman?" he said, wishing she would leave the kitchen so that he could think. He glanced at the clock. No time to cook more curry before they returned home.

Edna's lips curved downward. "Shameless, useless man," she began. "Total *namak-haraam*. My mother always said—"

"Damn your mother and her mother," he yelled. "Curse six generations of your family. Now go. Get out of my kitchen before I—" He picked up a spatula and raised his arm threateningly. "I'm telling you for your own good, Edna. Get out."

"I'm going." She opened the door and then looked back. "But if you serve that curry, I swear I will tell them the truth."

He stood holding on to the counter, tears streaming down his cheeks. How he hated them all—Gulab, Edna, Frank. How he wished he could get on a bus and simply get away from this village, with its sad memories and ghosts that rose up to darken his present. He eyed the pot of red liquid, lifted it, and poured it down the sink.

He would simply have to lie and say that he'd burned the curry.

CHAPTER 24

Frank was in a meeting when Ellie called him the next day. "What's up?" he said impatiently, and before she could reply, "I'll call you back in an hour, okay?"

Ellie sounded like she was at her wits' end when he finally reached her. "I'm so sorry, hon," she said. "But I thought it was better to tell you right away, in case you can still get our money back."

"Tell me what? What're you talking about?"

"It's Prakash. Turns out he's changed his mind about Ramesh going to Cleveland with us. He's convinced that we're gonna—I don't know—kidnap his son, or something."

"Did you try talking him out of it?"

"Actually, I didn't. I'm—I'm just tired of his shenanigans, to be honest with you. I don't want to deal with it."

Frank swore under his breath. "Okay. I'll talk to him when I get home. Stupid jerk. I thought he might pull something like this at the last minute."

"Edna's acting really weird, also. She's been scuttling around the kitchen like a mouse all morning."

He hung up, and although it was only noon, found himself craving a drink. A gin and tonic would be nice right around now, he thought, and then smiled as he recalled fixing his grandmother Benton her favorite cocktail at eleven in the morning while visiting her in Dearborn. "You know what hell is, honey?" she'd once said to him when he was a kid. "Hell is a warm gin-and-tonic—with a hair in it." He had squirreled that nugget back to Ann Arbor to feed it to Scott, had stood on the bed in his bathrobe and imitated his grandma in his best Bette Davis accent.

But now he stopped thinking about his long-dead grandma and was back to fuming about Prakash. He wondered if the cook had broken the news to Ramesh and how the kid was dealing with it. He thought of the strings he'd pulled to get Ramesh a visa, remembered the strained, awkward conversation with his mom where he'd told her he was bringing a young Indian boy home with them, a conversation that had ended with his mom saying, "Okay, dear. If you think that's wise." I'll call Prakash in tonight, he thought grimly. Ask him for an explanation for his ridiculous behavior.

But then, just as suddenly, his anger left him. In its place, he felt fatigue, an exhaustion that sank so deep into his bones, it felt like pain. He felt his shoulders sag, imagined his body made a hissing sound as he lost his fighting spirit, his outrage, his desire to bend Prakash to his will. He was tired. Tired of fighting all of them. All of India, it seemed to him, was ready to judge, disapprove of, or frustrate him. Of late, he had been feeling as if his hold on himself was slipping, that he was becoming someone he didn't want to be, was shocked by racist thoughts that sometimes rose in his mind like dark waves, was stunned at how easily an invective or a cuss could rise to his lips. The slightest provocation—someone cutting Satish off on the road, Deepak's blank, inscrutable expression during meetings, the close way in which Ellie always seemed to watch his interactions with Ramesh—bothered him. Ah, Ramesh. The kid was the only pure, unfettered source of delight in his life. He wished he could pick up the boy in the crook of his arm, bid adieu to the rest of them, and disappear. Everybody else seemed so goddamn complicated, and he was expected to feel sorry for all of them—for Deepak, who was making a fraction of his salary, for the workers who had suffered for generations at the hands of the moneylenders and the police and the government, for Prakash, who was a run-down alcoholic. Who, he wanted to ask, felt sorry for him? His own childhood hadn't been that hot—a father who beat him as a kid and abandoned him when he was twelve, a mother who moped around the house like a friggin' nun, a family business that spluttered along over the years, barely enough to keep them afloat. Yes, his luck had changed after he'd met Ellie, but those years were hard to recall now. Or rather, he didn't trust his memory of them because he saw them for what they were—the setup, the trick, the lull before the Fall. If Eden came with a snake, was it ever really Eden? If paradise could be lost, was it ever really paradise?

He continued in this self-pitying vein for a few more minutes and then realized what he was doing. He was holding a one-way conversation with Ellie, pleading his case to her, trying to convince her that the fact that he was white and male and American—*privileged*, in her parlance—didn't mean that he had to carry boulders of guilt all his life, didn't mean that he had to make excuses for every Edna, Prakash, and Deepak. "Screw you, Ellie," he muttered and then caught himself and laughed.

By the time he went home that evening, his mind was made up—they would not go home for Christmas. For weeks, he'd been trying to ignore the anxiety that he'd seen on his wife's face because his own excitement at taking Ramesh to America was stronger than her dread at going back. But Christmas without Benny was hard enough. Celebrating it in a familiar place with family would be too painful. Like Ellie, he didn't feel ready to face it, not without the crutch of Ramesh. Pete would be annoyed, but hell, Pete seemed annoyed at him all the time these days—he'd get over it. His mother and Scottie would be heartbroken, but maybe they could try going next June, when the weather would be better and there would be no holiday to celebrate. Ellie's parents—well, she'd have to deal with them and their disappointment. He suddenly felt lighter than he had in weeks. For once, he was about to suggest something that would put him on the same side as his wife, rather than opposing her. It was, he supposed, the best Christmas gift he could buy her.

As he had suspected, Ellie didn't seem too crushed by the change of plans. "Guess I'll mail all the gifts," she said. "I just hope they get there on time."

"Or at all," he said. "If some enterprising mailman does not pilfer them. It's a common problem here."

Another month went by and then it was time to plan their own holiday celebration. They invited Nandita and Shashi to dinner on Christmas Eve, and it was assumed that Ramesh would join them. Ellie insisted on cooking the meal herself, and Frank was happy to help her. That morning, Edna came to the door to sweep and clean as usual, but Ellie had sent her away. "It's Christmas Eve. Go enjoy with your family," she said.

Ramesh was in and out of their house the whole day. At one point, Ellie assigned him the task of shelling some walnuts. The boy looked at the silver nutcracker she handed him. "What for, Ellie?" he asked.

"To crack the nuts?"

Ramesh laughed. He ran to the door and placed the nut in the doorjamb. Then he half shut the door, cracking the shell open. "That's the way we do it," he said.

"A surefire way to break your fingers," Frank said. "I think we'll do it our way, buddy."

Around four o'clock, Ellie turned to Frank. "I bought a tiny plastic Christmas tree," she said. "How about if you and Ramesh decorate it?"

And just like that, their eyes filled with tears. They stood in the sunlit kitchen, holding hands, remembering the years they'd driven to Forest Farms just outside of Ann Arbor to chop down their own tree. Benny in his yellow parka, puffed with self-importance because Frank let him believe that he had actually helped his dad bring the tree down. Ellie warming the apple cider once they got home while father and son positioned the tree in its stand. Frank standing on a ladder to place the silver star on the top branch. The two of them staying up late every Christmas Eve wrapping Ben's gifts.

"God," Frank said, his voice hoarse. "Oh, God."

"I wasn't going to get a tree," Ellie said. "But I saw it in the market and couldn't resist." Her voice cracked. "I—I just felt like he'd want us to."

Frank nodded. "Okay." He made a visible effort to control his emotions. "But you'll have to help us decorate it."

It took them all of ten minutes to finish the task. First they strung some silver tinsel over the two-foot tree. Ellie had bought a small blue star that Frank placed on the top. They looked at the small, pathetic tree with dissatisfaction. Frank thought back on the twinkling, seven-foot trees they usually decorated in the living room of their Ann Arbor home. How far we've fallen, he thought.

Ramesh closed one eye and looked at their handiwork. "It need snow," he said. He turned to Ellie. "You are having cotton balls at home? That's what we put at school." And so they flattened cotton wool and laid it on the scrawny plastic branches. Frank felt a quick sense of regret that, thanks to Prakash's stupidity, Ramesh had missed the chance to see real snow this December. "Is snow as white as the cotton?" Ramesh asked.

"Whiter."

"Like vanilla ice cream, it is looking?"

"Guess so," Frank smiled. "Except it's flaky. You put a flake on your tongue and it dissolves. And did you know, no two snowflakes are the same?"

Ramesh thought for a moment. "In the whole world no two are the same?"

"Yup. Just like fingerprints."

The boy cocked his head. "Impossible."

"But true."

They left Ramesh to watch TV in the living room while they returned to the kitchen. Helping Ellie chop tomatoes, Frank thought to himself that children were like snowflakes—no two alike. Benny and Ramesh were so different from each other, unique in their personalities, and yet each boy was beautiful in his own way. He suddenly felt a great longing to see the two together in the same room, laughing and playing together. He turned toward Ellie. "Do you think Ramesh and Benny would've liked each other?"

Ellie's smile was evasive. "Benny liked everybody."

"I know. But do you think they would've been friends?" he persisted.

She pushed back a strand of hair with the back of her hands, which were covered in flour. "I think so. Though Ramesh may have bullied him a bit, being older and all."

He nodded and turned away, dissatisfied with her response. Though in fairness, what could Ellie have said that would have made it better? "I'm done with the tomatoes. What else needs chopping?" he said.

In response, Ellie looked at the kitchen clock. "It's quarter to five," she said. "Better send Ramesh home for a few hours. I'd promised Edna he'd be home by five."

He went into the living room to approach Ramesh. And maybe it was the angle of the sun in the room, maybe it was the light, maybe it was the chopped onions on the kitchen counter that had made his eyes burn, but for a split second, it was Benny sitting on the couch, his legs dangling. It was Benny fidgeting with the remote. There was Benny, his hair lit up from the side by the afternoon sun.

Frank blinked. And Benny disappeared, and Ramesh took his place. Frank felt his heart race. The world went completely silent. He stood for a moment, swallowing hard, unable to hear what the boy was saying to him. Then his ears popped, as if he'd descended from twenty thousand feet, and he could hear Ramesh jabbering away about the wrestling match he was watching. Seeing the strange look on Frank's face, the boy stopped. "What's wrong, Frank?"

"Nothing. Just—nothing." He stood staring at the boy, reluctant to issue the command for him to return to his parents, when it was so damn apparent that his real place was here, on the couch, in this house, with them. He knew that Ramesh was coming back to dinner at eight, but even three hours away from this boy on Christmas Eve felt like too much. He was about to argue with Ellie when she came in from the kitchen, wiping her hands on the apron.

"Hey, sweetie," she said to Ramesh. "Go visit with your mom for a few hours, okay? But make sure you're back by eight."

To Frank's surprise and disappointment, Ramesh didn't protest. "Okay, Ellie," he said, slipping off the sofa. "Bye."

Frank sat down heavily on the couch and closed his eyes. He was tired. Lord, he was tired. When he opened his eyes again, Ellie was standing in front of him, holding out a gift-wrapped box.

"What's this? Are we exchanging gifts now? I thought we were going to wait until the others—"

"Just this one," she said, sitting down next to him. "It's from Benny. The rest we'll open after dinner."

He opened the box and immediately recognized one of his old ties. The last two Christmases of his life, Benny had raided his father's closet, picked out a tie, wrapped it, and presented it to his dad. Ellie was continuing the tradition. "Thanks," he whispered. They sat on the couch, smiling awkwardly at each other. Frank kissed the top of Ellie's head. "He was like you," he said. "Gentle and sensitive."

She shook her head. "No. He had the best of his dad. Everybody said that." She got to her feet. "I need to put the pie in the oven."

Nandita and Shashi arrived at eight, minutes after Ramesh had showed up dressed in the new outfit Ellie had bought for him. "Wow," Nandita said to Ramesh. "You look so handsome I think I'm going to leave my husband and marry you."

Ramesh's eyes widened, and he looked questioningly at Frank, who pulled the boy near to him. "You tell her she'll have to pay you a huge dowry before you'll consider," he instructed Ramesh.

Ramesh gave Nandita a toothy grin. "I am having a girlfriend," he confided.

Nandita flopped down dramatically in a chair. "*Arre*, my *naseeb* is so bad."

The adults all laughed. They sat in the living room sipping their drinks, and Frank noticed with appreciation that Shashi made every effort to include Ramesh in the conversation, asking him questions about school and his favorite teachers. He beamed at how smartly Ramesh answered back.

Ellie had tried to make a semi-traditional Christmas meal—mashed potatoes, apple and raisin stuffing, green beans and apple pie for dessert. To give it an Indian twist, Shashi had picked up tandoori chicken and lamb biryani from the Shalimar's restaurant.

"Yowzers," Frank exclaimed. "Think we have enough food here?"

"What you say?" Ramesh said. "Yeeou what?"

Frank ruffled his hair. "All right, my boy. This ain't no time for an education. It's time to eat."

They moved back into the living room after dinner. Ramesh pointed out the small Christmas tree to the guests. "Me and Frank decorated it," he said proudly. "Ellie helped."

"Hon, how about some music?" Ellie asked. Frank plugged in the iPod and whistled tunelessly to "White Christmas." When he turned around, Ellie had disappeared into the bedroom. She soon returned with an armful of gifts. "A little something for everyone," she said.

Ramesh's excitement reminded Frank so much of Benny's. "I first, I first," the boy yelled, tearing off the gift paper that Ellie had so carefully wrapped his box in. And then, "Yeeeeeessss. Yes, Ellie, yes," as he held up a new pair of sneakers.

"Glad you like them, hon," Ellie said. "Try them on to make sure they fit."

As Ramesh walked around the room, they each opened their gifts. The Bentons received a beautiful carved wooden wall hanging. "It's sandalwood," Nandita said. "Smell it."

"It's lovely, Nan," Ellie said.

Ellie had bought Nandita a green silk kurta and a silver bracelet. Shashi, who they knew was a big Harry Potter fan, got a T-shirt that had the caricature of an Indian potter making a pitcher. Under the picture it said, "Hari Potter."

"I love it," Shashi said, laughing.

Out of the corner of his eye, Frank saw that Ramesh was still dancing around in his new shoes. "Excuse me," he said and went into the bedroom. He went into the closet of the guest room, where he'd hidden the big white cardboard box, and carried it out. He set it on the floor. "Oh, Ramesh," he said casually. "Come see. Santa has brought you one more gift."

He ignored the confused look that Ellie was throwing him, focusing on the boy. Ramesh broke into the box with eager hands, throwing the shredded paper packaging all over the floor. When he lifted the silver laptop out of the box, Ellie gasped. But Ramesh did not react, looked at Frank with a perplexed expression.

"It's a computer," Frank finally said. "For you. To help with your homework."

The boy squealed with joy. "For me?" he said. "For me?"

Even though he was conscious of the curious looks the others were giving him, even though he was aware of how silent it had gotten in the room, Frank could not keep the pride and pleasure out of his voice. "Yup. Your very own computer."

"Ae bhagwan," Ramesh breathed. "I am so happy."

Frank tossed his head back to laugh and caught the look that Ellie was exchanging with Nandita. He noticed that none of the other three had said a word yet, and the room felt heavy with their disapproval. He felt a shard of resentment shredding through his happiness. Fuck them, he thought.

But his tone was innocent when he finally spoke to his wife. "So what do you think, El? Don't you think this will help him with his homework?"

Ellie bit her upper lip and shot Nandita a quick glance. "It should," she mumbled.

"It was such a good deal," he continued. "I was ordering some computers for work and thought—well, it was such a good deal."

"Where will he put it?" Ellie asked. She gave a short, bitter laugh. "It's not like there's that much room in their one-room hut."

"Oh, we'll figure something out," he said breezily, determined not to let her ruin his pleasure.

"And what about Prakash?"

"What about him?"

"Should we have asked him first?"

Ramesh was looking back and forth between them, having at last detected some tension. Frank felt a flash of anger. Why was Ellie acting like this? Deliberately, he put his arm around the boy. "So what do you think, bud?" he said. "Do you think your parents will let you keep this gift?"

The boy grinned from ear to ear. "Yes, of course," he yelled. "I will tell them, Santa brought."

Ramesh's words changed the mood in the room. "Computers have become almost mandatory in schools now," Nandita murmured, while Shashi turned to Frank and asked, "What software did it come with?"

Only Ellie, he noticed, was still not participating. He got up and walked behind her chair and rubbed her shoulders. Bending low so that only she could hear, he said, "He shouldn't fall back in school because of the lack of a lousy computer, hon."

She exhaled. "Guess not," she whispered back. "I'm just worried about Prakash's reaction. It's such an expensive gift."

He sensed her resistance waning and gave her shoulders a quick squeeze. "Don't worry so much," he said. And turning to his guests, "What would everybody like as an after-dinner drink? We have Bailey's? Nandita, some sherry? Or Kahlúa?"

"I want to play my computer," Ramesh cried.

"I do, too," Shashi said, pushing himself off the couch. "Let's go set it up, shall we?"

Nandita and Ellie remained in the living room, sipping their drinks, while the three males crowded around the kitchen table, checking out the new gadget. "This is beautiful, Ramesh," Shashi breathed. "Will you share it with me?"

Ramesh balked. He looked at Shashi for the longest time as he considered the request. "You can play with it again next Christmas," he said finally.

Shashi burst out laughing. "This boy is a *pucca* businessman," he said to Frank. "I should hire him to work for me."

Frank smiled back, despite being slashed by two contradictory emotions—pride in Ramesh and affront at the thought of Ramesh working for Shashi at his hotel.

This boy is destined for greater things, he thought dreamily. This boy is destined for America.

BOOK FIVE

Spring 2008

Girbaug, India

CHAPTER 25

The sun was God.

Frank wondered why he'd never known this before. He had spent his childhood yearning to see the face of God, had always thought of him as an old man with a long, white beard, as Charlton Heston, and here he had been—hiding in plain sight. All those years spent following a false theology, believing in a personal God, praying to the Father and the Son—when all along it had been the Sun instead of the Son. He had believed the myths about Adam and Eve and the Serpent, about God as a personal savior, as if he was some damn accountant perched in the sky with a giant ledger book. All-powerful they called him, but really, their view of Him was that of a petty, vengeful tyrant.

But it was all clear now. Of course. Of course. The sun was God—life-giving but mercurial, sometimes soft and mellow, sometimes fiery and distant. This was the all-powerful deity they talked about. Wasn't everything controlled by the sun—the seasons, the weather, the vegetation, the animal kingdom? And yet, what a mystery. The beautiful star that affected every single life form on earth chose to remain hidden from us. And why wouldn't it? Why would it bother with an army of gnats? No wonder Icarus got his wings burned by flying too close to it. Flying into the face of God.

Shadow and light. All the things that human beings took personally—the ups and downs of personal fortunes, the roller-coaster ride through life's vagaries, was just a damn light show. When the sun went down, the world went dark. Every toddler knew this. But surely this cycle of dawn and dusk, the strictest law governing the universe, also governed individual lives? What we humans called fate was simple physics, a matter of degrees and positioning: sometimes the sun turned a benevolent eye onto a lucky mortal and showered him in its light, so that he was blessed, golden, untouchable. And then, it moved a few inches, gracing another with its attention, giving that person his moment in the sun, leaving the first person to feel the coldness of its shadow. How easily we accepted the rotation of the earth around the sun, the dissolving of day into night, the partitioning of the globe between darkness and light. And yet how we resisted the fact that this interplay between darkness and dawn also ruled each person's life.

Perhaps, Frank thought, we mistook the sun's consistency, its reliability, its unfailing rise in the east, for a kind of love. But really, the hallmark of the sun was its indifference to us. Our prayers, our piety, did not disturb it in the least. It didn't care if it ruined our picnics or weddings or even our lives. Tossing in his bed, Frank felt liberated by this thought. It was foolishness, conceit, this belief in a personal god, an indication of our puniness and weakness.

This is what had happened to them, to him and Ellie. They had basked in the sun's benevolence for an absurdly long time. How fortunate we are, they'd whispered to each other a million times as they lay in bed together. Every night they used to meet in Benny's bedroom and take turns naming three things they were grateful for that day. And after their son fell asleep, he and Ellie would walk out holding hands. Looking back at that young couple now, Frank saw how silly, how deluded, they were. The golden couple, expecting their time to last forever. Born on a planet pockmarked with war and famine and disease and ancient hatreds, they had somehow thought they could soar above it all, trusting only themselves and their love for each other. Thinking they could use their college degrees, their jobs, their beautiful home, their healthy bodies, their American citizenship, their white skin, to shelter them from the savage world that prowled outside. But it caught up with them, didn't it? The sun tilted away from them and smothered them with a blanket of darkness that snatched Benny away. A cheap trick, part of the repertoire of any two-bit kidnapper. And a ransom that they would pay the rest of their lives.

It was wonderful, really. Not to have to take it personally. To give up once and for all the old-fashioned notions of good versus evil, of fate and destiny, of wondering what they could or couldn't have done. To realize that there was no great scorekeeper in the sky whom they might have displeased. To know that the signature mark of the universe was indifference. No more praying to the Father and Son. The only son who really counted had been taken away. It felt good to no longer be burdened by the awful weight of heaven. If he thought of Benny in an afterlife now, he would imagine him glittering like crushed glass in the eye of the sun. Adding his tiny, holy body to the majesty and power of the sun, making it even more powerful, feeding it with his own coarse energy. Perhaps that's what global warming was all about, the destroyed energy of a million Bennys feeding the open mouth of a fiery beast.

He wanted to think harder, didn't want to wake up or open his eyes until he had understood it all, but his head was throbbing with pain. Beside, he wanted to share this new understanding with Ellie, explain to her how it wasn't their fault, that what had happened to them was not punishment but simple mechanics, like the turning of the wheel. He wanted to tell her that they could stop missing Benny, that he was playing peekaboo with them all day long, just like he used to when he was two, the little rascal. Looking at them, following their every move, like when he was an infant and had learned to turn his head, remember? For the last two years since his death they'd thought they were alone, while all along he had been slipping in through the windows, dancing on the ocean outside their porch in Girbaug. And not just that—Benny was keeping an eye on his grandparents as well as on Scott and Anne and Bob. He was no longer their own private Benny. They had to share him with the universe now. Why, he could feel Ben on his skin right now, hot as coal.

He needed to tell Ellie all this. Right now. He tried to get out of bed but felt as if he had been stitched on to the mattress, pinned down by invisible threads that only pricked when he moved. And the throbbing in his forehead was stronger than ever. Beside, he couldn't remember how to make his mouth take the shape of Ellie's name.

"Ell—Benny," he screamed. "Benny. Help me."

"He's delirious," Dr. Gupta said. "It's but natural. Result of the fever. He'll be all right as soon as he gets more medicine in him."

"I want to transfer him by ambulance to a hospital in Bombay," Ellie said. "I don't want to take any chances."

Gupta looked amused. He glanced quickly at Nandita, who was standing next to a very worried-looking Ellie. "Madam, please," he said. "It's a simple case of pneumonia. Very common here. A few days of my tablets, and he'll be back to normal. Strong antibiotics we're treating him with. Same as what the hospital in Mumbai will do."

Ellie opened her mouth, but before she could say anything, Nandita stepped up. "Dr. Gupta, let me talk to you for a minute." She pulled him aside while Ellie went and sat next to Frank, trying to calm him down. "It's okay, sweetie," she said. "You were just having a bad dream, all right? You're gonna be fine, I promise."

Gupta's eyes showed a new seriousness when he returned to the bedside, and Ellie suspected that Nandita had told him about Benny.

"Here's what I propose, madam," he said. "Let's give the antibiotics a chance to work for today. If the fever is not down by tonight, we can talk about shifting him to the hospital." As Ellie looked up at him, his face softened. "I'm just trying to spare him the road trip to Mumbai," he added. "Our ambulances are not as well-equipped as yours in America."

"I appreciate your help, Doctor," Ellie said. She cast about for Nandita. "What do you think, Nan? Does that sound reasonable, to wait?"

"It does." She smiled in Gupta's direction. "Shashi and I have blind faith in Dr. Gupta. He has wonderful diagnostic skills. I would trust his judgment on anything. If any guests get sick at the hotel, he's whom we call. And as you know, he's our private physician, too."

Gupta bowed. "Thank you for the vote of confidence," he said. He put a hand on Ellie's shoulder. "Don't worry, madam. I've treated more cases of pneumonia here than even a top infectious disease specialist in America. Your husband will be in tip-top shape in a few days."

"Okay," Ellie said. "We'll wait."

She walked Gupta to the door, and when she walked back, Nandita was sitting on the couch in the living room, patting the seat next to her. "Come get off your feet for a bit," she said.

"I will in a minute. Let me just check on him."

Frank had fallen into a deep sleep again. She stroked his hair for a few minutes, and when he didn't respond, she crept out of the room.

"He's sleeping," she said, and Nandita nodded.

"Good. That'll help him more than anything else."

Ellie sighed. "He's been running himself ragged. The labor situation has been so hard on him. He worked right through Christmas, also."

Nandita stared straight ahead, saying nothing.

"What?"

She shook her head. "Nothing."

"Come on. I know when you're trying to be diplomatic. What's on your mind?"

Nandita shrugged her shoulders. "We just saw our first case of diabetes among the villagers. I'm really upset about it. These were a people who had never heard of the disease, thanks to their consumption of the *girbal* leaves. God knows how these folks even knew of its healing properties—guess that's the kind of primitive, ancient wisdom that people who live close to the land develop over the centuries."

Usually, Ellie enjoyed listening to Nandita wax philosophical about the native genius of the local people. But she'd been up since early morning with Frank and was worried to death about his health.

"What's your point?" she said.

Nandita trained a level gaze on her. "My point is, Ellie, that it's downright unfair that HerbalSolutions owns these trees. This fact just sticks in my craw."

Ellie sighed. Everything about Nandita was irking her today. She's so goddamn self-righteous, she thought. "Well, you know that Frank has agreed to allow the locals to take a small share of the harvest. And in any case, it was the Indian government who leased the forest to HerbalSolutions. It is their job to protect their own citizens. So you can't fault—"

Nandita looked aghast. "Oh, come off it, Ellie. You know better than that. The bastards in the state government are so corrupt they'd sell their own sisters if the price was right. What do they care about a forest of trees in the middle of nowhere? Or about the fate of some poor, impoverished villagers? A few, well-placed bribes and they'll do—"

"Nandita, please. Nobody at HerbalSolutions offered any bribes. Frank would never stand for that."

"Don't take it so personally, *na*, El," Nandita said softly. "This is not about your husband or even one company and one village. I'm talking about how entire economies are being shaped and devastated by the forces of globalization."

"But you're trying to blame us for the corruption of your own leaders," Ellie said, tearfully aware that she had somehow slipped into the role of playing Frank to Nandita's Ellie.

"Who's 'us,' my dear El?" Nandita's voice was sad and weary. "I've never thought of you as one of 'them.' So why are you making these false distinctions based on nationality?" She jutted her hand out to stop Ellie from interrupting her. "Wait. Let me finish. This is not about white versus brown or America versus India, darling. This is simply about the powerful versus the powerless. And all of us get to choose where we throw in our lot, whose interests we want to support. As for the corruption of the Indian government—you're absolutely right. But holding one institution culpable doesn't mean you excuse the culpability of the other, does it? You can blame both sides, no?"

Ellie shook her head. She was tired and worried about Frank. Her earlier gratitude at how willingly Nandita had canceled her plans for the day and brought over Dr. Gupta now soured. She simply wanted Nandita to leave, so that she could crawl back into bed with Frank and forget about the world for a few hours.

As if she had read her mind, Nandita stood up. "Anyway. This is not the time to talk about these things. You go take care of Frank. And call me if you need anything, okay? You promise?"

Now that Nandita was standing up, ready to go, Ellie didn't want her to. Still, she said nothing, nodding mutely. They walked to the door, and Ellie turned to accept Nandita's hug. As always, she felt comforted by Nandita's warm, tight embrace. "I'm scared," she heard herself say. "I don't want anything to be wrong with Frank." Her throat tightened with fear.

"I know." Nandita's arms around her got stronger. "I know,

sweetie. But don't worry. He just has a fever, that's all. You're not . . . you're doing the right thing."

"I'm sorry for being bitchy with you—"

"Hey. Who the hell do you think you're talking to? I love you like my own sister, remember?" Nandita walked down the path that led to the door and then turned around. "Besides, love means never having to say you're sorry." She pulled that rueful, doleful face that always made Ellie laugh. "Another American expression of dubious merit."

Ellie felt a little lighter as she closed the door and went into the bedroom to check on Frank.

He felt like a baby, learning to walk again. He was amazed at how weak he felt as he got out of bed for the first time in days. Ellie was at his side, holding him up, and he tried mocking the terrible weakness in his limbs, but even that took too much effort. But slowly, with her help, he made it into the kitchen to sit at the table. Edna had placed a steaming bowl of soup for him and was fussing around so nervously that it made Frank feel jittery. She hovered behind him, urging him on with each spoonful that he swallowed, keeping up a steady chatter of inane conversation until Frank finally looked up and shot an imploring look at Ellie. "Edna," she said immediately. "Let him eat in silence for a few minutes. The doctor said not to make too much noise around him."

Edna's hands fluttered to her side. "Yes, yes, madam, of course," she said, hurrying back to the stove. "We have a nice roast chicken for dinner."

He put his spoon down after a few more swallows. "I'm full," he announced, and Ellie looked worried. "Okay," she said. "Maybe you can try again in a half hour."

He sat at the table with his eyes closed.

"Tell you what, sweetie," Ellie said. "Would you like to sit on the porch for a few minutes before going back to bed?"

So he sat on the swing, staring out at the sun gleaming on the water. He remembered his dream from a few days ago, but calling it a dream felt wrong, as if he was desecrating its power. It hadn't been a dream; it had been a vision, a revelation. A message to him from Benny. Despite the weakness of his body, his spirit felt light and strong. He felt free—free, not just of the terrible belief that Benny's death had been a punishment for some past sin but free of his belief in a moral universe. The arc of the world bent not toward morality but toward indifference. He didn't see this new way of thinking as a crisis of faith. Rather, he had found a new home for his faith. It was not that he had stopped believing in God; he had simply replaced the old, scorekeeping God with one whose signature characteristic was apathy.

He sat on that swing day after day as his body grew stronger, looking out at the sun on the water. The fever had long left his body, but his mind felt fevered as he tried to figure out what the vision had meant. He was now convinced that it was Benny he had seen on the couch on Christmas Eve, Benny come back to show him the way. It had not been an optical illusion at all, as he had then supposed. His son had come to lead him to the sun. He felt sad at the realization that he couldn't explain any of this to Ellie. Without the sweaty agitation of the sickbed, where the vision had been born, he could speak to her the words but never the music. She would never see Benny's incandescent body dancing on the waves or illuminating the sky, as he did.

He was talking to Benny and waving to him one afternoon when Ellie walked onto the porch. He knew she had caught him gesticulating with his hands while his lips moved. I probably look like a friggin' madman, he thought to himself, as he caught the concerned look that crossed her face. But really, he didn't care all that much. He mostly wanted to be left alone, so that he could figure out things, and all she wanted to talk about was whether he wanted his eggs fried or hard-boiled.

"A fried eye looks like a sun in the sky," he blurted out. "You ever thought of that?"

In response, she strode up to him and felt his forehead.

"I don't have a fever," he said.

Ellie was looking at him curiously. "You should take a nap," she said. "You're still pretty weak."

As it turned out, she was right. It took him almost another ten days to feel like himself again.

He went back to work on the twelfth day. For the first time since Mukesh's death and the strike that followed, he did not dread stepping into the factory. Benny was with him. And the vision made him feel less guilty about the events of the past few months. Mukesh had died because it had been his time to enter the darkness, that's all. It was nobody's fault. Nobody's fault, at all.

CHAPTER 26

For two months now he had been losing his son to a machine. Bad enough that he was forever fighting a silent battle with the American for his son's time and attention. But now Frank had set a trap for him so that even when he and Edna had Ramesh with him physically, the machine was controlling the boy, luring him away from his father, seducing him with its color pictures or with its blank screen that Ramesh filled with words Prakash could not read.

The child had come home with the computer on Christmas Eve. Prakash remembered the day well. He and Edna had spent the evening watching television, looking up eagerly each time the wind rattled their open door, thinking it was Ramesh come home. Occasionally, the tinkling sounds of laughter and voices wafted over the courtyard from the main house, making them feel even more miserable and isolated in their single room, making them feel like underworld creatures, like mice or roaches, living in the dark, while light and laughter poured out of the big house where the Americans were having their celebration. With their boy as one of the guests.

At nine o'clock he had asked Edna if she would go to a movie with him, but she shook her head. She was thinking about the Christmas Eves of her youth in Goa, he knew, and that recognition added to the closed-in, oppressive atmosphere of this single room. "Let's go get Ramesh and go to cinema hall," he proposed again.

"Are you mad?" she snapped. "No manners? He at a party."

What did he know about manners and parties? He had never been invited to a party in his life. Diwali celebrations, Holi processions, were all community affairs, and when he was a child he would enter people's homes uninvited, like a scrap of paper blown in by the wind. Most of the time nobody minded, and if they did, they let him know, chased him out with words or a raised hand. Edna's childhood, he knew, was different, with family parties and dances and socials. How low she had sunk since her marriage to him, how isolated he had made her life. By marrying Edna, he had orphaned her, also.

He was brooding on this long after Edna went to bed at eleven. But he was up, feeling trapped in the little house. He longed to go sit in the courtyard, feel some of the cool December breeze on his face, but was afraid of running into the Americans or their guests, afraid that they may think he was spying on them or worse, looking into the main house with envy. He sat on his cot in the dark and made himself miserable by counting the ways in which he'd made Edna miserable.

So he was already in a foul mood when Ramesh bounded into the house at eleven thirty and turned on the light. "Turn off the light," he snarled. "Your mother is sleeping." But Edna was already rolling on her side and getting out of bed.

Edna noticed the new sneakers immediately. "Let me see, Ramu," she said.

But Ramesh shook his head impatiently. "Look at this, ma. My new computer. Frank gave."

Prakash felt a flame of jealousy shoot through him. But before he could react, Edna squealed. "What? A computer? For you?"

Ramesh nodded proudly. "Brand-new. For me. For school."

The way they had gone on that night, mother and son, you'd have believed Ramesh had been given a new car, Prakash now thought. And a car he would've known what to do with. He would've known how to repair it, drive it, paint it, wash it. But this computer was like a foreign god who sat smug and fat and incomprehensible in his house. One who controlled his son, one whose light shone late into the night as Ramesh bowed his head before it.

Prakash now eyed the hated object. He was alone at home—the boy was at school; Edna had gone shopping with Ellie miss. He thought back to the evenings when he had wanted to take his son for a walk along the beach or to the cinema house. Ramesh would get a regretful look on his face. "I can't, Dada," he'd say. "I have so-much, so-much homework to do." And he'd go work on the computer.

Well, let the boy read his books instead. Prithviji, the oldest man in the village, who could recite part of the Mahabharata by heart, had told him recently these computers were tools of the devil, corrupting the village youth, filling their heads with dangerous ideas. And wasn't Prithviji correct? Prakash saw pictures of America on TV every day—women walking almost unclothed on the streets, priests doing wicked-wicked things to children, soldiers putting black bags over naked Iraqis and making them do unnatural things. If he had his way, he wouldn't even let the American teach his son. God knows what the man was saying to Ramesh during their morning runs or while helping with his homework.

Nothing he could do about the homework—Edna would leave him before she would allow Prakash to break that tie. Beside, he worked for the Americans, and he had seen how Frank looked at Ramesh with big, needy eyes. No point in lifting the rock that the snake was coiled under. No need to bring Frank's wrath on his head.

The machine was a different story. The computer was a guest in his home. One he could ask to leave. He went to the corner where he kept his toolbox and picked out a screwdriver and a pair of cutters.

He unplugged the laptop, turned it around, and deftly unscrewed the metal panel in the back. He stared at the miniature landscape of shiny chips and wires before him, so that for a second his fascination was stronger than his fury. Regret at what he was about to do nipped at him momentarily, but he shook it off. He began to work, systematically snipping whatever wires he could. He stopped after a few minutes, satisfied with his handiwork. Slowly, carefully, he screwed the silver panel back into place. Nobody would ever guess what had happened, what he had done. He plugged the computer back on and noticed happily that there was no light in the power cord.

He walked toward the kitchen area, pulled down a bottle of cheap liquor, and took a long, lingering swig. Then he walked out of their tiny house. There was a lift in his step that had been missing for months.

CHAPTER 27

Arthur D'Mello, HerbalSolutions' IT man, laid the laptop down on Frank's desk, a strange expression on his face. "Someone has chopped the wires, sir," he said, his voice reflecting the bewilderment he felt. "This is a deliberate job."

Frank glanced at the computer and saw the veracity of what Arthur was telling him. But his mind could not comprehend what his eyes were seeing. The machine was almost brand-new. Why would someone—? And who would—?

Even before he could complete the thought, he knew the answer. Prakash. It had to be. The fellow had destroyed the computer. No one else would be that spiteful and that reckless. But why would the jerk do this? Did he really not care about his son at all?

He had not been too concerned when Ramesh had showed up last night complaining that his computer was not working. "Can you repair, Frank?" the boy had asked.

"I don't know how to fix these things, bud," he'd replied. "But I'll take it to work tomorrow. I'm sure Arthur can figure out what's wrong." All the while thinking it was a simple software glitch, not sabotage.

Arthur was eyeing him curiously. "Are you all right, sir?" he asked, and Frank realized that some of the fury he was feeling must have shown on his face. "Yeah, fine," he replied, forcing his face into a neutral blankness.

"Who would do such a thing, sir?" Arthur continued. "Why?"

Even while his rational mind told him not to confide in a subordinate, Frank heard himself saying, "A total bastard, that's who. A jealous, insecure jerk who's afraid of his own child's success. I'm going to kill him when I get home tonight."

Arthur took one step back. "No, no, don't say that, sir," the young man said appeasingly. "You're just upset, sir, I understand. What to do, sir? So many stupid-stupid people in this country."

Oh, don't even get me started about this country, Frank thought. He looked at the man standing next to him. He liked Arthur—he was a smart, competent guy, one of the best hires Frank had made. Also, he was from Bombay and had a level of sophistication, indeed, a rhythm that the small-town people who made up most of Herbal-Solutions' midlevel office staff lacked. Still, he'd seen how startled Arthur had looked when he'd lashed out against Prakash. Better to be careful. How could he expect a perfect stranger to understand the extent of Prakash's vileness and perfidy?

He made a visible effort to control his emotions. "Well, is it fixable?" he asked, nodding toward the laptop.

Arthur made a face. "I could try, sir," he began. He shook his head. "But to be honest, there's a lot of damage done. Not sure if—"

"Forget it," Frank said, cutting him off. "Let's just junk it."

"We can save the hard drive and other parts, sir," Arthur said. "After all, it's brand new."

Didn't he know it? He remembered the joy on Ramesh's face on Christmas Eve and felt murderously angry all over again. He forced himself to focus on Arthur. "Whatever you wish," he said. "Thanks for coming in."

"No mention, sir," Arthur said. He picked up the ruined laptop and left Frank's office.

He spent the rest of the afternoon plotting what he was going to do to Prakash. By the time Satish picked him up for the ride home, he had come to a resolution: it was time to remind Prakash of who was boss. What he wanted from the man was a confession and a promise never to do such a thing again. If that meant threatening Prakash with filing a police report, he would.

Prakash was in the courtyard pulling the weeds from between the stones when Frank got home. His distaste rose as he saw Prakash's skinny, bent shape. Still, he ignored the man and went indoors.

"Hi, honey," Ellie called to him and he gave her a kiss before he went into the bedroom to change. He came out wearing a T-shirt and cargo shorts. Ellie looked up. "You have a good day?" she asked.

"Great," he lied. He didn't want any of the anger that he was feeling to be squandered in the retelling of the story to her. "I'm going out to the car for a minute," he said and walked outdoors.

Ramesh was in the yard, helping his dad with the weeds. Frank stopped dead in his tracks when he saw the boy, unsure of whether to confront Prakash in front of his son. But right then Prakash looked up at him and smirked. Frank took in the cagey eyes, the thin smile, and then he was almost upon the man, who was still crouching on the stones as he tugged at the weeds.

"Get up," he said. "Get up."

Prakash rose slowly. "Yes?" he said.

Frank could hear the mockery in the man's voice. "Why did you do it?" he asked, keeping his voice low. "When did you do it?"

Prakash's eyes widened. "Do what, *seth*?"

Frank was dimly aware of the fact that Ramesh had risen, too, and was staring at him. But he was past caring. He would get a confession out of Prakash if he had to beat it out of him. Prakash had started this provocation, but he, Frank, would end it. "You know what I'm talking about. Destroyed the computer. Tore out the wires. Why did you do it?"

Prakash opened his mouth, but Frank spoke first. "Don't lie to me, you scumbag. Don't. Because if you do, next thing you know you'll be talking to the police, not to me." He stopped, remembering something. "Or better yet, I'll turn you over to Gulab Singh."

He had instinctively chosen the right weapon to fight Prakash with. At the mention of Gulab's name, Prakash began to wail. "*Maaf karo*, Frank sahib," he said, folding his hands in a pleading gesture. "It was my mistake. Too much to drink, sir. Please forgive."

Prakash's wailing drew Edna out of her house. "What?" she said. "Frank sahib, what has happened?"

"Dada broke my computer," Ramesh yelled to his mother. "Purposely. Cut the wires, ma." The boy was near tears, his eyes flashing with rage. And instead of feeling sorry for Ramesh or protective of him, Frank felt a raw satisfaction. Let the boy know what his father is made of, he thought. It's time he knew his character.

"*Besharam*," Edna berated her husband. "Wormeater. *Kutta*. I curse the day I laid eyes on you."

As if to salvage his last remaining pride, Prakash turned on Edna with a growl. "Shut up, you whore," he yelled and raised his hand toward Edna. "Get back to the house."

Frank moved. His right fist landed on Prakash's chest bone at the exact moment that Ellie came into the courtyard to see what the commotion was about. Prakash staggered back five steps and then fell heavily on his butt. He stayed on the ground, moaning to himself, rubbing his chest with both his hands. The blow had landed harder than Frank had intended. He knew from how his knuckles stung.

"Frank," Ellie screamed as she raced toward where he was standing, towering over Prakash. For a full minute, she was the only one moving. The other four stood frozen, varying degrees of shock registering on their faces.

"Oh, shit," Frank said, staring at Ellie and then at Ramesh. "I didn't mean to——. I thought he was going to hurt her," he added, pointing toward Edna.

Ramesh was staring at him, an expression on his face he couldn't read. And then, still keeping his eyes on Frank, Ramesh went up to his father and sat down beside him, stroking his arm. "*Chalo*, Dada," he said. "Get up. Come into the house."

Frank felt his cheeks burn. He wished Ellie wasn't here to witness his shame, the obvious fact that Ramesh had sided with his father over him. He noticed the protective way in which Ramesh cradled his father, the careful way in which he was helping him get to his feet.

Just before hobbling away, Prakash looked at Frank. The contempt on the man's face took Frank's breath away. It was a look that said that Prakash knew what Frank saw—that even in defeat, he was triumphant. Because Ramesh belonged to him. Because the ties of blood could not be severed as easily as cutting the wires on a computer.

Edna, ever anxious to curry favor with her employers, must've dimly registered what had just occurred. "Thank you for saving me, sir," she said. "Not telling what that drunkard would have done." Getting no reaction from Frank, she turned toward Ellie. "He save me, miss," she said. "That rat was about to—"

"I know, Edna, I know," Ellie said dryly, and Frank knew that she was not convinced.

Ellie turned to Frank. "This is enough drama for one day, don't you think? Let's go in."

He followed behind her. As he'd predicted, she turned to him as soon as he shut the door behind them. "You *hit* him? Are you out of your mind? Can't you find someone your own size to—"

"Damn you," he said in a low voice. "You weren't there. You don't know what he did. He's a piece of shit. And I should've known that you'd side with that prick instead of with me." But what he was really thinking was, Ramesh went to his father's aid, not mine. Even after he found out what his dad had done.

"Frank," Ellie began, but he cut her off.

"No. Not today. Save the social worker act for someone else. You don't even understand or like these people. You—you just feel sorry for them, that's all." He turned around and left the room. He sat on the porch for a few minutes and watched the sea churning in the distance. But he was too agitated to sit still. He got up, crossed the front lawn, and ran down the steps to the beach. He tied one shoelace that had come undone and began to run along the water, the evening sun sinking to his left.

But no matter how fast he ran, he could not run away from the image of Ramesh sitting beside his fallen father, stroking his arm. Stupid, stupid, he chided himself. Hitting the bastard in front of the child. Leaving the poor kid with no choice. Frank made a fist and slammed it into his left hand repeatedly, punishing himself for his violence, for his lack of control. A few fishermen drying their nets on the sand looked at him curiously as he ran along, punching and talking to himself. He barely noticed them.

The sun had set by the time he got home, and he ran the last quarter mile in darkness. Ellie had left the porch light on for him. She was reading in the living room and looked up when he came in. He wanted to ask whether Ramesh had come asking for him but didn't have the heart to find out. Besides, he was pretty sure he knew the answer. The boy was probably home with his father, who would soak up sympathy like bread in a bowl of warm milk.

Pulling off his drenched T-shirt, he headed into the bathroom and slammed the door behind him.

CHAPTER 28

Ramesh was gone. Vanished. Disappeared. Along with his father.

Two days after Frank's altercation with Prakash, the latter had left the house to go pick up Ramesh from school as he usually did. He had mumbled something to Edna about taking his son for an outing and that they would be home late. Edna, happy any time Prakash paid attention to his son, had been glad. But at eight that evening Mulad, one of the village drunks, had staggered up the driveway, knocked on Edna's door and handed her a note. It was in Ramesh's handwriting but was dictated by Prakash.

Dear Edna, the note said, *I am taking my son away for a while. The boy needs to understand where he comes from. And I am needing to know my son. You please do all the cooking at the main house while we are away. Don't worry. We will return soon.*
Your husband,

Prakash

Edna read the note and then brought it over for Frank and Ellie to decipher.

What caught Frank's immediate attention was Prakash's two mentions of Ramesh as "my son." He looked at Ellie to see if she had picked up on the current of hostility that wound its way through the letter. But the expression on her face told him that she didn't see what he did—that this was Prakash's revenge for Frank humiliating him in front of his family.

"Where could he have taken the boy?" he asked Edna.

"That only I'm asking myself, sir. I'm thinking and thinking but not knowing. But the blue suitcase is missing. God only knows when Prakash took it out of the house."

Frank gritted his teeth. "Does he have any idea how it's gonna set Ramesh back in school, this little—adventure?"

Edna looked ready to cry. Ellie shot him a warning look. "I'm sure Prakash is aware of that, honey," she said smoothly. "I'm sure they'll only be gone for a day or two."

He barely heard her. He had just had another thought: What if the note was a ruse to buy Prakash some time? What if the drunken bastard had fled forever with Ramesh? In a country of a billion people, how would he ever find Ramesh again?

And all of a sudden, he knew, *knew* that that was exactly what Prakash had planned. He felt physically ill, unable to stand up, as weak as he'd felt while recovering from the pneumonia. "Frank, what is it?" he heard Ellie say, and he saw that the two women had noticed.

"He's gone," he blurted out, his eyes filling with tears. "He's taken the boy and run. Forever."

He didn't hear Edna cry out or see her hand flying to her open mouth. He didn't see the disbelieving look on Ellie's face. "Whoa, whoa," Ellie said. "Let's not get carried away here. Just because Prakash has decided to take his son on a trip . . ."

He felt as if he was looking down on Ellie from some great height, felt as if he was really *seeing* her for the first time. What he'd always thought of as kindness and compassion, he now saw for what it really was—silliness. A dangerous naïveté.

"Has he ever taken the boy on a—trip?" he asked Edna, not bothering to keep the sarcasm out of his voice.

"No, sir. Never. Prakash has hardly left Girbaug except one-two times."

"And how has he been since—since the day, y'know, we exchanged words?"

"He been acting very strangely, sir. One minute he all quiet and serious and then he's smiling at me. Like he knowing something I'm not knowing."

Frank turned to Ellie triumphantly. "There. You heard that."

"Well, so damn what? Prakash always acts a little strange."

He was suddenly tired of both women and their hazardous stupidity. Of their inability to look clear-eyed into the unyielding core of the universe. Of their failure to recognize malice even when it lived up close to them. Ellie was a psychologist, had been trained to look inside people's heads. And here she was, deceived by an illiterate cook.

He read the letter again. And suddenly realized that it was meant for him. Prakash had known Edna would bring the note to him. It was designed to throw him, Frank, off their scent while Prakash disappeared with the boy. He felt an urgent need to find Ramesh, to reassure him, to rescue him from whatever fate Prakash had in store for him.

"Well, nothing we can do tonight," he lied. "In any case, I have some phone calls to make."

Edna looked unconvinced. "Sir, he'll come back. He loves that boy. And Ramesh will want to be coming back, no?"

He looked at her absently. "I'm sure," he said vaguely. He turned on his heels and walked toward the guest room. "I have to make some work calls," he said to Ellie. "I'd like to not be disturbed, okay?"

Ellie looked skeptical. She opened her mouth to say something and then shrugged. "Whatever."

He shut the door behind him and sat on the edge of the sleeper sofa, cradling his head in his hands. The thought of Ramesh not being across the courtyard from him tonight, the image of the boy sleeping in some strange bed—or worse, in a field or under a tree— filled him with despair. The fucking bastard. Fucking coward. Prakash couldn't take him on directly and so was using the child to get back at him. What if he took him to a big city like Bombay or Calcutta and disappeared? They'd never hear from Ramesh again. The boy would disappear like a small stone thrown into the ocean.

He jumped up from the sofa. He had already wasted precious hours. If he was to find Ramesh, the time for action was now. Prakash already had a head start of several hours. He paced the room for a minute, trying to think clearly, to keep his panic on a leash. There was only one man who could help him. Only one man whose dislike for Prakash matched his. Only one man with the self-confidence and wherewithal to know what to do. He sat at the antique desk and dialed Gulab's number.

"Tell me," Gulab answered.

"It's Frank Benton," he said. "There's—there's a situation that I need help with."

"Yes, sir?" Frank could hear the animal alertness in Gulab's voice.

"It's that fool Prakash," he said. "He's taken his son and disappeared. I need your help finding them."

"Disappeared where, sir?"

Frank ground his teeth. "I don't know. He just left a note saying he was taking his son on a trip for a few days."

"Then we should wait. They will return in two-three days. The idiot probably doesn't have money for more than that."

Why was Gulab being as obtuse as the rest of them? "Look," Frank said. "The note is a ruse. The man has kidnapped his son, don't you get it? We'll never see them again if we don't move on this."

There was a second's silence, and when Gulab spoke again, something had shifted in his tone. "I see. Well, in that case, Frank sahib, I should contact the police chief. Try and find out where that *goonda* has smuggled his son."

"Okay. But Gulab, there should be no violence. I—I just want to find the boy, that's all."

"Understood. I will contact you in the morning, sir."

"But if there's any news tonight, I want you to call. Don't worry about the time." Frank made a mental note to sleep in the guest bedroom tonight.

"Yes, boss."

But sleep was not his country tonight. Frank lay in bed, trying to fight the images preying on his mind—Ramesh sleeping in some unsavory, unsafe place, Prakash getting drunk and hitting the boy, Ramesh scared and inconsolable in a big, alien city. Maybe it would be better if Prakash took the boy to Bombay, Frank thought. At least Ramesh would know something about the city. But when he thought of what flea-infested hotel Prakash would be able to afford, he almost cried out in rage. He wondered whether Ramesh at least had his sneakers on, repelled at the thought of the boy wandering through the dirty city in his plastic slippers.

He got up late the next morning, having decided before finally falling asleep that he would take the day off from work. For one blissful moment his mind was blank, but then he remembered and the bleakness fell upon him, as if he had pulled a blanket over his head. He got out of bed and, ignoring the pressure on his bladder, dialed Gulab's number.

"No news, yet, sir." He could hear the apology in Gulab's voice. "But not to worry. Police will start their investigations full blast today."

"Okay," he said. "But remember, no violence. Just find me the boy. Oh, and one other thing. I'm working from home today. So call me on my cell if there's any news."

"Very good, sir."

He peed and then opened the bedroom door and walked into the living room. He could hear Ellie in the kitchen. "Hi," she called out. "I didn't know whether to wake you. How come you're not at work?"

"Playing hooky," he mumbled.

Ellie walked into the living room with a large mug of coffee. As her eyes fell on him, her eyes widened and her mouth fell open in shock. Some of the coffee splashed onto the tiled floor. She barely noticed it.

"What's wrong?" he said, involuntarily looking over his shoulder.

She moved her mouth, but no words emerged.

"Ellie. What's the matter?"

"Oh, God. Frank. What happened to you?"

He looked at her inquiringly. "What're you talking about?"

"Your hair. Oh, God." She set the coffee mug down and came up to him. Taking his hand, she led him to the mirror in the bedroom.

He let out a cry when he saw his grandfather looking back at him. But, no, that wasn't it, exactly. What he really saw in the mirror was his own body and face, the body and face of a thirty-four-year-old. But the blond hair had turned gray. Overnight. It was like seeing his present and future selves at the same time, as if the mirror was a reflecting glass as well as a crystal ball. He felt as if he was a figure in a fairy tale, an apparition, felt that if he didn't dig his feet into the floor, he would float away, disappear.

Frank ran his hand through his hair and turned to Ellie with disbelieving eyes.

"What? How is this possible?"

"It happens. When people are under great stress. I've seen it in my practice." Ellie's eyes were moist. "Frank. What's going on with you? How is it that you're suffering so much and I am not part of it?"

He shook his head, not knowing what to say. He had the strange sensation of being aware of aging, as if he could suddenly feel every cell in his body becoming sluggish, turning as gray as his hair.

He let Ellie lead him to the couch, and she sat holding his hand. "Babe. Sometimes the hair reverts back. But you gotta let go of this stress. Talk to me. Tell me what's going on with you. Let me help you through this."

He looked at her face, so eager, so innocent, so beautiful, so *young*. What could he say to this face? This face had seen the ugly reality of the world but had not turned ugly. Had known the same searing loss and grief that he had but had not turned distrusting and fearful. Ellie had somehow risen above the tragedy that had befallen them, had reclaimed her place in the world. Whereas he, he had handed over the keys to his salvation to a nine-year-old boy. A boy who was now missing.

He shook his head. "I don't know. I—I'm just worried about Ramesh."

"Don't be, honey. He's with his father. And no matter what Prakash is, he loves his kid. They've just gone on a vacation, hon. Like we used to take Benny."

He didn't bother to keep the look of outrage from his face. How dare she desecrate the memory of their vacations with Benny by comparing them to Prakash's sneaky abduction of his son?

"What? What'd I say?"

"Did I ever take Benny on a vacation by myself?" His voice shook with anger. "Without checking with you? Informing you after the fact with a note?"

Ellie sighed. "Frank, I'm just trying to help—"

"Then leave me alone. This is not helping."

He ignored the hurt look in her eyes as he got up and walked out of the house. He knocked on Edna's door. "Any word from them?" he asked as soon as she answered.

"Nothing, sir," she said. "But maybe—"

He nodded, turned around and walked back into the house.

He spent the next four days at home. His days took on a pattern of avoiding Ellie, talking to Gulab several times, grilling Edna about any clues she may have as to where Prakash may have disappeared, falling into bed at night and sleeping fitfully. Ramesh's face kept haunting him. He imagined the boy in all kinds of dire situations, a beseeching look on his face, calling out to Frank for help. He would wake up in the middle of the night, his heart thudding, drenched in sweat.

His cell phone rang. It was Gulab calling. "Yes?" he said eagerly.

"Just got a call from the police, sir. Turns out Prakash bought a train ticket for Aderbad. The fellow who sold it to him was on leave. Returned to work today, only."

"What the hell is Aderbad?"

"A small town, sir. Nothing much there."

"Why the heck would he go there?"

"God knows, sir."

"Well, tell the police chief to send some of his men there."

There was a slight pause. "Out of their jurisdiction, sir."

Frank barked out an expletive. "They're investigating a kidnapping case. Nothing should be out of their jurisdiction."

Again, that pause. "They're saying a father taking his son is not kidnapping, sir."

Was Gulab mocking him? Frank gave his lower lip a savage pull. "Listen, Gulab. Tell the chief to send two of his men. I'll pay all expenses—plus *baksheesh*."

"That will work, sir. I'll phone him back right now only."

So why the fuck didn't Gulab come right out and tell him to pay those bastards off? Frank wondered as he hung up. What the hell was he being so delicate about? As if he, Frank, didn't know that the whole rotten country was a cesspool of corruption.

His house phone rang, but he ignored it. Ellie could get it. It was probably for her, anyway. He went to where Edna was sweeping the courtyard.

"What's in Aderbad?" he asked.

The woman started at him blankly. "Sir?"

"The town of Aderbad. Who does Prakash know there?"

"I never even heard of it, sir. Why you asking?"

"Because he bought a train ticket for there."

"Maybe one of his friends from the liquor shop is from there," she offered. But he was already turning away in disgust. Stupid, ignorant woman, he thought. Knows nothing about her husband.

Ellie gestured to him as he walked back into the house. "It's good to hear from you, Pete," she was saying. "And give our love to Janet and the kids, would you? Well, here's Frank."

The last thing he wanted to do was talk to Pete. But he had no choice. "I'll take it in the guest room," he said. He walked in there and waited until he heard Ellie hang up before saying, "Hey, Pete."

"Jesus, Frank," Pete's voice was close and hot in his ear. "What the hell is going on? I've been trying to reach you for days, and Deepak just kept putting me off. What are you doing at home, man? We have a huge order, and you guys are already running late."

Shit. The consignment had been due to leave Girbaug two days ago. He had put Deepak in charge of it, told him to handle things for a while. Obviously, his subordinate had dropped the ball. Why hadn't he called Frank to inform him? But then he remembered: he had told Deepak that he didn't want to be disturbed for a few days.

"I—I didn't know it hadn't left," he began.

"You didn't know? What the fuck, Frank? I have all these distributors breathing down my neck, and you didn't know?"

"I'd assigned the project to Deepak."

"Why? What's wrong with you? Deepak said you hadn't been in for four days. Why are you home, anyway?"

He decided to come clean with Pete. "There's a situation here. Ramesh—you remember him? He was gonna come to the States with us over Christmas? Well, it seems like his father has run away with him. They've disappeared. I'm—I'm trying to help the police find him. I need to be home to coordinate things."

There was a long, painful silence. "Hello?" Frank said.

"I don't believe it," Pete muttered. "You're sitting at home because a boy has gone somewhere with his own father? And in the meantime, my orders are—"

"Don't patronize me, Pete." He had spoken more sharply than he realized.

"Patronize you? Man, I'm ready to choke you. You're costing me thousands of dollars a day because—"

"This kid is important to me, Pete."

"Gimme a break, Frank. Hell, you showed up at work a week after Benny died. And here you are—"

Frank felt something snap. He remembered Pete's casual mention of attending his son's Little League game a few months ago. "Don't say my son's name," he heard himself say. "I don't want you to say Benny's name."

He heard Pete's intake of breath. "What the hell has gotten into you? I loved Benny like my own son. And now I'm not allowed to say his name?"

"You know what, Peter?" he said, his voice low, shimmering with anger. "You don't know shit about anything. We've been friends for how many years, and you can't cut me some slack for missing a few days of work? You're more worried about your bank balance than about a boy whose life may be in danger. You just go about your safe, happy, white-picket-fence life, man."

"I take great offense at that." Pete's voice was hard, angry. "You have no right to blame me for the fact that you are obsessed with some poor kid in India. I'm a businessman, Frank. And so were you, until you went off the deep end. If you want to play detective instead, well, don't blame me for that."

He was dying to get off the phone so that he could unfold a map and see where Aderbad was. And here was this dumb asshole who he'd thought was his friend, delaying him, droning on and on about business ethics and responsibilities. Frank felt a sharp pain shoot up his jaw and realized that he'd been clenching it. "Listen," he said finally. "I'll—I'll go in, okay? I'll make sure the orders go out by the end of this week. All right?"

"That's not good enough, Frank."

"I'll do the best I can." His cell phone was buzzing across the room, and Frank's eyes lit up. Surely it was Gulab, with some good news. "Listen, I have another call. I gotta go. We'll talk soon."

"No, wait. I want to—" Pete was saying as Frank hung up on him. He raced across the room and was disappointed to see that the caller was Deepak. Screw him, he thought. I'll call him in a few hours.

CHAPTER 29

They stood silently in front of the modest stucco house, the boy and the man. Prakash stared at the pink outer walls, the blue front door, the jasmine bushes to the right. Beside him, Ramesh shifted from foot to foot.

They had gotten into Goa this morning. Two nights ago, they had slept on a bench at the railway platform in Aderbad. Ramesh had balked at this, said he'd wanted to go back to Girbaug, but Prakash had told him that there was something he wanted him to see in Aderbad the next morning. After that, they would take another train and go to Goa.

When they woke up the next day, Prakash told Ramesh the story of how when he had ridden a motorcycle from Girbaug to Goa years ago, he had stumbled upon a temple along the way. "I'd never even heard of this Aderbad," he said. "*Bas*, stopped there for lunch, only. But then I saw this temple. And only Bhagwan knows why, Ramu, but I needed to walk in there. So quiet and peaceful it was. There was a big statue of Krishna, smiling and all. So I ask Him please to give me a beautiful wife. Two-three days later I met your ma."

"So why are we going there again?" Ramesh asked huffily. Even though his father was carrying the small suitcase, he was grumpy. His back was stiff from having slept on the bench, and the walk from the train station to the temple was long.

Prakash looked disappointed. "Don't you see, Ramu? To give thanks. I wants to thank God for giving me my family."

A shrewd look came on Ramesh's face. "Can I ask God to give me what I want?"

"Of course, *beta*. What you want to ask for?"

"I want my team to win the soccer match."

Prakash laughed. "*Bas*, that's all? Bhagwan will definitely grant you this wish." He caressed the boy's back. "I will pray bigger-bigger wish for my son."

Ramesh insisted that they catch an auto rickshaw back to the train station when they were done. "Dada, my back is hurting," he said.

Prakash fingered the bundle of notes he had in his pocket. He wondered if Edna had yet noticed that he had taken most of the money they had been saving inside a tin she kept in the kitchen. "*Theek hai*," he said. "Let's take a rickshaw."

Back at the station, he bought two tickets for an overnight train to Goa. Once aboard, Ramesh talked nonstop, thrilled to be visiting the place that his mother had talked so much about. But suddenly, he looked thoughtful. "Dada," he said, munching on the *batatawadas* Prakash had purchased at the last stop, "why Ma not coming with us?"

Prakash looked out of the train window. "It is a surprise," he said finally. He turned to face his son. "Do you know who live in Goa?"

Ramesh shook his head.

"Your grandma and grandpa. Your ma's mummy-daddy. We are going to see them."

Ramesh's face fell. "But Ma said they not wanting to see us."

"They will. Once they see you." Prakash reached over and ran his fingers delicately over Ramesh's face. "Once they see this *khubsurat* face."

And now they were standing on the bottom step, looking up at the house where Edna's parents lived. Prakash felt a nervous quivering at the base of his throat. He longed for a drink to steady his nerves, but he had vowed not to touch the bottle while he was on this trip with Ramesh. So far, he had kept his promise.

He took Ramesh's hand and climbed the two steps and knocked on the door. There was no response. He knocked again, a little louder. This time, they heard the shuffle of feet, and then the door opened and an old lady in a yellow dress peered at them. "Yes?"

Prakash cleared his throat. "Are you Agnes D'Silva?"

"Yes. And you are?"

"I is Prakash." Even to his own ears, his English sounded awful. To recover, he said, "And this your grandson, Ramesh."

Nothing happened. The old lady squinted a bit as she looked at Ramesh, but her face was impassive. The moment stretched on forever. "Wait," Agnes finally said and disappeared.

Father and son stood in the afternoon sun, not daring to look at each other. For the first time it occurred to Prakash that the situation he had been imagining—the teary reconciliation, the remorseful grandparents, the triumphant return to Girbaug—would perhaps not happen. But then he heard a second set of footsteps, and his optimism returned.

An old man stood at the door. He was tall, broad-shouldered, and square-jawed. He also had the coldest eyes Prakash had ever seen. Those eyes were looking at him now and then looking away, as if they'd been displeased by what they beheld. "So you're the bumpkin she married," the man said. The eyes flickered toward Ramesh. "And this is the bastard."

Prakash let out a cry of protest. "This is your grandson," he said, as if the old man didn't understand. "We came to—"

"You must be mistaken." The old man spoke carefully, deliberately. "I don't have a grandson. Because I don't have a daughter." He stepped back and shut the door.

They stood in shock, staring at the closed blue door. Prakash wanted to pound on it, tear it down, burst in and squeeze that old, grizzled throat until the man took his words back. But he suspected that in a fight with Edna's father, he would lose. He had no resources with which to combat such deliberate meanness. Beside, Ramesh had heard enough damaging words. He needed to be protected from any further cruelty. "Come, Ramu," he said, taking his hand. "Let's go. This *boodha* is mad."

They ate lunch at a beachside shack—prawn curry for the boy, chicken vindaloo for him. But the food tasted bitter to Prakash. To erase its taste, he ordered a glass of *feny*, the Goanese wine made from cashews. Then, another glass.

"Dada," Ramesh said, flashing him a worried look. "Don't drink so much, *na?*"

He looked at his son as if seeing him for the first time. He felt as if he understood his son completely—the pinched circumference of his present, the narrow limitations of his future. He felt an unbearable pity as he watched that young, eager face wolf down the curry rice. To obliterate that feeling of pity, he downed a third glass of *feny*.

He staggered out of the shack, Ramesh following at his heels. "You wanting to return to the hotel?" he asked the boy and was relieved when Ramesh shook his head no. The thought of returning to the run-down room with the peeling paint and the paan stains on the bathroom wall was too depressing. "Let's lie here, only," he said, flopping down on the sand. He was asleep within moments.

But not for long. He woke up twenty minutes later, the bitter taste still in this mouth. The idea for this trip had come to him as he had sat on his cot nursing the bruise where the American had hit him. He believed that Edna's parents would thaw once they saw their beautiful grandson. That they would regret the years of absence and would insist that the three of them move to Goa. He would've been happy to do so. The American's interest in his son was beginning to scare him. He wanted other people to claim Ramesh as their kin, wanted Ramesh to belong to a larger family—people with whom he shared the ties of blood.

Above Prakash, the sky was spinning and he cursed himself for having drunk so much *feny* so fast. He glanced to his left to where Ramesh was lying on the sand.

"Ramu," he said. "Are you sleeping?"

"No, Dada."

Prakash thought for a moment. "Ramu, don't you ever be poor like your dada. This world doesn't like poor people. You promise?"

"Promise, Dada."

"Good. And Ramu, another thing. Don't ever drink so much like your dada. Promise?"

"I promise, Dada."

He was silent for a long time, gazing up at the swirling, spinning sky. "And Ramu. Don't ever be an orphan like your father. Promise?"

"I promise, Dada." Followed by a little giggle.

Prakash turned his head to face his son. "You is making fun of your dada?"

Ramesh was screwing up his nose from the effort of trying not to laugh. "Sorry, Dada. But how can I promise not to be an orphan? That, up to you."

And suddenly, they were laughing, laughing so hard that Prakash felt a hot squirt of urine leak onto his pants. He immediately tightened his muscles. *"Saala,"* Prakash said, rolling toward his son and wrestling playfully with him. "Teasing your old father."

"I wasn't, Dada," Ramesh squealed. "But what you said was so funny."

The laughter and roughhousing did them both good, broke the

spell cast by Edna's father's mean words. Prakash felt something free up in his heart. Curse the old man to hell, he thought. If he cannot spot a Kohinoor diamond in the dust, his misfortune. I know my son's worth.

He sat on his haunches and pulled Ramesh close to him. Father and son sat in this position for a few minutes, staring at the water. He kissed the top of the boy's head. "You are my life," he whispered. "Always remember this."

"I know, Dada." This time, there was no mischief in the boy's voice.

"*Chalo,*" Prakash said finally. "Let's go to the market and buy your ma a few things. Some Goanese sweets I needing to get her. Then tomorrow morning, we will leave for Girbaug."

"I want to stay, Dada. I like Goa."

He kissed the boy again. "I know, *beta*. But so much school you're missing. And your ma will be waiting for us."

They arrived in Girbaug at nine the next evening, armed with goodies—*bebinca* and other sweets for Edna and Ramesh, two bottles of *feny* for Prakash, and two packets of Goanese cashews for Ellie miss. As he walked up the driveway, Ramesh skipping ahead of him, Prakash felt his chest tighten. Despite the failure of his mission, he had loved every minute he'd spent with his son. Now, he would once again have to share Ramesh with others. He forced himself to remember the sweetness of their time together.

He belongs to me, he said to himself. This boy is mine and Edna's. No one else's.

CHAPTER 30

Five days had gone by since Prakash had brought the boy back, and Frank was still smarting from the insolence of the man. Prakash had wandered back home as if he'd had every right to take off with his son. And now he acted as if he was completely oblivious to the havoc he had wreaked—the anxiety he had caused Edna, the expense of the police search, the lost days of work the episode had cost Frank. Prakash had, in fact, acted outraged when he'd heard that the police had been looking for him all over Girbaug and in Aderbad. "What, I don't have the right to go somewhere with my own son?" Frank had heard him yell at Edna. "Tell your 'Merican bossman to call off his pet dogs. What police charge me with? Taking my son on holiday?"

He had wanted to march out of his house then and smash in the bastard's face. Pulverize it and then stand back and watch in satisfaction. But many things had stopped him: the memory of revulsion on Ellie's face as he had gotten more and more involved in the police's search for Prakash. Her hostility toward Gulab, who had frequently stopped by the house with the latest reports. Also, the memory of Ramesh comforting his father after Frank had pushed him in the courtyard. And finally, a beaming Ramesh walking into their house, bearing gifts from Goa for them. Looking for all the world as if he'd just returned from an honest-to-goodness real family vacation.

Ellie had been touched by the gifts. Well, let her be duped. He knew better. Prakash had had every intention of running away with the boy. The train ticket to Aderbad had been a ruse, to throw them off his scent. The fellow was cleverer than he looked, he'd give him that. Though why he'd returned after five days was a mystery. Probably ran out of money faster than he'd anticipated. Or maybe he had another trick up his sleeve. Maybe he was lulling them all into complacency, so that the next time he eloped with Ramesh, nobody would be worried. Well, he would just have to watch the boy like a hawk. Maybe have Satish drop him off and pick him up from school.

Frank looked at the stack of papers in front of him. He couldn't believe how much work had piled up during the time he'd stayed home. Yet the thought of attacking the pile made his eyes ache. He also had over eighty e-mails in his in-box. Half of them seemed to be from fucking Pete, about the consignment that hadn't left Girbaug yet.

He rubbed his forehead and stared out of the window, trying to figure out a way to thwart any plans Prakash might have for Ramesh. His phone rang and he eyed it with distaste before answering it. "Hello?" he said.

The caller let out a sigh that felt like a gust of wind in his ear. "Frank? This is Pete."

"Hello, Pete."

"Listen, this is a quick call. What's going on with the consignment?"

So that's how we play it these days, Frank thought. No small talk, no asking about Ellie. And this from a man who had been in his wedding and a pallbearer at Benny's funeral.

"I think we'll have it shipped out tomorrow."

"You think? I need more of a reassurance than that, Frank. It's already been—"

"I know how long it's been delayed, Pete. I'm working on it."

"You're working on it? I don't believe this. Listen, Frank, you seem to have forgotten that you have a friggin' job. That we're not paying you to sit at home and—"

"And you seem to have forgotten the fact that I've made you more money than any other person in your company, Pete."

"So is that what you're doing? Resting on your laurels?"

"No. I already told you the order's just about ready to be shipped."

There was a long, painful silence. And then Pete Timberlake said, "You know what, Frank? I've been thinking about this. I want you to come home. I'm pulling you out of India."

"What are you talking about?"

"Just what I said. Your contract's up. And really, we need an Indian face to head the plant. It's time for you to come home."

"Pete, have you lost it? You know I'm in the process of negotiating the new machinery for the plant that will cut our labor costs by a third—"

Pete laughed. "Have *I* lost it? That's precious, Frank. You're the one who blows off a deadline and sits at home moping around because some poor son of a bitch takes his own son on vacation, and you ask me if *I've* lost it?"

His hands were shaking so hard he needed both of them to hold the phone. "Listen, Pete. I'll get the consignment out by tomorrow, I promise. Hell, even if I have to stay here the whole damn night I'll make sure it's done."

Pete sighed. "Frank, it's more than just the consignment. Look, with all the labor trouble you've had and stuff, I just think it's better if you're home."

"Better for whom, Pete?" Frank said.

There was no mistaking the coldness in Pete's voice. "Why, best for HerbalSolutions, Frank. For God's sake. Don't make this personal."

Pete, you asshole, we're friends, Frank wanted to scream at him. I've changed diapers on your sons. Who the fuck do you think you're talking to in this stilted, formal way? Instead, he said, "Look, Pete. Don't make me beg. Jesus, Ellie's gonna have a fit when she finds out."

"Frank." Pete's voice was quiet. "What're you gonna do? Live in exile the rest of your life? You and Ellie? India isn't your home, bud. You gotta face up to . . . what has happened and move on. You know? I don't think this is healthy, the fact that you even blew us off at Christmas."

He was suddenly glad that Pete was sitting halfway across the globe from him. Because he would've physically hurt Pete if they'd been in the same room. You damn, smug prick, he thought, sitting in your office with your life intact, lecturing me about what's healthy.

"Frank? You still there?"

"Yup. I'm just—" He tried to say more, but his voice cracked. His left eye began to twitch.

"Oh, shit," Pete breathed. "I'm not trying to hurt you, Frank. But my mind's made up. I need you back here. You can take—I dunno—two to three months to wrap things up over there. I can send Stan to help you, if you like."

"Okay," he said, wrestling with his emotions. He'd be damned if he'd break down in front of Peter Timberlake. "Listen, I need your word—you can't mention this to Ellie. I—I need to tell her at the right time."

"Yeah, that's fine. That's your business."

"So I have your word on this?"

"Yup. But you better tell her soon, kiddo. Two months will go by fast."

"Sure I can't get you to change your mind, Pete?" he asked, hating himself for the beseeching quality his voice took on.

"Afraid not, Frank."

"Okay. We'll talk later," Frank said.

He hung up the phone, and his first thought was of Ramesh. Leaving India meant leaving Ramesh behind. He tried to get out of his chair and couldn't. His legs felt like they were made of hay, his head felt stuffed with cotton wool. Shit, he thought, maybe he was getting sick again. But even as he thought this, he knew that the truth was that he suffered not from the illness of the body but a disease of the soul. If love could be called a disease, that is.

The intensity of his emotions stunned him. When on earth had Ramesh become this important to his life? How was it that the thought of leaving India and reuniting with Scott, his mom, all the other people who had always lit up his galaxy, gave him no comfort or joy? He admitted the answer to himself: Ramesh had become the brightest star in that galaxy, his sun, and without the sun his future looked barren and dark. Without the sun—without the son—there was only the Father, lost and lonely, with nothing to guide his path.

He thought of his rituals with Ramesh—their morning runs on the almost deserted beach; the monthly haircuts that he and the boy got at the salon at the Hotel Shalimar; the Sunday dinners at home, where Frank taught Ramesh how to use the proper silverware, even as Edna waited on them and beamed proudly at the sight of her son cutting into the chicken with his fork and knife.

And here was Pete wanting to take all this away from him. Wanting him to abandon Ramesh as if he was some litter that he'd picked up on the beach. He fought the urge to get on the phone again and plead with Pete or even threaten to quit. But he couldn't risk Pete calling his bluff. Fuck Pete. Maybe he'd get a job with another multinational in India. But then what? he thought. There were no other foreign companies in Girbaug. If he was very, very lucky he might get something in Bombay. But that was a long shot, and even if he did, he might be able to see Ramesh once a month. How soon before the boy fell back in his studies, how long before he forgot his table manners, before his English went from bad to worse? Losing Ramesh slowly, over time, as he succumbed to the pull of his culture and family dysfunctions, would be more painful than losing him all at once.

Losing Ramesh was not an option. No. Ramesh had to go with them to America. He had to figure out a way to make it happen. There was nothing for the boy here in Girbaug.

He needed to think, think. Needed to buy some time. One thing was for sure—Ellie could not know about Pete's ultimatum. He would have to carry on as if everything was normal. He looked around his office, still pinned to his chair. This is my life, he thought, and the bastard who calls himself my friend is destroying it. Making me renounce it. And I will—I'll give up the chauffeured cars and the live-in help and the free housing and all the baubles Pete had strewn my way when he had wanted me to run the plant. But I will never give up on the true treasure, the real gem. Ramesh.

CHAPTER 31

"So what's he doing that's making you so nervous?" Nandita asked as Ellie and she wandered through the narrow alleys of Agni Bazaar.

Ignoring the frenzied cries of the vendors, Ellie thought back to the number of times she'd walked into a room and caught Frank talking to himself, as if he was losing some furious argument. And the way he sat for hours on the porch, staring at the sea, looking almost comatose at times, wildly animated at others. And oddest of all was the tic in his left eye.

"He twitches," she said.

"What do you mean, he twitches?" Nandita asked.

"Just that. I mean, he's jumpy and anxious, his eyes dart about, and well, he twitches. Plus there's this weird thing his left eye is doing."

A skinny youth tried to brush up against Nandita, and she fixed him a baleful glare as she skillfully avoided him. "You think Frank is depressed?"

"I don't know. I'd love to put him on an antidepressant and have him try Xanax for a few weeks. But he won't hear of it."

"He's still under a lot of pressure, eh? But at least now that Ramesh is back, things will ease up."

"Yeah, maybe." Ellie paused for a second. "It's funny—I thought when he found out why Prakash took Ramesh to Goa, he'd be relieved. I thought it was such a sweet gesture. But if anything, he seems even more angry."

"Well, he probably feels a little foolish, don't you think, El? I mean, the police search and all that was a little excessive."

"Tell me about it. I begged him to not do it, but he was like a madman. Unstoppable." Ellie shuddered. "It was an awful, awful week, Nan. That first morning when his hair went gray overnight, I was so scared." She made a rueful face. "I had really hoped his hair would revert back to its original color."

Nandita squeezed her arm. "That's okay. I say he still looks like a stud muffin, even with the gray."

Ellie smiled. "You're shameless. I'm so glad you came with me today. I think shopping therapy is what I desperately need." She peered into a store. "Can we go in here for a minute?"

They entered together, trying to ignore the clamorous, aggressive sales pitch of the rival shopkeepers. The proprietor raced up to them, bowing and nodding. "Come in, come in, madams," he said. He snapped his fingers, and a teenage boy appeared. "*Arre*, can't you see we have two guests?" he cried. "Go get two cold Coca-Colas, quickly."

Ellie opened her mouth to refuse and then thought better of it. Experience had taught her that she was no match for the famed Indian hospitality—or the aggressive Indian sales pitch. "Can I see that turquoise ring?" she asked.

"Of course, madam, of course." The shop owner turned to Nandita. "And for you, madam? Nice-nice gold silver jewelry we're having."

They wandered from the jewelry counters to the cloth section.

Two men deftly unfolded spool after spool of brightly colored silks for them to inspect. "Enough," Ellie protested, surrounded by a multicolored sea of fabrics. "Please don't go through the trouble."

"No trouble, madam," one of the men grinned. "If you don't see, how you buy?"

"Now, don't buy anything out of guilt," Nandita whispered to her as they sipped their Cokes. "These people are *pucca* business-men."

In the end, she purchased the turquoise ring for herself, insisted on buying a silver chain for Nandita, and got talked into getting a men's silk kurta for Frank, despite knowing that he would never wear it.

The other vendors were thrown into a frenzy as the two women emerged with their shopping bags. "Madam, nice American products we are having," they yelled after her, not understanding that that was the last thing that would hold her interest.

"Ignore them," Nandita instructed her. "Don't make eye contact. Otherwise you'll emerge carrying ten bars of Hershey's chocolates." She shuddered visibly.

"Oh, you are such a snob."

"Guilty as charged." Like most upper-class Indians, Nandita thought American chocolates were awful.

"Like Cadbury's is any better. Or Lindt, for that matter."

"Careful. You're trampling on hallowed ground." Nandita pretended to look offended. "Next thing you know, you'll be insulting the queen," she sniffed.

Ellie grabbed Nandita's hand. "You're nuts. Now come on. Let's find an auto rickshaw. I need to get home."

"Hey, before I forget," Nandita said after they were in the rickshaw. "You know my cousin Divya? The one who lives in Australia? She's going to be in Delhi on the twenty-first. Will you go with me to see her for a few days? Shashi can't get away. So I thought it could be an all-girls outing."

"I'll have to look at my calendar," Ellie said.

"*Ae*, screw your calendar. Just say yes, why don't you? I've been wanting for eons for her to meet you."

Ellie laughed. "I want to meet her too. How long will it take to get there?"

"We can take the overnight train. I'll have you back home in six days, I promise."

"Well, it sounds lovely." Ellie sighed. "And I'd like to get away for a few days, Nan. The mood at home—I dunno, it's too heavy at times."

"Good. Then it's settled. I'll buy the train tickets."

CHAPTER 32

Somehow, he managed to shake Ramesh off. Told the boy he couldn't jog with him this morning. He made himself ignore the hurt puzzlement he saw in the boy's eye. It's for his own sake, Frank told himself.

And now he was sitting on one of the large boulders that were submerged in the water, the waves nipping at his bare feet. Staring at the sun rising from the water. Trying to talk himself out of the plan he was hatching even while he knew that he had come here to this lonely spot to put on the finishing touches. To work it all out, so that it would unfold like a play, like a poem, when the time came.

There would be violence. There would be blood. This he had to accept. He had come here to take his own measure, to take measure of his love for this boy. To ask himself if he was willing to pay any price, in order to have Ramesh. To weigh the joy of having Ramesh against the tarnishing of his soul.

There was no other way. He had to keep reminding himself of that. Lord, if there were another way, he'd take it. If he could've legally adopted Ramesh, for instance. But they—Prakash, Edna, Pete, Ellie—they had all blocked his way. Until there was no way but this. And *this* was what he had to work out. Work out every last detail, like writing up a business plan.

But that wasn't why he'd come here. The details of the plan he could work out in any setting—while Satish drove him to work, while eating breakfast, while lying awake in bed, Ellie breathing quietly beside him. No, he had come to this quiet spot for the reckoning. To hold his greedy human heart in one hand and his immortal soul in the other. To see which one he would favor, which way the balance would tip. To mark this moment, this precise spot where he stood between the Frank that he had been and the Frank he would become. To see what he would value—the sweet, turn-the-other-cheek religion he had been raised on or the liberating, amoral theology that had appeared to him when he was sick with the pneumonia. To ask what was fueling him—the thick, gelatinous hate that gripped him at the thought of Prakash or the light, effervescent love that filled him at the thought of Ramesh. To resolve the paradox that both his hate and his love were leading him to the same dark, bloody place.

Above all, he had come here to tax his imagination—to see whether he could imagine a life in America without Ramesh in it.

He tried. He sat on the boulder with his eyes closed, the sweat dripping down his face. And all he saw was emptiness. Darkness. Ellie and him growing old in Michigan, running out of things to say to each other, occasional words dripping out of them like drops of water from a faucet. Ellie and him not turning on the porch light during trick-or-treating, afraid of the flocks of happy, rambunctious children skipping down their street. Ellie and him staring hungrily at other people's kids at the mall, at parties, at the playground, until their parents, sensing that hunger, pulled them away.

He opened his eyes. The world looked hazy for a moment and then came back into focus with such sharp clarity that Frank gasped. He pushed himself off the boulder and hurried out of the water, shaking off the seaweed that had wrapped around his foot. He had wasted enough time already. And he knew exactly what he had to do next.

CHAPTER 33

"Thanks for coming on such short notice," Frank told the man sitting across from him. "I appreciate it."

For a moment the man who was built like a building—tall, wide, impenetrable, his face a blank facade—did not stir. Then, Gulab nodded slightly. "Of course, sir. My pleasure."

Frank looked away to escape Gulab's dark, reptilian eyes. His gaze caught on and followed the slow descent of a green leaf from a tree outside his window.

"Sir?" Gulab said. "You were saying."

"Ah, yes." Frank's voice shook a bit as he spoke. "Listen, Gulab. I wish to talk to you in confidence. Can I expect you to—"

"Sir. Everything you ever say to me is in absolute confidence. I am a trained army man, sir. I was taught to keep my mouth closed."

Frank nodded. He eyed Gulab's large, thick hands, remembered what he had once said—*I have killed men with my bare hands*. A long time ago, he had been repulsed by the brute force they represented. But ever since Gulab had helped him in his search for Prakash, he had come to see him as a trustworthy, capable ally. Today, he saw these hands as helping him carry Ramesh safely ashore to America.

"I don't know if you remember this," Frank said. "But many

months ago when you were at my house you said something about coming to you if I ever needed to take Ramesh back with us to America. What did you mean?"

Gulab's face was unreadable. "I said only to ask me if you were truly ready, sir." He looked deep into Frank's eyes. "Are you ready?"

"I am," he said, his voice firm. But his hands were shaking uncontrollably, and he was glad that his desk hid the fact from Gulab.

"Then it will be my pleasure to assist you."

"I want Prakash gone." The words came out in a rush. "I want you to—take care of him. For me."

Gulab's face was impassive. "Done, sir."

He had to make sure. "Do you understand what I am saying? What—what I'm asking you for?"

Gulab did not skip a beat. "Of course, sir. No problem."

Frank's left eye began to twitch, and he hoped Gulab couldn't see this. He felt the sweat bead up on his forehead and fought the urge to wipe it off. This was no time to act like a schoolboy. He struggled to recapture some of the clarity he had felt after coming to his decision at the waterfront two mornings ago. "What about Edna?" he asked.

Gulab shrugged. "I'll take care of her, also."

Frank permitted himself a pang of regret. He remembered Edna's eager, upturned face, her sincere pride in the interest Frank took in her son. But it couldn't be helped. Edna would cling even more strongly to Ramesh if her husband was dead. She had to be—dealt with—also.

"Are there any other relatives who could come forward to claim the boy?"

"Who, sir? You heard what Edna's parents said when the *chootia* dragged the boy to Goa. And Prakash has no kin." Gulab smiled. "Even if someone shows up, I will . . . convince them."

With nobody to claim Ramesh, he and Ellie could begin adoption procedures. Ellie was too softhearted to abandon Ramesh, he knew. And under the circumstances, he was sure that Tom Andrews would help them jump through the immigration hoops. Hell, he might have Ramesh with him in America by Memorial Day.

Frank realized he had been holding his breath. "If I were to consider this, where—how—would you carry this out?"

Gulab thought for a moment. "Best to do this late at night, sir. When they're sleeping. Easy to access their shack directly from the street. Still, better if you and your missus are out of the main house when it happens."

Frank nodded. "Here's what I've been thinking. Ellie's taking a trip to Delhi with a friend on the twenty-first. What if I take Ramesh out of town that same weekend? Can you do it then?"

"That will be perfect, sir. Will give me enough time to make preparations. You will leave Saturday morning, yes?"

He nodded, his mind racing. He had already decided that he would tell Prakash he wanted to take Ramesh to Bombay to see the All-India Soccer tournament. Frank's jaw tightened with anger at the thought of kissing up to Prakash. But it's only for a few more weeks, he reminded himself.

Gulab cleared his throat. "Sir, one other thing. You needn't worry about coming home and finding the . . . bodies. After the job is done, I will place an anonymous call to the police, saying I heard gunshots. They will check out the house and then will call you, sir. So your vacation will be interrupted. Unfortunately."

It's like we're planning a picnic instead of a murder, Frank thought. He imagined the stricken look on his mother's face if she overheard this conversation, imagined her dismay at how far her son, the altar boy who had sung at St. Anne's every Sunday, had fallen. But there is no other way, he reminded himself. Between Prakash's obstinacy and Pete's ultimatum, he was left with no options. Besides, he had to think about Ramesh's future. God knows nobody else was thinking of him.

"There's another thing, Gulab," he said. "You have to do this yourself. I don't want anyone else involved, no one. And this—this can never be traced back to me, you understand? I—believe me, if I could think of another way to settle this, I would. But under no circumstances—"

"Frank sahib," Gulab interrupted. "Don't worry so much." His tone had changed and was more relaxed, jocular. "This is nothing." He flicked his wrist. "Like killing off a mosquito."

Frank didn't like this flippancy, this carelessness. He wanted Gulab to understand the gravity of the situation, to give it the weight it deserved. "Listen, Gulab," he said. "This—what I'm doing—goes against everything that I know and believe in. Do you understand? I—we Americans believe in the sanctity of life. I was brought up to believe, Thou Shalt Not Kill."

Something bright flashed in Gulab's eyes. But when he spoke, his tone was flat, his face expressionless. "Yes, sir. World over, Americans are known for respecting life."

Was the guy mocking him? Frank peered closely, but Gulab's expression was as blank as a wall. "In any case, I want an assurance that you will—you will do this job yourself."

"No problem, sir."

"And—one more thing. How much—that is, what do you charge for this job?"

Gulab's smile was thin and stretched. "No fixed rate, sir. This is not exactly my profession, to bump off people. Just as a favor to you. So whatever your heart tells you to pay is good."

Frank felt the sweat forming on his forehead again. He felt weak, nauseous, and his hands fluttered in his lap. "Gulab, I have no idea what would be fair."

"Would one lakh be possible, sir? A special discount rate for you," he added.

One lakh. Frank did a quick calculation. That was about twenty-

five hundred dollars. He felt something twist in his heart. He now
knew the value of a human life. Of two lives.

Gulab was waiting for his answer. "That's fine," Frank said. "But
this money has to come from my personal account, obviously. And
I have to withdraw it without making my wife suspicious. So I need
to think about how——"

"Buy a carpet."

"Excuse me?"

"My friend has a shop, sir. Sells handwoven carpets. Good quality. You buy a very cheap one. He will give you receipt for one lakh.
You just give me a bearer's check next week. And I will get you the
invoice. Carpet delivered few days after—after the job."

So Gulab knew how to launder money. It shouldn't surprise him,
really, that someone as worldly as him would have the whole thing
figured out. This, after all, was a country where bribery was so
common that middle-class businessmen openly boasted about never
paying so much as a traffic violation fine. He himself had gotten
used to paying *baksheesh* for every doggone license and permit that
he needed at HerbalSolutions.

"One other thing, sir," Gulab was saying. "We should decide
now only the date you will pay me. Best I come here to pick it up.
After that, there should be no contact between us until—after. Safer
for you, that way."

"Okay," he whispered. "But . . . what if something goes wrong,
Gulab?"

Gulab sat up straight in his chair and threw his shoulders back.
"I don't know if you remember, sir. But a long time ago—when the
Anand situation was going on—you held me responsible for what
had happened to that boy. At that time you said that I owed you." To
Frank's consternation, Gulab swallowed hard, and Frank realized
that his careless words had deeply affected this man. "Well, Gulab
Singh doesn't like to owe any man, sir. So I give you my word, if

something goes wrong, I will not betray you. I will hang from the gallows before I do that. I will say I had an old score to settle with Prakash. Okay?"

And Frank had the unreal sense that in the space that it took Gulab to make his promise, the world had broken into a million jigsaw pieces and been rearranged again. This man whom he had thought of as a coldhearted killer had suddenly displayed the sensitivity of a butterfly; had taken his nonchalant Americanism—*you owe me*—and heard it as a challenge to his honor. He thought back to the revelation he'd had during his illness. A kindly old God with a long, flowing beard could've never created as complicated a being as Gulab; it took the randomness of an indifferent universe to have birthed a man who was this immoral and honorable.

"Okay," he said.

He sat in his chair for a long time after Gulab left. Multiple voices competed for his attention—his mother's voice, reading the Bible to him as he lay in his boyhood bed, Scott discussing Hegel and metaphysics with him when they were both young men, Ellie reading out loud passages from Father Oscar Romero's last sermon, Benny reciting the prayer that he said every night before going to bed:

Thank you for the world so sweet
Thank you for the food we eat
Thank you for the birds that sing
Thank you God for everything

He looked down at his hands. They looked dirty, stained, as if the deed that he was contemplating had already occurred. And then suddenly he was retching. He pulled the trashcan toward him, afraid he was about to soil his shirt. His mouth filled with the pungent taste of vomit, but he couldn't throw anything up. The foulness remained lodged, deep within his gut.

* * *

Prakash was walking down the street near their house as Frank got home that evening. The man was probably headed to the village bar, Frank surmised. "Stop," he told Satish. "I'll get out here. You go on home. I'll be right behind you."

He hopped out of the car. "Wait up, Prakash," he called and crossed the street.

Prakash stopped. A wary look came over his face.

Frank stood in front of him, his blue eyes looking into Prakash's dark ones. "Hey, look. I'm sorry. I shouldn't have pushed you. I—I wanted to say sorry."

The wary look never left Prakash's face as he stood silently.

Frank dug up a fifty-rupee note from his pocket and thrust it into Prakash's sweaty palm. He repressed the shudder that ran through him as his fingers made contact with Prakash's moist hand. "This is for you," he said. "As a way of saying I'm sorry." He turned his head in a conspiratorial way. "Don't tell Edna," he added.

He was rewarded with the thinnest of smiles. *"Achcha."* Prakash raised his hand to his forehead. "Thank you, *seth.*"

Frank waited as Prakash nodded, turned around, and walked away a few feet. Then he called out, "Oh, Prakash. One other thing."

Prakash stopped, the wary expression back on his face. Frank bridged the distance between them, keeping the smile on his face. "There's a big soccer match two weeks from now. I want to take Ramesh. He will enjoy it very much, I know." He watched Prakash watching him carefully. He made a downcast face. "Problem is, it's in Bombay."

He stood quietly, waiting for Prakash to say something. There was a long silence. Then, Prakash said, "You are wanting to take him?"

Frank gave a broad shrug. "I do. But I don't want any more tension with you. If you say no, I won't fight you. I'll—you can just tell the boy you don't want him to go."

Prakash stared at the ground. Then he looked up. The guarded expression was gone from his face. "Take him," he said simply. "No problem."

"You sure?" Frank said, wanting to prolong the moment. "You won't back out at the last minute?"

Prakash's eyes were clear. "I sure. Ramu love soccer."

And just like that, the final brick fell into place.

CHAPTER 34

It wasn't until eight on Saturday evening that Frank began to miss Ellie. He and Ramesh were walking along the seaside across from the Taj when the boy tripped on a broken sidewalk and cut his knee. To Frank's consternation, Ramesh burst into tears. He held the sobbing child in his arms, shocked at how openly Ramesh was crying in public. He examined the gash on his knee, dabbed at the droplets of blood with his handkerchief. He had seen Ramesh take tumbles that were much more severe when he and the boy had been engaged in an aggressive game of basketball. Then, the boy simply got up, dusted himself off, and resumed playing. So Frank was a little taken aback by this public display of emotion. He looked around helplessly, wishing Ellie was here. Passersby were taking in the scene—a white man holding and consoling a dark-skinned child—and shooting him curious looks. A gray-haired lady stopped and said to Ramesh, "*Su che, deekra?* Are you okay?" Ramesh nodded and pointed to his knee. "I fell," he sobbed, and the woman *tsk-tsk*ed a few times before resuming her walk. "You should take him home and wash the wound," she tossed over her shoulder.

"C'mon, kiddo," he said to Ramesh. "Let's go back to the hotel, and I'll clean this off for you." They stopped at the Taj's pharmacy on their way up, and he purchased some gauze and a box of Band Aids. But as Ramesh continued to cry in the room, it began to dawn on Frank that the boy's tears had nothing to do with the fall. And as if to confirm his suspicions, Ramesh said, "I miss Ellie." And then, "I miss my dada." Frank was crushed. Ever since they'd said good-bye to Ellie and Ramesh's parents this morning, he had endeavored to make sure Ramesh was having the time of his life—letting the boy hang his head out of the window as Satish drove them along the coast to Bombay, playing the wretched Hindi film music that Ramesh insisted on listening to on the car radio. At the soccer match this afternoon, he had allowed the boy to eat four samosas and drink two Cokes, until he was afraid Ramesh was going to puke. None of this had apparently been enough to distract him from homesickness. For the first time since he had hatched the plot with Gulab, Frank worried about how the boy would deal with his parents' death. He had been so busy grappling with his own conflicted emotions that he had not stopped to consider how Ramesh would handle the event that was about to befall him. Now, mortified by his own obliviousness, he wondered how he could've possibly failed to factor in Ramesh's grief. In a few hours from now, Ramesh would be an orphan. He flinched inwardly as his mind focused on that last word.

"Frank," Ramesh was saying. "Can we phone Ellie?"

"We can't," he replied gently. "She's on the train to Delhi, re-member? No cell phone reception there." Seeing Ramesh's crest-fallen face, he added, "She'll be back on Thursday. You'll see her then. Now, do you want to watch some TV before it's time for bed?"

"Okay," Ramesh said. "But I choose the show."

Frank pretended to grumble as he handed the remote to the boy. "You've become a world-class bully," he said.

At ten o'clock they were still watching a Jackie Chan movie. Fi-nally, Frank grabbed the remote and turned the TV off. "Come on, now. You have to go to bed. Go brush your teeth."

Ramesh looked surprised. "I brushed my teeth in the morning."

"Don't you brush again at night?" Frank asked, and Ramesh shook his head no. Once again, Frank wished Ellie were here. She had been in charge of the boy's nightly rituals the last time they'd traveled with him. "Well, you have to brush twice a day while you're here with me."

Ramesh shot him a dirty look but rolled out of bed and padded into the bathroom. "Finished," he said a few minutes later.

"Okay, off you go to bed," Frank said. He wondered if there were any bedtime rituals that his parents performed with the boy each night. Probably not, he thought. So he was taken aback when Ramesh came up to him and gave him a quick kiss on the cheek. "My ma always gives me good-night kiss," the boy said, grinning slyly.

Frank ran his hand through the boy's short hair. "Good night, pumpkin," he said and then regretted his choice of words as Ramesh convulsed with laughter. "Pumpkin," the boy repeated, holding his sides. "You said pumpkin."

"You are a silly boy," Frank smiled. "Now come on, go to bed." He turned off the lights.

Ramesh was asleep within five minutes. But Frank was wide awake. His heart had begun to thud loudly as soon as the room had fallen dark. He glanced at the digitalized alarm clock by his bed every few minutes. Time crawled slowly. He turned on the televison set again, hitting the mute button, so as not to disturb Ramesh. He needn't have worried. The boy's steady breathing told Frank that he was fast asleep. *Love Story* was showing on one of the channels. He watched part of it. He wondered where Gulab was at this moment, whether his heart was racing like his was. Somehow, he doubted it. He did a quick calculation. Gulab was to creep into Prakash's shack at about two in the morning. The plan was to . . . take care . . . of the couple before breaking into the main house and ransacking it a bit. Maybe take a small item or two and then drop it in the driveway, as if the thief had been scared into fleeing. So by the time Gulab made the anonymous phone call to the police and they investigated, it would be five or six o'clock before he heard anything. He would have to pretend to be sleepy, disoriented, when they called. As if they'd woken him out of an undisturbed sleep. He looked at the clock again. It was only midnight. He would not sleep tonight. He would lie awake, keep a kind of deathbed vigil while Ryan O'Neal and Ali MacGraw frolicked in the snow. The icy feeling in his stomach grew. Our Father who art in heaven, he caught himself praying. He turned on his side to face Ramesh. Tomorrow morning the sun will rise, he thought, and there will be two less people in the world. A wild, sharp feeling that he could not name tore through his heart. He eyed the boy sleeping trustingly next to him. "I'll take care of you," he promised. "I'll give you a great life."

His lips were moving as he fell asleep. Thy kingdom come, thy will be done, he chanted to himself.

The hotel phone rang at four thirty. Frank turned in bed, hit the snooze on the alarm clock, muttering in his sleep. Nothing happened. The ringing got louder. He suddenly sat up in bed. A spasm of pain bolted through his entire body. His jaw ached—he must've been grinding his teeth. He fumbled for his phone. "Hello?" he said.

"Mr. Frank?" a male voice said.

"Yes," he said. His heart was beating so hard he thought he was going to pass out.

"This is Inspector Sharma speaking. From Girbaug, sir. Sorry to say there's been an accident, sir."

"Accident?"

Sharma cleared his throat. "Um, yes. That is to say, two murders have occurred on your premises, sir."

He closed his eyes. So Gulab had done it. He was shaking with relief—and remorse. He was triumphant—and terrified.

There was a sound in the background, as if there was a scuffle going on. He heard Sharma say something in Hindi, and then there was a gasping noise on the phone. "Hello?" he said cautiously.

The nasal voice was immediately familiar. "Frank sahib," the voice sobbed. "We brothers now. *Arre bhagawan*. We have both entered the Age of Darkness, *seth*."

There was a roaring in Frank's ears. Prakash. Prakash was not dead? "Speak clearly," he ordered. "Give the phone back to—"

Prakash wailed in his ear. "We both widowers now, *seth*. We both—"

Maybe Prakash had been shot in the head. "Prakash," he said. "Stop talking rot. Give the phone to the inspector."

There was a pause—and Frank died and was reborn a hundred times in that pause—and then Sharma was back on the phone. "I'm so sorry, sir. He grabbed the phone—"

In the background, he could hear Prakash's sobs. "Inspector," Frank said, his eyes filling with tears. "What has happened? Who—who is dead?"

There was a crackle on the line. "The servant girl, sir. And—and your missus, sir. I'm desperately sorry, sir. Routine robbery, it appears to be."

He laughed out loud with relief. "That's impossible. My wife is out of town, traveling to Delhi tonight." She's safe, he thought, Ellie's safe.

"Beg pardon, sir. This chappie here says she didn't go. It—it definitely is your wife that is dead, sir. We have positively identified."

He hung up on Sharma. Ignored the urgent ring of the hotel phone as his fingers raced through the numbers on his cell phone. Shashi. He had to call Shashi. He would know what was going on. He glanced over at Ramesh. The boy was snoring with his mouth open. How the fuck can he sleep through this commotion? he thought with distaste. He looked away.

"Hello?" It was Nandita. A sleepy Nandita, but Nandita all the same. His stomach dropped.

"Nan? Why are you home? Why aren't you—"

"Who's this?" Nandita still sounded sleepy.

"It's Frank," he yelled. "Why are you home? Where's Ellie?"

"Oh, sorry. I didn't recognize. El's home. We didn't go today. Shashi's joining us. Last-minute decision. We're all leaving tomorrow instead."

He listened in horror, unable to take in what she was saying. "Frank?" Nandita said. "What's going on? Why're you calling me?"

His whole body began to shake. "You didn't go to Delhi?" he repeated. "Ellie was home tonight?"

"Yup. Are you trying to reach her?" Nandita sounded baffled. "She should be there. You can call her."

Why hadn't she phoned him yesterday to tell him about her change of plans? But even as he wondered, he knew the answer— Ellie had not wanted to intrude on his time with Ramesh.

The hotel phone was still ringing. He ignored it. "Frank," Nandita said again. "You can reach Ellie at home."

"I can't. I can't call her. I just got a call from the police. There's been a break-in at the house. Nandita, Ellie's dead. My wife is dead."

He woke Satish up, told him to drive as fast as he could back to the Taj to pick them up. They would leave for Girbaug tonight. Next, he went into the shower and turned on the water. He forgot to remove his clothes. Steam filled the bathroom, the heat scalding his skin. He leaned his face against the moist bath tile and bellowed. Beat the walls with his fist. Fell to the floor; banged his head against tile. He raised his wrist to his mouth and bit into the flesh. He wanted to inflict pain on his penitent body; wanted to experience such strong physical pain that he would forget for a blessed second, the agony of his soul.

He had killed her. Murdered the most precious thing in his life. The old Christian God, the one who kept track, kept score, the one who punished the wicked, had won. It was a moral universe, after all. He had tried to play his hand, winner take all. And instead he was left with nothing. Nothing. Just this empty void of a universe, emptied of the one person who had loved him, stood by him as steadily as a candle flame in the night.

He came dripping out of the shower, peeled off his clothes, which clung to him like skin, and got into a bathrobe. He walked into the bedroom, eyed the sleeping Ramesh with as much interest as one would a pile of bills. He tried to muster up pity for what had happened to this innocent boy, guilt over what he had stolen from him. But he felt nothing. More precisely, he felt a kind of anger at Ramesh. He had lost his Ellie in his bid for this boy. Had he gone mad? This sleeping, snoring boy didn't feel remotely worthy of the trade. The sacrifice had been too great.

He went to wake Ramesh up, but the thought of telling the boy what had transpired in Girbaug froze the words in his mouth. He let him sleep. Ramesh would wake up soon enough into an irrevocably altered world.

CHAPTER 35

Ellie miss was to have left for the train station at six in the evening, but at three thirty the phone rang. "Hi, Nandita," Prakash heard Ellie say. "I'm so excited—what? Oh, really? Well, I guess that's okay."

She spoke for a few more minutes and then came into the kitchen where Prakash was preparing the mutton cutlets she was to carry on the train for dinner. "Sorry for all this work," she said. "But there's been a change of plans. We're leaving tomorrow instead of today."

He was careful to keep the disappointment out of his face. This morning, Edna had told him that she'd been looking forward to a few days of rest while Frank and Ellie were away. "A little holiday for us, also, no?" Edna had said, "without having to do cooking-cleaning for them."

He had been anticipating spending the evening with his wife. Now, he would have to take care of Ellie miss. "Shall I put away the *kheema* in the fridge, madam?" he asked. "Or fry the cutlets for tonight?"

Ellie sighed. "We'll take them on the train tomorrow. But you may have to make a few more, Prakash. Shashi is joining us, also. And don't worry about dinner for tonight. There's plenty of leftovers."

"Yes, madam," he said.

"She not going to Delhi today," he announced as he walked into their hut a half hour later.

Edna was crouched in the corner of the shack, lighting the kerosene stove. "Don't talk nonsense," she said grumpily. "Of course she's going. All packed-pooked, she is."

"She change her mind. Going tomorrow instead."

"What for?"

He shrugged. "Because she American."

Edna curled her lip. "Don't you be starting today, you stupid," she said. "I'm not feeling well. No time for your nonsense."

He smiled. "You just missing our Ramu." Frank and Ramesh had left for Bombay early this morning.

She looked away. "Maybe." She paused, struck by a thought. "So this means I have to clean as usual?"

He took in Edna's tired face. "You rest," he said. "I will go over and do everything today."

Her face softened. "Many thanks, sweetie," she said quietly.

Sweetie. She hadn't called him that in a long time. His heart was singing as he crossed the courtyard and went back into the main house. Ellie, reading on the sofa, raised her head as he walked in. "Yes?"

"I will do cleaning-washing today instead of Edna, madam. She resting."

"Don't worry about it, Prakash. I don't need any clothes washed today."

He stood before her uncertainly. "So no washing?" he asked.

"Nope. No other housework, either. I'd already told you guys you'd have these days off. So enjoy."

"I will clean before Frank *seth* return on Monday night," he said, his Hindu belief in cleanliness outraged at the thought of a dirty house.

"Whatever."

"Shall I prepare the tea now, madam?"

"Prakash," she said. "I don't need anything. Really. Actually, I just want some priv—I want to be undisturbed the rest of the day."

He sighed and left the house. Despite himself, he felt a grudging affection for Ellie. She was nice, he thought. Kept her promises. Treated him and Edna as if she *saw* them.

Instead of going back into the shack, he decided to go for a walk along the beach, wanting to jiggle and treasure this unexpected gift of leisure, like silver coins in his pocket.

But the sea only made him miss Ramesh. He remembered bringing Ramesh to this beach the very first time, when he had been only six days old. Despite Edna's protests about the baby catching cold, he had brought Ramu to the same spot where he was now standing and held him up in his arm. "Look at this," he'd said to his son. "This all yours. Land, I will never possess. Your ma's land in Goa, you will not inherit. But this—this sand, this sky, this sea—this belong to you. No one can ever take away. You remember this."

During the Olaf years, the three of them would often come to the beach and take their supper on the sand, returning home after the sun went down. Or he and Ramesh would sometimes get a ride on a fishing boat on a Sunday morning. They would return home stinking of fish, and Edna would laughingly hold her nose while heating up water for their baths. That was the good thing about Olaf babu—he minded his own business. Give the man a clean house, hot meals cooked on time, pour him his Scotch exactly at seven in the evening, have that Gulab bring him a woman once a week, and *bas*—he was happy. Made no other demands on them. Didn't try and worm his way into their family life.

He was kicking up puffs of sand as he walked, resentment tearing tiny holes into the contentment he'd felt when he'd left the house. He decided to change tracks. He would walk to the market and buy his Edna a box of *ladoos*. They were on a kind of holiday, after all. They should celebrate.

Edna seemed touched but uninterested when he presented her with the gift. Setting the box aside, she said, "I'll eat these later. My tummy is paining right now."

"You want tea?" he asked but she simply shook her head. "I want sleep."

He sat watching her for half an hour while she slept. It felt strange having time on his hands and no one to spend it with. He had a sudden thought—he could go to a movie. He rose to his feet, wondering whether to wake Edna up. But she was sleeping so peacefully, he decided to go without her. His bicycle rested against the corner of the house, and getting on it, he pedaled toward the village's only theater. He spent the next three hours in the dark, his heart soaring during the romantic dance numbers, filling with outrage at the villain's chicanery. The man sitting behind him sang along with all the songs, which Prakash didn't mind, and recited all the dialogue spoken by the villain, which he did. *"Chup re,"* he hissed a few times but it didn't make a difference.

It was dark by the time he left the theater. He began to ride home, but as he passed the village bootlegger's shop decided to have one shot of *daru* before proceeding. There, he ran into Moti, the village cobbler's son, who bought him a second drink. Etiquette demanded that he reciprocate. A few other men joined them. This is good, Prakash thought, and so much more fun than drinking alone at home, under the shadow of Edna's disapproving looks. The men were friendly with him today, drawing him into the fold, and the lonely feeling that he usually felt around the villagers vanished. He was one of them tonight, not the orphan who usually stood at the outskirts of their lives. It was a powerful feeling, this sense of belonging, this camaraderie, and it made him want to drink to rejoice. When he finally staggered out of the joint, he was stunned to realize it was ten o'clock. He pedaled home as fast as his wobbly legs allowed him to.

He had braced himself for the gust of Edna's wrath as soon as he walked through the tin door. What he was unprepared for was the sight of his wife curled up in a fetal position on the rope cot. Her face was flushed and her forehead covered with sweat.

"Prakash," she gasped as she saw him. "Where have you been?"

"I went to see a film. What is wrong?"

"I don't know. Horrible stomach cramps I'm having. Maybe something I ate. Though truth to tell, not much I'm eating today." Her voice was so low, he had to drop to his knees to hear her.

Panic seized him. He wished his head wasn't spinning so much, so he could think of what to do. "Shall I call doctor sahib?" he said, even as he remembered that they owed the doctor two hundred rupees.

Edna lifted her head. "No," she gasped. "No doctor, I beg you." She had a deep fear of doctors, he knew.

"Wait," he said. "I be right back."

"Prakash, stay here, *na*."

"I come right back. Two minutes, total." He pulled his hand from hers.

The lights were turned out in the big house, and for a minute he worried that Ellie was not home, had left to meet Nandita memsahib for dinner, perhaps. Or maybe she had gone to bed. He banged hard on the kitchen door, and when there was no answer, banged again. To his relief, a light turned on. A second later, Ellie opened the door and blinked at him.

"What the—?" And then, screwing up her nose, "You've been drinking, haven't you?"

"Ellie madam, come quick-quick. My Edna is most sick." The words came out slurred, despite his best efforts.

He watched her forehead crease with worry. "What's wrong?" she asked, but before he could answer, she disappeared. When she appeared again, she had thrown a robe over her pajamas. "Let's go," she said and they hurried across the courtyard.

Edna was holding her stomach and moaning lightly. "Turn on the lights," Ellie ordered, and he did. Ellie sat at the edge of Edna's cot. "Tell me what's happening," she said gently.

Edna licked her upper lip. "I don't know, miss," she gasped. "Stomach is paining a lot."

"Do you have a fever?" And before Edna could reply, she turned to Prakash. "You have a thermometer?"

He stared at her, his drunken brain trying to conjure up the image of a thermometer. Ellie made an exasperated sound. "Never mind," she said, stood up, and left the shack. She was back a moment later. "Here we go." She smiled at Edna. "Let's stick this under your tongue, okay?"

There was no fever. "That's good," Ellie said. "And here are some pills for a tummy ache. Can you sit up to take these?" She looked to Prakash. "Go get me a glass of water."

She helped ease Edna back onto the cot. "Boil a pot of water," she instructed Prakash. "I'll be back with a hot water bottle."

By quarter to midnight the spasms had diminished, but Edna still looked terrible. Prakash sat propped up in one corner, trying his best to stay awake. *Ae bhagwan*, he prayed. Let my Edna be okay, and I will not touch this vile *daru* for one whole week.

Ellie sat on the cot across from Edna's. "Are you asleep?" she whispered.

"No, miss," Edna answered immediately. "Pain is better but still there."

Ellie looked around helplessly. "I think we should have Dr. Gupta come in."

Edna looked to the ceiling. "No, miss. I beg you. No doctor."

"But why . . . ?"

Edna folded her hands. "I beg you. No doctor."

"Listen," Ellie said. "Let me at least phone him, okay?" She was walking to the door before Edna could respond.

Prakash got up off the floor and sat holding his wife's hand. He didn't know how much time had passed before Ellie came back. "Okay," she said loudly. "I reached Dr. Gupta. He says as long as you don't have a fever, that's good. But he wants you to take two more of these." She held out the big pink tablets.

"Thank you, madam," Edna said. "You go home, madam. It's late."

In response, Ellie turned to Prakash. "Listen," she said. "I'm going to spend the night here with Edna. I—I'll sleep on the cot and keep an eye on her. You go into the main house. Take some sheets and go to sleep in the kitchen. Understand?"

He staggered to his feet without protest. As he rose, the veil of alcohol lifted for a second, and he saw his home clearly—saw how empty and shabby it looked compared to the opulent main house. He took in the filthy sheet that he covered himself with at night, the lack of a pillow on the rope cot. "Excuse, please," he mumbled and stumbled out of the house. Outdoors, he went behind the house, walked a distance, and took a piss against a tree on the street. He would've been too embarrassed to use the tiny bathroom in his own home with Ellie there, knowing it was separated by the rest of the shack by a flimsy door that didn't hide many sounds or smells. Next, he entered the main house and opened the linen closet. He picked out two sheets—one to drape over the cot, which he knew Ellie would find uncomfortable to sleep on, and the other to cover herself with. He wondered whether to fetch her her pillow but was afraid of touching her bed without her permission. He hurried back to the shack. Ellie was again crouching near Edna, stroking her hair. He used the time to make the bed.

"Shall I stay, also?" he whispered to Ellie. "I can sleep in the corner," he added hastily.

She peered at him. "It's too tight and hot in here," she said. A look of annoyance crossed her face. "Besides, you're too drunk to be of help. Better if you sleep this off and be fresh in the morning. I'm sure she's going to need your help tomorrow."

"As you wish," he mumbled. He went over and kissed Edna's forehead and received the slightest of smiles. "Go rest," she said to him. "So late it is."

As he crossed the courtyard, resentment at having been banished from his own home wrestled with gratitude at Ellie's willingness to spend the night with Edna. Not too many mistresses do this, he reminded himself. And by the time he placed a clean, lavender-scented sheet on the cool kitchen floor and fell asleep in the spotless, airy room, only gratitude remained.

The pressure of his bladder woke him up a few hours later. He was getting up off the floor to go pee when he heard it: *pop*. Followed by a woman's scream. And then, in rapid succession: *pop*. *Pop-pop*. A pause and then, another *pop*. Something crashed. Followed by an abrupt silence, louder than what had gone before. He had no idea what the popping sounds were, but his heart was pounding as he rose to his feet and rushed to the kitchen window. And he saw it: a man as tall as a tree emerged from the shack and disappeared into the black of the night. Prakash blinked a few times, wanting to decipher whether the shadowy presence was a *daku* or a *bhoot*, a dacoit or a ghost. But then, to his terror, he saw the figure moving slowly toward the main house. Prakash's trembling hands instinctively moved toward the light switch. He flipped it on, flooding the room with brightness. The figure stopped dead in its tracks and then moved away, heading rapidly toward the driveway. A ghost for sure, Prakash's alcohol-soaked, superstition-riddled brain told him. A ghost chased away by the purity of light. He thought he saw the figure leap over the low brick wall and onto the driveway, but it was too dark to be sure. He stood at the window a few more minutes. Then he remembered the scream. As he hurried across the courtyard, he heard the engine of a car fire up in the distance. He paid it no mind.

The door of the shack was open. He walked in. "Edna?" he whispered. No response. And then he heard it—a moan so low and horrible, it made the hair on his body stand up. He turned on the light. And saw the scene that he would still see when he was a seventy-year-old man waking up from his nightmares each night.

Edna was in a fetal position, cradling her stomach. But now there was a river of blood emerging from her stomach. In place of the red bindi she always wore on her forehead, was a bullet hole, the size of a rupee coin. Her eyes were closed.

He looked over to his right. Ellie was sitting up on his cot, leaning against the plastered walls. Her head was slumped against her collar bone. Her mouth hung open, a thin stream of blood trickling out. Her legs were splayed in front of her. The wall behind her was splattered with blood and some yellow—*ae bhagawan*—what was this puslike, yellow, alive-looking thing that was pouring out of her head?

And one of them had moaned. Who had moaned? One of them had been alive when he'd entered the room. "Ednaaaaaaaaaaaaaaaa," he screamed. "Madaaaaaaaaaaaaaaaaam." There was no response.

He fell to his knees in front of his wife. He picked up her hand, and when he lowered it, it dropped lifelessly away. She was dead. In his shell-shocked mind, the realization registered as fact, not as grief. Not yet. Still on his haunches, he scrambled his way toward Ellie. The floor was hot and slick and slippery with blood. "Miss Ellie," he cried. "Miss." He went to lift her arm, but something about its angle, the unnatural way in which it was bent, gave him the answer he needed.

Police. He needed to phone the police. He scooted away on his buttocks toward the door. He felt like he was being marinated in their boiling, steaming blood. For the first time, he became aware of the slaughterhouse odor filling this tiny room. Immediately, he began to retch and gag. Get away. He needed to get away. Call police. Breathe fresh air. He rose to his feet. And slipped on the slick floor. He steadied himself. He was almost to the door when his bladder betrayed him. With that release came another: he emerged from the protective shell of numbness that he had built around himself, into the dark continent of grief.

And so Prakash stood at the door, tears streaming down his blood-streaked face, hot piss streaming down his trembling legs, eyeing the mutilated female bodies that would haunt him the rest of his days.

CHAPTER 36

He ran. Down the steps of the porch leading to the front yard and across the lawn and to the steeper flight of stone steps that led to the beach. Onto the brown sand and directly toward the blaze of the mid-morning sun as it glowered like a scold over the protesting waves. And then, a sharp right away from the house and he was running on the dark, muddy flatness of the beach where the waves scuttled and lapped, timid as mice.

He ran. His shirt was hanging on the rocker on the porch back at the house, fluttering like a white flag in the breeze. The sun broiled the skin on his back, turning it a salmon red. By tomorrow he would be sunburned and the burns would feel delicious, an addition to the litany of ways in which he was trying to punish himself since Ellie's death. He focused now on how the sneakers were tight on his feet, how they were pinching his little toe, sending occasional sparks of pain that his brain hungered to register. Later, he would find the bloom of a red blister and he would cherish it, pick at its red heart to feel the lovely, tortured sensation. How clean, how uncomplicated, how free of irony, physical pain was. And what a great diversion from the mental anguish that he fought every second of his life to keep at bay.

He ran. Waited for that moment when his lungs would be bursting, when rivulets of sweat would fall from him, when exhaustion would make his calf muscles quiver and his mind would turn blank, mercilessly blank, a white sheet of nothingness. That magical moment when he would enter the zone, where he would stop being a thinking, tortured man and simply become an animal, a mechanical being, a sum of moving body parts—a heaving chest, a burned back, a straining thigh muscle, a pair of eyes watering from the sun's glare.

He had cremated her two days ago. Had ignored Anne's and Delores's pleas to have the body flown back to America for a decent burial. At first he had tried to reason with them, to explain how difficult it would be logistically, how he wasn't up to dealing with the Indian bureaucracy at a time like this. But Anne had immediately offered to fly to Girbaug to help. And he had recoiled at this. And pulled out the final weapon in his arsenal. Ellie loved India, he'd said. She had recently told me that she never wanted to leave. This— this feels right, leaving her here. I'm just honoring her wishes. And he didn't know how much of this was true and how much of it was convenience. Whether he believed his words or didn't. Whether his memory of Ellie saying those words was accurate or something he'd dreamed up. And the surprising thing was, it didn't matter. It was all evasive, ephemeral, merely words and thoughts that floated by as absently as clouds. The only truth that mattered was that Ellie was dead. They could fight over her body, could bury or burn her, could transport her body or keep it on this soil, and it wouldn't lessen the horror. Wouldn't change the fact that the Ellie whom he loved, the Ellie whose spirit rested in each one of his skin pores, the Ellie who gave shape and meaning to his life, that Ellie was gone.

Which is why when Inspector Sharma had driven him to the morgue fifty kilometers outside of Girbaug to identify the body, he didn't recognize her. His Ellie had a long, taut neck; this woman's neck was broken. His Ellie had eyes that shone like jewels; this woman's eyes were smudged glass. His Ellie had a chest that was smooth and uniform; this woman had two button holes down her breast bone, where the bullets had entered. Most important of all, his Ellie had an expression of peace and contentment when she slept; this woman's face was twisted with indignation and rage, as if she was outraged by the ugliness of what had befallen her. On the way to the morgue he had been sick with fear at what he would have to witness, had expected to look at the body just long enough to identify his wife. But instead, he found himself staring and staring at this body, waiting for Ellie to emerge, much as a sculptor waits for the sculpted form to emerge from the block of marble. He chipped away at this torn body with his eyes, looking for his Ellie. But nothing happened. Instead, the custodian of the morgue pulled the white sheet back over the body, and Sharma was tugging at Frank's elbow and escorting him out of the small room. It was only then that he paid attention to his own trembling body and realized that he was throwing up all over himself.

"We will catch the *badmaash* who did this, sir," Sharma was saying. "No fears, I promise we will get him."

And Frank understood the true horror of his situation. He would not be afforded even the normal diversion that accompanied most murder cases—the search for the killer, the putting together of clues, the choking anger and rage directed toward the unknown as-sassin. In his case, the killer resided within and so all his wrath had to be directed at himself. The crime and the punishment were one and the same.

Deepak stood beside him in an open field a few days later as he watched Ellie's body burn. The fire hissed and crackled as it hit fat; the sound of Ellie's bones popping reminded him of the sound of the pop of his BB gun when he and Scott pelted each other with its pel-lets as boys. The sounds the fire made repulsed him, so that he spent much of the time fighting the urge to throw up. But there was also something clean and beautiful about Ellie's body being devoured by fire, instead of entrusting her body to the whims and appetites of the fat-bellied worms. Instead of lowering Ellie's body into the dirt, he had raised it to the heavens, to where it was escaping in large billows of smoke. It was exactly the kind of lavish, grand gesture she would've loved.

Behind him, he heard a woman sob and turned his head slightly. Nandita was convulsed with grief, bent and leaning into Shashi's body. Frank was grateful. He himself was unable to cry. Nandita and Shashi were their Indian family, and Nandita's sobs appeased some of his guilt at having kept Ellie's and his family at bay. They had all wanted to rush to Girbaug, of course. But he just couldn't handle it. "Frank, you're not thinking of anybody else," Scott had reprimanded him gently, and he was right.

"Damn straight," he'd replied. "I—I can't. Can't think of anyone else. I need to . . . this is about Ellie and me. No one else. No one can understand."

The wind shifted slightly, and a strange odor filled the air. He gagged and then forced himself to stop. The breeze affected the trajectory of the flames, so that instead of shooting straight upward, they tilted and bent a bit. In the space created by their new direction, Frank saw the tall figure of a man standing on the other side of the pyre, staring directly at him. His stomach dropped. It was Gulab. And through the smoke and the flames Frank saw that Gulab was standing ramrod straight and at attention, as if he was inspecting a military parade.

It was the first time he had seen Gulab since the murders. He had fantasized about running into the man and going straight for his jugular. But now, as he watched Gulab staring back at him, a lump formed in Frank's throat. Gulab was here to apologize to him. And to honor the memory of Ellie. Something about his military bearing, his posture, conveyed this to Frank. Still, Frank couldn't bear to look at Gulab. Not here. Not now. He bent his head slowly toward the ground. By the time he looked back up, there was only air. Gulab had vanished. Frank looked around, even as he knew that he wouldn't see his chief of security again.

There was a final crackle of the fire, and then it was all done. Frank said the Lord's Prayer for Ellie's soul. He noticed that the man who had been stoking the funeral pyre was walking toward them. The man went over to where Shashi stood and whispered something. Shashi, his eyes blood-shot, came up to Frank. "He wants to know if you want to collect the ashes now. Or he can send them, later."

In response, Frank walked over to the pyre and picked up a pinch of Ellie's ashes. He rubbed the ash in his gray hair and then wiped his right hand on his left. She was on his skin, part of him now. Inseparable. Always.

He turned to face Shashi. "I don't want her ashes. I—I wouldn't know what to do with them." He stopped, struck by a thought. "In fact, if you don't mind, maybe I can ask you guys to sprinkle it in the countryside, after I'm—gone? She'd like that."

He saw them glance at each other. Nandita spoke first. "We will."

The three of them walked away from the smoldering pyre toward where Shashi's car was waiting. And then Frank saw them, huddled together and standing to the left, under the shade of a large tree. A group of men from his factory and other villagers he didn't recognize, including some children and teenagers. They were standing with their heads bowed and their hands folded. So they had come to pay their final respects to Ellie. He was surprised at how touched he was. Glancing at Nandita and Shashi, he walked up to the group. "Thank you," he said simply. His eyes filled with tears, and there was a lump in his throat the size of a baseball. "I—I sincerely thank you."

They looked at him blankly. He folded his hands and bowed his head and from their sudden smiles knew that he'd made a connection. "Ellie, miss, great lady," one young boy said. "She teaching me."

A young woman held out her hand and showed Frank a cheap golden bracelet. "She gave to me. From her hand."

Then they all spoke at once, and he felt overcome both by their obvious gratitude and loyalty to Ellie and by his realization that he had been blind to what Ellie had meant to them. What he had thought of as a fanciful indulgence on her part, the bored housewife volunteering her time, had changed something in the lives of these people. He felt a profound loneliness for what he had missed, an aspect of his wife that these people had known that he did not. He stood surrounded by the jabbering villagers, as each of the adult men took his hand in both of theirs and held it up to their foreheads, in a gesture he supposed was an offering of condolence.

Shashi and Nandita drove him home from the funeral. They parked in front of the house, and he knew that good manners demanded that he ask them in, but he didn't. Couldn't. He simply turned and said that he'd come by their house to say his final good-bye before he took off for America a few days later. "Don't leave without seeing us, okay?" Nandita said gently, and he smiled and assured her he wouldn't.

He turned the key and walked into the kitchen and saw it at once. A blue envelope on the floor. He knew what it was even before he picked it up. His heart thudding, he slit open the envelope with his index finger. And there was the bearer check that he had handed to Gulab almost two weeks ago. Upon his instructions, Frank had left the date blank and had made the check payable to bearer, which meant that its recipient could cash it. Harder to trace that way, Gulab had explained to him. So Gulab had left the funeral and driven here to slip the check under the door. It was his way of apologizing for how terribly wrong things had gone. And perhaps also to cover his tracks. Refuse to accept blood money, since the wrong blood had been shed. Frank had heard about honor among thieves. Now he realized that there was honor among murderers, also. He held the check up, eyeing his signature with distaste. He remembered how badly his hand had shaken when he'd signed this check—no, this death warrant. And yet, he'd done it, hadn't he? He had not woken up from his obsession with Ramesh, from the long dream of replacing one son with another, had not heeded the calls of his conscience because those calls had been covered by the incessant chatter of his desperate need.

Now, running along the side of the sea under the watchful eye of the overhead sun, he remembered the check. He had resisted the temptation to tear it into a hundred little pieces and had instead left it on top of the dresser in his bedroom, where it could torment him every time he walked by. One more way to flog himself, to feel the pinch of stinging guilt. In the days following Ellie's death he had flirted with the idea of turning himself in to the authorities. But the truth was, the thought of life in an Indian prison terrified him. So he told himself that he could devise far more exquisite tortures for himself. Also, the crime was his alone, and he didn't want others to pay for it. Both his and Ellie's families were devastated enough. Even Gulab—Gulab's sin was nothing compared to his. Gulab didn't deserve to hang for his, Frank's, sins. No, the tortures the world had in store for him were plenty. Like walking into a room and calling out for Ellie. And the lurching disappointment that followed as realization seeped in like black poison. Or rolling in bed in the middle of the night and his hand groping its way toward where Ellie should be. And wasn't. A million, trillion pinpricks of memory and forgetfulness, so much more painful than the swift slash of a knife.

He looked at his watch. It was 1:30 P.M. Satish would arrive soon. The plan was to stop at the Hotel Shalimar to say his good-byes to Nan and Shashi and then drive to an airport hotel in Bombay and rest for a few hours before catching the night flight to America. Looking down at his watch, sweat dripping from his forehead, he remembered Ellie's large, men's watch. She had been wearing it the night of the murders. The glass plate was shattered when the police handed it to him. She must have hit it against something—or something must have hit it. The broken dial had conveyed the brutality of the violence against his wife more than even her battered body had. So he had saved it, too. Placed it on top of the dresser, next to the check. Felt its shattered face watching him, accusing him, like a woman with a black eye.

The memory of the two objects on the dresser made him turn and begin the run back home. As he ran closer to the water, the waves tickled his ankles. A few of the bolder ones splashed his shins. He peeled off his wet sneakers outside the house and left them there. He would not need them again. He walked immediately into the bathroom and took a shower. His last shower in Girbaug. Then he changed into the silk kurta that he had found gift wrapped in his closet, after Ellie had died. He pulled on his blue jeans and went to inspect himself in front of the closet mirror. What shocked him was how unchanged he looked. He took in the blue eyes, as clear as a California sky; the way the full lips closed together in a line that indicated strength and integrity; the wide, uncreased forehead that conveyed clarity and innocence. He still had feet, not hooves. Yes, his hair was gray but he still had a thick head of hair and it did not sprout horns. His hands were burned bronze and there was no blood running down them. This was the final insult, this appearance of normalcy.

Self-loathing made it hard to continue looking in the mirror. He turned away and picked up Ellie's watch and shoved it into the pocket of his jeans. He folded the check in half and thrust it into the other pocket. Next, he unzipped his suitcase and placed the photo frame with Benny's picture in between some of his shirts. He took one last look at the bedroom. If he looked closely at the bed, he could still see Ellie's indentation. So he didn't permit himself a close look. Every day, for the rest of his life, would be a balancing act, weighing what degree of pain and pleasure he could bear. That would be his true punishment—caution. Never again would he be able to do anything spontaneously, or on an impulse. He would measure his life in coffee spoons.

Satish was in the courtyard when he stepped out of the house. "Sir," he said hurrying up to Frank, to relieve him of his suitcase. The driver opened his mouth to say more, swallowed. "I'm sorry, sir," he said.

Frank put his arm on the young man's shoulder. "Thank you," he said. They both stood in the courtyard for a moment. Frank eyed the small shack that had become Ellie's tomb. The shack was empty now. Prakash had refused to step foot into it since the night of the murders. Shashi had offered Prakash a job at the hotel, and father and son were currently living there. Turning away, Frank looked back at the sweet little cottage where he and Ellie had spent two years together. I hope you were happy here with me at least part of the time, he said to himself. I hope I made you happy sometimes.

They drove to Hotel Shalimar, and Nandita burst into tears as she hugged him good-bye. "I can't stand this," she sobbed. "It's hard enough without Ellie. But now you too are leaving us, Frank."

"You guys were wonderful friends to us," he replied. "I'll never forget that." He turned toward Shashi. "One more favor to ask. Is there a private room where I can talk to Prakash and Ramesh for a few seconds? And then I'll be on my way."

He waited alone in an unoccupied hotel room, and a few minutes later there was a soft knock on the door that he immediately recognized. "Come in," he called, and they entered.

He had barely spoken to Ramesh since the drive back from Bombay. Back at the hotel, he had simply told him that his mother and Ellie were both sick, and even that lie had been unbearable. The desolation that he saw on Ramesh's face at the thought of Edna being sick had been a wake-up call. The mad self-absorption, the crippling delusion that had made him plot the murders, the fog of insanity that had made him ignore the fact that he would be inflicting on Ramesh the most grievous injury a child could suffer, lifted during that long ride from Bombay to Girbaug. He was mortified, guilt-riddled. And so he had avoided Ramesh. Also, his grief over losing Ellie was so blinding, he couldn't bear to acknowledge that Ramesh was hurting in the same manner as he was. He might have been able to handle either guilt or grief. Together, they were too heavy a load for Frank to carry. He felt his obsession with the boy ebbing away, like a fever leaving his body. Now, he saw the child for who he was—an extraordinarily smart kid but perhaps not college material; a sweet, bright boy, but certainly not someone who held the key to his happiness.

Now, as if aware of his fall from grace, Ramesh looked at him silently. Frank forced himself to acknowledge his presence. "How are you, Ramesh?" he said softly.

The boy shrugged.

"I see. Yes . . . well . . ."

"I am missing my mama. And Ellie, too," Ramesh blurted out.

Frank looked away. His eyes focused on where Prakash was standing. The cook looked as if he'd aged by about ten years. An image of Ellie's haggard face at the hospital when Benny was sick flashed unbidden through Frank's mind. People don't age with time, he realized. They bend with grief.

He walked up to Prakash. "I'm very sorry for your loss," he said. He pulled the check out of his pocket. "This—is for you and for Ramesh. For his education. Maybe you can even buy a small house, somewhere. In any case, I hope it helps."

Prakash stared at the piece of paper, and Frank realized that the cook was illiterate. But Ramesh was at his father's side, and Frank saw his eyes widen. *"Baap re,"* the boy breathed. "Dada, this is for one lakh rupees."

Prakash looked bewildered. "I don't understand?"

"It's for you," Frank said urgently. "A gift from me—and Ellie."

"I am a millionaire? A *lakhpati*?" Prakash said.

Frank smiled. "I guess so." He waited for his words to sink in and then said, "Listen, Prakash. Put this money in a bank. Don't drink it away, you understand? This is your chance to—"

Prakash placed his hand on Ramesh's head. "I'm swearing on my son," he said. "Frank *seth*, I haven't touched one drop since—since that day. May worms eat my flesh if I ever touch that *daru* again. It is the devil's brew."

"Good. Look, this is your money. But I'm going to give you some advice—ask Nandita and Shashi for help. They will tell you how to invest it."

Prakash still look dazed. "I will be forever in their debt if they help, sir," he said. "What do I know of banks and things?"

"Okay," Frank replied. "I'll let them know." He stared at Prakash for a moment, wondering why he'd ever disliked the man so much.

Ramesh wove his hand into Frank's and looked up at him. "I will miss you, Frank."

For a second, he felt the old connection again, and his heart responded to Ramesh's simplicity and innocence. How happy this boy had made him for a little while. "I'll see you sometime," he lied.

"You are going home?" Ramesh said.

"Yes," he lied. He had no idea where home was or where he was going. His ticket said he was going from Bombay to New York, but it all felt like a dream to him right now. He might decide to get off at London. Or he might oversleep in his hotel room in Bombay and miss the flight and lose himself among the eighteen million people who called that strip of an island their home. Or he might actually arrive at JFK and be met by Scott and his mother. In a way, it didn't matter where he went, because wherever he went, he would be alone and homeless. He had had only two homes in his life—Benny and Ellie. And they were gone.

A month ago, the thought of turning his back on Ramesh and walking away had been unimaginable. Now, he was doing it. Without a backward glance.

He hugged Nandita one more time. "Will you stay in touch?" she cried.

"Yup. I'll send you my information as soon as I'm settled," he said. But what came to his mind was not the house in Ann Arbor or Scott's condo in New York. What came to mind was wandering. That's all he wanted to do, wander, walk and walk until his legs gave out, the mechanical movement of his feet keeping rhythm with the hectic pace of his mind, until there was only blankness, until his thoughts stopped pestering him like tiny insects. The thought of a desk job where he sat in meetings or moved paper; of living in his home, where he was controlled by the tyranny of the coffeemaker and the dishwasher and the television set; of being around people whose skins were unlined and minds unburdened, frightened him. He had been ejected from that world, into a rarer world—one occupied by ascetics and sadhus and wanderers. He needed to move, move, to escape the menagerie in his head.

Back in America, there were people who loved him—loved him for himself and because he was their last link to Ellie. Who wanted to care for and console him, to draw him back into the fold of human company. He was unworthy of their love. They did not know that they would be bringing a killer into their midst. The normal consolations of bereavement were not open to him. He did not deserve them. Even between him and Scott there would now be a secret. He would not—could not—avail the luxury of confession. Perhaps the only person who would understand him—no, the only person he, Frank, would understand—would be his father. Who also knew a thing or two about betraying the ones you love.

Maybe I'll look for him, he said to himself as he got back into the car. Maybe I'll—but he didn't finish the thought. Like so many of his thoughts these days, this one shivered and died, like a fish washed to shore.

"Ready, sir?" Satish said.

"Ready," he answered. He looked to where Nandita, Shashi, Prakash, and Ramesh were standing at the entrance of the hotel. He waved and then rolled up the window. In a minute the car approached the hotel gates. He looked back, and they were all still standing there, as distant as stars. Then Satish made a right turn, and they fell away.

Out of the blue, he remembered something his grandma Benton had once said to him in one of her boozy moments. The old lady, gin on her breath, had bent toward the startled eleven-year-old boy and said, "You know the most dangerous force on earth, darlin'? It ain't the atom bomb. It's a man who is truly free. That's who you gotta watch out for."

Frank leaned back in his seat as Girbaug erupted in bursts of red dust and occasional green around them. He felt free and dangerous.

CHAPTER 37

The sky dripped gold that evening. And reds and purples, as rich as blood. As twilight fell, the colors dropped onto their skins, breathed fire into his and Benny's blond hair. The sand had turned the color of copper, and they ran greedy fingers through it. The ocean rustled like autumn trees, sighed in contentment. They were at Captiva Island in Florida, and each night they had slept deeply, their breathing in unison with the breathing of the ocean.

It was their wedding anniversary. Benny was three years old. Right now, he was playing by himself, digging up the wet sand with his yellow shovel and filling up his little green pail. He squatted a few feet away from them, jabbering away to himself. The setting sun had turned his skin a rich shade of bronze.

Ellie was sitting across from Frank on the blanket, the summer breeze running through her hair. He took in the delicate curve of her neck, the sharp nose that was sniffing the salty air, the dark vein running down the slender arm. He felt a lump grow in his throat, felt something in him ache with longing. It didn't seem possible to love her even more than he had the day he'd married her. But he did.

"Whatcha thinking?" he whispered.

She smiled and turned her head away from the ocean and toward him. The sun trembled in her eyes. "Of a quote by Shaw that I came across recently. It says, 'A happy family is but an earlier heaven.'"

Involuntarily, they turned toward their son. He was now picking up the wet sand with his hands, flattening it into a patty, and then flinging it away. "You'll have to give him his bath tonight," Ellie said wryly. "I'm not touching him."

He lay back on the blanket and stared at the sky. The sun was coughing up colors that any self-respecting painter would have been embarrassed to use on a canvas. He watched the moving, flowing crayon streaks and then said, "Here's a saying for you: 'The sky is an upside down ocean.'"

"Who said that?"

"I did. Frank Benton Shaw."

They giggled. Benny looked over, and Frank sat up immediately. "Hey, sweetie," he said. "You wanna come sit with us for a few minutes?"

They moved closer to each other, their knees touching, as Benny tottered over to them. The boy sat in front of them, and they both threw one arm around his chest. "Are you cold, honey?" Ellie asked, and Ben shook his head no.

They sat that way, drinking in the last, sweet drops of the day. The sun hovered at the edge of the horizon, declining to go down, like Benny refusing to go to bed.

All around them, the earth was sighing. They joined in its miraculous breathing.

ACKNOWLEDGMENTS

The following (in alphabetical order) helped this novel happen:

Dr. Blaise Congeni, director of pediatric infectious diseases at Akron
  Children's Hospital, for sharing his medical expertise with me
*The Baker-Nord Center for the Humanities at Case Western Reserve
  University,* for a much-needed fellowship
Kim Emmons, for long talks on long walks
Sarah Gridley, conspirator in mischief and creativity
Mary Grimm, who suggested turning a short story into this novel
Eustathea Kavouras, who never stops believing in me
Kulfi and Baklava, superhero cats
Annerieke Owen, wife of the U.S. Consul General in Bombay, for a prompt
  resolution to a specific question
Marly Rusoff, the most hardworking agent on the planet
Noshir and Homai Umrigar, my forever people
Claire Wachtel, my irrepressible editor
Sarah Willis, thoughtful critic, generous friend

Some people go to priests; others to poetry; I to my friends.

—VIRGINIA WOOLF

Me, too.

—T.U.